'Well, Zlobec?' Bor's voice was impatient.

'We have a disaster on our hands.' Zlobec felt himself near to tears. He hadn't expected any sympathy from Bor, but a little would h

'*We*
dam
Ther
and c
to be
all the
wires c . . .

'Commissioner . . .' Zlobec hesitated. It was obvious to him that Commissioner Bor had no idea of the magnitude of the disaster at Postojna. He took a very deep breath. 'The caves, Commissioner.'

'Postojna . . . what about the Postojna caves?'

'Collapsed.' Zlobec could think of no other words to describe the happening. 'The visitors are all trapped. Commissioner . . . for God's sake, we need immediate help!'

Bor was silent for almost a full minute. 'Zlobec, listen to me. Tell me about the caves . . . what exactly has happened?' Bor was aware of the popularity of the grotto in mid-tourist season. He was hoping for an answer that would please him, but inside he knew what was to come . . .

Also by Forrest Webb

THE CIRCLE OF RA

and published by Corgi Books

Forrest Webb

The Sealing

CORGI BOOKS
A DIVISION OF TRANSWORLD PUBLISHERS LTD

THE SEALING

A CORGI BOOK 0 552 11718 8

First publication in Great Britain

PRINTING HISTORY
Corgi edition published 1982

This book is set in 10/11 English Times

Corgi Books are published by
Transworld Publishers Ltd.,
Century House, 61-63 Uxbridge Road,
Ealing, London, W5 5SA

Printed in Great Britain by
Hunt Barnard Printing Ltd., Aylesbury, Bucks.

The Sealing

1

The foot dangling in the lukewarm water of Piran harbour in Yugoslavia belonged to Joe Catlin. The harbour wasn't the cleanest or wisest of places to dangle anything. The comings and goings of the fishing boats, and the small tides, gave just enough current for the debris of the village to collect in the odd corners of the harbour, or to drift across in patches acting as parasols for the miriads of minute fish who scavenged beneath the slightly oiled surface. Sewage from the houses and hotels spilled out by gravity at the peninsular's point five hundred yards to the north of the fishing village; some of it drifted back. Occasionally the sewage gave a few unwary holidaymakers something more to think about than the ancient beauty of the old town.

A porbeagle shark, eight feet in length and weighing around three hundred pounds, was cruising a half-mile-long slick of blood, scales and fish guts, trailed by a fishing vessel just tying up alongside the quay. A small crowd of restaurant owners were already making loud and aggressive offers for the boat's catch. The porbeagle had rounded the head of the Adriatic, just beyond the shark nets lining the coast from west of Trieste in Italy, to the Yugoslavian border. Tourists were not informed of the shark nets by either the tourist boards, or the travel agencies who sold them the tickets. Shark incidents were rare, but just frequent enough to make the nets essential. There were few anti-shark nets once you crossed the border into communist Yugoslavia. Shark nets are an expensive luxury in a country short of western currency.

Catlin lay on his back in the bottom of the small dinghy. It smelt of fish, and was normally a tender for one of the larger fishing boats with the elegantly upswept bows that showed their classical origin in the Nile estuary dows of over two thousand years before.

The water was tepid, so close to blood heat he was almost unaware of it around his foot and ankle. He stared up at a cloudless sky and tried to forget his work as an oil well fire fighter, tried to escape from the death of Mike O'Donovan. The hire of the dinghy had been an attempt at escape; it hadn't worked, wasn't working, at least not yet. Unwinding took longer with each job. He'd witnessed death before, most kinds of death. The slow and insidious death from disease, the terrible noisome death of war. He'd once stood on a hill in Korea, himself and a whole machine-gun company, and heard the whistles and the shouting, and then watched several thousand North Korean soldiers hurl themselves to their deaths against the rapid firing guns in their concrete positions. Only the first wave of Red troops had carried weapons, and they carried them knowing they would die, and that the rifle, pistol or submachinegun they carried and used, would be picked up by the second wave, the third or fourth. Catlin had wondered, at the time, if they said to each other before their attacks; 'Hey, Hook Fo, you keep a steady eye on my back, and when I go down, you will be fortunate enough to inherit all my worldly possessions - my four grenades, my rifle, and my ten clips of ammunition.' They'd come on and on, blowing whistles, shrieking in agony, dying, crawling. They'd come on staggering, leaking deep crimson blood, bits blown off them, until, like it or not, Catlin had to shoot wounded men to save himself. They hadn't retreated, they were just shredded and blown away, and the snow of the hillside held their blood until the thaw several weeks later; when the snow melted, the blood blackened and the ground stank.

He had seen men die fighting renegade oil wells. It happened: Sometimes through carelessness unfamiliarity, over confidence. Or like Mike O'Donovan, one of the best troubleshooters in the business, for no good reason at all.

Murphy's Law had killed O'Donovan.

The law states: 'No matter how perfect you make a piece of machinery, no matter how foolproof you devise a piece of equipment, no matter how safe you compound an explosive, one day it will break, twist itself inside out, disintegrate, suffer from molecular decay, fracture, be inserted sideways, upside down, explode unexpectedly.' Both Catlin and O'Donovan had known that even systems were only as safe as the law of the mythical Murphy would allow.

O'Donovan had been six feet three inches in height, weighed in at a little under 190 lbs, was clean shaven, Catlin's only close friend, and had died a wealthy man.

The oil well responsible for his death had formerly been the property of United States Middle East Products. It belonged now to Sheik Hussad Mohamet Amou'ahd, producing its liquid gambling assets to be spent largely in the casinos of Europe, and only fractionally for the education and well-being of the Sheik's deprived third world subjects.

Sheik Hussad Mohamet Amou'ahd's oil well had been ablaze. To be accurate, only one of his many wells shot a column of flame and black smoke into the desert air, making the ground shake and the air vibrate with the thunderous roar of gas and oil escaping under great pressure. But it had been burning for five days, and twenty million dollars worth of roulette and poker chips trailed an evil smoke mist across hundred miles of raw desert. His other well-head pumps nodded wisely and productively in the stinking fog, like knowing mules.

Catlin's circus, as it was known internationally, tamed renegade oil wells. It was self-contained. Team One, headed by Catlin himself, arrived in their own aircraft, a ten-year-old Hercules that had once seen war service with the Army Air Corps. Now it carried, with no greater comfort, a four man team, its pilot, and several tons of assorted equipment. Most of the latter was neatly stacked a quarter mile upwind of the burning well. Mohamet Amou'ahd's company provided the explosive. Carrying nitro, or plastic, on board the aircraft presented too many problems at on-flight fuelling stops. Mike O'Donovan had checked the Arab charges; gelignite, sweating in the desert heat! O'Donovan had little imagination. Catlin preferred his men that way, it make them more reliable and predictable.

O'Donovan was sweating like the explosive, and for the same reason. The harsh sun of July forced the temperature up to a hundred and ten. The breeze, a hot movement of air drawn towards the burning well, as it sought oxygen, brought no relief, only a flour-like dust that became red mud on the men's bodies when it mingled with their perspiration.

The heat, the vast roaring flame, the vibrating ground and throbbing air, no longer impressed O'Donovan. He'd been impressed with the first few wells that had broken away and run wild, but he had seen Catlin cut them down to size, tame them, bottle them up and stopper them. They were giants with no ambitions.

There was no point in talking. Catlin, ear-muffed, only two yards away, could not have heard him even had he screamed until his lungs burst. Their silver, heat-reflecting suits made them look like astronauts. They moved as clumsily.

Catlin nodded, briefly, then swung his headgear over his shoulders. The narrow strip of mica in the visor reflecting the orange flame of the fire. O'Donovan shrugged his way into the folds of heavy asbestos cloth. The roar of the well softened.

There were ways of snapping out the flame, and Catlin's was personal. It could be done by robot, or by placing explosive against the mouth of the well at the end of a fifty foot pole. In Catlin's view neither was satisfactory. He fed the tiger by hand, placing the explosive in the exact spot that he knew would guarantee a first-time successful job. Fast, neat, tidy; dangerous.

Nearer the well-head, the ground became a jelly, quivering beneath the men's feet. O'Donovan clenched his jaw muscles to stop his teeth chattering. Sweat coursed the valleys of his body. The men carried the insulated box of explosive between them, picking their way across the last few yards of rubble and twisted wreckage at the foot of the shrieking inferno. Jake Harley, two hundred yards behind them, paid out the wire he would couple to the detonating generator when the men returned to safety.

The two men did not hurry, but there was no hesitation in their movement. They had made this trip often, in other places.

What had been a hot breeze a hundred and fifty yards from the inferno, was now a gale, threatening to drag them into the column of the fire. As Catlin had once said, if a man ever wanted to know what Hell was like, then he need only stand a few yards from an oil well fire.

Catlin stopped and, with his free arm, waved downwards. They were still thirty feet from the base of the flames. Very little of the original rig remained in its place. It would be a dirty and difficult job to cap, even when the flame was out. A local Arab crew stood by their truck, half-a-mile away, nervously waiting in their protective clothing.

The two men knelt. O'Donovan crouching low to minimise the effects of the heat while Catlin crawled forward, pushing the box in front of him until he reached the rim of the small crater which the well had dug itself, like a budding volcano. This was a job for one man, the other holding himself ready should some unforeseen emergency arise; there were many unpleasant possibilities at this point.

Catlin was now almost belly-flat on the trembling ground, inching his way toward the fire. He had little time. The heat inside his suit was almost unbearable. Soon, even the aluminium and asbestos would become red-hot and his body begin to cook. He eased the box up the quivering slope of scorching sand and pebbles until it reached the rim. It slid from sight. The specially protected cables would withstand the heat for only fifteen minutes at most. Catlin wriggled hurriedly backwards, then turned and got to his feet. He gave a vague thumbs-up signal with a heavily gloved hand.

Murphy's Law had already begun to operate. When the local explosive had been placed in the heat insulated container, the outer layers should have contained no detonators. The greasy blocks had been stacked in place like gold bricks in a vault. But the explosive had been in use before, prepared as demolition charges should terrorist forces decide to make an attack against the oil field. The attack had never come and the charges had been dismantled, but one block of explosive still contained a live detonator placed only fractionally below its surface. The block was one of the outer pieces of explosive, its side pressing against the thickly insulated lining of the steel container. Catlin's own detonators were deep inside the charge, well away from the sides of the metal case.

It should *still* have been safe; would have been, but for yet another factor determined by the Law of Murphy. The inch-thick insulating material had a single joint within the steel container. Normally the joint was scarfed, it's two ends overlapping. The Texan fitter who had built the container for Catlin, not even aware of it's future use, was at the time thinking of his chances of seducing the canteen girl who had agreed to accompany him to a drive-in that evening. The joint made by the distracted fitter was butted, instead of overlapping. Now, a warping of the outer case of the container in the ferocious heat of the fire had drawn the joint apart.

The vibration of the ground shook the plastic explosive. Already too soft in the desert heat, the weight of the top blocks flattened those below. The hidden detonator was forced into the gap between the two ends of the insulation material. It was pressed against the heat-blueing metal of the outer wall.

Even so, the two men were now twenty five yards from the well. It was Murphy's Law again that determined Mike O'Donovan should be in the wrong place at the wrong time.

The overheated detonator and the thirty five pounds of explosive erupted without warning. The force of the explosion tossed the two men further away from the wreckage of the well-head, bundling them like rag dolls across the scorched desert. A sheet of quarter-inch steel plate, part of the rig-flooring, 400 lbs in weight and twice the size of a house door, spun, as a child flicks a piece of roofing slate, away from the centre of the explosion, arcing toward the stunned men. It fell, edge on, a white-hot guillotine blade that dissected O'Donovan from right shoulder to crutch, frying and cauterising the sliced flesh. O'Donovan felt his death, it was not instantaneous. There was time for one silent scream of agony behind his mica and asbestos hood. His left arm and leg died last, twitching and kicking in the smoking oil mud, as black rain poured from the sky above the extinguished well.

It had been the 12th of July . . . just three days ago, thought Catlin, sadly.

There'd been a brief inquest the afternoon of O'Donovan's death . . . the day of his burial . . . you didn't waste time getting a man underground in desert temperatures. The verdict at the inquest had been one of accidental death; no blame for negligence. Cause of death; premature explosion, reason unknown!

There'd been a will. Joe Catlin had packed O'Donovan's gear . . . and there hadn't been much of it. Moving around a lot meant limiting personal possessions. Two suitcases of clothing and an army surplus duffle bag of work-gear. A valise of paperbacks, mostly unread, and a single bottle of Beefeater gin, which Mike drank neat when work was over. And only the will. No parents alive, and no wife. He'd left every dollar he'd earned, every dollar that had remained unspent over eleven years, accumulating interest . . . to the company! To J. J. Catlin Incorporated! He'd have argued: 'Why not, they're my family; friends and family. It was all company money, anyway.'

Catlin had torn up the will; claimed he hadn't found one. There'd be relatives somewhere, and no matter how distant they might be, blood family was where the money should go.

Strange, Catlin thought, you did a job you liked, did it well, and charged the going rate, and suddenly there was more money than you ever needed. Catlin was like O'Donovan with money — he used it rather than spent it. Most of Catlin's money was churned back into the business; there was always new equipment required and two offices to staff and furnish . . . one office had to be in Dallas where it had all started, and the other was in

Leith, Scotland, to take care of the new North Sea oil exploration companies. Lately he'd been favouring the Scottish business, it had something of a fascinating quaintness about it all, like Ma Enid MacDougal who always insisted he drank tea, although it tasted to him like waterhole-pumpings, and in a motherly fashion she'd check to make sure he was adequately dressed in what she referred to as: 'This wee cold northerly winter.'

Catlin was an inch short of six-feet. A bulky man in his middle forties, he had missed the European war, and caught Korea. He knew most about two things; oil and explosives. His body showed the hard way of learning. Out in the sun the right side of his back tanned normally, as did his chest and right leg. The left side was fire-scorched, the skin tortured and burnt, mottled purple and white, twisted into obscene tattoos. His lips were thickened like those of a boxer, his nose flattened and offset. A denture replaced the three front teeth that remained embedded in a piece of pine planking he now used as a paperweight on his Dallas office desk top. The roar of escaping gas had taken the edge from his hearing, and the fumes of burning oil added a rasp to his voice. Had he been a smoker, he would have been warned to give it up; no-one would have dared suggest he gave up oil taming.

He had the reputation of being nerveless, but in truth he squeezed the nerves until they were dust-shot hidden somewhere deep inside him. With each job he squeezed harder, and every time he did so it took just a little longer to soften the compressed pellets.

Mike O'Donovan he had liked, trusted. He'd expected the man to retire, one day long in the future. Mike had been no keen young buck, bursting to get his ass blown away. He'd been careful, slow and methodical; the way to be if you wanted to see sixty in the oil business.

And no close family; another thing he and O'Donovan had shared. Both orphans, both unmarried. Catlin never really thought of himself as an orphan, for although his parents had died when he was young, he remembered them both. He remembered them dying together, on a Saturday night; it was as though they had gone out and left him alone deliberately. It had been several years before he had understood there was no intended hurt in their deaths. Sideswiped by a drunken driver while they waited at a bus station. There had been only two mangled bodies and a tearful, alcoholic-dazed teenager, who served a prison sentence when the manslaughter charge stuck. Catlin was brought up by the State, fathered and mothered by it, and later pushed through college. He was grateful they had troubled. Lots of the orphanage kids grew up with a fiery resentment inside them; Catlin just thought 'thanks', and was happy to pay his taxes, though he'd have admitted they hurt sometimes.

He'd got into oil, through war. He'd thought about the Marines and decided he could do without having some bootneck drill sergeant yowling at him for months of training. He chose the engineers and they taught him demolition. He was commissioned in the field. By the time he left Seoul and the war had ended, he knew almost everything about explosives, from old-fashioned blasting powder which the North Koreans seemed to love, to the most modern European plastics. He had been young, then; enjoyed the thrill of detonation, the considered risks in dismantling a live bomb, the neat placing of a cutting charge to chop a slender tree, or drop the legs of a viaduct away as clean as a power-cutter, and a thousand times quicker. He enjoyed the notoriety, the way the men would point him out in a bar to the Korean hostesses: 'See that guy, that's Catlin. Take a close look at him baby, he's already dead.' There was a mess joke, wry and grim, saying there was a coffin, made and waiting, with his name, rank and number already painted on the lid. It was a special miniature coffin, because there wouldn't be much left of him to ship home. It was known as Catlin's casket, and the guys would shout: 'Joe, you'll be wanting your casket today?' He'd laugh and reply: 'Maybe.' He'd outlived many of them.

The army had also taught him responsibility. You didn't take chances when other men's lives were at stake, and it was this responsibility that had prevented him from marrying. He'd thought about it several times. There had been women he loved, quite a while back. He'd nearly married Suzy Brickness, a girl from the same State orphanage. She'd been a year younger than himself, and he hadn't really noticed her until he came home on leave from the army. There she was, Suzy Brickness, a pert, attractive blonde, and not dizzy. She was helping out at the school in her free time, having recently qualified as a teacher. They dated on all his leaves until his first one back from Korea. He knew about death by then, and responsibility. If Suzy Brickness wanted him, then she'd have to wait. Bringing up a family wasn't easy for an army widow, and there were already too many of them. He told Suzy to go out and find herself another man; anyone in a safe job. He loved her, but never said as much. Six months later she wrote she'd met a short-sighted journalist with flat feet and no ambitions to be a war correspondent. They'd married the previous week. It wasn't a 'Dear Joe' letter, though it began with exactly those two words. It was warm, and friendly. She was happy and there were no hard feelings. Suzy and the myopic journalist got themselves a mortgage, raised kids and credit, and lived happily ever afterwards.

There had been other women, most good, a few bad, and not too many he classed as indifferent. Some he might have married in other lives, but it had taken him only a few years to realise that so long as he went on taking risks for a living, it was cruel to expect the risks to be shared by a partner you respected. Had he raced cars as a job, he'd have felt the same. He knew it was better for everyone if he just didn't allow himself to get involved emotionally. It had been a game he'd had to learn. It was just as cruel if you allowed your partner to fall in love, but stayed cool yourself. Now, it was: 'That Joe, he just isn't a marrying man . . . but what a helluva feller.' He had plenty of women friends; none he would call an enemy.

Big Mike O'Donovan had arrived from another war, from Vietnam. His qualifications and his background, excepting that he never knew his parents, were so similiar to Joe Catlin's own that Catlin had hired him immediately. The two men could almost read each other's mind. After a few months of training with Team Four, Catlin had moved him up. O'Donovan trod on no-one's toes; the other men respected him, and not because of his size.

It had been almost three years before the two men realised they were friends. It was a moment decided by the quantity they might drink when they were together. For a long time Big Mike didn't get drunk with his boss, nor Joe Catlin with his employee. Catlin made the first move. He got boozed stiff after a three month job in the heat of the Red Sea. Mike O'Donovan made no comment. He carried Joe out of the Cairo bar, checked to see that his wallet was still in place, and got him back to the El Borg Hotel in a rusty and battered Egyptian 'tax'. The next night Big Mike let his hair down, and Catlin stayed sober enough to get them both back to the hotel. That was the way it always was; one relaxing, the other keeping an eye on things. It was responsible as well as friendly in the kind of bars they did their drinking.

'Jesus Christ, O'Donovan, you're a miserable turd,' said Catlin, to the heavy azure sky seeming to sit only a little way above the rocking dinghy. If Big Mike was up there then the bastard would be laughing himself sick at the sight of Catlin lying in a small boat in a Yugoslavian harbour, with his foot dangling in the scummy water.

'What the hell am I doing here?' Catlin spoke aloud again. His gravel voice was pitched deep and he wasn't always easy to understand. A couple of large green blowflies, who seemed to live on the sickly smell of long consumed fish offal in the dinghy, flirted around his head. He said: 'Shit,' and jerked his peaked cap forward over his face. He could still see the bright sky through the weave of the material. The dinghy caught his sudden movement and bucked soporifically.

There had been no need for Catlin to hang around in Mhalluka for the final capping of the defeated well. That was Jake Harley's responsibility, and he was quite capable of handling operations on his own. Harley would use the local crew and complete the job in a few more days. Catlin, the hard nerve pellets inside him compressed even more tightly than usual by O'Donovan's death, had needed time on his own. He'd sent two cables; one to Dallas, one to Leith. They were brief but sufficient. 'Taking a break.' He'd signed them 'Cat'. He'd had few vacations over the years, but knew the offices could function without him for a while. He only employed competents.

He had packed a single suitcase and left his others with O'Donovan's and the remainder of the crew's, on the company 'plane. He'd catch up with them somewhere.

The airport at Mhalluka was a flattened section of desert with a single cross of runways rising to a slight hill in the centre, so any large aircraft was forced to accelerate over the hill and make its take-off travelling down the slopes. There were few hangars, and those existing were mainly workshops for the Mystere fighters continually patrolling the country's borders. There was a control-tower built of steel scaffolding with concrete bunkers around its base, and similar bunkers interspersed with machinegun posts surrounding the entire perimeter of the airfield. Troops continually patrolled the high wire entanglements beside the roadway, as though the country was actually at war; its ministers would claim it was, if asked.

The airport terminal was a camouflage-painted Nisson hut, first erected by the British Royal Air Force in 1941. Besides the airport offices, the corrugated-iron building contained the only booking agency in Mhalluka. There was no duty-free shop, although two Arabs with trays of small souvenirs, and imported rugs draped over their shoulders, appeared from the shade at the side of the building as soon as Catlin climbed from the jeep. He brushed the salesmen aside and found the booking office. The clerk spoke moderate English.

'I'd like the first plane out of here,' said Catlin.

'To Moscow?'

'It goes to Russia?' Catlin was surprised.

'Eventually with certainty, Sir' The clerk was obviously amused by the expression on Catlin's face, but he was trying to be helpful. He was a slightly-built man in his early twenties, and wore neatly pressed western clothes, below a desert Arab's head-dress. He checked a pile of documents on his desk, and then looked at Catlin again. 'It is probable to arrive here in approximately one hours, Sir. It will refuel itself and then be flying to Yugoslavia, then Czechoslovakia and eventually the Soviet People's Republic.'

'Whereabouts in Yugoslavia?'

'Ljubljana, Sir.' The clerk was curious as well as helpful. 'May I be asking, Sir, why you apparently want to depart to no-where in particular?'

'I need a vacation.' Said Catlin. The clerk's interest did not provoke irritation. 'Anywhere, I guess. Just a few days break. I've been working on the well-fire.'

'Yes, I know, Sir.' He noticed Catlin's quick look. 'This is small city, Sir. We do not have too great many Europeans over-stopping here. I was on duty when your aircraft was brought through. Naturally, all people have also heard of the terrible accident.' He was embarrassed as soon as he mentioned it, and tried to make amends by quickly changing the subject. 'Ljubljana . . . Yugoslavia, Sir, is supposed to be a most beautiful country. I have male cousin who stay there for a long while; he was at Ljubljana University, Sir. He spoke highly of the country. It is seemingly very green and mountainous, and it is possible to swim in a beautiful sea. I understand they have an open country for the west. It is possible for a Western European to travel there and stay as visitor, without many restrictions. There are aircraft from Ljubljana to other western countries. Also regular flights to France, Germany, Italy, Britain, and if required you will be able to get for yourself a visitor's visa, at Ljubljana airport immigration.'

'Okay, I'll have a ticket.'

The clerk frowned, briefly. 'Alas there may not be a seat available on the aircraft, Sir. Regrettably, we must adjourn a decision until it lands. I would be surprised, however, if it were not possible. You will be paying in western currency?' Catlin nodded. 'Then I am very certain we will manage to load you on-board.'

Seven hours later Catlin had landed in Yugoslavia, in Ljubljana. A small Renault, used as a cab, took him to the centre of the town. It was already dark, but contrary to Catlin's expectations of a communist country, the town was not deserted after nightfall. There were restaurants and bars open, and tables placed on the sidewalks were occupied by people drinking and talking. Lights shone in the store windows and people window-shopped and strolled. It was a warm night. He was deposited at the Solin Hotel, and found himself a room. He ate a mediocre meal and took a short walk in the town. He had changed dollars for Yugoslav currency at the airport, but felt disinclined to visit the town bars although he wanted a drink. He returned to the hotel half an hour later and drank at the small bar beside the reception. The barman spoke a little English; enough to take Catlin's orders for drinks. He retired to his room at midnight, and for the first time in several days slept well.

He met Lisetta Irano shortly after he had breakfasted the following morning. He had viewed Ljubljana from his room window; it seemed an unattractive city. Stark outlines of cheap and ugly apartment blocks contrasted sharply with the softer architecture of older buildings and he could smell the fumes of vehicles from the narrow roadway below that was noisy with traffic.

'Some place for a vacation,' he thought. He found the hotel restaurant. He wasn't hungry, so the light continental breakfast was sufficient; the coffee tasted stewed. The thought of a flight, on to the USA, was tempting. There would be only one change of aircraft; at London's Heathrow. Maybe he could even fly out through Germany, and make the Atlantic crossing direct from there? He decided to check-out and walked to the reception area. The girl, studying a directory beside the counter distracted him.

She was lightly built, almost boyish in jeans and a sleveless tee shirt. She wore no bra and the shirt moulded itself to her body. The skin on her shoulders and neck was pale olive, her hair dark and cut short like a man's. She turned as he stopped beside her and looked towards him. Her eyes, dark as her hair, moved quickly across his face, as though she hoped to recognise him. He guessed her age as somewhere in the early twenties, and decided she was one of the most attractive women he had seen in many weeks.

She looked back at the directory.

The clerk behind the counter spoke.

'I beg your pardon.' Catlin wasn't sure what language the man was using, but it was unfamiliar. By apologising, he hoped he would encourage the man to reply in English. It usually worked, but this time it didn't.

The man repeated himself, his palms flat on the desk top, his body weight pressed forward as if he were about to vault to Catlin's side. He articulated each word carefully, mouthing the vowels slowly.

Catlin shook his head, and the man shrugged and lost interest.

'He no speak American. What you want to know?'

For some reason the girl's voice beside Catlin embarrassed him and he felt himself blush. He'd never been clever at languages and even after months in some foreign country usually only learnt enough to get his wants across to a local barman. He felt somehow the girl had instantly recognised the weakness. Her eyes met his, enquiringly. 'You are American, yes?' The voice, Catlin realised, held no criticism. She spoke softly, her voice pitched just a fraction lower than the average woman's.

'Er, yes ma'am.' Catlin hoped he wasn't leering stupidly. Damn the woman, she even made him remember his broken nose and thickened lips.

She smiled back and Catlin felt himself relax a little. Women had rarely made him feel self conscious. If he'd been holding a cap in his hands he knew he would have been twisting it, awkwardly, like a young countryboy meeting a sophisticated town girl for the first time.

'Perhaps I help you?' The dark eyes held his own. The girl's mouth was wide, and her teeth square and perfect. There was no makeup on her lips or the flawless skin of her cheeks.

'Yes . . . I'd sure like that.' She stood waiting. He tried to remember what he had been going to ask the clerk. 'I, er . . .' His thoughts wouldn't link and he knew too long a time was passing between his words. The girl interrupted him by laughing at his brief confusion. Catlin was startled but her amusement was infectious. He laughed back and the embarrassment left him.

'Good god,' he said. The girl had her fist to her mouth, and there were tears in her eyes. A group of people across the reception area had turned to watch. Catlin grinned at the girl. 'I was going to ask him if there was somewhere I could buy a decent coffee.' The girl's face was totally open, animated, every emotion instantly obvious. Catlin was mesmerised.

'Not here. No good coffee in hotel. You come with me. I show you.' She led him from the hotel. Catlin expected her to stop on the sidewalk and point to some distant cafe, but she didn't. She walked briskly beside him, threading a path through the people and forcing him to stretch his pace to keep up with her. It was a warm morning and Catlin was sweating by the time the girl led him to a small square, one side of which was occupied by three busy rows of meal tables shaded by sun umbrellas. Waiters hurried between them balancing small trays, delivering drinks and snacks, collecting money.

She saw a vacant table and beckoned Catlin to follow her. When they reached it she turned and held out her hand. Catlin took it automatically. He thought she was about to leave him, instead she said: 'I am Lisetta Irano. Will I have coffee with you?'

'Of course.' The girl didn't release his hand immediately.

'You are doing it again.' She was smiling.

'Doing it? What?'

'Going red.' She let go his hand and sat down.

He sat facing her and saw by her eyes she was teasing him. Catlin hadn't been teased for twenty five years. 'My mother was frightened by a communist!' Damn, he thought. He couldn't have made a more stupid remark. He'd forgotten Yugoslavia was an Iron Curtain Country, and the girl was entitled to react angrily. He cursed his thoughtlessness; he'd be sorry if she left him now.

'My mother, also.' To his relief she contnued to smile at him. 'But I no go colour of Russian flag. What your name, please?'

'I'm sorry, I . . .' began Catlin. He gave up. 'Joe,' he said, weakly. 'Joe Catlin.'

'And you are tourist, Joe?'

'No . . . yes, I guess I'm a tourist.'

'You not know.' She was teasing again.

Get a grip of yourself, Catlin told himself. The girl was making him feel like a schoolboy again. 'Sure I'm a tourist, but I wasn't really expecting to take a vacation in Yugoslavia.'

The girl called to a waiter, then turned back to Catlin. 'Why?'

Catlin found himself explaining the past few days. He didn't make a big issue of O'Donovan's death, the loss of a close friend, but he saw the girl understood.

She didn't speak for a while when he had finished. He watched her, wondering if he had said too much. Eventually, she asked: 'And now?' There was interest in her voice and he knew the question was genuine.

'I wasn't sure what to do next,' he admitted. 'I was going to ask the clerk for an airport timetable.'

'To leave Yugoslavia?' She sat forward, concerned.

'Yes.'

'That bad idea.' She rested a small hand maternally on his own and spoke positively. 'You need rest. Here will be good for you.'

It was beginning to look better, thought Catlin.

'Go to seaside, take rest in sun. You swim; no think of work. You drink, dance,' she ordered.

'I won't get much pleasure dancing on my own. I don't know where to go to find your sea, and you've seen how much trouble I can have trying to understand your language.' There was as much inference as Catlin dared to risk. If he laboured the innocent tourist bit the girl might feel he considered her naive or cheap.

The girl knew what he was hoping for in her reply, and smiled at him. 'You will go to the town of Piran, it is beautiful sea there. I will arrange all for you. You drive car? I will find! You need hotel; I make booking. Last week I could come with you; even next week is possible. But now, it is not. I must make journey to my parents.' The girl saw disappointment on his face. 'I think maybe we meet, Joe. We make arrangement. How long perhaps you stay in Yugoslavia, now?'

It was tempting bait. 'A week,' said Catlin lightly. 'Longer, perhaps.'

'You go Piran one week or more. After four days I find you.'

Catlin decided not to press his luck.

It took three hours for her to get him a hotel booking and arrange the rent of a car. It was a small Fiat into which Catlin levered his bulk with difficulty. Lisetta waited in the Ljubljana hotel foyer while he settled his bill and then outside the entrance leant through the window of the car.

'In four days, Joe, we meet.'

'Okay.'

'You rest.' She kissed his cheek. 'And mind for Yugoslav

driver; he most dangerous.'

'Sure, honey.'

She stepped back and waved him off.

Lisetta had bought him a map; Piran was not far away. The journey looked simple and it was. He was in Piran less than two hours later. He parked the car in a narrow street at the side of the harbour and found his hotel within a few minutes of arrival. He checked in at a desk where the clerk was lethargic and unhelpful. The room was not as clean as the one he had vacated in Ljubljana. The carpets of the Piran hotel were threadbare in patches and the place had a positively run-down air. Plastic-covered tables in the reception area showed cigarette burns on the edges. The paint-work was fly-spotted and needed freshening. No-one offered to carry his bag or direct him to his room. He was handed a key attached to a large lump of chipped rubber. He found his room on the second floor. It faced the sea. He pushed open the windows and stood on the small balcony, the view was beautiful. The room faced a wide bay, to the left was the entrance to the harbour; the sea was like gin. The sun, now a little after mid-day, was high and beating down on the sunbathers along the edge of the rocky beach. For a while he stood and watched them. Family groups with children playing in the short waves, the odd swimmer wearing mask and flippers, beating the water forty or fifty yards from the shore. Brown backs; stout women in bikinis who should have known better. Stouter men in baggy shorts. Lithe youths lying beside equally slim young women whose bra-straps lay unhooked on the rocks beside them. Suntan oil being smoothed into olive skins. Sunburn on paler bodies. Black-haired and dark-eyed Italians and Yugoslavs, blonde-haired and blue-eyed men and women from the northern countries. The sounds of their mingled voices reached him as a continuous indecipherable murmur.

There were a lot of people, Catlin thought, perhaps too many. They were holidaying, enjoying themselves. This wasn't exactly what Catlin was seeking. He wanted only to unknot the nerves; unwind somehow. He wasn't sure how it should be done. It had been easier with O'Donovan around. Together they drank the tension away . . . sometimes silently, sometimes with a coarse rough humour they both understood. It had been a long time since Catlin had unwound alone. The girl's company had been good, but the tension had returned with the drive from Ljubljana. Four days alone wasn't too much, he tried reminding himself.

She'd said, in four days she'd come to Piran. At the time he'd believed her; wanted to believe. Now he wasn't sure. A girl like that wouldn't be lacking company. Why the hell should she be interested in some middle-aged guy? His thoughts depressed him. Maybe he shouldn't have let her sidetrack him; maybe he should be on that aircraft now.

He left the hotel, found the people. He walked the length of the sea front, the route laborious between strolling families carrying their towels, beachbags, holiday paraphernalia; eating icecreams, fruit, local sweetmeats. He passed the bars, the tables beneath sun-parasols, crowded. Laughter and beach games on the rocks; beach balls and frisbies. Couples chasing in the waves; splashing, relaxing, holding hands, kissing.

Catlin felt outside it all; lonely, and taut. He thought briefly of taking the Fiat and driving it to Ljubljana, but the car had been hot, even with all it's windows open. Driving it again today was not appealing.

He found the small dinghy by late afternoon. It was moored beside a commercial fishing boat. He pointed at it and then himself, and one of the fishermen shook his head and waved a negative hand. Catlin persisted, peeled some money from his wad of Yugoslavian dinars and tried again. The man shook his head as determinedly as before. Catlin shrugged and began to walk away.

The man called: 'Englisi?'

Catlin stopped, turned and said: 'Americano.'

The man held up his hand to indicate Catlin should wait for a moment while he consulted with the other fishermen. He did so noisily, then spoke again. 'Got mark. .lira. .pound. .dollar?'

'Dollars.' Catlin had already found western currency was more acceptable than the eastern state dinar. Apparently the dinar could not be used outside Yugoslavia, at least, not in a western country, and Italy was only a few miles away where the border was formed just outside Trieste. Yugoslavs could visit, stare at the plushly decorated windows in the stores, but buy nothing unless they had western currency. A dollar could buy far more than its true value in dinars, in Yugoslavia.

The man held up both his hands, fingers spread wide. 'Dollars.'

Catlin could recognise this game; laughed, and held up two fingers, wondering if the man would also know it as a mild insult. The man did so and grinned; his companions watched him keenly. He held up seven fingers and Catlin replied with five. The man hopefully added another but when Catlin half turned away, he quickly matched Catlin's. Catlin handed him a five dollar bill which he stretched towards the sun and then examined. He nodded as Catlin climbed into the dinghy and then untied the bow rope, tossing it into the boat. He made signals so Catlin knew when he returned he was to tie the dinghy back in the same place.

The oars were as old as the dinghy, split, rough, and unequal in length. It had been a decade since Catlin had rowed. It brought back memories; ten years before, a hot September afternoon on Central Park lake. God, why had he chosen New York in a hot September? It had been as sweaty as a sauna, the humidity so high that if it had risen a few degrees, New York would have been waterlogged. He remembered he'd just completed a contract with Western United Oils; a big contract. It had looked good, but worked out bad. But why Central Park lake? Josie, that was why! She'd lasted about the length of time of the contract. Another dark girl, she claimed she was half Sioux, but he knew she was that percentage Puerto Rican. He let her keep up the illusion as that was what she wanted, though he wouldn't have minded whatever her ancestry. She'd been good company, lively, bright and intelligent. Just not quite intelligent enough to know he didn't give a damn about race, colour, creed or background.

There was a large rock tied to a length of rope, resting in the bow of the dinghy. Catlin knew it was intended as the anchor. He rowed the small boat slowly out past the end of the harbour wall. The sea was glass calm, a little oily on its surface. It smelt of sea plus garbage. The scent of a harbour; the dinghy stank of fish.

He made sure he was away from any route used by the larger vessels, and then let the rock slide over the side. The water was clear enough for him to watch the yellow stone sinking below for many feet, before it disappeared from view. He payed out a few extra yards of rope, then looped it around one of the rowlocks.

He lazed, thinking the day away. There were still too many oil fires in his mind; there was still O'Donovan. Sometimes there was Lisetta Irano, and she was just a little more real than most of the other thoughts.

The great porbeagle, sleekly torpedoing the water beyond the harbour entrance, had no real thoughts of attacking anyone. It had experienced few contacts with humans during its lifetime. It had seen swimmers, but avoided them; they did not look like food, only danger. It found most of its meals amongst shoals of sardine and other fish. It would drive in swiftly, its great jaws apart, slashing, to turn and slash, slash again, until the sea surrounding it was full of torn and ripped fish. Then it fed leisurely on the protein-packed debris. Sometimes it trailed the wakes of the cruise liners up the length of the Adriatic, snatching tidbits from their waste. This it had been doing for the past few weeks until a Spanish ship had led it to Trieste, and it had turned eastwards then south on its present course.

It had no predetermined intentions. It did not plan far ahead. It was an opportunist. It ate what it found to eat; it avoided trouble.

Its last turn, at a line of rocks only ten or twelve feet below the surface, brought it nearer to Catlin's dinghy. It saw the long line of the anchor rope first, picking up the sunlight. The dinghy was a dark object moving gently on the mirror surface above. The shark, curious, flicked its powerful tail. The movement drove it closer. Something paler than the large object attached to the rope, moved in the water's surface. The shark sensed it was alive, might be edible. The great fish angled a fin and coasted a wide arc, hesitantly.

Catlin splashed his foot in the water, then shuddered. He experienced a strange incongruent feeling, for he seldom shuddered unless he was cold, and there was no chill in the air or his body now. He did not understand the primeval signal of hidden danger, perceived by a deep and mysterious part of the mind; an unrecognised faculty without which the human race could never have survived, but now buried beneath the thick cloth of civilisation. For no reason he could determine, Catlin drew his foot back into the boat. The soft touch of the sea water seemed to have become unbearably hostile. He had a brief feeling of unjustifiable guilt at the action as though he had stepped aside to avoid walking beneath a ladder. He moved himself to a more comfortable position, his back against the thwart, the warm air quickly drying his foot and leg, leaving a thin powdering of salt on his skin. The afternoon sun was dropping away.

The shark had seen the movement, but simultaneously had experienced the feeling of transmitted contact. Some vague primitive part of two unequal minds had met, touched, read, understood, and acted. The sleek fish turned its head, adjusted its lateral fins and powered itself away from the harbour towards the deeper water out at sea. It sensed rather than experienced the distant vibrations of the screws of a cruise ship heading south towards the Greek Archipeligo. The shark would join it for the duration of its voyage, or until another and better source of food attracted the fish's interest.

2

There is seldom an accurate way of defining the beginning of an event. For a great brown hawk circling a thermal perimeter three thousand feet above the dry hills of the Yugoslavian Karst it began late. The bird viewed the catastrophe emotionlessly, as he winged the shimmering uplift that was the gift of the late morning sun. But for many who were involved it had begun early . . . days or weeks before, in distant offices, bedrooms, lounges, clinics, studios, factories, automobiles, subway trains. It began with their plans, schemes, and ideas; their employers' rewards to them for faithful service, their self-indulgence for the few weeks of rest won after a year of toil. It began in brochures, and with bookings and deposits; confrontations with city-imprisoned clerks selling the mysteries of travel as though they were soap powder.

It did not begin at all for some people, unless a beginning can also be an end.

On the evening of the 12th of July, the day of O'Donovan's death, Senta Kaguri was in his home town of Hosokai, a functional and concrete industrial chequerboard, some eighty miles out of Tokyo, in Japan.

There is nothing externally attractive about Hosokai. It is not an old town. It has no ancient but carefully preserved Shogun's castle, no magnificent Shinto temple, no carefully landscaped civic lake with attendant geese and ducks. It is mostly factory; mostly the factory of Morei Yoshuabi. It makes bicycles, millions per annum, a steady stream that flows from the benches to the production lines, to the packing and despatch departments, and to almost every country of the world. Were they all treated with radio-active paint, and then photographed from outer space, it would appear as though the globe was in the grip of a gigantic octopus, its heart centred on the Japanese town of Hosokai, not yet twenty years of age.

Hosokai also manufactures drugs. A large chemical plant produces fertiliser, aspirin, food colorants, and industrial dyes. Cherry trees, planted in small suburban gardens flower each spring. So do chrysanthemums, and exotic shrubs carefully bonzai'd. They have no discernible scent. Hosokai smells only of chemicals.

In winter when the wind blows along the valley from the sea, it meets the harsh concrete blocks of Hosokai's buildings. They do not bend like the mountain pines, they meet the wind in head-on conflict and divide it, separate it, wound and anger it, until it tears its way through passages, along narrow streets; a vengeful blast striking viciously at the flesh and the bones of those who live and work within the town.

There is one street of pleasure. It contains the town's three cinemas, two hotels, nine restaurants, a dozen bars and five amusement arcades. Apart from the neon caligraphy it does not look Japanese. The two hotels are of the international kind. An occidental businessman, visiting to purchase Hosokai's goods, or even wishfully attempting to sell the industries his equipment, may stay in either of them, and apart from the facial and physical appearance of their staffs can feel as much at home as in the Deep Falls Holiday Inn, or the Munich Hilton.

One restaurant is not conspicuous. It is called simply 'The Old Way'. It has no street sign and is reached along a narrow alley that does not encourage the stranger. It is an alley like a thousand others in the city; windy and chilled even on a summer evening, possibly leading only to the rear entrance of a warehouse. The street door to 'The Old Way', is painted green. It is the first of three doors.

Behind the first two are the courtyard and garden of an inn. It has no genuine sky, but above the tree and shrub-surrounded lake distance fades to darkness and the hint of stars set somewhere in a lofty and disguised roof. There is the sound of water, the movement of waterfowl upon the pool, the lazy swirl of feeding carp beneath its surface. There is scented air, clean and purified. Wind bells of fine porcelain ripple soft music. Listen carefully and there is the most distant sound of praying monks, as though the breeze carries their words from high upon the unseen holy mountain.

The visitor must cross a narrow curving bridge towards the Inn's verandah ahead of him. Any other guests he meets will be like him in their traditional dress. He should pause now, in the garden. There are stone seats amongst the shrubs, close to the small lake. His wooden zori will clatter on the cobbles and he may walk a little slower with their unaccustomed clumsiness. Eventually, he approaches the third door. He slips off his footwear, knocks softly and passes through.

He is inside the Inn. If any Japanese of reasonable status from the past thousand years were to find himself within this place, it would be familiar. It is as it has always been. This is the Sanctum of Hosokai; 'The Old Way'. It costs fifty cents a minute to breath its exclusive aromatic air. Food, saki, entertainment, are very much more expensive.

Senta Kaguri was fifty-two years old. He had degrees in accountancy, had been a commissioned officer of the Imperial Navy in his youth and once swore holy allegiance to the Emperor Hirohito. His family were always of the Samurai class, leading their own armies, carrying their ancestral weapons, until the uprising late in the 1800's. There were many heroes amongst them, and their mons can often be seen on the dress of warriors in the fine woodcuts of the libraries and art collections. Kaguri is Assistant Managing Director of Yoshuabi Industries.

There were four of his friends with him, one of them the Managing Director himself. The actual founder of Yoshuabi Industries is now nothing more than a pension-drawing figurehead seldom seen at his factories, he spends most of his time in retirement in the distant and beautiful mountains. A deeply religious man, he was not one of the five men present.

The meal had been excellent, the saki plentiful and good.

Kaguri felt satisfied; almost. He pushed himself backwards a little on the firm tatami and stretched his ankle joints.

'You will find it interesting, Kagsan.' It was the Managing Director using the familiar form of address. 'And well deserved. It has been a fine business year. We have made the highest profits ever. Much of it due to your hard work.'

'Thank you.' Kaguri nodded his head. It was unnecessary to disagree with the Managing Director, he knew his remarks were no more than the truth.

'The Europeans will expect you to eat with hashi, from a bowl, and treat you like a barbarian,' said one of the other men. They all laughed.

'It will be interesting for me,' admitted Kaguri. He sucked at his teeth to clean them and the movement hollowed his thin cheeks even more. 'It is not the first time I have been abroad, remember Detroit is almost as well-known to me as Hosokai. There are things I like as well as dislike. I enjoy the travel.'

'But this time it is for pure pleasure,' advised the plump Managing Director. 'You must not forget that, Kagsan. No engineering . . . no accountancy . . . no profits and losses; simply pleasure.'

'I am most grateful to yourself and our company. It is a generous reward, and unexpected.'

'They tell me there are places in Hamburg, and in Paris, where . . ' began one of the men, his voice blurred with the wine.

'We know of them also in Tokyo,' laughed the Managing Director. 'I have no doubt Kagsan will have a few tales to tell us on his return. I hope they are not all of long-nosed and yellow-haired women who are dead fish in his bed.' There was a kimono-dressed girl kneeling, waiting, a few yards away. The Managing Director nodded towards her, she stood gracefully and left the room to discreetly arrange the signing of the bill. 'It is time I returned to my house.' He grunted a little, a heavy man, as he pushed himself to his feet. He smoothed the folds of his clothing.

'I think I shall remain longer,' said Kaguri. 'My vacation has already begun. I do not need to be at the airport until tomorrow night. My bags are packed. I shall stay here.'

'Then do so, and travel with pleasure, my friend.' The Managing Director was swaying. They had consumed several flasks of hot wine throughout the meal. The other three men joined him at the door, bowed their departure to their friend, wished him satisfaction and a good flight on the following evening, and left him alone.

Kaguri allowed himself the private luxury of briefly stretching his legs. Too many years working in a modern office and making use of westernised equipment, chairs and desks, damaged the old training. At one time, he would have been able to sit for a complete day on his heels, without feeling any discomfort.

He was pleased, however, that he had gathered his feet beneath himself once more when the girl returned a few minutes later. She showed no surprise at him remaining alone in the room. Kaguri frequently visited 'The Old Way'; he too was an account customer whose bills were always settled monthly, by Yoshuabi Industries.

'I will be sleeping here,' Kaguri informed the girl. She nodded.

The girl had a very flat face, of a type which Kaguri did not find particularly attractive. His own wife, who would not be accompanying him on the trip to Europe, remaining at home with their three teenage children, had a more pleasantly pointed face. Her temper, though, was unpredictable. She had a degree herself, in Occidental literature, and they had met at University after the war. She was sufficiently liberated to resent the cage of domesticity, and the freedom of the male in her society. They had loved each other deeply in the first years after their marriage, but somehow their family, and then her husband's success in business had drawn them apart. There were times now when Kaguri even wondered if his wife hated him. He knew for certain she disliked his only hobby, Kendo, and the time he spent in the dojos teaching his young pupils. But Kendo had been almost a way of life for him since he had been a child; the quiet reverence of the practise room, the sudden clash of weapons against the black armour, the exuberance and the feeling of satisfaction at the end of a contest, were too important to him. Wisely, however, she had never forced him to make a choice between Kendo and their marriage.

The flat-faced girl brought him a flask of delicate wine flavoured with rose petals. He sipped it. 'Would you like music?' The girl's voice was paler than the wine. He shook his head.

The low table before him was already empty apart from the wine flask and his single thin porcelain bowl. The hidden air-conditioning had already cleansed the atmosphere. It was as fresh as a mountain woodland, as though pine forests stood beyond the windows whose artificiality was undetectable.

'Will I stay, or leave,' asked the girl, softly. The tone of her voice gave no indication of her own wishes.

Kaguri considered her question. She had been discreetly efficient throughout the evening, but he had hardly considered her as a sleeping companion. He had not recognised her; she must be some new addition to the staff of the Inn. To ask for another girl would be an insult which she had done nothing to justify. She could hardly be held responsible for the fact he found her face over-flat. On the other hand, he could tell her he wished to sleep alone, but this was not so. If he wished to sleep without companionship, then he might as well return to his own bed.

He let the cool wine slide across his tongue. It's faint taste of roses was refreshing. The wine had been chilled to the temperature of spring water.

'Stay,' he told the girl.

There was the slightest movement of her lips, and a fractional lowering of her eyelids and he knew she too had considered the possibility he might send her away. She was relieved by his decision.

He drank in silence for another half hour, conscious of the girl's dark eyes watching him, interpreting his facial expressions to requests. The wine flask was not yet empty, but he wanted no more. The girl was instantly beside him as though she read his mind. She held a small box of warmed damp cloths for his hands and face.

Later, in the sleeping section behind the sliding wall on one side of the cool room, he lay and watched her. She undressed modestly, but slowly enough and sufficiently openly for him to enjoy watching her should he so wish. Gentle artificial moonlight bathed the sleeping area and made her cream flesh translucent with its shading. Her breasts were small and well-formed, her waist slender and her slim thighs pleasantly rounded. There was no hair on her body and Kaguri wondered whether she had shaved, or in the ancient way had plucked the hairs from herself. Later, as his fingers searched the soft flesh between her warm thighs, he knew that like the Inn itself, she too sought to provide the authenticity of the ancestors.

For Kaguri, it was beginning.

Despite the plush brochures of the tour companies, Yugoslavia is *not* the most beautiful country in Europe. On its northern frontier, it does have attractive mountains and charming lakes, but the mountains are not as spectacular as the Swiss, French, Italian or Bavarian Alps, nor are the lakes surrounded by the sophistication of those to be found in Italy, Switzerland or Austria, though they may rightly claim to be less polluted by the oil of outboard engines. The Yugoslavian villages are certainly interesting, particularly those in the southern region, but a tourist will find that whereas an Italian village may absorb and digest its guests, one in Yugoslavia can remain somehow aloof. Some Yugoslavian cities do have buildings of great architectural interest, but there is not the wealth of style or the overwhelming density of history that a visitor can find in Florence, Rome, London, Paris or Athens.

Yugoslavia has little in the way of national wealth in the form of minerals, oil, large gas or coal deposits. It does not have vast seas so rich in fish, it can compete in the world's fish markets. It might have been better. Yugoslavia could perhaps, by now, be in the same high scoring class of industrialised countries who benefited from the major injection of capital from the western powers at the end of the Second World War. The gift of the Gods was not made to Yugoslavia for one very simple reason: The late Josip Tito, communist leader of the country at that time, chose to ally himself with the Soviet Union. His dream was a Communist State, an Utopia where all men and women were free and equal, where education was available for all, and where land was not the privilege of the rich; a country where a free man might stand on a hilltop and stare across the long valleys and truthfully say: 'This is all *mine*.' A country where people would not be exploited, and where profits of industry could be returned to the people in the form of hospitals, health services, education, culture and the comfort of the many public utilities. It has not worked that way.

Tito attempted to weld together a series of small nations who, in some cases, were traditional enemies. Six small countries in all; most with their own language, and fiercely loyal to their original heritage. They still hold themselves apart. The Slovenes of the north look to a history when they were under Austrian rule and learnt the elegance of the Austrian people. Their own last king continued to rule in exile in England over a pitiful court of emigres to whom, even to the last, he handed out his traditional orders and decorations — purchased for him by his friends from the shops of London who specialise in selling such interesting secondhand paraphernalia to collectors. The Slovenes do not number greatly in the population of Yugoslavia, though proportionately they seem to produce a very large number of educated intellectuals. There are said to be a hundred poets to the square mile in Slovenia. But to be Slovene in modern Yugoslavia is to be frustrated, for there are far more Serbs and Croats. If you are Slovene, then you will find few books are published in your language and you are therefore forced to learn Serbo/Croatian should you wish to read your national literature. And Croats, you may feel as a Slovene, are little more than swarthy peasants.

Serbs and Croats, on the other hand, have little love for the paler Slovenes. They too remember the Austrian rule, and consider the Slovenes almost Germanic, certainly snobs.

To attempt to blend so many nationalities with so many differing cultural backgrounds, is like trying to produce a clear colour by mixing together all the primaries; it is impossible, the result is an unpleasant soup.

Yugoslavia's problems are even more complex than simply a

matter of an amalgum of race; they are political. Tito, who loathed capitalism and loved Communism, stepped towards Russia. Russia, in turn, welcomed with open arms a country which would provide her with much needed land for military bases and even ports within the Mediterranean Sea. With Yugoslavia under her control she could build massive offensive sites at the very doorstep of the western world itself, cutting Europe completely in half and allowing her to overshadow and perhaps subsequently dominate Turkey, Greece, Austria, southern Germany, Italy and the Chinese satelite Albania.

To say that Tito realised his error, is simplifying matters too much. He still wanted his Communism, though not the Soviet domination. Like a fish caught on a light line, he twisted and turned, wriggled and shook himself. The hook remained firmly embedded and the line was tightened.

For more than thirty years he managed to keep the prowling Soviet wolves from his country. For his successors it has been even more difficult. They remember Czechoslovakia and Hungary, who thought they had found freedom within the jurisdiction of the Soviet Union, but at the very moment when the freedom seemed real, in rolled the Soviet army, its tanks and battalions. Blood was spilt in the streets as the Soviets 'liberated' their serfs once more. The Soviet wolf has been breathing heavily on the neck of Yugoslavia since Tito's death. Their military action in Afghanistan has indicated that with the slightest encouragement the Soviets may decide to 'liberate' Yugoslavia. It is not a happy situation to live with if you are a Yugoslavian citizen!

And so Yugoslavia has received little or no aid from anyone, eastern or western. The price of her communist independence is high. She is not a very industrialised country. Her agriculture is not technically highly advanced. Her intense communism of the early days did not work. It had to be relaxed. At first, one could own nothing more than personal possessions, and they were few; nothing much was produced for home consumption, few raw materials were available. People working for the state barely bothered to work. The free education for all introduced its own problems. Thousands upon thousands of young men and women who might otherwise have had only a normal education found they could go to university. They did so, and studied hard and qualified in many fields. So many became 'highly educated', that it became difficult to find people willing to do the normal manual jobs of the state.

'Steel workers are needed at Zagreb.'

'I have a degree in psychology.'

'We have no jobs for psychologists, only steel workers.'

'But I have been at University for three years. I have been educating myself for the past fourteen years. I speak three languages and my rated I.Q. is one hundred and thirty eight.'

'Perhaps you could go back to university and study for your doctorate.'

'What will I be able to do then, in another three years?'

'There may still be jobs at the steel factories!'

The communism of Yugoslavia today is hardly communism in the Soviet sense. You may travel freely, providing you can somehow find western currency. You can actually open a business of your own with few restrictions other than that you may not employ more than five people; this, incidentally is a restriction which in itself is damaging to a country's economy. The businesses most likely to succeed are those begun by individuals with the drive and enterprise to do so. By limiting their staff Tito strangled their ambition, expansion and output, no matter how much revenue they might eventually be able to return to the state. The Yugoslavs are fiercely individualistic and independent. They do not want the state to intervene; they keep their businesses small and therefore unprofitable, nationally. Or, they leave Yugoslavia to work abroad, and only return to visit their families.

Why then, after all this criticism, do people still travel to Yugoslavia from western Europe?

Because it *is* beautifully inexpensive! Wine, although not perhaps the quality of French, German or Californian, is good . . . and *very* cheap. Should you wish, you can get drunk for a pound. Food is excellent, especially sea food. The sea is mostly clean, clear and warm. Beaches are mainly rock or concrete in the north, but there are golden sands; enough for the tourists. You can visit Yugoslavia and find the sun, get a wonderful tan, drink yourself to regular hangovers, and eat like a prince — at the lowest prices in Europe. It is the package-deal paradise. Yugoslavia gets her western currency from tourism, and July and August are the peak of the Yugoslavian tourist season.

While Catlin was dangling his foot in the water of Piran harbour, Ljubljana's airport had been working furiously to cope with the increased air-traffic of the holiday season. The traffic controllers, under great pressure and mindful of a miscalculation which had caused a fatal two-plane aircrash only a few years previously, were pale with tension. The periods of duty, packed with decision-making requiring continual concentration, flew past and left them mentally and physically exhausted.

Tight control at the immigration and customs departments was impossible. Each plane landing brought in a couple of hundred more tired visitors, every aircraft leaving the tarmac took with it an equal number of bronzed and usually satisfied holidaymakers. The officials in their heavy uniforms barely coped.

Two aircraft in particular landed that afternoon. A Tri-star of European Airways delivered 187 Americans to the Ljubljana immigration authorities. They were an average cross-section of international tourists; businessmen and their wives on vacation, retired couples, newly-weds on honeymoon, bank clerks, school teachers, two photographic models and a fashion photographer, people you might find and meet in any American city. Both the tourist and first-class sections of the Tri-star had been full.

The passengers were hot, sticky, and a little fretful; many were mid-way through a frantic tour which had already taken them to England, France and Germany. They would spend two days in Yugoslavia, resting, then fly south-west to Italy before recrossing the Atlantic.

The second aircraft was a Lufthansa Airbus. It landed only six minutes after the arrival of the Tri-star, and disgorged its passengers at a neighbouring terminal. It carried a greater variety of nationalities; German mainly, five Swedes, three Danes, and thirty seven Japanese of both sexes, including three children.

A number of long coaches, hired by the various tour companies, each with its own courier, carried the now separated groups from the airport to the hotels around the Slovene city of Ljubljana.

3

Martin Bor was sitting at his table in the living room of his Ljubljana apartment. He had just eaten salami and rye bread, with a plate of sliced tomatoes, salted, peppered, and lightly dressed with olive oil and wine vinegar. He washed them down with a bottle of chilled Yugoslavian beer from his refrigerator. His son, a gangly and narrow-shouldered youth of nineteen was lounging in an armchair watching a football match on Italian television.

Bor was fifty-eight years old, and a Commissioner of the police for the Slovenian area which included the sector bordering Italy, and containing some hundred and sixty villages and two dozen small towns including Postojna, Idrija, Pivka, Sezana and Piran. Being a frontier area it also held more than an average amount of the military, with several barracks, some with artillery and armoured units. These, apart from any civilian misdeed which military personnel might at some time or another commit, were outside his control. But he was an ex-military man himself, a former partisan who had fought with Tito's comrades in the long war, and he therefore viewed the military coming and going in his region with the interest of personal experience.

When Bor allowed himself to think of the past, which was often, it seemed to him somehow the glory that had been hard gained, dangerously won for Yugoslavia, had slipped away over the years. He looked at his son, watching the Italian football, his shoulders hunched forward, his fists gesticulating as he encouraged the Milan team in their World Cup elimination match, and he could see little resemblance between the boy and himself when he too had been the boy's age.

He could remember his own nineteenth birthday. It was the first he had spent away from his parents; they had been farmers. 'Farmers' was perhaps an exaggeration. They had scratched a bare living from a hectare and a half of exhausted ground. One hectare was vines, and his parents were too poor even to own the equipment necessary for pressing and making the wine, they sold the crop of grapes at low prices in the open market; someone else made the profits. The remaining half of a hectare was a vegetable patch from which the family mainly existed. They had a few chickens, and several goats which provided milk and were grazed along the sides of the narrow roads. He could remember his mother's burning ambition to own just one solitary house cow. She made goat's cheese and sold this from a basket each morning, walking a round of the local villages. There were three plum trees at one end of the vineyard, and each year when the fruits were ripe, his father made slivovitz, a harsh and fierce liquor, carefully stored for six years before being brought out as though it were liquid gold itself, on special occasions. The slivovitz was the one luxury he could remember.

When Martin Bor had been nineteen years old, he could read and write only with difficulty and a great deal of concentration. He had spent just three years of his life at school, a small village establishment where lessons took second place to the requirements of the villager's land. If crops needed to be planted, or harvested, vines required pruning, or dung had to be spade-turned into the ground, then school work was of little importance. Reading and writing did not fill empty stomachs in those days.

One thing Martin Bor could do at nineteen, was kill. He was able to do it efficiently, and totally without any emotions or feelings, other than those of great satisfaction. He killed Germans, and on his nineteenth birthday he was sitting at the entrance to a small cave, cradling a captured German machine-pistol in the crook of one arm, while behind him a small group of colleagues hand-printed a liberation newspaper which was distributed with terrible risk to all those involved. On the morning of that day he had forgotten it was his birthday. He didn't feel nineteen, he felt much older. He had already taken part in several harassing attacks on German convoys making their way across the mountains on what had once been the Austrian border. He had watched the soldiers, in BMW motorcycles and sidecars, roar their machines around the bends of the mountain roads, to encounter taut telegraph wires stretched across at neck height, trucks and vehicles destroyed by captured mines concealed in shallow holes dug in the road surfaces. He had seen blood, heard the screams and cries of the wounded, hurled grenades at the

loaded transports and stood high on the rocks, or in the trees, his gun chattering in his hands as he poured long bursts into the torn bodies of the enemy below him.

The cave where the newspaper was printed was not high in the mountains. It was right under the noses of the Germans, in a strange rock-bound fortress not far from the town of Postojna, the town of the great grotto which mysteriously winds its way through seventeen kilometres of the mountain.

The unique rock castle was at the village of Predjama. It sat, like an eagle's nest, in a tall crevasse in a high cliff. It had once belonged to the robber baron, Erasmus, in the fifteenth century. The cave within the castle had been inhabited for much longer. Before the war, discoveries had been made linking it with paleolithic occupation. Much later, the Koblenzl family had built the present renaissance castle pressing itself into the face of the cliff. And hidden inside a cave in this fortress, so obvious to Germans who often visited the place, but so carefully concealed almost by its own blatantness, was the vital equipment of the Nanos Partisan printing press.

It was easy for Martin Bor to return his memory to that particular cave; the cave, complete with its original equipment and its ancient British typewriter, and even some of the partisan's personal possessions, was open to visitors even today. The tourists never really understood its significance; never knew the bravery required to operate the underground news-sheet, never knew the real cost in lives. They just wandered through the winding corridors of the romantic castle, and thought little of the most important part, not the caves of the robber Erasmus, but the place where men had produced liberty.

On the morning of Martin's nineteenth birthday, Jon Goetz, one of the older men, tall and broad-shouldered from a lifetime of heavy work in the fields, and with a great red beard, had walked into the cave and slapped the boy on his back. The blow had jerked him so hard he had almost fallen. Goetz was unaware of his own massive strength.

'Here Martin! A gift from your mother and father. They send you their thoughts today.' The man spoke like a mountain bear, his voice seeming to come from a pit deep in his barrel chest.

'Today? Why today?'

'Your birthday, young idiot. They tell me you are nineteen. Here . . . ' He thrust a small package into Martin Bor's hands. The packet was soft and Martin opened it carefully. It contained a pair of fingerless gloves, knitted in raw black wool. He pushed his hands into them and flexed his fingers.

'Don't worry, you'll still be able to fire your precious sub-machine gun, and pull the pin of a grenade.'

Martin had grinned self-consciously. Goetz had embarrassingly read his mind. 'They're fine,' he said. 'The weather is getting colder. I can make use of them in the mountains this winter. It's good to have your own gloves rather than those from a dead man.' He looked down, almost ruefully, at the thick leather boots on his feet. They had come from the body of a German infantryman whose corpse now rotted somewhere in the pine woods. 'Are my parents well?'

'As well as can be expected,' replied Goetz, his face now more serious. 'Those Nazi dogs keep them short of food, and fuel. Your father has been forced to work with them on the railway. At least he is at home, not taken away in the labour force. He is with your mother most nights.'

'He'll get his slivovitz, then,' smiled Martin Bor.

Goetz's face hardened more. 'No slivovitz, no wine in the village. They searched every house and confiscated it all, along with any preserved meat and grain they could find, and more than two thirds of all the livestock. The bastards!'

That was his nineteenth birthday.

By the time he was twenty, Martin Bor was almost an old man. Much had happened in one short year; a lifetime. The Germans had been storing petrol and fuel in the incredible cave system of the Postojna grotto. Working with courageous determination and under great difficulties, a group of the bravest partisans had penetrated the system through a little known passage behind the main entrance. They had succeeded in forcing their way through narrow crevasses, slits in the wet rocks, crawled their way in darkness through forests of tall but hidden stalagmites, swum dark pools and uncharted underground rivers, to bring themselves behind the heavily guarded petrol dump. They had laid their charges and destroyed thousands of gallons of vital fuel. Like the printing press, the evidence could still be seen; smoke-blackened walls in the first few hundred yards of the heavily visited cave system, the slight smell of carbonised fuel even after all these years.

Retribution had been terrible at the time.

An enraged German Commandant had taken many hostages. If any family was known to have connections with the partisans, then they died; shot in village squares, hanged by barbed wire or meat hooks under their jaw bones, tortured, bayoneted, taken away to the labour camps in Germany, and to Dachau and Auschwitz, the extermination camps.

'You are the father of Martin Bor?'

'That is so.'

'You will call me Herr Kapitan, and you will remove your hat when spoken to by an officer of the Third Reich; insolent peasant.'

'Yes, of course, Herr Kapitan.' Alessandro Bor had not known the rank of the man, and had forgotten he was wearing a cap. He always wore his cap, even when in the small house. He only took it off when he went to bed. He removed it now and held it awkwardly in his hands.

'God, do these people never wash,' the officer said to a sergeant at his side. He looked back at Alessandro Bor. 'Your son has been named as one of a group of local partisans.' Alessandro Bor remained silent. Someone had talked, but he knew it would have been only under torture. He would not now commit himself and bring the risk of death to his wife who stood a yard away silently watching, her eyes wide with fear. 'When did you last see him?'

'We have not seen him for almost two years,' said Alessandro Bor. This was not true, they had seen the boy, the man, only a fortnight previously. He had crept into the village at night, to tap lightly on their darkened window. They had been expecting him. They had embraced him, the mother weeping silent tears as she watched him sitting at his own place at the table, eating a small piece of her cheese and drinking a mug of the fresh milk of the one remaining goat. She would have loved to feed him meat, given him wine and fresh bread. They were no longer available, even if they'd had the money.

'You lie,' said the officer. He struck Alessandro Bor a sharp blow across the face with his stick, and his wife gave a low moan. "We have reliable information you have been meeting him regularly. That is consorting with the partisans and is an offence carrying the death penalty as you well know. Do you think we make these rules for our amusement?' He struck Alessandro Bor again. 'Sergeant, put this man with the others.'

Martin Bor's mother had cried: 'No . . . ' A wail of anguished desperation. She had clutched at his father, and one of the grey uniformed soldiers had thrust her roughly away. The village priest had cradled her in his arms, his old and dusty habit muffling her sobbing.

Alessandro Bor had met his death bravely, with five other of his friends from the village, facing a German machine-gun on its tripod. The priest was amongst them, for it had been decided he too was guilty of consorting with partisans, because it was known he had given absolution to one who had died after being hit by a grenade fragment. The six men stood in an uncertain line against the wall of a vineyard, only forty metres from the small fifteenth century church with its medieval murals of Christ and the Holy Virgin.

The priest, his head high and his hands clasped in front of him as though he were speaking from the pulpit of his church, was murmuring prayers; not for mercy, but for the forgiveness of those who were about to murder them.

Alessandro Bor was wearing his cap. Across the road he was watching the remainder of the villagers. They had been ordered there by the Commandant to witness the execution. Alessandro could see his wife, Caterina. She stood with the wives of the other condemned men, a close group in their black Sunday clothes, their heads down. He knew the clothes would smell slightly of camphor, because they were her only best clothes, and lived all the other days of the week in the old pine chest in the small bedroom. He wondered what would happen to *his* best suit of clothes, and his nearly-new flannel shirt. He hoped it would be given eventually to his son Martin, just as he too had once received his father's best clothing. His only boots were on his feet.

He wanted Caterina to look at him. With a terrible yearning bringing him momentarily close to tears, he wanted just once more to see her dark eyes. It had been so many years since he'd held her close in his arms, and had told her he loved her. Now, suddenly, the brief meeting of hands was not enough, the casual touching of their arms as they walked to church together was insufficient. He wanted to hold her, tell her, so much. He did not fear death, he feared only her misunderstanding.

There was the ominous metallic sound of a belt of cartridges being fed into the breach of the machine-gun. Hard leather-soled boots stamped to attention. A single word of command snapped out in the silence. The guns began.

Alessandro Bor screamed his words as loud as he could in Slovenian. His wife looked up, startled, her face white. For a brief second their eyes met, then bullets hit Alessandro Bor in his chest, smashing him backwards against the now crimson splattered wall. He stood, his jaw muscles clamped hard, his lips pressed together. For seconds he tried desperately to live, or to die with grace. His eyes never left the face of Caterina. He could contain the pain no longer. His face muscles relaxed and his jaw dropped. Blood gushed from his mouth. The image in his eyes dimmed. He slumped to the ground. An officer, his pistol drawn, walked forward.

The villagers, men and women, screamed. But for Alessandro Bor, no more bullets were necessary.

'What did he shout,' asked a shocked German private who had witnessed his first execution and sincerely prayed he would never see another. He had wished only to fight enemy soldiers, in the correct field of battle.

'Some stupid patriotism; they are all mad,' replied his corporal.

Alessandro Bor's final words on earth had been words he wished he could have said in private. It had taken far more courage than he knew he possessed to shout them in front of all the villagers, all his old friends and neighbours. 'My Caterina, I will love you forever.'

There is one village in northern Yugoslavia which is famous for a most terrible thing; it is, or was at one time, a village without any men, without even a male child. It was a village of women. Every male, regardless of age, was exterminated by the Gestapo as retribution for helping the partisans. The women, like black clad ghosts, went about their work in grief-filled silence. For the fighting partisans, the village and its women became a symbol; the reason for fighting. The Third Reich created many such martyrs.

Martin Bor had killed before his father died. He killed very differently afterwards. He had joined the partisans as a boy, as a youth; he became a man and a killing machine. He did not seek danger, but he sought the enemy. He formed his own group, proving himself a keen and able leader dedicated to liberating his country, totally loyal to his commander Tito, and willing to die for the new Yugoslavia Tito envisaged for his followers at the end of the long struggle. He was trustworthy and dependable. He did not argue the new principles, he listened and he believed explicitly. In the long hours of waiting between attacks on the increasingly harassed enemy, he improved his own education. He polished his reading and his writing. He studied. He killed ruthlessly and efficiently, and he survived.

He learnt English. A British officer, skilled in the art of guerilla warfare, had been parachuted into the mountains to work with Bor's own group. Bor was more impressed by the quantity of explosive and new weapons that were dropped a few days later, than by the man himself. But he found he was wrong. The Englishman's ideas of warfare were not exactly those of Martin Bor, but he was forced to admit they were effective. The officer had spent many months in military college, in special training camps and with the commando; he spoke fluent Slovene. His main task was to radio back information to the advancing allied armies. They were not too far away. The man was young, only a few years older than Bor. They had become friends. The Englishman spoke of many things, but never mentioned politics. He fought well, and faced danger with a grim humour. He spent many long winter evenings teaching Martin Bor English. Bor never forgot it, and it had been very useful when the British army at last arrived in Yugoslavia.

Bor had been wounded again. It was his third German bullet. The first had passed through the muscles at the back of his neck; a clean wound which healed easily, leaving only two puckered marks just below his hair-line. They were obviously bullet wounds and he carried them as a Heidelberg student might wear his duelling scars. The second bullet hit him three months later, in his right buttock. It was not a romantic wound, and he did not enjoy the weeks of lying face-down on a hard lice-ridden straw bed in a mountain hideout. The wound became septic and festered like a huge carbuncle, because the bullet had been left deep inside the muscle. There were few doctors in the mountains. At last it healed, and he walked with a stiffness that remained even when the bullet was later removed in a British military hospital.

The third bullet was Yugoslavian. . . at least, it was German, but fired by a fellow Yugoslav. The Germans had retreated, left the country. The British and other allied troops had arrived. Bor's fight now became political. His was a communist partisan group, but other partisans within the area did not share Tito's views nor wish to participate in his plans. Fighting broke out between the left and right wing groups. The allied forces were powerless to intervene. It was settled quickly and ruthlessly; Tito's men proved themselves superior, perhaps because they found within themselves a driving force compelling them to win. Martin Bor fought his last battle on a Yugoslavian hillside, where he had once exterminated a complete patrol of German soldiers. Now, he fought against sixteen right wing supporters of the King.

It was a bitter fight, for there could be no prisoners and no escape for the losers. It began at dawn on a Tuesday morning, and continued sporadically until Friday. By eleven o'clock on that day only three of the right-wing partisans were left alive amongst the rocks. Six of Bor's men were either dead or severely wounded. Bor had spent the last four hours working his way above the men hidden in the rocks. It had been a slow and silent business, the grass between the rocks too short to give him cover should they suddenly look in his direction while he inched himself forward. The men were below him, twenty metres away. He could hear them talking between shots. He guessed there were two of them, and he was wrong.

He pulled a grenade from his pocket and worked out the pin. He let the lever go, taking it clear with his left hand so there would be no clatter against the rock. He heard the fuse ignite, hoped it would be unnoticed by the two men below, counted three and then got to his knees and tossed the grenade, underhand. He dropped flat on his face. The grenade exploded in mid-air, only a few yards from the concealed men. Bor leapt to his feet when the shrapnel had whistled and hissed its way past him. The shattered bodies of the royalists lay sprawled on the rocks. He cheered loudly and waved his hands to his men a hundred yards further down the slope. A pebble clattered to his left and he turned quickly. A man faced him, a Luger automatic pistol held firmly in his hand and aimed at Martin Bor's chest. The man said one word, almost spat it from his lips: 'Communist!' It was a curse. He fired and the nine millimetre bullet hit Martin Bor in the chest, lifted him clean from his feet and somersaulted him backwards into darkness.

A communist partisan, with a rifle, killed the standing man before he could fire a second shot. The war was finally over for Martin Bor and his men.

His recovery took many months and this time it was in a civilian hospital where he was treated as a hero. The bullet from the Luger had gone clean through him at that short range, but it had done terrible damage to his ribs and lungs. He had not been expected to live, but Tito had personally shown interest in his follower, and had insisted the man be given the best possible medical treatment.

The local Communist Party was now, and for the first time, in a position of power. And Bor, as an ex-partisan communist leader, was amongst its most honoured members. He was able to act in a senior capacity, for very few of the older members had any formal education at all. While the allied troops remained in Yugoslavia, Bor worked with them as a local administrator and translator. He knew the villages and towns, and was known, respected, and even a little feared, by their inhabitants. When the British finally left, and handed over control to Tito's party, it was almost natural that Bor should be chosen to reform a sector of the police force. This he had done with the same amount of cold efficiency he had used in the fighting. He was not a man to argue with, not a man to cross, but he was fair.

Unlike most rural Slovenes, he hadn't married a girl from his village, for now, although his mother still lived in her old age in the same small village cottage, he could no longer identify himself with an agricultural peasant. He could not picture himself in the fields with a spade in his hand, or a pruning knife, tending the vines and pasturing the goats. He needed a wider sphere of activity, and a woman who could help him in both his work and party activities. He found her, Annina Corec, a young Party secretary whose family were tailors in Ljubljana. By his country standards they had been wealthy. Annina was well-educated and had the sophistication of a town girl. She was red-haired and light-skinned, and her mother's parents and her mother had been Italian. She was bi-lingual in Italian and Slovene, and had a smattering of Serbo Croat. Like most Yugoslavs who had survived the war, she understood German, but would never speak the language. Her approach to Communism was as fiery as the colour of her hair.

'You must read yet more, Martin, if you are to understand. It is essential. Ignorance is not the way of true Communism. It is the duty of a citizen to be educated, particularly in all aspects of the party's work and aims. If you are to marry me, then you must study. I am prepared to help you, but you must work.'

He worked, and they were married. With the arrival of their only child, the boy whom Martin Bor had named after his dead father Alessandro, the zealous enthusiasm which Annina had shown for her Communism diminished slightly. She was very maternal, though all signs before her pregnancy had seemed to indicate that any children born to her would play second fiddle to the party. She was disappointed when no more children were conceived, but compensated by devoting perhaps rather more of her time to her only child than was necessary.

Bor was successful in the police. This was not always the case with the initial party members who suddenly found themselves in positions of responsibility, partly as reward for their loyalties. Many industries and utilities which had been profitable before, ran down quickly under unskilled administration. But the police was like the army, and Martin Bor was a natural, though not trained, soldier. He studied other police forces, used their methods and chose his subordinates carefully. It was not the best of police forces and he was aware of its inadequacies. It had its corruption, especially at the lower levels; but it functioned moderately well.

He was now in his late fifties. He had been a sturdy country lad, now he was burly. Annina was a good cook and his position gave him enough money to live well. He could get hold of a little foreign western currency, legally, and this enabled him to make a trip to Italy once or twice a year to shop with Annina and Alessandro, and to buy luxuries not yet available in the shops in Yugoslavia. He was still a Communist, still strongly loyal to the ideals of his dead leader. There *had* been improvements on the old way of life. People no longer starved to death as they had years ago. People could get education, and have medical treatment. In his eyes, Tito's Communism was working, it would take time before it was perfect, but it was surely working. The danger to it lay now in the country's youth; boys, unfortunately like his own son, who looked to the affluent west and were dissatisfied with the ties with the east. Where would they lead the country when it was their turn to rule? Martin Bor did not know the answer to that question, though he had turned it over in his mind many times.

Sometimes the old wound in his neck stiffened. His face was lined now, and his hair grey. He wore a moustache which drooped slightly at the ends, and which was stained brown beneath his nostrils, from the smoke of his cigarettes. He smoked too much for a man with an incomplete lung. On damp days he limped from the bullet-ripped muscle of his buttock. Even had he wished it otherwise, he was seldom allowed to completely forget his war.

The Italian football match on the screen ended. 'Turn off the set', ordered Martin Bor.

'There's an American western on next,' Alessandro complained. He made no move towards the television.

Martin Bor said angrily. 'You listen to more Italian than

Yugoslav. Those programmes are rubbish. Education is what you need, not capitalist propaganda!'

'There is little propaganda in sport, despite the Soviet attempts to make it so,' replied the youth. 'And as far as American western films are concerned, there is little propaganda in them either. They are simply a form of myth; a young culture seeking an inheritance.'

'We are a young culture,' raged Bor. 'I, and many thousand like me, made our inheritance. . . your inheritance. We gave our lives. . . '

'. . . you can see our graves marked in rock in the hillsides,' said young Alessandro Bor, quietly.

'You can see our graves. . . stormed Martin Bor.

Alessandro stood, walked to the set and switched it off. 'I am going out, Father.'

'Where to?'

'To meet some of my student friends.'

'At a cafe?'

'A cafe!'

Martin Bor shook his head slowly. 'Do you have *no* ambitions, boy?'

'Some, Father,' said Alessandro Bor, softly. He left the room. Outside in the narrow hall he stood for some moments, then reached for his jacket and draped it across his shoulders. He knew it would not be too long before he must leave home and find a place of his own; perhaps an apartment shared with two or three other of the students. At one time he had thought of working abroad; lots of his friends had already gone; there was good money to be made in Germany or Sweden. He had decided otherwise. There *could* be equally as good opportunities in Yugoslavia. . . it only needed changes in the present system. . . a more liberal approach. As the older men retired different ideas were introduced by their younger successors; each generation of government made its minute improvements. For the young to leave the country was a betrayal of its future; increased freedom could only be obtained by pressures exerted from within. Alessandro Bor knew that he and many of his friends were still fighting a kind of partisan war, though his father would not have understood the similarity and would have been furious at a comparison. It was just that the new war was more subtle, might take longer, and should not be fought with bullets. He closed the apartment door behind himself, and ran lightly down the steep flight of steps to the street. He paused at the kerbside and waited for a break in the traffic. A man joined him and Alessandro Bor glanced sideways and recognised him, by his clothing, as a foreign tourist. The man ignored the quick look, and together they crossed the street, dividing on the opposite side, young Bor striding towards the square where his friends were waiting.

Unknown to either of them, just as the minds of Catlin and the shark had briefly touched, so had the pasts of the two men. But this time there was no reaching-out, no hidden knowledge of recognition, for the pasts were of their fathers.

Carl Struger was German. He had arrived only two hours before on the Lufthansa Airbus. He had travelled alone, was transported with other airline passengers to their hotel, and had been unimpressed with his accommodation, a small single room overlooking a main street. He knew it would be noisy. He had partly unpacked his suitcase, rinsed his face in the small basin in the corner of the room, not bothered to change his travel clothing, and left the hotel for a walk through the town. He did not think he would be impressed by anything he was likely to see in Ljubljana, and enjoyment was not the reason for his visit to the country. Struger was thirty-eight years old, of average height, slim, and balding at the front of his head. He was not particularly Germanic in appearance, and could have passed as a citizen of any western country. He was used to his partial baldness which had begun when he was only twenty six, and had not increased much since; when he was younger, he had been pleased at the rather studious air it gave him. He taught history at a school in the town of Mannheim, on the Rhine. He normally spent his vacations in the mountains; climbing in summer, ski-ing in winter. Yugoslavia had been one of the few countries in Europe he had no real desire to visit. He was here making a delivery . . . to a destination he knew he would never find.

It had begun a few days before with the death of his mother. Although a widow, she had left considerable assets to be equally divided between her son Carl, and his elder sister Frieda. Struger's legacy made him wealthy. In the mother's will there had been a request that her son should lay flowers, and her wedding ring, on his father's grave. The thick gold band was in a ring box in Struger's luggage, the flowers had yet to be purchased, and Struger knew the grave did not exist. Struger's father, a stern-faced and neatly moustached man whom Struger knew only from a pair of photographs, one in uniform and the other in casual sporting clothes — both with frames draped in the black ribbon of mourning — had been an officer in the Transport Corps. His family would have preferred a more distinguished regiment, but Herman Struger lacked one important qualification; he was not a member of the Nazi party.

He was killed in Yugoslavia. He had not been a fighting soldier, he was an administrator: milder and much more gentle in his manners than either his superiors in the Corps might have preferred, or the occupied people of Yugoslavia would choose to remember. He had died in the partisan attack on the petrol dump in the Postojna cave system. He had never enjoyed the dark, though it was a childhood fear which he had subdued with age, nor the claustrophobic atmosphere of caves and caverns. He died in a terrifying billow of white flame, which he had just enough time to see and feel, before the enormous explosion of the fuel tanks turned the entire first kilometer-and-a-half of passages into a furnace. When they were cool enough to enter many days later, there were no signs of the troops who had been stationed within the cave system guarding the precious fuel, even the metal of their badges and buckles had been vaporised by the intense heat. Oberleutnant Herman Struger's grave was in the dust that the dry summer winds swirled like spinning dervishes across hot Slovenian meadows.

Carl Struger didn't care about the war. It had ended before the age of personal memory. But for his late mother it had been as though her life had ceased its forward motion on the day she received the news of his father's death. Her younger sister was far more of a mother to Carl and Frieda than the confused, gaunt woman who spent most of her life alone in the attics of the old house.

Struger was engaged to be married, and the ceremony was already planned for the coming October. His fiancée was eleven years younger than himself, the daughter of a hotel owner at Kitzbuhl. He had met her two years previously on a skiing holiday; like himself, she was a school teacher, and the long vacations gave them opportunity to spend a lot of time together. He was missing her now, wishing they were walking or climbing together somewhere in the Tyrol, instead of his time being wasted on a pointless mission.

He didn't hate his father, or the memory of the man, though he had felt from childhood that somehow the figure staring out of the black ribboned photographs had contrived to steal away the woman who should have been all love and care for her children, and left instead a haggard figure roaming the house at night like a phantom.

His sister, his aunt and other relatives, had sat and listened to the flat voice of the lawyer reading his mother's will. There had been no change of tone as he pronounced the request to her son. Afterwards his aunt had said: 'You should go, Carl. Perhaps it is the only way they will both rest in peace.' His aunt knew, quite as well as Carl, the grave did not exist. That night she had placed the ring, in its small purple box, beside his place at the dinner table and Carl knew that so far as the ring and his late mother's request were concerned, the ritual must be seen to be carried out. The next day he booked a return flight to Ljubljana. He had only a vague plan in his mind. He knew the situation of the Postojna caves from the study of a map of the area. He would visit them and take with him a small posy of flowers that would not be too obvious. Somewhere, if it was possible, he would put the flowers and the ring together where they might remain undisturbed. He could think of nothing else appropriate.

He checked his stride on the Ljubljana street, realising he was walking purposely, but to nowhere in particular. A hundred yards back along the road he found a small bar. There were tables outside, one of them unoccupied.

He decided he would enjoy a cool beer, and sat down. He signalled a waiter. The man understood his German.

At the next table there were four men and a girl. Struger thought they might be students; they were of that age group and too untidily dressed to be office workers.

The girl, he heard one of the men call her Lisetta, had dark eyes, set widely apart below a broad forehead; her jaw was too square for her to be classically beautiful, though she was certainly attractive. Three of the men with her had the same slight Mediterranean sallowness to their skins, but the fourth, sitting closest to Struger, was blond enough to be northern German.

Struger's eyes caught those of the fair-haired man and held them for a fraction of a second before Struger turned his head in politeness, then moved in his seat to face more directly out towards the roadway. Carl Struger would never know that the stranger whose eyes he had briefly searched, was the son of one of the partisans who had killed his father.

4

The Ljubljana hotel accommodating most of the American tourists who had been on board the Tri-Star, was the least imposing they had visited so far on their trip. It had been built within the last five years in what could be best described as Communist concrete and questionable taste. Even the Yugoslavian Tourist Board would not have called it a first-class hotel; it had been built to cater with the package trade. Few wealthy Yugoslavs, and there were some, would have stayed there. It was a package-deal hotel; cement and plastic. There were no carpets in the reception area, the dining room, bars, or corridors; the only floor coverings in the bedrooms were small patches of rug on either side of the beds. The bathrooms were small, and just adequate, containing a shower, which splashed water around the complete bathroom and then took an hour to drain away, a wash basin and a toilet. There were no balconies to any of the rooms and for the main part the windows faced the rather tatty industrial sector of the town. There was no air-conditioning, and although it was possible to open the windows, they did not have the usual louvred shutters allowing the rooms to be ventilated and yet shaded from the sun.

The Americans had been travelling hard. For many there had been long journeys in the United States before they even joined their party at Kennedy Airport, and it seemed to them they had been continually on the move since the time they had left their distant homes. This was, in part, true. They had covered vast distances in a very few days. Jet-lag was now a part of life and they tended to wander from capital to capital, great city and historic building to the next piece of impressive scenario, in a hazy dream. Like so many other visitors to Europe they would return home eventually and then puzzle over their developed photographs.

'See, honey, this is Rome.'

'No, Charles, that was Florence. Well. . . maybe Florence, perhaps it was Paris.'

'Jesus, Annabelle!'

They'd have to consult the guidebooks and compare their pictures before they could fix them in their albums with any degrese of accurate titling.

Now they were tired; almost exhausted. The tour itinerary promised: 'Towards mid-term of this exciting excursion into Europe, we venture behind the Iron-Curtain to the romantic country of Yugoslavia with its beautiful and unspoiled lakes, impressive pine-covered mountains, and picturesque coastline. Here in Slovenia, you will find peace and rest amongst some of the friendliest folk in Europe. For those who wish to make the most of their visit to this charming country, bus tours will be arranged. Bookings may be made on arrival in Ljubljana; just check with your courier. Others amongst you may care to rest during their stay in Yugoslavia and we recommend. . . '

'The guy at reception said, "Poy-stoy-nia," ' said Sheila Hubertson to her husband Ralph. He was forty six and a little paunchy from twenty eight years of working in an office, in life assurance. The pair of them had raised three children, three girls, all of whom were now living lives of their own. This was the second major vacation the couple had managed, the first had been their honeymoon at Niagara Falls. They hadn't lived too far from them for all their married lives; Jamestown, New York State. 'Poy-stoy-nia,' Sheila Hubertson said the word again as though committing it to her memory. She was a stoutish woman who found the heat uncomfortable. Winter-time she wore a girdle, and felt more at ease. 'It's a grotto,' she added.

'A grotto? Hell, I didn't travel all this way to look at a cave. I came to see Britain. Remember, all my family were British. They came from a place called. . . '

'Dawn of Day, and it was in Wales, not Britain,' Sheila Hubertson managed to look superior and bored at the same time.

'Wales *is* Britain. . . well, part of it,' grumbled Ralph Hubertson. Being the only male in a family of four women hadn't totally subdued him, though he'd been happier as each successive daughter found herself a man of her own to pester and had left the family nest. 'It does a man good to trace his roots, sometimes,' insisted Ralph Hubertson. 'I would have like to tread the good earth that spawned my forefathers.'

Sheila Hubertson changed the subject back to the cave by thrusting the tourist brochure under his nose. 'Look, honey. . . ' She jabbed it with a short, rounded finger with a bitten nail. 'Just look at that.'

Hubertson was unimpressed: 'A cave isn't essentially European. We have caves back home. What's that thing in the other picture?'

'A castle, but it's at a place called Bled.'

'It isn't much of a castle, we saw better in London, and in France. . . at. . . '

'Versailles, where the two ladies once met the ghosts of the French court, walking in their pretty crinolines around the gardens.'

'Stuff and nonsense,' said Ralph Hubertson, firmly.

'You wouldn't enjoy the castle, would you, dear,' wheedled his wife. "I'm certain you'd prefer the grotto.'

'You know, Dad would have liked me to go look up my ancestors.'

Sheila Hubertson began to feel exasperated. This was the opening of a conversation she'd had several times in the past few days. 'Ralph, honey, your Father's dead . . . been dead for three years. If he is so darned keen to make contact with his ancestors, he's better placed to do it than you. They're probably all together, right now.' She closed her eyes briefly, and remembered Ralph's father, a short, stout and aggresssive man who would snatch at some point of a conversation like a hound at a rabbit, then hold on for grim death. She added: 'Arguing!'

'Now see here. . . ' began Ralph. He had retained some, if only a few, of his father's characteristics.

'This. . . ' said Sheila, ignoring him, 'Poy-stoy-nia. It's a cave, and caves are cool and restful. We've had a lot of hard travelling and a cool and restful place would do us both good.' She made her voice just a little seductive. 'If we go to the caves we can breakfast late. Lie in a little . . . have a cuddle, maybe, and then just join the tour. You don't *have* to do anything. We can just stroll around and do what we please when we get there. They'll pack lunches. You could buy a bottle of beer. It would be very nice. . . and restful.'

'Restful. . . ' replied Ralph. He knew he had lost. He moved determinedly to the bar.

There were no package tourists in the bar of the Cene International, Ljubljana's top hotel; it rated four stars in the European guidebooks. Its guests needed to be wealthy to pay the hotel's charges; the majority did so on expense account. . . international businessmen, their wives and mistresses, leaders of trade delegations, a few upper-bracket tourists or jet-setters on brief stopovers.

The peach tinted mirrors of the bar, symbols of the hotel's origin in the mid-thirties, reflected a tall, pencil-slim girl a million times, making her appear the closest of a never ending production line of animated dolls.

Angela Zubrecht; New York model on assignment in Europe for Lady Ahead magazine.

Eight days before, Angela Zubrecht had been working — naked.

'For God's sake, don't tease me, Angie. Stick them out a bit, honey.'

'I don't have much control of my nipples. I'm not a tassel dancer.'

'Well, think about Fred's penis.' The photographer moved one of the spotlights, swore as the cable tripped him, then brought up his camera again. 'Oh, Jesus.' He lowered it in exasperation. 'Look, honey, these prints are going to be twenty by ten. Twenty by ten feet, Angie . . . of your breasts *without* nipples. Nipples should be the size of a derby on a twenty by ten. Your tits will look like ass, without nipples. Do you want me to get you a piece of ice?'

'Who's Fred,' asked the girl. She was tall, her hair frizzed out and her lips generous. Her cheek bones, accentuated by diet, were mid-European, but her mouth from a more southerly continent.

'What do you mean, who's Fred?'

'The Fred you just mentioned! The Fred with the penis!'

The photographer sighed. 'Fred is fiction, honey. Fred is any guy with a ten-inch prick who makes your nipples stand out for my pictures. Fred is your vibrator, if that's what turns you on. . . maybe, Fred is even your girl friend. I'll get the ice.' He put the camera on a chair, said: 'Relax a minute,' and disappeared past the hot lights. He returned with a towel-full of ice cubes, and handed them to the girl. 'No. . . for Christ's sake, not yet. Let me get the lighting right first. Okay. . . now just rub the ice on your tits and then dab the moisture off fast. . . got it?'

'I've done it before.'

'Then do it again, before I get thoroughly pissed off and telephone your agency. Why in God's name did Cathy Marchant get mumps?'

'Listen asshole eyes, I'm here as a favour right? I don't do this sort of picture. I'm only here helping out K.G. Models whom I happen to like as an agency. I don't give a monkey's balls for your twenty by ten. You can roll it up and stuff it. . . '

The photographer back-pedalled quickly. The girl was right, she *was* doing someone a favour. . . and it certainly wasn't him. His call had been late and urgent when his booked model had gone sick. They'd warned him this girl didn't usually do nudes — wouldn't in fact, unless there was a guarantee her face and name weren't to be used. The photograph of the breasts was a commercial backdrop for part of an advertising campaign for Hudson's beer. The work was urgent, already late. It was the 'tits only' and double the fee, that had got Angela Zubrecht to his studio.

'I'm sorry, honey. You're a big name. I apologise. Would a little music help? Perhaps you'd try the ice now . . . great . . . great . .' His camera clicked. 'Again . . . super, honey. Jeez, that's more like it . . . turn a bit . . . up . . . up a little.' Click. Click. Click. 'Relax again, while I reload.' He unsnapped the camera and flicked out the film. 'You got plenty of work, I'll bet . . .'

'Tomorrow, Europe: London, Paris, Berlin, Rome. Me and Fudge Kelly. For Lady Ahead.'

'Great.' said the photographer, threading the new film. 'Who's got the camera job?'

'Berkley: Who else?'

'Yeah, who else! I like the bastard's work.' The photographer spoke with unconcealed envy.

'We get a lot of assignments together.'

The photographer swung up his camera and aimed it. 'Okay baby, a bit more. . . Jesus Christ!'

'What?' Angela Zubrecht looked startled. The effect was artistically superb, her eyes wide and beautiful.

The camera clicked and clicked again, the man thumbing the lever quickly. 'Your nipples, honey, your nipples. No ice. . . so it's David Berkley turns you on.' Click. Click. 'You'll never make him, honey. . . I swear it, he's a fag.'

Angie Zubrecht glanced at the studio clock. 'One hour the agency said, and one hour it is, buster.' She stepped out of the lights and the set, swinging a silk robe around her shoulders.

The photographer groaned as she strode towards the dressing room, her long thighs tossing the soft folds of the robe aside. She was out three minutes later, dressed in jeans and an old faded and threadbare sweater, a collection of god-knows-what in a deep snakeskin bag almost touching the floor as she walked. She paused at a desk by the studio door.

'This it?' She read a model release form, used the felt tip to write in 'breasts only — no indentification', then signed it. She held her own agency form towards the photographer. He scribbled in the start and finish times and put his name and studio stamp at the bottom. 'Thanks.'

'You're welcome, Angie. Maybe we'll work together again.' He moved to open the door for her. 'Have a good time in Europe.'

'I will.' She paused in the doorway. 'One thing you should know, baby . . . Berkley fucks as well as he photographs . . . believe me.'

There were four of them in the Lady Ahead team. Angie Zubrecht, Fudge Kelly the other model, David Berkley, and Colette Marishall the Lady Ahead Fashion Editor. Angie Zubrecht was the most beautiful, the most startling. She had high, almost oriental cheekbones, which produced incredible effects with the right kind of lighting. She was tall, slim, and cool looking. She had a dark, latin, skin colouring and gently sloping eyes, but generous lips that gave great sensuality to her pictures. Her ancestry was an amalgum of several races. Her father, a truck driver, had told her maybe it was Greek. . . but the name was central European and her grandfather had spoken with a thick accent which even his family had found difficult to understand. He had come from Vienna, when he was a youth. He might have been Jewish, but if he had been then he never mentioned the fact. In America he was staunchly Presbyterian, as were most of the people in the small community in which the family established themselves. Angie Zubrecht had known she would be a model since she was thirteen. She was now twenty-one. She had been the most dated girl of her age in the town; very popular. The attention had made her blasé about relationships with men. She had been given compliments by them since she first became a teenager.

'Just look at that Zubrecht girl. . . she'll be a beautiful woman soon.'

'Angie, you look super tonight.'

'Angie, you're coming to the dance with me. I can't go without you. Gosh you're a great looker, Angie.'

About the same age, they began to try to seduce her.

The first man to really try, succeeded. She was fourteen and a half and he was twenty-two. By good luck and the grace of God, she didn't become pregnant. She thought he was a real man at the time; that had been the attraction, he hadn't been fifteen and pimply. His name had been George Ewell, and he was in the Navy; a lieutenant home on leave. They'd gone out of town in his Chevrolet. . . a long way out of town. There had been a place he knew with a live band. They danced, and he bought her a few drinks. She looked old enough to fool the barman. On the way home he stopped the car in some woods at the side of a quiet road and told her he might get killed on his next tour of duty. She had let him undress her, and was self-conscious she had such small breasts; they never did get much bigger, and she was almost the same height then as now. He had kissed her shoulders first, then gradually moved his lips down her body. Afterwards, she couldn't remember how she'd got into the back seat, but it was there he seduced her. It hurt a little and didn't feel very good. It had been four more years before she made love again. By that time she had already moved out town, arrived in New York with a few hundred dollars saved and a girl friend who wanted a job as a secretary. She studied at a model school for a few weeks, and just as her money ran out she got her first modelling assignment. It paid a little but not a lot. The modelling school acted as her agent and recognised her exceptional beauty. It needed only the right job, with the right magazine and right photographer to get Angie well up the ladder to modelling success. It happened. She made the cover of 'Super Girl.' Six months later she could pick and choose her jobs from the agency. She had met Berkley about this time.

They didn't go to bed on the first assignment. Had he tried to make her, she would have backed away, fast; it would have made him like all the others. She picked and chose her men like she picked and chose the work. No-one ever made Angie Zubrecht now, she made them. . . when she felt like it. Berkley almost ignored her. It succeeded where an advance would have failed. She went home from the job and wondered what was wrong with her; a feeling that didn't happen often. Maybe she had some flaw that didn't appeal to him? Maybe there was a physical fault others had overlooked, but which the expert Berkley had spotted? Maybe. . . maybe? She thought about it quite a lot for several weeks.

They had a second assignment together; it was in Paris. The magazine wanted pictures of her wearing the latest French fashions set against the background of the Eiffel Tower. They could have used a blow-up, but it would have been cheap. This had to be authentic, and in any case it was partly backed by three of the top international French fashion houses. She and David Berkley flew out together. Apart from greeting her, he hardly spoke. In the aircraft he just sat and read. The first day they met the designers from the three French houses. The following day they began shooting. It took three more days and at the end of that David Berkley had still barely spoken to her, other than to give photographic directions. He wasn't being deliberately unfriendly, but was totally absorbed with his work. They completed the assignment on a Thursday.

'We could change flights,' he suggested, suddenly, on the Thursday evening when they were finally alone and the work was finished. They were due to fly out, Pan Am, the following morning. She waited for him to continue. 'There's another flight Sunday: Get us into Kennedy by nightfall.'

She said: 'Yes' in a tone of voice that was almost nothing more than a soft gasp of surprise.

That evening they'd taken a taxi to Montmartre and found a small restaurant with dim lighting and a girl who sang like Edith Piaf. The wine was good and the food excellent. The atmosphere soft, warm, lapping around them like gentle waters against the night beach of Pacific island. They returned to the hotel, late; to his room. He had not asked her and she had not volunteered. They made intense and exciting love throughout the night, and slept until mid-day. It was the same Friday, and then Saturday. Sunday they returned to the States, and neither had followed up the experience. There was no longing and no resentment. It had been good; very good.

Fudge Kelly the second of the Lady Ahead models was pure Irish, second generation American, born in Queens, New York. She was a model simply because someone had seen her in the hairdressing salon where she was training after leaving college. She was a year younger than Angie Zubrecht, and totally unlike her in temperament. Nothing was cool about Fudge. Life was one great adventure, to be lived and enjoyed every second of the day. Living, travelling and working with Fudge Kelly was unpredictable, fun, exhilarating and exhausting. It began from the moment she awakened in the morning, and didn't end until she collapsed on her bed at anytime between midnight and dawn.

'She'll ruin her looks,' swore the older models. 'Her figure, too,' agreed others. 'She never diets, and she drinks absolutely anything!' 'Has gin for breakfast!' The latter remark was untrue. Fudge Kelly drank a little, but didn't need alcohol. She got her lift from the sheer wildness of her way of living.

Fudge Kelly was even taller than Angie Zubrecht; five feet ten inches in her bare feet — which was most of the time. She had black hair that shone dark blue in certain lights and which looked so sleek it could have been greased. Her eyes were grey, and in contrast to her jet hair they looked pale. Her face was freckled, which she hated, and her mouth wide and continuously smiling. 'For heaven's sake, Fudge, be serious. Think of something terrible,' the photographers would say. Fudge Kelly laughed, tried to keep her face straight, and collapsed as soon as the shutter clicked. Men flocked to Fudge Kelly; she liked them around her, but never led them on. She made it clear she enjoyed playing the field. She didn't sleep around. A man had to be something quite special to get Fudge to bed. Her Catholic background made it important to her.

Colette Marishall, Fashion Editor, was the third woman in the Lady Ahead team. She'd graduated from out of state newspapers, to an eighteen month stint on a third-rate city magazine specialising in mushy teenage stories. She'd been a good sub-editor, but had wanted to work on fashions. She joined Vogue's rival, Lady Ahead, and was now a trusted member of the staff. Twenty six years old and about five feet two inches in height, she was not fat, but slightly buxom. She wasn't ugly, but even the less spectacular models could make her feel uncomfortable and self conscious. As compensation, she presented herself well, her chestnut hair always neatly cut, her make-up carefully applied, though it wasn't easy to put on eye make-up when you wore spectacles and couldn't see much with them off. She'd thought of contact lenses, but decided they'd be inconvenient. Her spectacles were slim, gold-framed, and so if she wore jewellery at all, it was also gold. She didn't wear the eccentric type of clothing affected by the models, hers would be in place whether she was at a cocktail party, a director's meeting, or simply in her own office. Her shoes were mostly sensible.

Her hazel eyes and freckled, sallow skin, showed French ancestry, and in fact one of her great-great-grandfathers had been a mountain man, and had passed his name down the family line. She had inherited a little of the fire and determination that had first taken her forebear into the uncharted forests and mountains, amongst the so-called savages he had learnt to love as brothers.

She knew she was not beautiful, and that David Berkley was. She had met him shortly after joining the staff of Lady Ahead. He had stepped into her office casually one morning, his blonde hair neat and his clothing obviously not that of the regular staff; pale cream slacks and a casual shirt. She had noticed he wore a pair of canvas shoes but no socks.

She had thought about him quite a lot, envying the models who seemed to share his life. He had never tried to date her, she hadn't expected it, nor had she tried to encourage him. David Berkley was David Berkley; he'd marry, if he married at all, someone with a lot of class. A top model from somewhere. They'd cruise the world together, be everywhere fashionable, parties, nightclubs, the Riviera, Bermuda. . . David Berkley was someone else's dream. She dismissed him as nothing more than a co-worker with Lady Ahead.

He was thirty-two years old, five feet seven inches in height and usually shorter than the women he photographed. He was youthful and athletic in appearance, almost effeminate in his movement, which sometimes led to the inaccurate assumption Berkley might be a fag. He was one of those rare non-athletic men, born with total athletic co-ordination. Had he trained, he could have been a great track man, a fine swimmer, a good baseball player, perhaps an international sportsman. He did not like or enjoy sport. His one passion in life, which had totally absorbed him since childhood, had been photography.

It had not been an easy profession to enter; even more difficult a field within which to find success. He might have succeeded earlier if, in fact, he had taken up a sport and then used his reputation to find him a good position within a major photographic agency. He had done it the hard way.

He was the son of a family living in the suburbs of Chicago. His education was nothing special. His father worked in the meat trade and his mother was a housewife. The family was wealthy enough to own one good car, but not two. They ate well and worried a little about the cost of living. The father, conscientious, tried to avoid buying on credit but would do so, one item at a time, grudgingly. He was not a mean man, but was careful, remembering a difficult childhood of his own with a father who was kind, but alcoholic. Most years there was enough money saved to permit a two-week vacation somewhere away from the city. The family rented a cabin. Father and son fished or hiked, while mother and two daughters sunned themselves on the bank of some quiet river or lake. Evenings were fun, sitting around a barbeque while Dad told yarns he had heard as a boy, or adventures he had experienced while fighting in the Phillipines. They sang old songs, and the woods around them absorbed the sounds. David Berkley always took a camera with him; the first had been a birthday gift from his parents when he was nine years old. They had thought him a little young for a camera, but the boy had insisted that it was the only thing he wanted. 'A real camera, Dad, not a toy. One with lens adjustment and different shutter speeds. . . '

'How on earth does a nine-year old know about technical details?'

'He reads camera magazines all the time; that's where he usually is, at the library, reading camera magazines.'

Berkley got his first camera. He got a job, too. Helping at the supermarket on Saturdays, when he earned a couple of dollars. A year later he traded in his camera for one with more sophisticated refinements. Because developing and printing was expensive, he saved harder, bought his own equipment and did his own work. By twelve he was more than competent, but by sixteen he was expert and supplying photographs to the local newspapers. He had one or two pictures used in exhibitions. Vietnam happened just at a time when he was establishing himself in a small business, specialising in wedding and social engagements. It wasn't in any case, what he wanted as a photographic future, but it was commercial experience he needed. He had planned to stick it out for three years and then try for a position in New York. Vietnam actually helped him.

The Draft Board had interviewed him; tried men who seemed bored by the endless procession of youth.

'We see you're a photographer.'

'Yes, Sir.'

'What kind of a photographer?'

'Any kind, Sir. Portraits, wedding groups. . . a little industrial work.'

'Hmmm. Any other skills?'

'I, er. . . well, I guess not.'

'What about hobbies? Interests outside your work?'

'Only photography, Sir.' He was hoping he'd get in to aerial reconnaisance.

They trained him as corpsman with the infantry. He saw, and tasted, blood and gunsmoke. He hated it, but stuck it out. His break came in a strange manner. As always he had been taking photographs; not of the war in Vietnam, but of the odd corners still beautiful, the out of the way places the war had somehow missed. He managed to find the exotic, the rare and the fine, in a devastated country. There were a group of international news correspondents stationed in a small town, half a mile away from the infantry camp. He knew amongst them were photographers and they had set up a darkroom for their printing. He sought them out.

'Sure kid, help yourself.' The news photographers were vaguely interested in the kind of photographs a corpsman might have taken. He would have been in the thick of the action and maybe had something they could use.

Berkley printed up his films.

'Let's have a look, kid.' The newsmen had taken the clean prints and passed them around. 'I don't believe it,' one of them had said, slowly.

'Don't believe what?'

'That this is Nam. . . you take these here, or on leave in Japan? You make this hole look like paradise! No war. . . no bombs, no blood.'

One of the newsmen suddenly said: 'They'd make a feature.'

'They'd toss them straight out of my offices,' another murmured.

'No, I think we could use them. It's a different side of Vietnam; unusual today. A soldier who just doesn't see the terror and the horror. A guy who can find the beautiful where there shouldn't be any. . . you'll sell them?'

'Under my own name, sure.'

'It's a deal. . . exclusive, mind. . . I'll do the story and captions. You'll have to take pot luck with payment, God knows what they'll give you for these. Maybe nothing. . . they might not use them.'

They did. The magazine printed thirty photographs. They also acted as agents; the feature was printed in nine languages in seventeen different countries of the world. They also wanted Berkley as a staffman when he finished his service.

He arrived one day in New York, already known, and on salary to the magazine. He worked with them two years, then joined another agency. He was able to work with beauty, with women. He had a kind of sensitiveness that could bring out the best in a temperamental and frequently fairly stupid model. He became known as The David Berkley and bought out the agency for himself.

There was one disadvantage; there was absolutely no way in which he could expand the business. No-one wanted his assistant to do their work, no matter who the assistant might be, nor how talented the man or woman might show themselves. They wanted *only* David Berkley; his name, and his skills. He could use whoever he liked in his darkrooms or as technicians, but when it came to the photography, clients insisted it must be him. So his business was limited to the number of jobs that could be done in any one day, or week, or month, by David Berkley himself. He became very expensive; they were still happy to pay. He knew it wouldn't last for ever, and stached his money away. Still, it looked like being good for a while yet.

'What have we got left?' David Berkley swung a camera and aimed it, empty, at a fellow guest sitting alone at the far end of the narrow mirrored bar. There were surprisingly few bottles on the shelves behind the counter and Berkley knew the barman had felt uncomfortable when he was unable to make a whiskey sour. Berkley wasn't talking about the lack of drinks now, he addressed his remark to Colette Marishall.

'Half a dozen outfits here, that's all; Knickerbockers and woollens.' She was checking a list and frowned above her lenses.

'Knickerbocker outfits in a temperature of over ninety! That's a task and a half — aren't they supposed to be winter gear? They'll look out of place in a beach setting and in mid-summer.'

Colette nodded. 'I have an idea though. There are some big caves not far from here. I saw something about them at the reception desk. Lots of stalactities and things. . . underground lakes. Pretty impressive.'

'We'll never get permission to do fashion shots in a location like that, not in the little time we've got.' David Berkley knew the problems involved. Most places didn't mind you taking amateur shots, but the minute it was professional, then there were difficulties, people wanted to receive payment and issue permits. It all took time; time they didn't have.

'We do it the free way.' said Colette. 'Ordinary flash; in colour. Just one set of clothing to each girl. They wear them in, and you take what shots you can.'

'It's a risk. We may get nothing.'

'You're the expert; you'll get something.'

'Okay.' Berkley took another imaginary shot of the bar, to the consternation of the bartender. 'If it doesn't come off, maybe we'll get something else. Worst comes to the worst we can double them up in Rome . . . Trevi fountain or something.'

'With a schedule like ours we can't afford to have you waste your time.' Colette took off her glasses and tried looking at him. His face was a blur so she returned the glasses to her nose.

'Lady Ahead are a tight fisted lot of . . .' began Berkley.

'Only on time schedules,' interrupted Colette. 'Because we always have deadlines to meet. International fashion is as hot as news. It just means we only have one chance at places like Postojna.' She pronounced the town Pos-toj-na.

'Like where?'

'The place with the grotto.'

Zlobec was thirsty. It was evening now, but it had been a hot and busy day for himself and his men at the Postojna caves. It was always hot and busy during the tourist season and he was pleased when it ended in early September. He was wearing his complete uniform, jacket over shirt and tie. It wasn't necessary because at this time of the year shirt sleeves were permitted, but Emil Zlobec preferred a more formal appearance, even if at times he would stand in the hot sun and feel perspiration trickling down between his shoulder muscles, or the centre of his chest. It never showed on the outside of his uniform as it did through the shirts of his own men, it evaporated in the heavy material.

Zlobec was Inspector of Police for Postojna, the caves and the small town. Most of the people worked in factories, some were farmworkers, either in the disintegrating collectives, or working their own small exhausted patches of soil. Some were shop workers or in the local administration, and others ran restaurants and bars both for the local trade and the tourists who visited the grotto and castle. There were a number of pensions, private houses who supplied rooms and beds to visitors, and a couple of hotels; the best and largest, the Hotel Jama, was situated at the mouth of the cave system itself. The Jama, a name which itself meant 'Cave', was the newest hotel in the region. It was a good hotel even by international standards; first class. A little out of place perhaps, its modern six-storey and galleried design pressed against the backdrop of the mountain with its steep slopes clad in pine trees, but nevertheless a luxurious hotel. Beneath the hotel itself was a parade of shops, a restaurant and a snack bar, to cater for the hundreds of visitors who came to the caves each day. It was here where Inspector Zlobec spent most of his time, for it was within the crowded precinct most of the regular police work of Postojna was done.

He often wished it might be more adventurous, for at the age of thirty-seven he seemed to have done little more than control the busy traffic, find missing children and relatives, shepherd people to their correct coaches, and take laborious reports of cameras, clothing, wallets and passports that had been stolen. Only seldom was an arrest made, for the visitors went away and prosecution was difficult unless they were prepared to remain, or return, and appear before a court some weeks later to give evidence. Very few did, unless they were Yugoslavs themselves, in which case it was unlikely they would have had much property to interest the thieves who picked pockets and mingled with the tourists.

Of course, some thieves Zlobec already knew. When he recognised them he warned them off and sent them away, but there were always new thieves, coming from distant parts of the country, itinerant rogues who followed tourists like hyenas waiting for a meal; they were almost impossible to catch, unless you actually saw one of them with his hand in a tourist's pocket or handbag, or forcing the door of a vehicle.

The caves were now closed for the day. The last of the guides was already on his way home, and the women cleaners were polishing the windows of the ticket offices, sweeping the debris from the floors in the entrance foyer, and folding and tidying the heavy blankets which the tourists wore around their shoulders when entering the damp and chilly caverns.

There were still tourists wandering and strolling in the area of the caves, but these were the ones staying at The Jama Hotel. The evening was warm and they sat on the terraces or lounged on the lawns beside the winding river Pivka. Soon, as hungry mosquitoes would begin their evening hatch at the water's edge, the tourists would amble back into the hotel, shower and change their clothing, and make their way to the hotel's restaurant or bar. A few might visit the town itself, looking for local atmosphere and colour; there was little of it around.

There would be a few drunks in Postojna town; not tourists, generally. The tourists who stayed at The Jama were not the sort to get themselves fighting drunk, or require restraining and a night in the cells. The drunks were usually Yugoslavian, and usually the same men. They drank mainly because of frustration, and Zlobec, who was not an insensitive man, understood their reasons and whenever possible avoided bringing them before a court.

Zlobec, round-shouldered and slim with an angular clean-shaven face, did not find the Postojna cave system fascinating. He had seen too much of it; always coupled it with the daily problems he faced. At times he wished it wasn't there, or that he had lived in another part of the country and not been born in Postojna. He had visited the caverns as a child, and had been impressed then. He had visited them later, when he was courting his wife, and he had taken his four children to see them when they had been old enough to enjoy the experience. He knew a lot about the cave system. You couldn't live in Postojna all your life and not know quite a lot. There were a large number of people employed to work in the grottoes: The guides who showed the tourists the wonders of the vast caverns, the drivers of the small electric trains which carried the visitors for the first one and a half kilometers under the mountain, the technicians, the booking office staffs, the cleaners, the car park attendants, the bar restaurant workers; dozens of people all employed in the service of taking paying guests into the deep heart of the mountain.

There was no need for Inspector Zlobec to memorize the books and tourist literature about the caves; he'd learnt about them in primary school. Every citizen of Postojna knows all their details.

The Postojna caves are very old. The entrance caverns have been known to local people for many years. There are signatures carved into the stone dating back to the thirteenth century, and man used the caves long before that date. There are more than three and a half thousand caves in the Yugoslavian Karst, but the Postojna Grotto is the largest and the most beautiful. The Karst is a strange area. It began as a flat limestone plain whose origins in the distant past must have been beneath great oceans. Eventually it rose above sea level and the rivers flowed across carrying their silt and spreading it over the wasteland in their floods.

The earth's crust crumpled and the plains rose yet again, now high above the Adriatic, forming indented plateaus and strangely shaped hills. The rivers changed their courses and began to flow towards the interior of the country. Others cut down through the layers of limestone, working their ways back towards the oceans, cutting and tunnelling the soft rock: Fissures, pot-holes, tunnels, caverns, abysses, all formed by the slow but relentless action of the water. It drained down through the rock, seeping, dripping within the caverns, each droplet of water carrying with it the mineral salts and limestone particles that form the great pillars and sweeping curtains of the growing wonders beneath the earth.

Man discovered the caves, lived and hunted from them, built his hearth fires in their safety once the savage bears had been driven from their dens.

The true wonder of the Postojna caves was not really discovered until 1818, when a guide who was showing the Austrian Emperor, Francis, around the then known system, climbed a high cliff within the Great Hall and shouted that he had found 'paradise' beyond the opening to a small cave.

Since those days, a lot of exploration has been done. Passages have been made to link many of the great caverns, some almost large enough to hold a fair sized cathedral. A concert hall is contained within one cavern and the accoustics are unique.

The visitor is carried by train for one and a half kilometers into the mountain, and then walks five more, before returning to a small underground railway station with a bar where welcome cups of hot coffee and glasses of warming slivovitz can be purchased.

But, the tourists see little of the actual cave system that runs through more than seventeen kilometers of the mountain. Hundreds of small passages, many still unexplored, run off from the main tourist route. Behind thin walls, within certain caverns, are believed to be still undiscovered parts of the system. And below it all, for seven kilometers underground, flows the Pivka River, a stormy torrent where rocks squeeze and funnel it through a hundred hidden lakes and siphons.

The caverns are the most beautiful in Europe; a hidden wonderland of mystery and delight, far below the harsh and uncomfortable terrain of the arid Karst, with its unproductive red soil.

Those are the facts taught in the Postojna schools, but Inspector Zlobec knew a little more about the caves. He also knew more than most people about the foreign tourists who visited the vast underground system.

Zlobec straightened his tie, then took a slim, silver cigarette case from his pocket. The case had been a wedding gift from his wife, and it was now in fact unsuitable for the cigarettes which Zlobec smoked; they were king-size whereas the case had been intended for those of standard length. This meant it could hold half-a-dozen, tilted sideways to permit them to fit. Zlobec was forced to replenish it several times a day from packs he kept in his office. It had one big advantage, though; it lay very flat in his pocket and did not spoil the trim outline of his uniform. That was why he used it. He extracted a cigarette, straightened it where the elastic of the case had dented the side, then lit it slowly, inhaling the smoke deeply into his lungs. He began walking towards the hotel bar.

'Inspector! Inspector Zlobec, Sir . . .'

It had been a long day. Zlobec kept walking towards the hotel, hoping that if the person who was calling him was on a relatively unimportant mission he would be deterred by Zlobec's purposeful departure.

'Inspector . . .' The man arrived at Zlobec's side.

Zlobec stopped. 'Can't you see I'm in a hurry, Nagorni?'

'Yes Sir . . . sorry Sir . .'

'Well?' Inspector Zlobec dropped his cigarette in the dust, then moved his foot hurriedly aside as Constable Nagorni stamped on the butt with a large, steel-studded boot.

'We're detaining a man you will probably wish to charge . . . he's from Belgrade . . . one of the campers on the site near the river. He was fishing for trout without a permit.'

'Oh my God,' said Zlobec.

'Yes Sir.'

Zlobec looked at his watch, it was seven-thirty p.m. He had been on duty for eleven and a half hours. 'Nagorni, if we charged every Yugoslavian who fishes the rivers without a permit, then we'd charge half the fishing population. Anyway, in theory, the rivers belong to the people. How old is he?'

'About eighteen.'

'Have you ever fished the Pivka for trout . . . without a licence, Nagorni?'

The constable looked uncomfortable. 'I, er . . . possibly, when I was young, Sir.'

'So did I.' Zlobec remembered the quiet deep pools, edged by rocks and overhanging trees. There had been one occasion when an unwary trout had taken the grasshopper he was drifting on the surface, and had been caught, killed, cooked and eaten, all within the space of half an hour. 'Let him stew for a few more minutes, then go back and tell him not to get caught doing it again.'

'Yes Sir . . . I'll make sure he knows never to fish again.' The constable saluted then began a semi-military about-turn.

'Wait.'

'Sir?'

'I didn't say that, Nagorni. I said, tell him not to get *caught* doing it.'

5

The new day did not look particularly inviting, seen through the blinding hangover which Joe Catlin was experiencing. The sun shone, far too strongly, through his hotel window. The balcony beyond, with its view across the bright sea towards the distant coastline, had no appeal. The three front teeth on their titanium palate, were on the bedside table and he looked at them in disgust. The thought of anything being put into his mouth at the present moment was enough to make his stomach churn. He groaned and lay back on the square pillow which, no matter how aggressively he had punched it, always remained an uncomfortable rectangle. He suspected it was filled with flakes from old car tyres.

He could remember returning to his room; just. It had been a long haul from the bar across the town's small square where he had sat alone, watching a group of students making their single glasses of pale reisling last the evening, while they sat in earnest discussion. There had been very little joviality between them; they were a serious group of young men and women, and bore little resemblance to the noisy youngsters he knew throughout America, or the Yugoslav girl he'd met in Ljubljana. Catlin had not been the only one attempting to drive away his depression in the bar. A few other men worked at it with a savage determination that had astonished him. Catlin drank slowly and steadily, but some of his fellow drinkers wanted their oblivion fast.

He now realised his drinking mistake of the previous evening; it was the mixing of beer, red wine, and some white spirit with an unpronounceable name. He'd drunk them in rotation. At the time the combination of taste and the effects of the differing types of liquor on his tongue had been interesting. He had not forgotten Lisetta Irano, but as he had become more drunk he had begun silently toasting the memory of O'Donovan, and equally as frequently wishing the tall man was with him. But O'Donovan was dead and gone.

Big Mike would have had a hangover this morning, too, thought Catlin, wrily.

He pushed himself up slowly, edged his feet over the side of the bed, and stretched. The headache exploded behind his eyes and his stomach wavered. He belched and felt better. He wished for Alka Seltzer and knew there were none in his suitcase, not even aspirin. Catlin seldom used medicine, but if he did it was for hangovers. He mused uncomfortably over alternatives, and thought of raw egg and Worcester Sauce. His stomach rose again and he fought it down. Getting to the bathroom entailed careful movement, for his legs were still unsteady. He swilled his mouth and then scrubbed his remaining teeth and rinsed again. He sucked his lips in against the gap at the front, rubbed his hands against his cheeks and felt the sharp bristle, then stared at the mirror. The red-eyed image, peering back was ugly. He sighed and splashed tepid water over himself, changed his mind and ran the shower, cold.

An hour later he felt he could face breakfast. It was just ten o'clock. Coffee, in quantity and strong, helped. He forced himself to eat a single bread roll and a thin slice of salami. It was difficult, but he managed to get it down and keep it there.

Another pot of coffee followed the roll.

He wondered how to pass the day. Outside, the holiday makers had already been improving their tans for the past two hours. The ice-cream eaters had been guzzling, and the frisbie players skimming their discs along the shingle beaches. Some were swimming; some were always swimming, thought Catlin.

He wandered to the reception desk. A clerk was working on a ledger and did not look up until Catlin said: 'Hey . . .'

'Yes?' The clerk did not believe in saying 'Sir' to anyone. He was about twenty-seven, untidy and with long greasy hair. He had a suntan suggesting he spent too much of his time out on the roof and away from his post at the desk. Catlin had noticed the previous day that it was frequently unattended. The man had dirty fingernails and should have had a closer shave. He might have lasted about five minutes in any reasonable American hotel. Catlin would never have employed him; a man who was careless about his personal appearance was usually careless about his job.

'What can I do around here?'

'A lot of people go to the Postojna caves,' said the Clerk putting down his pen.

'Postojna?' That was the name of the town Lisetta had said she was visiting; where her family lived. She had written down her address for him, but he had assumed it was some place hundreds of miles away from Piran and was the reason he had begun to doubt if he would see her again. 'How far is Postojna?'

'A little over an hour from here if you take a bus. Less if you have your own car.'

'And the caves?'

'A big series of grottoes,' said the clerk with the exaggerated enthusiasm he reserved for tourists. 'They're *very* interesting. I can recommend them. They are *very* beautiful. Well worth a visit . . . but Postojna town has nothing to offer.'

Nothing for you, maybe, thought Catlin. So Lisetta was less than an hour away! There was every possibility she did intend to keep their arrangement. The thought cheered him. 'Are these caves difficult to find?'

'Not difficult at all. The road is well signposted. Just drive inland from here.' He picked up the pen again and pulled one of the hotel reception cards from a box. He wrote on the card and handed it to Catlin. 'Postojna . . . just look for Postojna. When you are near, you will see the signposts for the caves.'

'Thanks.' Catlin took the card. It was superfluous, he wasn't likely to forget the name, but the clerk deserved courtesy for brightening Catlin's morning. He'd visit the place, have a look at the caves . . . he couldn't remember ever having visited any before . . and afterwards he'd have a walk round the town itself. He wouldn't try to find the girl, but it would be interesting to see something of the place she said was her home.

Catlin was still on the road, his body wedged into the narrow seat of the small Fiat, when the buses containing the American, German and Japanese tourists arrived at the coach park across the main road from the Hotel Jama and the entrance to the cave system two hundred yards further along the valley. It had not been planned for all the coaches to arrive at the same time, and it was in fact, inconvenient for everyone. It would have been better for the tour couriers, and the tourists themselves, if they had reached the terminal at better spaced intervals. Now, they were certain to have to wait for a little time even though each of the couriers held passes to the cave system for all of their charges.

The couriers, who all knew each other, met briefly to discuss the situation. None felt their own particular charges should be kept waiting; not that it made any difference to the reputation of the tour company, which for all the coaches and couriers was the same one, and state owned, but it might well make a difference to the amount of tip the courier would receive from the tourists when they were returned to their respective hotels. The argument was considerable, and obvious to the waiting and overheated tourists.

Eventually, and because one of the guides was a senior Communist Party member, it was agreed the Germans and mixed nationality tour would enter the cave system first, followed by the Americans, and finally the Japanese; the latter known to be patient people who never complained about anything and who tipped badly anyway.

In all there were seven coaches and a total number of two hundred and sixteen tourists of the various groups, the largest single group being the Americans who, including five children, numbered one hundred and twelve. The tour guides did not intend to enter the cave system, it was a chance for them to escape from the responsibility of their charges, and to have a brief rest.

Within three quarters of an hour, most of the coach tourists had joined other visitors who were already below ground. There were now almost four hundred people inside the Postojna cave system.

The tourists had ridden into the underground railway terminal, at the end of the kilometer and a half tunnel, in awe. They could feel the weight of the mountain pressing down upon them. Riding in the open carriages had been like the ghost train of childhood fairgrounds. As it rattled along its narrow track, lights were lit ahead of it, illuminating the weird shapes and formations in the walls and the tunnels; strange and fantastic shapes that might have been the invention of a Disneyland sculptor. Parchment-thin curtains of coloured rock reflected the lights; strange growths, looking like faces or figures, hid in glistening niches. Pillars from temples, columns from cathedrals, lined the route. Above, only inches higher than their heads, was the chiselled roof of the tunnel, except where occasionally it widened briefly into floodlit wonderland caves with dark smooth pools.

It was cold inside the cave system, but before entering the visitors had all been issued with thick blankets to wrap around themselves as protection against the chill and the dripping roof.

Those who had found themselves too lightly clad, still retained the blankets and wore them like sinister monks, the heavy cloth wrapped tightly around their shoulders and draped as hoods over their heads. The air was dank and still; voices, although they created a steady indecipherable murmur in the cave, were hushed.

There were a number of signposts in the first cavern, and each designated the language that would be spoken by the cave guides who were to take the party on their walk around the vast grotto. The majority of nationalities were covered by the signposts, for guides were required to speak at least two European languages. The Japanese were unlucky, there were no Japanese speaking guides and so their party split themselves up, some choosing to travel with a German speaking guide, most with the English tour, and three young Japanese who might have been students, stood beside the sign reading 'Francais'.

One of the American couples, on honeymoon and very much in love, shared their blanket and cuddled beneath it, the young husband enjoying the soft roundness of his new wife's breasts. They were only inches from the taut back of a thin woman who was travelling alone, and who looked as though she would scream if a man happened to accidentally touch her.

Sheila and Ralph Hubertson, the middle-aged couple from Jameston, were engaged in an unlikely conversation with some new acquaintance from Louisiana, comparing the cavern to the Niagara Falls. A painfully thin man, Paul Ukley, of Oregon City, who had spent the previous two months recovering from a severe bout of bronchitis, was complaining to his wife of the damp atmosphere of the cavern, and regretting his foolishness in deciding to accompany her. He knew he should have waited in the dry air of the sunlight above ground.

A cave guide, a tall slouch-backed man with the loping gait of a mountain walker, suddenly called in a thick accent: 'All Engleesh speaking peoples, please.'

The voices hushed. One of the American children shrieked, to hear its echo in the wide cave; it was immediately batted on the head by its mother. A small group of Japanese looked on in horror at this atrocity.

Struger had seen the tour to the Postojna cave system advertised at the reception desk of his hotel. As he had no transport it seemed sensible to make use of the tour facilities rather than go to the trouble of renting a vehicle. He had considered himself lucky to be able to purchase the last ticket available for that day - all the others having been taken by the package deal companies. There'd been other German tourists on his coach, but he had felt apart from them; they were on vacation, while his visit was enforced by circumstance. It made him feel different.

There was no emotion to Carl Struger's first sight of the Postojna cave entrance. It was not an attractive building, and resembled a railway station; if anything, it spoilt the rising slope of the mountain which seemed to hang above the white stone construction. The train platform, below ground, had the tiled appearance and the same rank, damp scent of any city's underground transport system; all it lacked were the graffiti and advertising posters. But once the train began moving along the illuminated tunnels, a terrifying feeling of depression seemed to descend on him. With horror, he saw the walls of the tunnel were still, after all these years, blackened by the smoke of the explosion and the fuel fire which had followed. The stalactites which hung down from the roof of slightly larger caves on the first section of the route, were not of milk-white limestone, but were black fingers of soot from the carbon fuel. Somewhere in this dreadful place, his father had been killed. At this second, perhaps, the train was rattling across his ashes. The soot above must also contain the dust of the incinerated men, he imagined he could taste them with each breath.

Struger had bought a small bunch of anemones from a florists near the hotel, that morning. He'd wrapped them so the flowers didn't show, and carried them as though they were some tourist souvenir he had purchased. He knew he should toss them from the train now, here in the tunnel where his father had died . . . he should toss them into some secret place, along with the wedding ring. The two items should be together. He didn't have the courage. There were too many people, the train rattled and jolted along and there was no opportunity.

Panic built up inside Struger and rapidly became terror, as though he was to experience the same fearful death as his father. He had never previously suffered from claustrophobia, but he was having a bad attack of it now. The smell of the burnt fuel began to suffocate him, the sound of the train's wheels on the track grew out of all normal proportions, with the echoes tossed back from the walls and roof — which seemed determined to squeeze Struger's life from him.

He could feel the stems of the fragile flowers crushing in his tightening palm. Even in the chill air, and the breeze of the train's movement, perspiration ran down his face. He shut his eyes, screwing the lids so tightly together that the muscles of his face were painful. He dropped the bunch of flowers on the floor of the train, pressed his head between his knees and clasped his hands over his ears. He could hear terrible sounds mingled with those of the train . . . marching men, the echoes of their boots resounding through the silence of the long cave; shouted orders . . . a distant explosion and then an increasing roar as though an express locomotive was tearing its way through the darkness towards them . . . and then light, a white ball of rolling flame . . . the shrieks of men in their last agonised seconds of life . . . Carl Struger stifled his own scream by clenching his teeth on a thick fold of damp blanket.

The train jerked to a stop; Struger remained hunched in his seat. He felt a hand on his shoulder. The hand gripped harder and then shook him.

'Are you sick?'

He looked up, slowly, to see the concerned face of an elderly woman tourist. She spoke to him with a north German accent.

'Are you feeling ill, young man? Can my husband and I help you?'

Struger swallowed; the panic was receding. He pushed himself back in the seat. He could feel his clothing soaked in sweat, clinging to his body. He tried to smile, reassuringly. 'No, I'm fine thanks. I think it was . . . perhaps the change from the heat to the cool.'

'Here . . .' The woman's companion, a white-haired man, unscrewed a small hip flask and poured some liquid into the silver cap. 'Schnapps. You young men think you'll live forever. You look as though you have a fever.'

Struger took the cap, knowing his hand was shaking. He drank the schnapps quickly, feeling the liquid burn his throat. 'Thank you.'

'You must take care,' the woman told him. 'Hot days and cool evenings are not good for you. Remember to wrap up well if you go out at night.'

'I will,' promised Struger. The woman sounded like his aunt. He stood and stepped out of the open carriage, onto the platform. The concrete was somehow comforting.

The woman pointed behind him. 'I think you've dropped your package.'

6

Joe Catlin stopped the rented Fiat. He was about a quarter of a mile from the base of the mountain and had just passed yet another sign which indicated the direction to the cave's parking lot. He could see the terraced, modern, block of the Hotel Jama surrounded by the trees of the wooded slope rising behind the building. There were a lot of people in the area, walking, strolling, peering into the windows of the shops below the hotel.

Catlin had a strange feeling the panorama he saw was unreal, like the illusion of a sequence viewed on a movie screen.

He didn't know why he had stopped the car, for the parking area was still more than three hundred yards away. He sensed something unfamiliar ahead, an invisible barrier blocking the roadway. The fine hairs on his neck bristled uncomfortably.

He cut the engine, opened the door and stepped quickly out.

The ground moved.

For a moment he thought he was about to faint. He remembered the previous night's hard drinking and as he did so the horizon of mountains and woods blurred and quivered.

Catlin said: 'Jesus,' under his breath. He wondered if he was having some sort of a heart attack, but he felt no physical discomfort or pain.

The Fiat began a soft squeaking, and a door panel beneath his hand picked up a growing vibration. A plastic skeleton on a piece of elastic, the good luck charm of some previous driver, began a macabre dance below the rear-view mirror. The ground rippled. There was a deep rumbling . . . the sound of a complaining wellhead under increasing pressure; the moment before the explosion. To Catlin this was a familiar sound of danger. Instinctively he threw himself away from the car and dived for the meagre grass beside the roadway. The ground beneath him seemed to swell, to

rise and fall, as though he rode a half inflated airbed on ocean breakers. The rumble grew to a roar. Automatically, he covered his head with his arms to protect himself and tried to press himself closer to the moving earth. A voice inside his head warned: 'This oil-well is really going to go; a big one, Hang on . . . and pray like shit!'

Emil Zlobec had been standing in the shade of trees in the gardens, some fifty yards in front of the Hotel Jama. Like Catlin, he was initially unable to understand what was happening. The ground moved and he grabbed at the thick trunk of the tree for support. The trunk shuddered but he managed to hold himself upright, although with difficulty. With horror, he watched the slab roof of the concrete arcade opposite him fracture, split and grate itself into fragments, before collapsing in a cloud of dust onto the terrified people beneath. The highest section of the hotel, the two top floors of the four-tiered guest section dropped suddenly downwards to scatter debris onto the lower buildings. Later he might swear it all happened in an uncanny silence; people died, crushed, soundlessly, the buildings crumbled like falling playing cards, without even the whisper of breaking glass, rupturing concrete and twisting steel; but there *was* sound . . . the sound from the earth, from the mountain, and it was so great and vast a noise that it smothered all else, so nothing was distinguishable from the deep earth-sound itself.

He clung desperately to the trunk of the swaying tree and saw the terror. Men and women, children, falling, staggering, crawling . . . dying. The collapsing building reached for them. A woman, stumbling to her feet, grabbed her small baby from its toppling buggy, and for some inexplicable reason ran straight into the falling wreckage to be immediately buried beneath twenty tons of masonry. He saw a young couple appear briefly on the high restaurant balcony before it broke clean away from the front of the hotel building and dropped downwards, the couple still standing on the falling section, their hands gripping the rail in front of them, their faces expressionless. They disappeared from sight in the rolling pall of dust now billowing upwards and outwards from the wreckage.

Zlobec fell to his knees. A car was being driven down the dancing roadway, rocking crazily, swerving and bouncing. It ran into the side of a parked delivery truck. There was an explosion of orange flame that enveloped the two vehicles.

The roots of the tree Zlobec was holding started to tear themselves from the stony ground. The tree began falling, and Zlobec, unable to get to his feet, rolled sideways to avoid its thick trunk. It fell, its branches interlocked with another which had suffered a similar fate.

Zlobec shouted, but could not hear his own voice. He raised the shout to a scream . . . but it still seemed to him that there was only silence.

A four-ton stalactite broke its feet free from the limestone roof of the cavern, and with only a sigh of warning speared down a hundred foot into the centre of a party of Austrian tourists, smashing with the explosive force of a large bomb on the concrete plinth of the waiting area. It ground aside pulped and twisted bodies, smashing bloody flesh across the damp and dripping rocks, now freshly crimson.

The cavern echoed the explosion and the screams, then picked up and amplified the demented howl of the mountain.

A large section of cavern wall tumbled outwards, carrying with it a bridge on which had been standing a party of Italians. The wall with its delicately sintered limestone curtaining, the bridge and the Italians, dropped into the deep crevasse below. More parts of the cavern roof broke away to fall onto those in the waiting area. People crowded in terrified groups, too stunned to move, shaken to their knees by the vibrating earth, tumbled into writhing and agonised heaps, the dead with the living, the undamaged pressed into the crushed and quivering bodies of those who had already died.

The concrete platform cracked across its centre, humped upwards, then fell three feet.

An elderly communist guide, on his knees and with his face buried in his hands, screamed a prayer for mercy to a non-communist but forgiving God.

The yellow lights flickered, dimmed, flickered again and were extinguished. There was no dust from the grinding of the porous waterlogged rock below ground. Water in the pools leapt into sharp spikes of wavelets, as though being shot upwards by the force of repeated blows from deep beneath.

The small train which had been entering the underground station, with another load of tourists, shook itself free from the narrow-gauge track, rolled on its side and threw gigantic sparks from its live rail, tossing blue-white lightning into the shadows.

The mountain moved and settled. Sixty million tons of limestone rock tilted, slid sideways and re-arranged its stratas.

Catlin now knelt and watched the face of the mountain ahead of him. He knew what was happening, although he had never before experienced an earthquake. He watched the destruction of the Hotel Jama, its terraced roofs slipping, collapsing in a vast cloud of pale dust. Something exploded; black oil fumes rose with the dust. Further along the valley he saw another building, older and with an arched terrace in front, lean outwards and then disintegrate as the arches shivered themselves to brick rubble. Orange coloured pantiles showered the paved court. Gay blue and white sun umbrellas at tables spun crazily away. A steep and rocky hillside, close behind the building, shook slim pine trees from its meagre soil, then seemed to drop twenty feet, twisting as though to deliberately shrug its rock and boulders into the wreckage.

A road bridge, only seventy yards beyond Catlin, rocked, shuddered then, suddenly shed its concrete and Macadam cladding into the river, leaving only bent and warped girdering and reinforcing steel to span the foaming water.

The ground became still.

There were several seconds of real silence; no sound from the tortured earth and rocks, no movement of any form of stunned life. No birds shrilled their fear, no cricket chirruped in the dry grass. Catlin held his breath, involuntarily.

There was only the silence at first; the terrible silence.

Catlin stood, carefully. The ground was solid earth again, once more familiar. He looked towards the hill. The whole lower area was obscured by a settling cloud of fine dust, while above, a complete forest seemed to have been felled by a maniac with no plan or reason, the trunks shattered and lying in all directions.

Then he heard them; the distant screams.

A figure ran from the dust cloud, its arms above its head as though it surrendered to its impossible enemy. Others followed, stumbling, limping, screaming, shouting.

Catlin, swore, viciously.

7

The degree in law, which Inspector Emil Zlobec had taken when university education became freely available to all Yugoslavs, was of no use to him in the present situation.

He could hardly believe the incredible destruction and loss of life he had just witnessed. He was still living the nightmare. He couldn't find half the men who should have been on duty at the cave site. A nerve-shattered and stuttering witness told him he thought two of them were taking a coffee at the time in the Hotel Jama bar; those, he believed, were still under the wreckage and were probably dead. Another, had become hysterical and, despite threats from Zlobec, took an abandoned bicycle from the park and rode furiously away to check the safety of his own family. There should have been seven more officers on duty, making a total of ten in all. Three were with him now in the small, wooden police hut which, because of its light construction, had somehow survived the tremors and then the massive earthquake. The other four of Zlobec's men were missing.

The telephone lines were miraculously still intact, though the posts leant at crazy angles across the fields. He was now through to Division Headquarters, but it had taken a long time.

'Inspector Zlobec here. Get me Commissioner Bor. Yes, damn you, of course I know there's been an earthquake. Just get me Bor. . . er, the Commissioner. All right, I'll wait.' He drummed his fingers on the desk. His uniform was white with dust, as were his eyebrows and hair. There was brick grit in his smarting eyes. He could not remember losing his cap, but it had disappeared, and his short cropped hair showed a permanent ridge around his head where the cap normally rested. He licked his lips and could taste the dust, acrid and bitter. Zlobec felt in his pocket and pulled out his silver cigarette case, it was buckled and twisted, the contents crushed. He flicked his fingers at one of the three constables and said: 'Cigarette?' The man nodded, reached into his breast pocket and produced a battered pack. He eased out a cigarette and passed it to Zlobec, then struck a flimsy wax match on a sweat-damp box, several times. The match bent in his fingers, soft with the heat, but finally caught. Zlobec dragged on the cigarette and pulled the smoke down into his lungs. He felt he needed the comfort of the tobacco, badly.

Bor kept him waiting another twenty minutes. There were many people to deal with of greater importance than Zlobec.

'Well?' Bor's voice was impatient and Zlobec could picture him hunched over his desk, the portrait of the late Tito on the wall behind him in a position where it could stare accusingly down at any malevolents who might be brought before the Commissioner.

Zlobec, nervous of Bor and his uncertain temper, hesitated in replying and Bor said again: 'Well, Zlobec? Don't waste my time!'

'We have a disaster on our hands,' Zlobec felt himself near to tears. He hadn't expected any sympathy from Bor, but a little would have helped.

'*We* have a disaster, Zlobec? The whole damned northern region has a disaster! There are reports of thousands of deaths and casualties, everywhere. You're lucky to be able to speak with me; practically all the telephone system is destroyed, wires down everywhere. Calls are coming in all the time, by radio from the police and military units. You want ambulances? There are none available. Zlobec. . . and if there were, I doubt if they could get through. Roads have been destroyed and bridges are down between you and Ljubljana. Try locally, and commandeer any useful vehicles you can find. . . farm trucks, tractors and trailers, delivery trucks. Call Colonel Taufer at the Zagon barracks. . . ask for *his* transport. Everyone is in the same position. This is a catastrophe, Zlobec, far worse than the coastal quakes of '79.'

Bor had dealt with more than thirty similar calls for assistance in the past hour. Any help he might have been able to provide had been given in the first twenty minutes; every man and vehicle he could spare was already somewhere out in the devastated region. He didn't know where half of them were, or what difficulties they might have encountered. The tremor had been felt in Ljubljana, but apart from cracking the walls of the old buildings, and breaking a few windows, damage and casualties were small. He had hoped it would be the same throughout the region, but as the reports had come in, it had become clear that the earthquake had been massive. One from the Ljubljana College of Geology, gave a first estimate of nine, on the Richter Scale, with the epicentre somewhere in Zlobec's district of Postojna. Bor could understand Zlobec's concern, but there was no help available until the President pronounced the region an official disaster area, then Bor would be able to call in assistance from the neighbouring regions. The announcement would be made any time now.

Bor had been sickened by the earlier reports from villages nearer the centre of the disaster. Complete townships had been shaken to ruins, villages totally destroyed, factories wrecked. At Prestranek a coach-full of people, mostly school children, had been rocketed over the side of a mountain road and crashed a hundred feet down onto the rocks. . . all of the occupants had been killed. People lay buried under the rubble of their houses, offices or factories, in dozens of small towns and villages. Fortunately, a great many of the region's inhabitants worked in agriculture, and at that time of the day had been out in their fields; nevertheless, the estimated figures for casualties were enormous. Fortunately, Bor realised, it was a mid-summer, and at least accommodation was not likely to be so great a problem as it would have been in winter . . . though difficulties already existed for medical supplies and would soon arise regarding food and water. . . perhaps there would be international help?

'Zlobec . . . ' continued Bor. 'Zlobec, you must do whatever you can, without outside assistance . . . for the moment anyway. Naturally we'll get to you as soon as possible.'

'Commissioner . . . ' Zlobec hesitated. It seemed obvious to him that Commissioner Bor had no idea of the magnitude of the disaster at Postojna. He took a very deep breath. 'The caves, Commissioner.'

'The Postojna caves?' Zlobec could almost hear Bor's realisation. 'Postojna . . . what about the Postojna caves?'

'Collapsed.' Zlobec could think of no other word to describe the happening. 'Commissioner . . . for God's sake, we need immediate help.'

Bor was silent for almost a full minute. He spoke again, but now very calmly as if he knew that all it required to tilt Zlobec over the edge into total inefficiency was one harsh word. 'Zlobec, listen to me. Tell me about the caves . . . what exactly has happened?' Bor was aware of the popularity of the grotto in mid-tourist season. He was hoping for an answer that would please him, but inside, he knew what was to come, and a situation involving foreign tourists needed careful handling.

Zlobec said, flatly: 'The visitors are all trapped.' There was a break in his voice. 'The whole mountain moved.'

'All right, Zlobec. I understand. Now tell me . . . can you get to them?'

'No, Commissioner. The entrance . . . the terminal, has collapsed.' Zlobec was horrified to find he was crying, and could feel tears running down his face. He glanced, embarrassed at the men who were with him in the room. Two of them were staring blankly out of the window. The third who was watching him also had tears streaking the grey dust on his face. As Zlobec's eyes caught his, the man buried his face in his hands and sobbed. One of the two who had been looking out of the window turned, and put his arm across the man's shoulders. Zlobec knew the policeman's brother was an underground guide. 'The hotel also, Commissioner . . . terrible . . . terrible. Half the damned mountain has slid across the entrance to the caves . . . dear God, Commissioner.'

'Zlobec . . . Zlobec, can you still hear me? Good; one more question, Inspector.' Bor used Zlobec's rank, deliberately. 'Do you have any idea how many tourists were in the caves at the time of the disaster?'

Zlobec could no longer control himself. He leant forward and rested his hands, one still containing the telephone receiver, on his desk. Tears welled into his eyes and he knew that for a moment at least, he could not speak. He could hear Bor's voice, urgent, demanding, distant, in the ear piece. Eventually he raised it and held it to his head. 'I'm sorry, Commissioner.' He swallowed hard. 'At this time of the year, the cave's normal receipts would show perhaps four hundred visitors an hour. There could be as many, if not more, underground. They may be alive, or dead. There are many more buried beneath the terminal, and at the Hotel Jama site.'

'Your own men?'

Zlobec explained.

'Get two of them to check with the coaches and cars in the car parks,' suggested Bor. 'That will help to establish the number of persons who may be missing in the caves. Send another man up to the stone quarries; give him an official authority and if necessary threaten them with the harshest possible state action if they fail in any way to co-operate. Get what men and equipment they have available down to the cave entrance. Try to find local volunteer labour; I will personally get in touch with the Commandant of the Predjama Military, and Colonel Taufer at Zagon. Leave the army to me. And Zlobec . . . in the circumstances I will try to be with you in two hours.' Bor hoped a helicopter would be available for his use.

Zlobec breathed: 'Thank you,' but the telephone was already dead. He jerked his handkerchief from his pocket, blew his nose and wiped his face. He was aware he had already allowed himself too much emotion. He braced himself, turned to the three men and said, sharply: 'Smarten yourselves up. Mikoc, take my jeep. Go up to the quarries . . .'

He repeated Bor's instructions in a brisk and formal manner.

There were few men with direct access to Minister Kalin. Martin Bor was one. He and Baraslev Kalin were of the same generation; Kalin was, perhaps, three years his senior, but they had both been partisans, both been party members since its official formation. Kalin had the advantage of more formal education and had been closer to Tito during the fighting years, but Bor was not envious of the man's position. They had once been close friends, and Baraslev was still a member of the Slovenian Regional committee, as well as the Presidium.

Bor spoke cautiously and described the Postojna catastrophe. 'Minister . . . my friend . . . we need all the assistance possible. I am flying down to Postojna now, but I wanted to make certain you knew the details before I left; it may not be easy to contact me in the area.'

'I believe you're inferring there may be political repercussions. . .' Minister Kalin paused. 'You're right, Martin. I'm glad you've contacted me so quickly. Is there anything else I should know?'

Bor had been aware he would not have to explain his views deeply to Baraslev Kalin, the man was quick-minded and astute. The political difficulties of the situation had occurred to Bor even during his conversation with Zlobec. He had decided it was essential that the Regional Committee should be informed as soon as possible. A Commissioner of Police had responsibilities, but there were limits . . . success was in knowing when responsibility should be conceded. 'There may be a party of Russians inside the caverns.'

'From the Leningrad Trade Mission?'

'Exactly! They've been in Ljubljana for the past week. I've had men guarding their hotel; I believe some of them wanted to visit the Postojna caves before leaving.'

'How do you know that?'

'They asked one of my sergeants if it would be possible to make the visit official . . . that way they can save the price of the entrance tickets and the transport.' Bor did not attempt to hide his dislike of the Soviets. 'I replied that it wasn't possible; I didn't want to set a precedent . . . a Trade Mission doesn't warrant the courtesy, they're trying to sell us goods, not buy them.'

'I hope to God they didn't go to the caves today,' said Kalin. He'd had personal experience in dealing with angry Russian diplomats; it was like trying to bargain with hornets.

'We can expect a full spectrum of other nationalities,' Bor continued. 'Americans, British, Germans, Italians . . .'

'I know . . . it's going to be unpleasant and difficult.' Kalin knew that once the information was released there would be pressures from fifty different directions. Every Embassy whose citizens were involved would be using whatever leverage they could find. 'The Regional committee,and the Presidium, will be informed, Martin.' Kalin paused. 'Are you able to cope for the moment?'

'Only for the moment,' answered Bor. 'We badly need assistance from the other regions. I don't know the full extent of the casualties and damage in the various towns and villages, but I should hear in a few hours.'

Kalin had been thinking while Bor talked. He interrupted him. 'I believe you should stay away from Postojna . . . don't visit the caves immediately.'

'No?'

'They're not important when considered as part of the entire disaster. We must make sure we keep things in proportion. You are obviously expecting high casualty figures in the region?'

'Unfortunately, yes. There have been estimates as high as five thousand dead . . . many more injured.'

'Mmm! Good organisation is going to be needed, Martin. Organise . . . you're good at it. Leave the problem of Postojna to me for the time being. The press! of course, newspapermen . . . Postojna will be the kind of story they like . . . they'll be there like a flock of vultures. Who do you have in charge at Postojna?'

'Inspector Zlobec.'

'Is he any good?'

'Reasonable . . . capable in normal circumstances. I don't know about this kind of situation.'

'Handle the press yourself, then,' said Kalin. 'Set up a press office in Ljubljana . . . I'll get someone from the Information Ministry to help you. Keep them away from Postojna.'

'Of course.'

'I'll talk with Kunoski at the Ministry of Defense, and try to arrange for military engineers to come into the Region, and I'll arrange the kind of supplies you need as soon as you can give me more details. And I suggest you keep an open line to this department.'

There was a naked foot sticking upwards from the rubble. Catlin stood astride it, and took hold of both ends of a slab of concrete weighing around two hundred and seventy pounds. He braced himself and lifted. He was naked to the waist, and sweat and dust had given his body a coating of dirty grey mud. He felt his jaw and neck muscles tauten as the rock moved. He twisted his powerful body, almost feeling pleasure in using muscles he had lately neglected, but which he knew were still good. He let the weight of the slab pivot him at the waist and dropped it clear. He leant forward, then stopped and groaned aloud. The leg ended at the thigh in a bone splintered mess. It's owner had once been a woman.

There were a group of soldiers working in the rubble a few yards away, one of them with a red cross on his armband. Catlin shouted: 'Hey!' and beckoned the man; he was little more than a boy and obviously had no need to shave. He stumbled over the ruins and paled when his eyes followed Catlin's pointing arm. The youth turned, retched and then vomited. 'Jesus Christ,' swore Catlin. He stooped, picked up the bloody limb and carried it to a patch of grass twenty yards away. The youth, and the other soldiers watched him. He laid the limb down carefully, as though it were still alive, and then wiped the blood from his hands on his trousers.

He spoke to no-one, and there was no need. The job to be done was in front of him, totally occupying his mind, wiping away his former stress, destroying recent memories. He worked until he was exhausted and unable to lift another block of rubble. Sometime during the afternoon, someone had tossed him a safety helmet and he wore it although it was a little small on the ginger stubble of his bullet head. Sharp pieces of stonework and rough bricks had grazed his arms and body, drawing blood, but he didn't feel them. By late afternoon, there were many workers in the area. Mostly they worked in gangs, keeping to their own sections of the debris. Some were soldiers, in either grey or khaki uniforms, the officers, most of them in their early twenties, toiled alongside their men. In the evening, two bulldozers arrived with an English made JCB with a long-necked grab making it look like a mechanical dinosaur. One of the machines failed to start, but one bulldozer and the JCB began lifting the heavier blocks of masonry from the debris. Every now and then a group of men would pause, listen carefully, and then speed their work to reach some injured man or woman who cried from the depths of the rubble. At other times there would be a sombre silence as a mangled corpse was carried away from the wrecked buildings. As the evening sun dropped, a group of military engineers began rigging flood-lights to illuminate the site.

Catlin eventually staggered from the rubble. His muscles ached and kept cramping, and his legs were unsteady. A tall man, his face bronzed with continual work outdoors, came over and took him by the arm. He spoke in Yugoslavian and Catlin shook his head said: 'American . . . Americana. Non capitch.' The man replied in a friendly tone of voice and escorted Catlin to a tent that had been erected some hundred yards away. It was lit by a kerosene pressure lamp and the smell of the oil and the yellow glow reminded Catlin of his days at camp as a boy. He was too tired, though, for more than a brief recollection. The man led him to a table, and sat him on a collapsible canvas chair. He was back a few moments later with a huge bread roll filled with salami, and a tin mug of red wine. He put them in front of Catlin, patted him on the shoulder, and left him alone.

Catlin's throat was full of dust and grit. He took a deep swig of the wine, rolled it around his mouth, and then let it wash down his throat. It felt good. Catlin had few feelings at that moment; he was too exhausted. It had been the same in Korea; men claimed there was exhilaration after a battle, a satisfaction that you were still alive. Catlin had not found this so. He had been an efficient soldier, but when the action had been completed, or when he had defused some tricky piece of explosive weaponry, he only felt exhaustion. The relief probably came later, but was never immediate. He didn't enjoy death, or carnage, but the sight of blood didn't have the same sickening affect on him that it had on many people. A body was a body, once living but now dead. Catlin respected bodies; anyone's, friend or enemy. Someone had once enjoyed it.

He walked to the counter where he waved the empty mug at a stout woman in a long apron. She smiled at him, nodded with understanding, then refilled it. He had yet another before his mouth was moist enough to cope with the salami-filled roll. He ate it walking back to the Fiat. He clambered inside, put the remains of the bread on the passenger seat, and was asleep within seconds. He slept until one thirty a.m., then awoke stiff and cramped. The work, by floodlight was still continuing. He climbed out, stretched himself several times and went back to the rubble.

Fourteen of the sixteen members of the Regional Committee had met at eleven p.m. that night, in Baraslev Kalin's Ljubljana committee rooms. Not all the members were representatives in the National Presidium, although Kalin himself, held Presidium office.

It was now almost midnight. The fourteen men and women sat around the long, mahogany conference table, grim-faced and aware of the problems now confronting the Region. Some had been more directly and personally involved than others; several owned properties in the devastated areas, and two had families they had been unable to contact since the earthquake. Much as they would have preferred to leave Ljubljana and spend the time trying to reach their homes, it was not yet possible. The network of services upon which the normal running of the region depended, had been torn apart, and their duties as representatives of the people were quite clear.

Minister Baraslev Kalin, Chairman of the Regional Committee, was speaking. He was deliberately making his voice authoritative and strong. He had always been an ambitious man, prepared to be ruthless in his dealings with his fellows within the League of Communists, if such ruthlessness furthered his own political aims. Already a member of the Presidium, the national committee which consisted of twenty three men and women representing the six Yugoslavian republics, two minor autonomous areas and the military forces, Minister Kalin had been planning a final political assault, on the Presidency of the country. The Presidency consisted of eight men, and it was from these that the Vice President of the country was chosen, and from it, too, would certainly come the next President. Kalin was a political opportunist, and the present situation, he knew, could be exploited. It must be seen by all the country's leaders, that Minister Baraslev Kalin was a man of courage and decision; that he was capable and able in his handling of the present Slovenian disaster . . . and even more important, that he was a man of strength upon whom the Presidency, the Presidium, and the Republic could depend.

'You must realise the delicacy of the present situation. Since Tito's death, we have become even more vulnerable to intervention. International events have shown the West's assurances to be questionable. This is a time when our country must show no weakness to the jackals on our frontiers.' Kalin was referring to the Russian satellite countries, and to the Soviet Union itself. He made it clear in his next statement. 'The Soviet Union barely tolerates our separate existence. If we are to be allowed to continue on our present path, then we must avoid giving them an opportunity to find a weakness in our system which they will undoubtedly exploit.' He paused for effect, as though he were speaking before the senior members of the Presidium. Mentally he was, for he was aware that at some future time he would wish to make his present decisions and actions more widely known. 'Slovenia must not be the door which opens to allow the passage of Foreign armies . . . Slovenia must show a solidarity that is an example of the determination of all Yugoslavians to continue to act as part of an independent republic.' He gave his audience time to consider his words.

'I do not see the present situation as an excuse for Soviet action.' The speaker was a youngish woman, perhaps in her middle thirties. She was attractive, but appeared deliberately to hide her good looks behind thick-rimmed and masculine spectacles which she took off occasionally and twisted between carefully manicured fingers. Her clothes were fashionable and Italian. She was the daughter of Marshal Morolec, a former Minister who had died five years previously from a heart attack. 'The Soviets have been aware, for a long time, Comrade Minister, that if they were to invade, we would fight.'

'They are also aware, Anna Morolec, that they would win . . . in a matter of days.' Pieter Luchochvitz, the representative from the town of Maribor near to the Hungarian frontier, spoke sourly. His area was one of the most heavily fortified in the republic, and was considered to be the front line in the event of Soviet invasion. He was the same age and wartime generation as Kalin and had no illusions concerning the strength of the Russian military forces. He ground out a wet cigar butt in a glass ashtray in front of him. He was the only person in the room who had been smoking, and the blue haze and the strong smell of Turkish tobacco was his responsibility. 'It has been calculated it would take them only four days to defeat us. Their armour would roll across our country, they would drop paratroops on all our airports, and then move in to take control of our towns. They could come at any time they choose, and for any reason.' He continued to grind the life out of the butt as though it were an enemy. 'And we should remember that there are some of our own party members who would make them more than welcome. What Minister Kalin has said, makes good sense. We can *never* afford to show the smallest sign of a weakness.'

'I fail to understand how we can provide them with *any* excuse.' The speaker was one of the youngest members of the regional committee; he had been a member of the Youth Presidium at University, and was now an educationalist.

Kalin answered him as though he were an idiot. 'There is an emergency meeting of the Presidium tomorrow morning.' The Minister glanced at his watch. '*This* morning . . . what I recommend will determine the Presidium's action. You have all probably heard the Belgrade broadcast?' He gave them no time to answer. 'There have been offers of assistance from a number of countries; Italy, Austria, West Germany, Czechoslovakia. In another few hours there will be further offers . . . from other countries, and amongst them will be the United States of America, and the Soviet People's Republic.'

Kalin continued, more slowly. 'I wish to suggest to the Presidium that Slovenia does not enlist *any* foreign aid.' He was pleased to see the startled looks on the faces of the listeners. He said, dramatically: 'Slovenia can show the world that Yugoslavia can solve all her own problems.'

Anna Morolec almost exploded. 'Refuse foreign assistance? That is insane! Comrades, people will die as a result of such a decision. Charity it may be, but at a time like this, a small country cannot be proud. We should be glad there is such a thing as international charity. It is the feeling of people for people, regardless of race. We will badly need medical supplies. We must have emergency food and temporary living accommodation — remember how almost a hundred thousand people had to sleep in the open after the coastal earthquake of 1979?'

'Accept help from one country, and you must accept it from all,' Kalin looked carefully round the long table, searching the eyes of all the representatives. 'And that will be an invitation to the Soviets.'

'Minister, you over-dramatise the situation,' Anna Morolec observed, coldly. As the daughter of one of Tito's former colleagues, she knew the shortcomings of the older generation of ministers with their memories of the armed struggled against first the German occupation forces, and then the rightwing partisans of the former king. They could find spectres in every cupboard. 'The Russians know world opinion would be *totally* against them. They would not dare act.'

'Opinion didn't stop them in Czechoslovakia or Afghanistan,' said Rasic, who had visited Moscow eight years previously, and watched the formidable May Day parade. He was uncomfortable with the knowledge that the armed forces of Yugoslavia were pitiful when compared with those of Soviet Russia. It was not difficult for him to visualise the heavy tanks and rocket-launchers grinding their way through the streets of Zagreb as impressively as they had roared across Red Square. He also knew the armies of Nato, and of the United States of America, would do nothing to save them. No major power would risk a global conflict for the sake of one small country, however valuable it might be strategically. The days of gunboat action had died; for the Americans in Vietnam, and for the British and French at Suez.

Angelo Brucevic was one of the oldest representatives present. There were no records of his actual age — few peasants of his parent's generation had bothered to register their children — but it was generally accepted he was in his middle seventies. He was grey-haired, slightly-built, and always looked like an old professor in his untidy suits. He fluttered his hands, like bat wings. 'I, for one, will not countenance *any* decision which might make Slovenia responsible for inviting to Yugoslavia any forces of the Soviet People's Republic . . . no matter how they might appear on their arrival.'

'But they would send technicians, doctors, medical help,' insisted Anna Morolec. She had seen, in the past, how the older generation Communists would always support each other in any arguments with her contemporaries. Once an 'old-comrade' clique was formed, it could never be broken, and its members would remain inflexible in thought no matter how sincere or just on argument.

Angelo Brucevic smiled condescendingly at her. 'My child, technicians may also operate tanks, guns, rockets. It is quite obvious that if the Soviets were to send personnel, they would include members of their armed forces; it makes sense . . . we would do the same, perhaps. And can you, Anna Morolec, identify a machine-gunner when he is wearing the uniform of an ambulance driver? I agree with Minister Kalin. We accept *no* help.' He sat more upright in his seat, squared his shoulders and pushed out his chest. 'We are Slovenian.'

There were murmurs of agreement with the old man's views. Minister Baraslev Kalin had been watching their faces, carefully. He knew that the majority of the representatives would now support him. He leant towards them and spoke in a confidential manner which was calculated to increase their warmth towards him. 'My friends, I see you all understand why this matter is one which concerns the security of our country. We *cannot* take the risk, even if it *is* minimal . . . hypothetical, perhaps. One single chance in a million is a chance too many when the future of Yugoslavia is threatened. I agree with Anna Morolec, it is true that a few people *might* die as a result of this decision . . . but how many more millions *would* die in a war?'

'What are the present casualty figures, Minister?' The question came from a woman on Kalin's right.

'Regrettably, they will be very high. Reports are naturally confused at the moment . . . there is a tendency to exaggerate the deaths and the casualties. Between three and five thousand . . .'

'Deaths?'

'Yes, deaths. But, ignore the radio reports . . . especially those coming in from Italy . . . they are guessing . . . taking figures out of the air. And figures are of little consequence. But, before I end this meeting, I would like to word your recommendation to the Presidium . . .'

'One moment, Comrade Minister.' Anna Morolec stood, speaking determinedly. She peered at Kalin over the top of her spectacles. 'Are you unaware of the disaster at Postojna?'

'Postojna?' Pieter Luchochvitz, the Maribor representative, looked at her, curiously across the table.

'The caves at Postojna,' she repeated.

'I have been informed of Postojna.' Kalin angrily wondered how she had heard about the caves, no information had yet been released. It was obvious from the quizzical looks on the faces of the other representatives that they knew nothing. 'Postojna is not important. The Postojna caves are a very small part of the crisis.'

'I do not understand you, Comrade,' Anna Morolec said, with her voice icy and her eyes hard and unblinking, meeting those of Minister Kalin. 'There are many foreigners at Postojna, buried beneath the earth. How can you consider *them* to be a *small* part of the problem?

'Because, Anna Morolec, they are regrettably dead.' Kalin was close to losing his temper with the woman. 'The Postojna caves were at the epi-centre of the earthquake. Seismographic readings prove this. There was a major ground movement in the area. According to witnesses at the site, a large section of rock strata was involved.' Kalin made no attempt to be technical and kept his explanation simple. 'The entrance to the caves was in a part of strata most affected by the movement. It is the belief of the Ljubljana geologists that in all probability most of the underground system has collapsed; the ground above the system has sunk. This can be seen from the air, and I have photographs that were taken from a military helicopter a few hours ago, which show the settling.'

Anna Morolec had remained standing when Kalin began speaking. She interrupted him. 'Minister, representatives of the international news agencies will be less concerned by the state of the mountain, than with the tourists who are trapped beneath. And you cannot be certain they are dead.'

'The press . . . the news agencies . . . do we run our lives and country for the benefit of the newspapers? It is unfortunate a number of foreign visitors have died in this catastrophe but it is unnecessary to consider the attitudes of the foreign press.' He waved an arm to encompass all the representatives. 'We know about the world press from the Skopje earthquake . . . the Italian Udine earthquakes . . . the air crash we had a few years ago, north of here. We know about journalists, comrades. The international media acts quickly and emotionally; it forgets equally as quickly. A man, or woman, who is influenced by the press is a fool.' He stared at Anna Morolec, pointedly for a few seconds before he continued. 'It is our job to get Slovenia back to normal as quickly as possible. And, Comrades, with effort from all of us, it can be done.' The tone of Kalin's voice made it clear he had nothing more he wished to say, but Anna Morolec persisted in her questioning.

'Am I to understand then, Minister Kalin, you are personally suggesting we totally ignore Postojna Jama . . . pretend it hasn't happened?'

Kalin allowed his anger to show in his voice. 'Of course not, woman.'

'Comrade . . .' Anna Morolec corrected him.

'Comrade . . .' he almost shouted the word. 'There will be salvage and rescue work done at the caves. The tourists' bodies will eventually be recovered . . . if it is humanly possible.'

'And what if they have been trapped below ground, but are alive?'

Kalin did shout. 'They are dead, Anna Morolec . . . dead. I am more concerned with the living.'

'So you accept responsibility.'

Kalin raised his eyes and made a hopeless gesture with his hands. He glanced at old Angelo Brucevic who made a non-committal shrug. 'It *is* my responsibility. As a member of The Presidium, representing Slovenia, it *can* only be *my* responsibility.'

'Comrades, I believe wrong and immoral decisions have been made at this meeting, tonight,' said Anna Morolec. 'Decisions which are not in the interests of either Slovenia, or Yugoslavia.'

Minister Baraslev Kalin spoke deliberately. 'I will ensure your objections are minuted, Comrade Morolec.'

It was dawn, at Postojna. A large tent, normally a field mess for the local troops, had been erected near the car park in front of the demolished Hotel Jama. It contained one hundred and eighty six bodies, wrapped in camouflaged military groundsheets. They lay in tidy rows within the tent; some of the bodies bore no resemblance to the corpses of human beings, but were just lumpy, evil smelling bundles the bloodstained rescue workers found hard to carry even on stretchers. On top of each wrapped corpse was a small pile of belongings; items found within the clothing of the dead person, or close beside in the debris and rubble. They would help identification. The names of one hundred and seven of the dead were already known. They had been carrying either passports or papers which made identification almost certain. A soldier with an automatic rifle stood unnecessarily on guard at the tent entrance.

There were now approximately one hundred and fifty workers at the site. Many were local volunteers, others were troops. More of the military could have been brought in, but the Commandant was using his men sparingly and working them in two hour shifts at the site, and then allowing them four hours rest. Many of the soldiers were very young, conscripts at the beginning of the national service and barely trained in foot drill. They worked willingly and would have stayed longer at the site had they been allowed.

There had been no more equipment brought to the area, other than the lorries of the military, and a fire engine from the town of Postojna. Roads had been destroyed in places, making the movement of heavy transport difficult. The injured, those few who had so far been found under the wreckage alive, were being taken to the Ljubljana hospitals in tracked vehicles capable of circumnavigating the damaged sections of highway, and fording bridgeless streams and rivers. There had been some miraculous escapes from death amongst the tourists and day-staff at the hotel. A thirteen year old girl was found unhurt, apart from minor bruises, between the smashed bodies of her parents. There had seemed no reason why she should have escaped a similar fate. A woman and a man, both in their late fifties, were found standing upright, in a space not more than two feet square and six feet tall, beside a steel support disguised as a pillar. They too had suffered only scratches though both were suffering from shock.

The party of Russians from the Trade Mission had, in fact, visited the caves that day, but early, and had actually reached their coach and started the drive back to Ljubljana when the earthquake began. The driver stopped the vehicle but the passengers stayed inside. They had been bounced around as the vehicle swayed and leapt on the churning earth, but apart from an unpleasant and brief form of seasickness, none had been injured in any way. The reactions of those who had survived without injuries were mixed. Visitors to the site who had experienced the destruction, but who were not staying as guests in the hotel, had attempted to leave. Most had eventually succeeded. The military engineers had bridged the river Pivka and the road towards the coast was intact apart from three sections where it was possible to drive vehicles across sections of farmland. Tourists wishing to return to Ljubljana in their own transport, found that although they were only a little over thirty miles from the city, to reach it on passable roads meant a journey of five times that distance.

The quake had been felt as far north as Klagenfurt in Austria, but it had been slight and dismissed by most people as nothing more than the vibration of passing traffic. It had been felt, too, as far west as Venice. In the Italian town of Trieste, nearer the centre of earth movement, the bells of two churches had begun ringing on their own, and some structural damage had been done to a number of buildings, though there were no casualties.

A few of the visitors, like Catlin, had remained to help. In some cases because members of their families were still trapped beneath the buildings, in others because they too felt they should help as long as they were needed. They toiled away alongside the local volunteers, their holiday clothing torn and shredded by the heavy work.

Commissioner Bor *had* visited the Postojna caves, despite Minister Kalin's suggestion he should stay away from the area. He had decided that for the sake of his reports, he must have some personal knowledge of the destruction, and also, contact with all his police sections throughout the devastated region was important. He had not, however, as he had promised Inspector Zlobec, arrived within two hours of Zlobec's desperate call. He visited Postojna the following day, at dawn, and not by helicopter but in a military jeep. He stayed less than an hour, remarking to Zlobec that he should be grateful he wasn't experiencing the problems of some town authorities where water and electricity supplies had failed, and there was risk of outbreaks of disease as a result of damage to the sewerage systems.

Inspector Zlobec had hoped Commissioner Bor would arrive and immediately assume command; this had not happened. Bor had strode rapidly around the area, stared at the rubble and watched the rescue workers on the debris of the hotel. He barely glanced at the demolished terminus, or the mountain with its bare rock and wrecked forest.

He said to Zlobec: 'No press . . . no journalists; keep them away from here.'

Zlobec thought he had misheard. 'No journalists?'

'No press, what-so-ever!'

'But, Commissioner, we have a couple here already . . . the Italians who arrived last night.'

'Then get them off the site immediately. These are Minister Kalin's personal instructions. And if any more journalists attempt to visit Postojna Jama, they are to be sent away at once. Direct them to my offices in Ljubljana.' Bor had seen the puzzlement in Zlobec's eyes and decided he should give him an acceptable reason for the order. 'It's for your own benefit, Zlobec. The Minister does not want work at Postojna hampered by pressmen.

No information is to go out from here, only through my office. Do you understand?'

'Of course, Commissioner.'

'And lists of the dead, the injured . . . survivors, Zlobec, they too must go out through my office. It keeps it all tidy; official . . . no conflicting reports.'

More pressmen had arrived shortly after Commissioner Bors's departure; one a stringer for the London Daily Express, the other an agency man. They were anxious for information, knowing that they would be followed by the main body of newsmen. Zlobec refused them permission to enter the area. They argued until Zlobec threatened to have them arrested. In anger, they began the long round-about drive to Commissioner Bor's office in Ljubljana. Zlobec set up a police post a few hundred yards out on the main highway. That was the closest any journalists would get to the Postojna caves.

The British-built JCB with its heavy shovel, had been moving concrete slabs from the debris of the terminal building. As a result of this, three clerks and one guide who had been having a siesta in the building at the time of the earthquake, were released alive and uninjured. The bodies of nine others had been brought out into the sunlight. Two of the terminal staff, a man and a woman, had been found with terrible injuries; they would only survive with major surgery and a lot of luck. A little after mid-day, the JCB had reached the communications section of the terminal, a small room with telephone wires running back into the cave system and through which guides could make reports, or the workers at the railway terminals or bars demand tools, equipment or additional food to be sent in on the small railway.

The driver of the JCB was curious when the bucket of his vehicle dragged aside a slab of reinforced concrete flooring and disclosed one section of the communications room. The equipment immediately below his poised bucket looked expensive. He cut the motor and climbed down into the wreckage; there was a modern telephone receiver dangling on its cables, his intention was to cut it free and keep it in the JCB cab until he finished his spell of driving. It was better than the more old-fashioned hand-set in his flat in Senozece. He pulled a knife from his pocket and opened it.

'What have you found?'

The JCB driver looked round, guiltily. The speaker was a

soldier, standing above him in the wreckage. The driver hid the knife. 'It looks like it's the telephone exchange.'

'Anybody trapped in there?' The soldier climbed down. He wore the white lightning flash of a radio operator on his uniform. He called a name back over his shoulder and a minute later was joined by a colleague. The JCB driver slid the knife back into his pocket and hauled himself into his vehicle again. He started the motor, reversed the wheels and pulled out of the wreckage.

The soldier spoke to his friend. 'Fitting this type of equipment was my civilian work. I'll be glad to get back to it.'

'It looks complicated . . . so many wires.'

'Not so many; they're colour coded. You can trace them easily.' The switchboard was tilted forward exposing the wiring behind. 'See . . . red to red along the casing . . . any colour is traced right through.' He ran his fingers over the sockets. 'It's simple work. Easier than radio.' The soldier picked up the earphones and set them on his head. He pushed a plug into the socket marked 'interior terminal', then pressed the call switch. He was about to remove the headset when his jaw dropped and his eyes widened. 'Holy Mother . . .' He waved wildly at his colleague, and then shouted . . . 'Get them to stop the machinery.' His friend stared at him blankly. The soldier pushing him away, violently. 'Go and get them to stop the machines, I can't hear properly . . . but there are people alive inside the mountain . . . hundreds of them alive . . .'

8

At the moment when the earthquake had begun, David Berkley, Fudge Kelly, Angie Zubrecht and Colette Marishall, had been standing together near the signpost which indicated the assembly point for the English speaking tour. Berkley was carrying two cameras, a Canon which he had used for several years and with which he was very familiar, and a new Leica purchased only weeks before in New York. He also had an automatic electronic flash; a sophisticated piece of equipment which limited its power output to the requirements of the camera. The latter was important, for shooting a series of pictures in the conditions he expected to encounter within the cave would give him no time to make flash adjustments manually.

The two models, Fudge and Angie, wore the knickerbocker outfits that Lady Ahead wanted included in their feature. The two girls had been hot and uncomfortable in the cab on the trip from Ljubljana, and Colette Marishall had spent the waiting period, before entering the caves, straightening their outfits and attempting to make them appear salon crisp. Once they had entered the caverns, the two girls felt cooler and Angie, more conscious of her appearance than Fudge, freshened her make-up in the poor light while they had stood and waited for the small train.

For Angie, the visit to the Postojna caves was just another part of the assignment. Her preferred pleasures were good restaurants, expensive clubs, dancing until dawn and fast cars. She did not enjoy sub-standard hotels, and caves were definitely not her scene. Fudge Kelly however, was as excited with the trip as if she had been taking a vacation. She liked any form of travel, and the hustle of the assignment had been fun. She found the crowds of people interesting, and had liked visiting the European capitals. For her, the work only interrupted the pleasure of the trip and the visit to the Postojna caves was a welcomed experience. She chattered like a schoolgirl, continuously, squeaking and gasping with pleasure at the sights within the caverns as the train rattled through its long tunnel.

Berkley's professional eye had been working overtime. There had been strange grottoes in the tunnel, incredible colours and lighting, and he had viewed it with the depressed feeling that he was not going to have the time to produce the quality of work the caverns deserved. He was tempted to try to persuade Colette to cable her office and obtain permission to break the trip, quit the tight schedule and spend a few days working on a good artistic feature. He had found an illustrated guide book in one of the hotel shops, and this had given him some idea of the layout of the great cavern system and the type of picture he was likely to obtain.

He had already taken a dozen for his own collection, and had decided a scene of the two girls in the crowded and rather mysterious waiting area, with its damp rocks and winding paths, was worth a couple more. 'Just ignore us, please,' he called to a group of half a dozen tourists who had paused to watch them. They recognised his professionalism and turned away from him to continue their conversations. He signalled Kelly to move to Angie's right, and said: 'Try to do something with Angie's hair,' to Colette. The two heavy blankets the girls had been wearing had flattened Angie's near-Afro hairstyle. Colette now had the blankets over her arm and leant forward to re-arrange the disturbed hairstyle.

Berkley stepped sideways, peering through the viewfinder of his Canon. He pressed the shutter release. The flash illuminated the group of tourists, bouncing to the furthest walls of the cavern and making the coloured rocks seem pale. He thumbed the winder, aimed the camera again, squatting close to the ground to make the models seem leggier. Again he pressed the shutter release.

At that precise moment, the stalactite broke away from the roof. The ground began trembling. Angie Zubrecht said loudly: 'My God, what . . .'

The stalactite hit the concrete platform thirty yards away from them with a tremendous explosion of sound. Fudge Kelly screamed; an automatic reaction. She screamed on roller-coasters . . . it was the last sound she ever made, and it was unheard.

A piece of rock, twice the size of a household table careered past Berkley, its sharp edges tearing the blanket from his shoulders and spinning him sideways. Like some gigantic and prehistoric monster it caught the two girls, gathered them in razor teeth and swept them ahead of it until it disintegrated in a mess of shattered limestone and pulped flesh against the foot of another giant teetering column.

Fragments, like shrapnel, hissed through the disturbed air. The signpost which had read 'English' was torn from the ground by a wedge of hurtling limestone carbonate weighing at least four hundred pounds.

Berkley, horrified, saw part of a body slide across the concrete, spilling blood and intestines onto the damp surface. He could hear screams now, screams that were echoed by others . . . terrified screams of pain and agony.

The mountain began its roar. Automatically, Berkley took pictures, his hands operating divorced from his brain and emotions. He was conscious only of the difficulty he was having breathing as unexpected fear tightened the muscles of his throat and chest.

The ground began to heave, rising and falling. Berkley's hands fired half a dozen shots before he lost his footing and dropped to his knees. He balanced himself with one hand while the other still attempted to work the camera; it was an impossibility. His mind regained control. He knew what he was experiencing; had somehow understood, from the very first movement of the ground. This was an earthquake; he was in the middle of it. It was happening all around him. He had tried to record it, but had failed.

The lighting in the cave began flickering . . . on, off, on, off, until the effect was of the strobe lights in a discoteque. People staggered, fell, moved, rolled on the ground, were killed, in the odd, jerky movements of an old-time movie.

There was so much sound from the mountain that the voices, screams, cries of terror from those inside its belly, were overwhelmed. The old-time movie was silent. Berkley was now lying on his side. Colette had grabbed him and clung to him, desperately. As the lights flashed he could feel her head pressed against his chest, as she attempted, childlike, to dismiss her terror behind closed eyes. He looked for the two girls, shouted their names, but there was no sign of them, and his voice was lost in the thunder of the caves.

More rock fell. He watched an enormous section of the distant cavern wall drop slightly, shuffle itself, then lean outwards before crashing to the quivering and broken ground beneath. More of the roof stalactites hurtled downwards as white thunderbolts, to smash on the stalagmites waiting below. Smooth polished stone glanced and ricocheted from glistening surfaces that became broken, jagged and tortured. Bright splinters swirled into the shadows, catching the flickering lights and fading like the sparks of a firework display.

The electric lighting in the cavern was extinguished, but was almost immediately replaced by cold white and blue light dancing against the rocks; the arcing of live metal to earth.

The groans and roars of the mountain diminished, and the human cries grew. The white flashes stopped. The sound of rock grinding against rock ended and brought the screams of the fearful, the injured and dying suddenly closer. The ground no longer trembled and heaved. Berkley wriggled himself into a sitting position, dragging the distraught Colette with him. He pulled her upright until she was sitting facing him in the blackness. Her head was against him. She was sobbing, loudly. He shook her. Her sobbing did not lessen. He spoke to her sharply.

'Colette . . . Colette, damn you . . .' He shook her again. 'The two girls, Colette.'

The thought of the others quietened her. Her sobs became stifled, controlled, and then ceased.

'What . . .' Her voice was small. She didn't finish her question.

'Earthquake,' answered Berkley. 'It's over; finished. Are you hurt?'

She didn't answer at once and then said, her voice a little firmer; 'No . . not hurt.'

The screams of terror had ended and now there were only the awful cries of the injured, mostly from Berkley's right where the giant stalactite had exploded on the concrete platform. There were shouts, names; husbands seeking their wives, wives their husbands, and children. There were the sounds of distress, of pain.

A few yards away, a strong voice was calling repeatedly: 'Kristoff . . . Kristoff . . . Yacho Kristoff . . .' It was answered eventually from fifty yards away in the darkness and a shouted conversation began in Slovene.

Colette asked: 'Angie . . . Fudge?' Her voice was still taut with fright. David Berkley's flash gun exploded white light. Although the flash lasted only a micro-second, it impressed a horrifying scene on his mind. Few people stood. Those who did so were like the blind, their arms stretched before them, their eyes staring in the sudden and brief light. People huddled, lay in groups together, were stretched arms and legs widespread on the wet and bloody rock as though pinioned, or clutched wildly at each other. A guide in his distinctive uniform was standing with his arms held slightly out from the sides of his body facing someone yards away, his mouth open as he shouted.

Berkley tried to use his camera flash again; it failed. Time became distorted; minutes passed like hours, then a lamp beam threw an orb of white against the cavern wall. There was more shouted conversation and another beam was waved as a signal to a fellow guide. A match flared and an emergency candle was lit and placed on the rocks, to be joined in minutes by eight or ten more. Berkley could smell burning wax in the air . . . overlying the metallic scent of blood and fear. He clambered to his feet.

The few guides who had survived now stood in a close and uncertain group, their voices hushed but urgent. He saw movement in the gloom, a horrific seething as though the fallen rocks writhed and crawled. Men and women, searching, unsteady in their movement groped their way across the shattered ground. There were groans, anguished cries as bodies were found and recognised. There was the sound of prayer and of grief and pain.

He tried to locate himself, attempted to recognise the place on the buckled platform where the two girls had been standing. There was nothing familiar, it was a new and terrible landscape.

'David?' Uncertainty thinned Colette's voice.

'Wait . . . just stay there. Don't move.'

He picked his way carefully across rubble that slid and moved beneath his feet. Ten yards away it piled itself against the roots of a decapitated stalagmite, the limestone stained deep rose in the feeble light. There were shreds of cloth draped on the sharp rocks. He picked up a bloodstained fragment and felt the harsh chill of dismay as he recognised it as part of the clothing Fudge Kelly had been wearing. There was more amongst the shards of limestone . . . things he didn't need to examine closely; things he associated, in nightmares, with shell and bomb craters, the paths of gunships. The chill became a shudder.

Colette watched him return, trying to read his face. His lack of expression warned her; she needed only confirmation. He shook his head, then squatted beside her.

'Dear God, no.' He put an arm around her and felt her body, taut. She repeated 'Dear God,' then said, softly: 'Fudge . . .' He knew she couldn't reconcile her memories of the two girls with their unexpected deaths. She put her hands quickly to her face and sobbed. He let her cry, feeling her soften against him; drawing herself closer to him.

After a while he said, gently: 'We have to help. People need us.'

She responded to his voice, stifling her sobs. 'Help . . . people?'

He pushed her a little away from him, so he could face her. 'There are a lot of people injured . . . I was trained as a medic, a corpsman in the army. They'll want all the help they can get.'

She said: 'Yes,' dully, then her voice hardened. 'Yes. I'll be fine . . . I'm all right now.' He stood, paused for a moment then started to move toward the group of guides. Her voice, suddenly urgent, stopped him. 'David, wait. Perhaps I can help, too.'

Yacho Kristoff was fifty three, the oldest and most senior of the cave guides. He had worked in the cave system for over thirty years; since the end of the war. He had not been a partisan, but only because he had been forced into a labour gang by the Germans, and by the time he was liberated he was in no fit condition to fight. He had, however, been an active though not educated member of his local Communist Party. When the caves had been re-opened, he had applied for a position. The members of the Cave Commission agreed, because he had learnt German during his time with the labour gang, and a smattering of English after the liberation; he was appointed mainly to deal with the German speaking tourists. This was not easy for Kristoff; he had not loved the men who forced him to work sixteen hours a day building their concrete bunkers, making him smash great boulders to fine gravel with a four-pound hammer, turning his hands into two great calluses cracking and seeping blood as he worked, while his body grew thinner from lack of nourishment. The years had softened the hands and the memories, but German tourists still found their guide sullen and reluctant to talk. He got a few tips from them, but was always helpful and friendly with any groups of English speaking visitors.

He had been injured by a piece of rock bouncing from the cavern wall during the earthquake, and now hunched himself forward in an attempt to deaden the sharp pain beneath his ribs. 'Where are the others?' He stared at the small group of guides. There should have been six of them underground, he counted only four, including himself. He guessed that there would have been over four hundred visitors in the caves at this time of the day, each guide's tour could number between eighty and a hundred visitors.

'Perhaps still in the system,' said another guide. He was younger than the other three, squarely built, powerful. Unlike Kristoff, Serge Irano would never be promoted to senior guide, though he had a formal schooling and spoke more than two foreign languages. He was not a member of the Communist Party, and had made it obvious he had no time for their weekly meetings with the endless pressing of political dogma. In state industries, promotion was party-linked. 'Dneser was late getting his last tour away . . . he was due back a while ago. I don't know about Rucht.'

Kristoff winced with the pain of his injury and then said: 'The train crashed . . . the power cables were probably cut by the wreckage.'

'Don't worry, Comrades,' said one of the other two guides, cheerfully. He was a burly, round-shouldered man. 'In an hour or two we'll all be going home to our suppers.'

'Shut up, Hans' growled Kristoff. Hans Mallek was the cross which Kristoff bore; the man was slow thinking and blundering. Mallek had been employed only because his father's brother worked in the Cave Commission offices. Mallek barely spoke Italian, the second language his uncle had claimed Mallek knew when he was given his job. There were always complaints from the Italian tourists when they had been taken through the system by Mallek. Kristoff turned and spoke to Serge Irano. 'Have you seen the tunnel entrance? It's buried under fallen rock! Perhaps the entire tunnel has collapsed.'

'You think we're trapped?' Tor Sarbo's face was anxious. Of the underground guides, he was the most nervous. Others, in free moments, might explore odd lengths of unopened passages, but not Tor Sarbo. He kept to the known routes and was glad to leave the caverns at the end of a working day.

'Maybe not trapped,' said Irano. 'If the tunnel *has* gone, we may still be able to link up with the Pivka system, through the Black Cave.' He was thinking of the route by which the partisans had reached the German petrol dump in 1944. 'There are a lot of tunnels and passages. We'll be able to find a way out. I think it's more important that we find a way in . . . to get medical help to the people who are injured. Some of them can't be moved until they've had treatment.'

Serge Irano, a Slovenian, loved the caves. They had been his hobby since childhood. He was just thirty years old, but had spent hundreds of hours exploring the Postojna system with other members of the local speleology club. He had wormed his way through crevices so narrow he'd had to remove his clothing so his wet and naked body might squeeze between the rock. He had hung precariously on thin wire ladders over unplumbed depths, swum siphons by taking a deep breath and trusting to luck that his air would last him until he reached some unknown and undiscovered cave ahead of him, and climbed smooth slippery rocks beneath the waterfalls as thousands of gallons of ice-cold mountain water thundered down around him. Now he had a strange pessimistic feeling, not the relief he had half-expected when the earthquake had finished and he had found himself alive and unhurt. 'We must do what we can for the injured, first. Perhaps Mallek is right, we will be home to supper tonight. If not, then there will be time for me to start looking for a way out.' Irano noticed Kristoff's pain for the first time. 'You're hurt?'

Kristroff shook his head. 'Indigestion.' He spoke to the other two guides. 'We've talked about this possibility . . . we've known it could happen even since Skopje; since the Dalmation Coast earthquakes.'

'Rucht said it was a gamble, but the odds were always in our favour,' interrupted Mallek.

'The odds, yes . . . but we always knew it might happen. I've even discussed it with our manager. He said there were predetermined and official ways of dealing with such things. Of course there are . . . and while we're worrying down here, people will already be trying to reach us. Irano is right . . . first, the tourists. Mallek and Sarbo, there is medical equipment in the emergency stations. Bring all you can find, and the candles and spare batteries, if they're undamaged. Irano, search the passages and see if you can find Dneser and Rucht; we need them with us.'

Irano waited until the other two guides had left he Kristoff and himself alone, then he said: 'I think it would be sensible to see how much food and drink we have in the canteen.'

'Food and drink?' The tone of Kristoff's voice changed as he realised the meaning of Irano's suggestion. 'You think we could be here that long?'

'There have been some rock falls before in some of the tunnels, even with the slightest past tremors,' replied Irano. 'This is bad rock; soft and unreliable. It is possible we could be here for a *very* long time.'

Kristoff straightened himself slowly, as though giving himself time to think about Irano's warning. He rubbed his hand over his stomach; the pain had not lessened. He stared across the great cavern, his eyes now more accustomed to the gloom. 'Then I must do something about the dead,' he said, quietly. 'The dead must be separated from the living.' He looked quickly at Irano. 'I will do that now, Serge. I have seen bodies before.' His eyes hardened slightly in the candlelight. 'I will get the German tourists to help.

Dneser and Rucht were dead. Irano found Rucht's body at the entrance to the section known as The Big Mountain. The Big Mountain had moved, to roll itself sideways on to Rucht and the thirty six tourists who had been following him. There was nothing of them to rescue or help. Gigantic boulders and slabs of limestone had rolled over them, ground and smashed them. Rucht's head, wedged between two huge rocks, stared up at Irano with glazed eyes, its mouth contorted by pressure into a terrible grin. Irano looked for a few minutes in the beam of the flashlight he was carrying, then gently moved a piece of broken slab so it covered Rucht's face.

Dneser had gone, somewhere into the depths, with all but two dozen of his party who had scrambled and staggered back to the reception area, bloody and terrified. The Russian Bridge, so called because it had been built by Russian prisoners in the First Great War, had collapsed while the guide and party were standing on its narrow span. Those who had survived, mostly Swiss, had been hanging back marvelling at a stalagmite which they felt resembled a small owl, when the earthquake had begun. They had seen the bridge collapse, the party hurled into the crevasse below, and then watched as thousands of tons of rock had dropped from the roof to bury any who might have survived the fall.

There was no movement of air within the cavern and this, for Irano, was not a good sign. It meant the system was sealed. He lit a candle in one tunnel, hoping he would see the flame flicker when he stood it on a rock; hoping also he would feel even a miniscule breeze against his sweat covered face. He had visited the blocked tunnel entrance. The twisted steel of the railway tracks ended beneath a pile of rubble. A new fault had appeared in the rock above the tunnel entrance and the fresh strata had been exposed by the vibration of the earth; the fault showed a five meter difference between any single line of fractured strata; this meant the entire mountain, or at least this part of it, had dropped by as much. Irano had not yet discussed it with the others, but he was convinced the tunnel no longer existed. The one and a half kilometers from the entrance was probably now solid rock.

There were no doctors. Kristoff was dismayed. He had hoped that amongst so many wealthy foreign visitors, there would be at least one qualified doctor. There were two German nurses who had been travelling together, and an English Veterinary Surgeon. There were also two Japanese with some sort of medical training. By using an English speaking Japanese as a translator, Kristoff found one of the men to be a recently qualified Dental Surgeon, with a little general medical experience. The other Japanese was a member of a Nagasaki volunteer service who normally helped with road accidents. Several Americans had first aid experience, military and civil, and were helping with the injured, but the British Veterinary Surgeon was the nearest Kristoff found to a qualified doctor.

The Veterinary's face would have been florid in daylight, but in the semi-darkness of the caves, he seemed dark-skinned. Robert Spark was forty-seven. His companion, a woman of twenty-nine, had been named in divorce proceedings by his ex-wife; neither Spark, nor Eileen Bathurst cared. They had been married the previous weekend in a Registry Office in Cheltenham, England. Spark was a country vet, preferring the company of the farming community to the more lucrative life to be found amongst the pets of townspeople. Eileen Bathurst had been the proprietress of a riding stables not far from his practice, and he had met her through his work with her horses. The trip to Yugoslavia, the fortnight package, had been their honeymoon; Robert Spark's first holiday abroad in fifteen years. He was a humorous and easy-going man. He had qualified as a vet prior to a short service army commission, and had been a veterinary officer in the last animal transport section of the British Army during the Malayan campaign in the early fifties. Spark had finished his military service at the same time as the British Army had disposed of the last of its mules. The mules had developed his sense of humour!

He had not been terrified during the earthquake, though he had been conscious of the fears of his new wife. The occurrence had astonished him; he had experienced the shaking earth, the roaring and groaning of the rocks, with more awe than horror, and when it had finally ended, he had picked himself up from the rocks and found his hands as steady as ever. It was not a question of him being phlegmatic, simply interested. The terrible injuries, and the deaths of his fellow tourists, had not become obvious until the guides lit the candles and returned some light to the cavern. He was pleased when Kristoff called for people with medical experience, and had volunteered at once. His wife, Eileen, had insisted on helping him, and with the two Japanese and the German nurses, and the American Volunteers, they worked as a team in an area which had been turned into a kind of field hospital. It was pitifully equipped; a few bandages and splints, sticking plaster and antiseptic ointment. The kind of things kept in the caves to deal with minor injuries which would be treated correctly when the injured visitor was brought to the surface. Blankets salvaged from the bodies of the dead were being used to comfort the injured. Two hundred and seventy nine people remained alive in the Postojna cave system.

Only twenty three Japanese had survived the earthquake. Some of their party had been on board the small train, most of which had been buried within the tunnel. It had spilled its terrified passengers against the walls just before the major earthshift took place and completely buried them. Passengers in the front section were thrown clear, though the driver, a middle-aged man who had been a close friend of Kristoff, had been electrocuted. The guard was somewhere back in the collapsed tunnel with the other crushed passengers.

All but eight Americans had survived. Fortunately most had been standing on a section of the platform which had escaped major destruction. A man from Detroit had been decapitated and, perhaps mercifully, the same long sliver of rock had penetrated his wife's chest and she too had died almost instantaneously. Three others had been crushed when the earth beneath the platform had buckled, opening a chasm into which they dropped a few feet before its sides closed back together again. The remaining three had been killed by the falling rocks, Fudge Kelly and Angie Zubrecht dying instantly during the earthquake, the other a few minutes later in the darkness. There were forty two with injuries, mostly cuts and bruises from flying rock splinters and fragments; with medical help they would all survive. Six had serious injuries; one a woman who had been face-down on the concrete platform when an eighty pound stalactite had fallen across her pelvis.

The greatest casualties were amongst a tour party of Austrians, who had been standing close together when the first huge stalactite dropped from the cave roof. There had been sixty eight of the Austrians; only five were now alive. They had entered the system earlier than the American, German and Japanese parties, and had been waiting inside the caves, for a guide, for almost half an hour. The five survivors huddled themselves together in silence, too stunned even to communicate amongst themselves. Three German women were attending to them, giving them sympathy and trying to break through the barrier of grief and shock.

The German group had lost seventeen members. The survivors behaved, at first, in a strange almost isolationist manner. They drew themselves together, rapidly found a spokesman; lined up their own dead and covered the bodies. They attempted to deal with their own injured. Fortunately, the establishment of the field hospital area had encouraged them to mix with the American party. Now, the two groups were intermingled. Amongst all those alive in the cave were thirty seven children.

For most of the survivors the catastrophe removed whatever national prejudices that might have existed. They were conscious their future survival could depend on those trapped with them, be they German millionaire, American factory worker, Japanese businessman, or Yugoslavian cave cleaner.

Carl Struger was unhurt, apart from bruises. When the earthquake had begun, he had believed for a few seconds he was reliving the death of his father; and then he had recognised the movement of the earth for what it was; it had been no less horrifying. It seemed to him the mountain was attempting to kill yet another generation of his family, and the malevolence contained in the earthquake was aimed at his personal destruction. Struger had been only a few yards from the point of impact of the first huge stalactite which had killed so many of the Austrian party. The body of a man, partially crushed by the falling rock, had thrust Struger between two boulders and protected him from other hurtling missiles as more of the roof collapsed. Struger fully expected to die, and when the cavern lights were extinguished and he found he was unable to move, he had even thought for a while that he was dead. Warm rivulets of liquid had run down his face, trickling around his neck; he knew if it was water seeping into the cave, it would have been cold. His mind had sought an explanation, and found it with horror. The liquid was blood. The smashed body of the man, wedged above him, drained itself. Struger had shrieked and forced it away from him, scrambling out of the rubble in the final seconds of the earthquake. In the first terrible minutes of silence that followed the roar of the mountain, Struger had hysterically stripped the blood soaked clothing away from his body until he was naked. Reason came soon afterwards when the glow of the guide's candles brought light to the cavern. Struger wrapped himself in a blanket, collected his clothing and washed it out in one of the many rock pools. He wrung most of the water from the material, and dressed again. The clothing was wet and uncomfortable, but he hoped the heat of his body would dry it out. He was now ashamed he had panicked; in all the years he had climbed and ski'd the mountains there had never been a second when he had lost control; it was disconcerting to know there was a breaking point.

Serge Irano searched the caves alone for seven hours before he returned to the main cavern and found Kristoff again. Kristoff's thin, sallow face was even more drawn and taut with the pain of his injury and the strain of the past hours. He sat on a beer crate beside the wreckage of the small bar on the platform. Beside him were several metal containers and a stack of fruit squash, lemonade and liquor bottles.

Serge Irano lowered himself to a rock next to him.

Kristoff jerked his head towards the wreckage of the bar. 'They were both killed; Herta and Staluca. One of the gas cylinders exploded when rock fell on the canteen. I didn't hear it with all the other noises.' Kristoff's voice sounded exhausted, and he slurred his words as though he had been drinking, though Irano knew this was not the case. Kristoff never drank — not even during celebrations. 'Did you have luck?'

Serge Irano shook his head. 'Nothing, so far. All the section beyond the Russian Bridge has collapsed; I might be able to force a way through in time, but not alone. It's impossible to reach the Black Grottoes and they were our only chance of getting to the Pivka system.'

'What about the Upper Tartarus?' asked Kristoff.

'Again blocked . . . also the tunnel to the Little Grottoes and the Crossroads.' The Upper Tartarus was a passage leading to part of the caves which were believed to be linked with yet another series of unexplored systems. The Crossroads was an entrance leading to a point deeper in the railway tunnel.

Kristoff scowled, the shadows darkening the lines on his face until they seemed to have been drawn in charcoal. 'Keep your voice down, Irano; I don't want the tourists to hear our conversation. Some of them may speak Slovene.' He dropped his own voice to a whisper. 'It is bad . . . very bad unless we can get out quickly. I have gathered together all the food . . . every item of food that anyone was carrying; biscuits, chocolate. I have it all together, here. But shared equally between almost three hundred of us, it will be only a few morsels . . . too little even to ration. Our food will be gone in ten hours from now. Water is no problem, there is too much of it down here; and there are the drinks. They may be useful for the injured. The medical people are using slivovitz as an antiseptic.' He hesitated before speaking again. 'If things are really bad, and they . . . outside . . . can't get to us, then people will begin to die. We will all die.'

'I have no intention of dying in this cave system,' Irano said fiercely. 'The earthquake destroyed a lot of the old caverns, but it has opened new ones. I need partners to work with . . . men to accompany me. I will find a way out eventually, Kristoff, believe me.'

'None of the guides can help you,' Kristoff answered heavily. 'And I am not much use to you at fifty three years of age. Already my joints are stiff with the damp of this place. Sarbo is afraid of the caves . . . I don't know why he carries on with this work, he is always talking of leaving.'

'Mallek is strong.'

'And also very stupid. The first time you give him a rope to hold, he'll let go to pick his nose the minute you're hanging over a chasm. I barely trust him with the tourists.'

'Perhaps there are cavers amongst them,' said Irano. 'I shall ask.'

Kristoff nodded. 'If you wish, but don't make them more nervous, they're frightened enough.' He looked at his watch. 'It is night-time . . . I have cut down the number of candles we are using and twice a day I will extinguish most of them for a few hours. Take Sarbo and Mallek's flashlights; whatever you need for your exploring. There is a rope, from the emergency stores.'

Had Irano wanted skiers, canoeists or swimmers, there would have been some, but, as with the doctors, there were no experienced cavers. There were however, a Japanese and a German who had done some rock climbing, and an athletic-looking American who had also volunteered.

Irano was the English speaking guide; he had learnt English at school and improved it with the long hours of conversation with tourists in the resort bars of the summer seasons. He spoke it fluently and enjoyed using it. Eventually, he chose the German and American, turning away the disappointed young Japanese because of the language problems. The German spoke English.

They borrowed suitable clothing, anoraks and boots from tourists better equipped than themselves, collected the rope from the stores which Kristoff had gathered, took a dozen of the precious candles and, like the final assault group making an attempt at a mountain peak, disappeared into the darkness of one of the caverns.

Their fellow tourists watched them go, silently. For a few minutes the beams of their flashlights flickered in the tunnel, casting their shadows tall and grotesque at the cavern mouth; then the lights faded and they were gone.

An American voiced the thoughts of all those who were tó wait, in a whisper that carried the length of the great cave: 'God help you. God help us all.'

Kaguri had been startled, but not frightened by the earthquake. It was not the first he had experienced. Earth tremors were frequent in some parts of Japan, and he had spent much of his youth in a small town that was periodically wrecked throughout its history by such events. He had been frightened only once in his life, and then not for his own safety. It had been on the day when the Japanese radio had announced the atom bomb attacks on Nagasaki and Hiroshima. He had been afraid then for the safety of the Emperor, and the people of the Japanese nation.

When the earthquake had ended, Kaguri had climbed slowly to his feet. He knew better than to act hurriedly. Earthquakes had the habit of renewing their ferocious assault within seconds of the first lull. Beneath his body he had sheltered two young children. He had instinctively grabbed them to him when the huge stalactite had shattered on the rocks. Their mother, had reacted more slowly, but had then thrown herself to the ground next to him. When the earthquake showed no signs of returning, he pulled them carefully to their feet and comforted them, explaining what had happened, calmly, against the background of agony. They said nothing, made no sound, but as their mother called to them in the darkness nearby, they reached for her desperately.

Kaguri had anticipated the devastation which was apparent when the guide's candles eventually lit the cavern. The sight of the terrible injuries and the death did not surprise him, but brought back memories he thought he had left far behind. For a few seconds, until he recaptured control of his mind, he was again on the deck of the carrier, seconds after the first salvo of shells from an enemy battleship twenty miles away had landed full on the crowded superstructure. The screams were the cries of his men, the jumbled rocks were smashed zeros, the bodies seemed to be clad in white Naval uniforms striped with blood. He had scrambled across the debris of the rocks to reach the nearest.

Order, if it could be known as such, had come later; much later. The corpses were identified, carried away, the injured tended and moved to the hospital area, the grieving comforted. Kaguri found no satisfaction in noting his compatriots behaved more stoically than the other foreign tourists; anguish and pain were as deep, no matter how they appeared on the surface. He knew that the slight woman a few feet from him, rocking herself silently on a rock, was as torn by her grief at her husband's death as the Italian woman sobbing loudly twenty yards away.

Some hours had passed but Irano had not yet returned.

'What time is it, Kristoff?' Tor Sarbo was wearing a watch, but used his question as an excuse to speak with the old guide. Sarbo had been sitting in near darkness, for Kristoff had ordered most of the candles to be extinguished. It seemed to Sarbo as though he had been in darkness for days, but in fact it was less than forty-five minutes. He had been in a kind of trance, thinking of the outside world; the trees, the vines on the slopes, the high corn in the fields. Sarbo's father was a farmer. The family land was less than three hectares — a little more than six acres — and life on the land was hard; his parents rose at five a.m., and worked until after mid-day before having a two hour siesta, then began chores that continued until dusk. And for what, Sarbo wondered. They couldn't afford a car, or a television! Sarbo had both . . . in his small flat in Postojna there was an almost new television; a portable television which he had purchased in Trieste! It was Japanese, and its small screen brought him Italian transmissions with no difficulties. He also had a Renault; second-hand, but still a good car. For what reason should a man work on the land? Sarbo knew the answer; you worked on the land, because the land was yours, and because you were working outside, in the sunlight, or the beautiful rain! Tor Sarbo swore that if he ever managed to escape from this terrible dank, dark tomb, then nothing on earth would ever persuade him to return to its depths. He rubbed a squat nose and felt his unshaven cheeks rough against the back of his hand. He knew he had been living a mistake; a terrible mistake. Had he listened to his mother, he would now be out in the fields, looking to the vines or the second cut of hay. He could remember his mother's exact words: 'Tor, you are foolish, like all the young people. God gave us the land.'

'God gave us nothing, mother. The land is the people's, by right of law.'

'You are wrong, son. The land was given by God, and it is our duty to tend it well. Money is not important, only the land of God, is important,' He had never tried to continue the argument. His mother and father were still staunch catholics, although any form of religion was discouraged by the state. Tor was not religious. He had made the decision many years previously when he was at school; God was for the old people. The young needed politics. Now he regretted his decision.

Kristoff had not answered and Sarbo repeated his question. 'What time?'

Kristoff said: 'Shut up . . . be silent.' A match grated and flared, and Tor Sarbo was grateful for the light. Kristoff put the match to a candle, holding it sideways until the wick caught the flame and wax dripped to the damp ground.

'What . . .' began Sarbo for the third time. The force of Kristoff's broad hand over his mouth almost knocked him backwards from the rock on which he sat.

'A bell . . .'

Sarbo pushed Kristoff's hand away from his face. He decided old Kristoff was becoming insane. He could understand it, for only with difficulty was he managing to keep control of his own emotions. There had been times in the past few hours when he had to grip the rock tightly to prevent himself from leaping to his feet, shouting and screaming in terror, tearing at his hair and clothing. So Kristoff was already mad . . . soon they would all be insane. Kristoff was just the first.

The sound was faint, but now Tor Sarbo heard it, too. The electrical buzz of a muffled bell; a broken and damaged bell that buzzed somewhere. The two men were now on their feet. They were not the only ones to hear the sound, others were stirring. More candles were being lit. A murmur of conversation began to grow and was instantly hushed as Kristoff shouted a command for silence, in Slovene, that was understood by all.

'It's at post eleven,' Kristoff's voice was excited. The sound of the faint buzzing had come from his left, from an emergency station which had been demolished by a fragment of the giant stalactite. Mallek had rummaged through its wreckage earlier, and recovered the first aid equipment and forty meters of climbing line. The telephone was buried somewhere beneath wet rubble. He scrambled towards it now, and Tor Sarbo followed.

Kristoff was on his knees, a crowd gathering around him. Fifty hands pulled at the wreckage of the small hut, hurled aside lumps of rock glistening in the candlelight. Candles were held aloft like the flares at a night festival. No-one spoke now.

Kristoff heaved aside a square section of metal. The buzz became a ringing tone. He scrambled desperately in the limestone sludge. A section of the rear of the small hut remained vertical. Attached to it, and by some strange miracle still in place, was the telephone receiver. Kristoff, his hands trembling, pulled it off. He paused and carefully shook rock particles from the mouthpiece, and almost as though it was some charm of incredible religious significance, brought it close to his ear.

His voice was almost inaudible. 'Yes . . . Yes . . .' The voice became a shout that echoed across the great cave. '*Yes* . . . Kristoff.' Only the Slovene speaking guides and a few of the tourists understood him, but all those in the cave knew his words. 'We are alive,' he shouted. 'Yes, Comrade, many of us . . . almost three hundred . . . we are alive.'

9

Catlin was resting. The work was hard on his muscles but he could already feel them hardening, regaining tone and definition as the labour toughened them and ate away the superfluous fat. He lay, his shoulders against the trunk of one of the fallen trees bordering what had been the parking lot.

There was a woman walking towards him; there were several around the site working alongside the men. Like the others, this girl's face was dust-coated, her hair was hidden beneath a tight head scarf. He had been reminded of photographs of similarly dressed women, Soviet women, doing a man's job in the railways or working in road construction gangs. There had been a woman working near to Catlin, one of a gang tackling the rubble nearest the entrance of the caverns. He had admired the way her efforts equalled those of the men she laboured beside; how she heaved at the rough slabs of rock and concrete, tossing the pieces back to a gang beyond the wreckage.

The girl walking towards him quickened her pace, she held two large bottles of beer in her hands and as she approached him paused and wiped both sides of her face with the sleeves of her upper arms, in a feminine shrugging movement.

'Joe . . . it me, Joe . . . Lisetta, Joe.'

He was on his feet quickly, but she reached him almost before he could steady himself. Her two arms clasped him around the waist, the beer bottles clanking behind him. The dust-covered face pushed upwards. He kissed her, surprised at her arrival, and the unexpected warmth of her greeting. The lips were soft. He could feel her slender body against his naked chest. He made the kiss last.

She pushed herself away, but only enough to enable her to look up at him. 'You see, Joe, I find you . . .' He was conscious of the pressure of her hips against his thighs. 'It good you come here . . . today is all good for me.'

Catlin asked: 'You came looking for me?'

The girl pouted. 'No not look here . . . not at Postojna Jama,' she admitted. Her face brightened. 'But I say I find you . . . and I find you.' She freed herself from his arms and offered the beer, then half pulled him to the ground beside her. 'I hear only a few minutes ago. Men say American, big American with red hair is work with them. I ask, is this American look like boxer with funny nose? When they say yes, I know it my Joe, and I come quickly and find.' She moved closer to him until their shoulders were touching. 'Good, eh? What you say to Lisetta, Joe?'

Catlin smiled. 'You taste of mud!' His mind tried to assess her feelings, she obviously liked him, maybe quite a lot . . . hell, he had to admit he was old enough to be her father! But even with layers of dust and grime she was still a very beautiful woman . . . and good to be with. He was glad she was here.

She grimaced, jerked at the bottom of her shirt, pulled it free and wetted it with beer, then scrubbed the material against her mouth. 'Now try, Joe.' She tilted her head towards him and half closed her deep eyes. Catlin kissed her again, this time longer and with more care, as though his rough strength might damage the delicate fashioning of her face. 'You like taste beer better?' She smiled back at him. 'Drink now . . . you need drink more than kiss.'

Catlin tilted the bottle to his mouth. The liquid was iced silk as it slid down his throat. Lisetta watched him for a moment, enjoying his satisfaction, then sipped her own beer. Catlin drank half the bottle before removing it from his lips. The cool liquid ran down his chin and then his neck; he let it go, it felt good. He closed his eyes for a minute and rested his head back against the trunk of the tree. He could still sense the girl close to him, her Latin need for contact.

'When earthquake happen, I think Joe go . . . he go away from Piran. All tourist go away. It make me sad. I think I no see my Joe Catlin again.'

Catlin said: 'Humph . . .'

'What this humph? You no believe?' Lisetta sounded hurt.

'I believe you.' She was so obvious, so open. Catlin knew there was no way this woman would ever be able to hide her feelings or emotions. She would never be able to lie, disguise love, anger, even hatred.

'You no want me find you?'

Catlin opened his eyes quickly. 'Sure. Hell, yes, I wanted you to come. I was counting days in Piran.' He paused. 'I got drunk as a hog the first night.'

'Good. Much drunk was what you need, Joe. First drunk, then much sleep.' She jerked her head towards the wreckage of the hotel. 'This bad for so many people . . . maybe a bit good for Joe Catlin, eh?' She gave him no time to speak. 'Bad here, much bad for many miles. My town is all wreck. Not many house left. My family safe . . . house not fall. Many relatives in house now. All young people help. I help, too.'

'It's bad,' agreed Catlin. 'A bad quake.' He hadn't previously heard of the damage to the surrounding towns or villages, but had guessed it would be severe.

'But now I hear some most good news . . . just now.' Lisetta's voice became excited. 'Down in cave people is *alive*. Many peoples. Nearly three hundred . . . all alive.'

'Take it easy, honey.' Catlin deliberately kept his voice flat. He knew the danger of optimism in disasters. You could congratulate yourself, or get happy, when they were over; when all the work had been satisfactorily completed. You didn't celebrate prematurely. 'When are they going to be brought out?'

Lisetta frowned. 'What you mean, Joe? They come out when we get them out, I think.' She was puzzled by his question.

'Then they aren't necessarily alive. They're only alive when they see daylight, maybe not even then. They're alive when they're standing right out here on solid ground, with a sky over their heads.'

Lisetta dropped her eyes and her mouth twitched. 'My brother is down with them, Joe.' She said softly.

Catlin sat forward, angry with himself. 'I'm sorry. Guess I'm tired. Maybe I'm losing my faith in everything. Sure, they're alive, and we'll get them out.'

There were tears in the girl's eyes now, and Catlin felt a bastard. He cursed himself inwardly for his tactlessness and for forgetting Lisetta's sensitivity.

'You right, I know you right,' she said, slowly. 'They will only be truly alive when they are out of the mountain. You work hard at the wreckage. The other workers, they think you must have friends in the caves. I tell them no, you work because you good man . . . kind man.'

'You've made up your mind pretty quickly about me, Lisetta.

Maybe I'm not so good.' People in the oil business who paid Catlin compliments to his face usually wanted favours. He knew it wasn't the case with Lisetta, but he was still finding it difficult to understand her. She was a rare kind of person, a type he'd never met before. He realised he would have to learn about her carefully; treat her quite differently from any woman he had known in the past.

'You good. I see it in eyes, on face. I have strange feeling like I know you much well.' She pointed at her forehead. 'I feel it here . . .' She hesitated and then moved her finger to her breast. 'Also I have feeling here.' The dark eyes found Catlin's again. 'Joe, my brother, he is cave guide in there.' She looked beyond him at the mountain. 'He is down in there.' Her voice was steady now, controlled. 'Today they have talk; on underground telephone. Soldiers make contact. There are many, many of your countrymen inside.'

'I knew they were in there,' said Catlin. He had been thinking of them while he had been working; felt sickened as he realised how futile and puny his efforts were to dig his way into the rock. 'I spoke to a guy last night; one of the coach drivers. But . . . well, hell Lisetta, you aren't going to get them out with the handful of workers and two miserable tractors you've got here. You need several hundred skilled demolition men, experienced tunnellers and plenty of heavy machinery, or those people will stay under that damned mountain forever.'

She nodded miserably. 'Inside me, I know this also. That why I speak with my friends in Ljubljana.'

'Two hundred and seventy nine alive!' The acknowledgement was an exclamation. Martin Bor waited until Minister Baraslev Kalin spoke again. He knew Kalin liked time to consider his words before speaking. There was some sort of static on the radio link, probably a storm in the distant mountains. Kalin sounded as though he were speaking with his head in a resonant metal canister. 'Alive . . .' The Minister repeated the word. 'Then, Martin Bor, you must do everything possible in your power, to get them out.'

'I need the kind of heavy equipment we don't have in the Postojna region, Minister,' said Bor. He had not slept in his bed for two days, and his voice was heavy with lack of rest. He had managed a couple of hours on a narrow bunk in the Military Barracks at Zlid, and that had been all. His eyes were sore both with fatigue and the dust from the many wrecked villages he had visited. When he closed them, all he could see were the processions of demolition workers passing bodies back out of rubble to waiting ambulance teams. 'According to the latest report from the geologists, Minister, there was a landslip at Postojna which has moved the strata. The entire tunnel leading to the caverns is probably blocked. There may be sections still open, but it is likely most of the tunnel is impassable. To reach the people trapped inside, we must cut a completely new tunnel deep into the mountain. We need tunnellers; as much labour and all the heavy equipment as can be sent in from the south.'

'Is it not possible to reach them by means of passages in from the other cave systems?' The tone of the Minister's voice surprised Bor. It was almost disinterested, as though the trapped people within the mountain were nothing more than an irritation.

'Perhaps, Minister,' agreed Bor. 'We have two speleologists searching the area above the caverns. They are having a lot of trouble; much of the sunken ground is unsafe. It has not finally settled and in places it collapses under the weight of a man. The known pot-hole entrances are blocked. They will try to enter from the Pivka direction later today, but it is dangerous and slow work, Minister.'

'Of course, and by the way, Bor, I don't want any more information on the caves released,' said Kalin. 'At least, not yet.'

Bor was astonished. 'But the news is good, Minister. The people were believed dead, and now we have proof that they are alive. There will be relatives who will be glad of the news . . . families . . .'

'No,' interrupted Kalin, firmly. 'In good time, Bor, in good time. There is no point in raising hope, if there is no possibility of rescue.'

'There is possibility, Minister. I'm not an engineer, but with men and equipment, tunnels can be dug.'

'Think, Bor . . . be logical. The tunnel on the Dravograd highway which was opened recently; how long is it?'

Bor hesitated. 'A little under one kilometer.'

'Exactly! A little under one kilometer. Bor, the Dravograd highway took fourteen months to complete.'

'But it is a two lane tunnel, and lined and surfaced.'

'No matter how small a shaft you try to drive into the Postojna mountain, Bor, you are talking of a distance of a kilometer and a half. I know the caves well . . . the entrance tunnel twists and turns . . . it is not a straight line, Bor. Would the new shaft be straight, or would it follow the bends of the collapsed tunnel? Either way, it cannot be dug in days . . . not even weeks!' Kalin paused to allow Bor to consider his words, and then continued. 'I intend to visit some of the towns tomorrow. I suggest we travel together. Will you be in Ljubljana tonight.'

'I was intending to visit Postojna again, today, in view of the news. Inspector Zlobec needs a certain amount of direction.'

'Stay in Ljubljana, Bor,' advised Kalin. 'It would be sensible if we met . . . we can have dinner together and discuss tomorrow's arrangements. You can suggest a route that is passable for our vehicles.'

Bor was silent and then said: 'Yes, Minister . . . as you wish. And Postojna?'

'Let the work carry on as it is. If equipment becomes available from the towns and villages, by all means have it moved to Postojna; the same with the labour force. I'm relying on you, Martin. What arrangements have been made for the people at Dolvas?' He was referring to a village which had been completely destroyed by the earthquake.

'The people have been evacuated,' answered Bor. 'Some to relatives' homes, others to Vrhnika military base. There may be some still buried in the rubble, but the rescue work will continue until we can account for all the people.'

'Good,' said Kalin. 'That's the sort of action I want, Bor. Positive action with positive results. We must get western Slovenia back to normal as quickly as possible. Follow my orders regarding the press, Bor, they've more than enough to keep them occupied. Let them visit Dolvas or one of the other towns if they want to see how things are moving. And come to my house, this evening. Eight o'clock. We can talk more, then.' The Minister hung up before Commissioner Bor could reply.

Bor lowered the telephone and replaced it on its rest. He had an uncomfortable feeling Kalin had somehow arranged that he should be the scapegoat if the rescue work in the region was ever criticised. He could see the Minister's point of view that Postojna was not so important that equipment should be taken away from equally deserving work in the wrecked towns and villages, but Bor had never lost the Slovenian peasant's concern for his guests, and at the back of his mind was the thought that in many ways the tourists were more important than his own people. Twenty-four hours before, Kalin had promised much more heavy equipment and supplies, but very little had yet arrived in Slovenia. There was already a shortage of anaesthetics and drugs, in the hospitals. In another couple of days the situation would be critical. He'd heard that in some casualty depots, it had become necessary to use sterilised strips of bedding for bandages, and most of the hospitals were now full and any suitable buildings were being used to house the hundreds of injured survivors who were being brought in continually, from the outlying districts. And there was a growing problem with the dead . . . individual graves were no longer possible in many of the towns, and corpses were being buried, without coffins, in communal trenches.

Bor swore so harshly that Breschev, his aide who stood nearby, jumped. Bor said: 'I don't understand government. I ought to be in any one of a hundred places in Slovenia tonight, but Minister Kalin invites me to dinner. I should have refused him.'

Breschev looked at the Commissioner's worried face, then shook his head. 'I don't think that would have been wise.'

The telephone had rung within seconds of Minister Baraslev Kalin replacing the receiver. He now held it well away from his ear; the woman's voice was sharp and penetrating.

'Two hundred and seventy nine lives, Baraslev Kalin . . . do you hear me? Nearly three hundred of them alive in that . . . that pit. What are the cave commission doing? What are we going to do, and Minister Kalin what are *you* doing?'

Damn Anna Morolec, thought Kalin. And damn whoever gave her the information about the survivors in the Postojna caves. It wouldn't have been Martin Bor, he would never disobey one of Kalin's orders, but perhaps it was someone in Bor's office or a contact at Postojna Jama. Kalin decided he would arrange to have all of Bor's senior staff checked by security as soon as possible. With difficulty he made his voice soothing as he answered the woman. 'My dear Anna Morolec, I assure you I gave instructions, personally, to Commissioner Bor, not two minutes ago to . . .'

'You must reverse the recommendation to the Presidium, Minister Kalin. Now we are certain the people are alive, everything possible *must* be done to get them out. If *we* are not in a position to supply the necessary engineers and equipment, then we must *ask* for help from other governments.'

'I made my feelings quite clear regarding foreign aid. And remember, Comrade Morolec, my views are shared by all other members of the Regional Committee.'

'Minister, we are dealing with humanity now, not a political situation. I refuse to acknowledge the reasoning of your argument. If we do nothing to save the people at Postojna, we commit a moral crime.'

'There is heavy equipment at Sporec and Hvania, where the motorways are being constructed. I have already ordered *all* of it to be sent immediately to Postojna.' This was not true, but Kalin could easily turn the lie to fact if necessary.

'And how long will that take?'

'Three or four days at the most. There are grading machines, heavy bulldozers and many different kinds of soil moving equipment.'

'Soil and soft earth equipment?' Anna Morolec's voice was scathing. 'To move a rock mountain? And in three or four days! What are you, Baraslev Kalin, a representative of the Presidium, or an executioner?'

Kalin reacted angrily. 'That is unnecessary, Anna Morolec! I have always been conscious of my duties.'

'To the State, or to the people? Or perhaps only to the Communist Party ideals! And *your* ideals, Minister Kalin. You will not necessarily appease the anger of the public once it is known you are deliberately delaying assistance to the foreigners trapped at Postojna. It is quite obvious, Minister, that for some obscure reason you would prefer them dead, and you *intend* to let them die. I will see they live.' She banged the receiver back onto its rest, sat back in her chair and allowed her anger to fade. She picked up her thick-framed glasses and saw her hands were shaking; there were not many people who could exasperate her as much as Minister Kalin. She had crossed swords with him on other occasions; the man was pig-headed. She rang for her secretary and when the girl appeared, asked for an urgent long-distance call to be put through to a Rome number.

A few moments later the girl returned to apologise for a possible delay; international lines were fully occupied. The operator would ring back. It was forty five minutes before the girl at the international exchange routed the call to Anna Morolec.

The telephone was answered in Italian. Without effort, Anna Morolec switched languages. 'I wish to speak to Signore Marcus Alistair, the American Ambassador. He will accept my call, please inform him it is Anna Morolec.' She waited.

Three seconds later, the telephone connection was cut. Anna

Morolec hammered furiously on its rest, but it was completely dead. Angrily she stormed through to her outer office and picked up the telephone on the secretary's desk; it too was dead. She pushed open the outer office door and began to walk down the corridor. Two young men in their early twenties stepped out of the elevator. The burliest of the two moved in front of her. 'Comrade Anna Morolec?'

She said: 'Yes?'

The man took hold of her upper arm, his fingers were hard and strong. 'You are to come with us.'

The slimmer man held his hand forward. It contained his State Police warrant, a blue plastic-backed card with his photograph and the insignia of the Ministry of Law and Order. 'Security Directorate,' he said, almost apologetically.

'What are you doing with your rucksack, Alessandro?' Annina Bor watched her son lashing his sleeping bag to the aluminium frame of the pack. Her husband, Martin, had left the apartment only half an hour before, having returned for just long enough to wash, and change his clothing. She had been upset by his worried appearance, and the exhausted look in his eyes. Although he had claimed otherwise, she felt certain he had not slept or rested since the day of the earthquake. The fatigue had aged him, darkening the area beneath his eyes and pulling at the muscles of his jaw to make his cheeks look drawn and hollow. He had glanced at the bed as he had dressed, and she knew he would have given much to be able to throw himself on it and sleep for a few hours. She was concerned, too, by his unwillingness to discuss the problem that was obviously disturbing him. Normally they shared their worries just as they shared their pleasures. She knew that whatever Martin Bor had on his mind at the moment, it was perhaps more serious than anything he had encountered before.

'Going to help,' Alessandro replied. He didn't turn to face her as he spoke, and she knew from the way he had stiffened his shoulders, he was expecting her to argue with him. Children, she thought, they never realise how well their parents know them. You study them from the minute they are born and learn to recognise every movement of their bodies as signals. 'I heard on the radio they were asking for volunteers.'

'Good, I think you should help.'

He was surprised by her answer. 'Branko Lassowavitz had a

call from a friend at Postojna; they need workers there. A few of us are going together.'

Branko was one of her son's closest friends, they were students at the same college. 'Postojna? I thought they wanted the volunteers to assemble at Vrhnika.' She knew of the deaths of perhaps four hundred tourists in the Postojna caves, and Martin had mentioned to her the day before, during a telephone call, that his men were having difficulty dealing with dozens of enquiries from people trying to establish if their friends or families were amongst those who had died underground. In many cases it had been impossible to help, because some enquiries were from people whose friends had been camping, or caravanning in the Postojna parks . . . and the parks had emptied immediately the earthquake had ended. People had fled from the area and there was no way the police could account for their whereabouts; they could be buried beneath the mountain, or safely on their way home.

Alessandro hefted the rucksack to test its weight. He seemed satisfied and leant it against the wall beside the apartment door. 'I took a little food,' he said.

'What about money? How will you get there?'

'On the back of Branko's motorcycle. I have some money . . . enough for a few days.'

She decided not to attempt to change his mind. He was old enough to make his own decisions. His father had been a freedom fighter at his son's age, and had been forced to make decisions which were life or death to himself and his companions. 'Have you taken sweaters and your anorak,' she said.

'It's mid-summer, mother!' The boy smiled. 'I have them packed. And spare socks . . . and handkerchiefs.'

She hugged him and felt him move slightly away from her in embarrassment. 'Wait.' She found her purse and pulled out a few notes. 'For emergencies. If you need it, use it. If not, give it me back when you return.'

He swung the pack upwards, easing it onto his shoulders, then opened the door. 'Take care, Alessandro,' said his mother.

10

There were seven candles burning in the cavern; seven yellow flames separated by pools of ominous half-light where dark silhouettes, distorted to stunted troglodites, moved amongst the glistening stalagmites and strange rock formations.

Kaguri knelt on a small piece of wood salvaged from the wreckage of the bar. He had placed it on a flat rock in a narrow crevice at one side of the cavern, twenty yards from his fellow countrymen. In the darkness he looked like a slim Buddha, motionless, his eyes closed, his back straight and his hands resting lightly on his thighs. He had remained unmoving in this position for the past three hours. For the last ten minutes, one of the young Japanese had stood facing him. Kaguri was aware of the man for his shadow had passed across his eyes and he had noticed the slight change of light, and sensed the man's proximity. He said nothing, nor did he open his eyes. Instead, he let his mind play over the intruder's presence in a form of relaxed contemplation. He could feel the man's anxiety, just as he had been able to sense the nervousness of an opponent when he practised his sword play in the dojo in Hosokai. In his youth, Kaguri had been a champion, considered almost unbeatable in competition. Now, he devoted some evenings of his week to the teaching of the younger generation. He found them soft and undisciplined compared to the Kendoka of his youth. Once, a dojo had been a place where men remained silent and respectful, apart from their shouts in times of practise or contest. Now, even with the discipline the old teachers tried to establish, the atmosphere had changed. Kaguri had studied the art of the sword, not because he considered it to be a sport or competition which he should win, but because it was traditional; the old way, and therefore he became a champion. Nowadays youth wanted the honour which winning contests could bring. They did not understand their teachers and although they might beat other young men, they could never equal the older generation who were dedicated to Budo by their background.

Kaguri decided he would let the man who stood in front of him speak first, and so he remained unmoving as though the intruder did not exist. Eventually the man coughed politely, as if he were attempting to wake Kaguri from sleep. Kaguri nodded but did not open his eyes.

The man said: 'Sensei, will you allow me to talk with you?'

The form of address, Sensei, was unusual. It was the term 'master' used by pupils in schools of the martial arts who wished to speak with or refer to their teacher.

'You are the Sensei Kaguri, of Hosokai,' said the young man, his voice indicating his immaturity. His words were not a question.

Kaguri said: 'I am he.' He deliberately chose an archaic manner of answering. It suited his present contemplatory mood.

'I am . . . was, a student of Sensei Maroda in archery, and also Sensei Morei in Kendo, at Waseda University. I heard your name mentioned by one of our party, and thought you must be the great Kendoka. Forgive my intrusion into your privacy.' The shadow of the man moved slightly and Kaguri knew he was bowing. 'I have competed against your pupils in the championships,' said the young man.

Kaguri asked: 'Is Moreisan well?'

'He is a lion,' answered the young man. 'He is still one of the greatest Kendoka. Even at sixty years of age, we cannot beat him.'

You never will, thought Kaguri. He could picture Morei, a slim, grey-haired man who would never consider wearing western clothing, stringy-muscled, lithe and fast, who could play with this young generation of kendoka as though they were children, knowing that were he carrying a real katana against them in battle they would be bloodless meat on the earth around him. It was a feeling Kaguri himself knew well, and occasionally allowed himself to enjoy, but with a sadness at the changing ideals. 'I am glad he keeps himself strong and fit,' he said. 'Marodasan, the Kyudo master, I also know. He is a fine archer; a traditionalist.' He had watched Maroda many times. The man could make archery so beautiful it was a poem in movement. Where his arrow struck the target was of little importance, but with Maroda it would always be within the diameter of a yen from the centre, no matter the range.

'I am honoured to speak with you, Sensei,' continued the young man. 'But we seek your aid.' Following Kaguri's example, the man now spoke very formally.

Kaguri opened his eyes. The man had moved to one side and it was now possible to see his face in the light of a candle that burned some yards away. He was probably only twenty two or three, short but with broad shoulders that held the damp blanket squarely. He had a thin, dark moustache. Kaguri thought the young man would also have liked to grow a beard, but was probably unable.

'I feel I am hardly in a position to help anyone.'

'We wish to take advantage of your strength, Sensei,' said the young man.

Kaguri laughed. 'Am I then a tree, or a boulder of granite that you may place your hand upon me and draw from within the secret strength of mankind . . . the hidden ki?'

Surprisingly, the young man said: 'Yes, Sensei.'

'Nonsense. I am a man. A very ordinary man, with too many failings.'

'The others have asked me to speak with you. You are known to them. They wish you to be our leader.'

'Leader?'

'A leader is necessary, Sensei. You are of an honourable family, from an ancient line of Samurai. You are also a successful businessman of the Yoshuabi factory; you are General Manager.'

'Assistant General Manager,' corrected Kaguri. 'I am also an accountant. Figures and money are my business.'

'You were an officer in the Imperial Navy, and commanded a submarine in the Coral Seas. It is known you received the highest honours from the Emperor, for your bravery.'

'The highest honour, is sometimes thought to be death,' said Kaguri. 'You know much about me young man, and you have not yet offered me your name.'

The man bowed again and spoke apologetically 'Forgive me, I am Mihunokada, second son of Morei.'

Kaguri permitted himself a slight sound of surprise. 'Morei's son?' Then this young man would have been brought up within a household as traditional as his own. He might not be quite as brash and westernised as some of the modern youth. It explained the man's knowledge of Kaguri, for his father Mihunokada would have spoken of his contemporaries. It would be the reason why the young man had been chosen to approach him when there were others much older and of Kaguri's generation within the party of tourists. 'Why is there this feeling of a need for leadership? Leadership in this situation is the responsibility of the guides. This is familiar territory to them.'

'There is a lack of confidence in the foreigners,' explained Mihunokada.

'You may share my rock,' said Kaguri. 'Sit close.' The young man took his blanket from his shoulders, folded it into a neat square and placed it on the ground. He knelt carefully and Kaguri was pleased to see he did not sit cross-legged which would have indicated he was more used to western furniture. 'Tell me more, Mihunokada.'

'There are twenty three of us. Two are injured, and seven are women. There are three children. Some of our party are old. The old and the young are concerned with their survival.'

'But *you* are not concerned?'

'Of course I am concerned, Sensei, but I am not afraid.'

'I did not ask if you were afraid.'

The young man lowered his face a little and Kaguri sensed his blush of embarrassment. 'We do not feel we are being considered by the other nationalities. Our offer to assist in seeking a new way out of this place was not accepted. We all sit here in this darkness just waiting for death. We wish to have a leader, one who will direct us, one who will at least let us die attempting to survive.'

'It may not be necessary. Rescue work will be taking place at the surface. We may be out of here in hours.' Kaguri had spent quite a long time considering his present situation. He did not believe rescue was imminent, but lied deliberately.

'There is no more food, Sensei. I had a look at the stores; there are so many people down here. They will starve.'

'A man may last several weeks without food, if he has spiritual strength and determination.'

'But not children, and not the aged,' said Mihunokada, firmly. 'The food should have been kept for the children.'

'True.' Kaguri did not think it necessary to mention he had refused his own share. 'What did you read at Waseda?'

'Economics. I qualified only a month ago. This trip is my family's gift. I hope to work for Honda on my return; I have already attended an interview.' The tone of Mihunokada's voice became enthusiastic. 'Sensei, there are more of *us* here.' he emphasised the word *us*. 'Two more kendokas, a karatega and an aikidoka. Others of the older men served in the Imperial forces. You must lead us and speak for us all.'

'You may tell your friends, and those who sent you, I shall consider the matter.' Kaguri closed his eyes again and the young man bowed his head very low, knowing Kaguri had already agreed.

Ralph Hubertson had said nothing for an hour. He was sitting on the stump of a shattered stalactite which somehow seemed to have the ability to pump water up inside itself and remain constantly wet. Like Kaguri, he had balanced a piece of wreckage on the top, and this kept him reasonably dry. His wife, Sheila, had just returned from the section of the cave which by mutual consent had become the communal toilet area. It was nothing more than a deep crevasse which offered a slight degree of privacy. A candle burned continuously in its depths, but with so many people making use of its facilities, the visit was now sufficiently unpleasant to be delayed until necessity made it imperative.

Ralph Hubertson was surrounded by other Americans. He could even smell some of them in the still air. There was a portly woman a few feet away who exuded an aroma of expensive perfume, while next to her, a man who was her husband, smelt of cigars. He had smoked them continuously for the first few hours, but his supply seemed to be exhausted, and he now smoked cigarettes which he had managed to scrounge from a fellow tourist. A man sitting only a yard away on Ralph Hubertson's right suddenly said: 'Oh Jesus Christ, the bastards!'

Ralph Hubertson looked at him. The man pointed. 'That little yellow bastard over there.' There was a Japanese squatting thirty feet away, his back towards them and his blanket drawn close around him. For a moment Ralph Hubertson thought the Japanese was defecating and that this was the reason for the fellow American's complaint, but then the man said: 'He just put that damned thing on his head.' The Japanese had tied a white cloth over his head like some woman at her housework. Ralph Hubertson couldn't see that it was of any importance. He watched his wife Sheila picking her way through the group towards him and looked at her questioningly.

'It's worse than ever,' she said, sitting next to him on the damp stalactite.

'Watch your piles, honey,' he commented softly. She hustled her shoulders as though annoyed by the remark.

'I shall die if I can't shower, soon,' she said.

The man to Hubertson's right spoke again. 'I shot those bastards, on Guam. You never forget the things you've seen.'

'Huh,' said Hubertson non-commitally. He wasn't particularly interested in the man and was more concerned that his wife Sheila should be kept calm and in a reasonable humour. He knew she hated dirt.

The man was unprepared to drop the subject. 'I've seen them dressed like that, before, too.' His accent was a Galveston drawl, town and not country. 'They wouldn't surrender, not even when we had them beat. Our Lieutenant was wounded, and those little yellow assholes bayoneted him. That was just after we quit the beach. I saw them toss away their helmets and uniforms, wrap those white cloths round their heads, then charge us . . . straight onto our guns, naked like a lot of dumb savages. Those white head-cloths are a sign of trouble.'

'We've enough as it is,' said Ralph Hubertson. He didn't believe a third world war was likely to break out inside a Yugoslav cavern.

'Remember Pearl,' warned the man.

'Sure.' Ralph Hubertson turned his back on the man and spoke softly to his wife. 'You want me to speak to that British animal doctor; ask him if he's got aspirin?'

'I don't have a headache, Ralph. I'm a little hungry, but I feel fine . . . dirty, but fine. You know, we'd be in Rome by now, but for this.'

'Sure, honey, Rome,' said Ralph Hubertson. 'Rome would've been great.'

'They'll take us on to Rome when we get out, I'd say. After all, we paid to see Rome. You remember what Martha Smith told us? We'd just got to see the Vatican, because it's the centre of the Christian religion.'

'Roman Catholic,' corrected Hubertson. 'You're Christian Scientist.' Asked his own religion, he would have claimed to be atheist, but privately he had a feeling there might well be some kind of a God, who was certainly forgiving enough to be denied occasionally.

'I am,' agreed his wife. 'The very second it all started, I said to myself, now what would Mary Baker Eddy have done?'

'Stayed at home and written a sermon.'

'Pah! Don't be facetious, Ralph. I draw great comfort from her teaching, and so should you. God is love, I said to myself, and the earthquake stopped.'

'We should have shot *all* the bastards,' the man on Hubertson's right said at the top of his voice.

'Turn the other cheek, and forgive, is part of the teaching. But mostly that God is love. Trust in God, and believe that he is within us all, and our power is unlimited.'

'The only good Jap, is a dead Jap,' insisted the man, his voice echoing.

'I beg your pardon,' replied Sheila Hubertson.

'All Jap bastards should be dead.'

'That is positively dreadful,' said Sheila Hubertson. 'Did you know that Mary Baker Eddy . . .'

'Stuff Mary Baker Eddy.'

'Now see here. You have no right to insult . . .'

'Be quiet, both of you,' said Ralph Hubertson, so loudly he startled himself, and people a few yards away turned to see what was happening. He looked at his wife, and spoke firmly. 'Sheila, just shut up about God being love; and you . . .' he glared at the man on his right. 'Knock it off about Japanese or I'll break your jaw.' He had never threatened anyone with physical violence; it had always seemed childish. It was his belief everything could be settled by reasonable discussion. He was surprised the man did not react to his challenge, but seemed to shrink slightly on his rock before turning his head away and shuffling his shoulders uncomfortably.

Ralph Hubertson sat awkwardly for a few minutes, unsure how to break the barrier of silence he seemed to have built between himself and his wife. She was always very sensitive about her own religion. He was just about to apologise when he felt her own moist hand close over his and give it a hesitant squeeze.

'Ralph, dear, you're such a strong person. You make me feel so secure,' she whispered.

There was one man whom Colette Marishall thought would die soon. His thigh had been badly smashed by a large piece of flying rock. The bone had shattered and pieces had ruptured the large veins. The thigh was little more than pulped flesh, and the man had lost a lot of blood through flesh wounds. He had been travelling with his wife and fifteen year old daughter, both of whom had survived the earthquake with no serious injury. They sat beside the man, leaning over him as though they both wanted to hide his tortured breathing. The wife was in tears, but somehow the young girl was finding the strength to comfort both her parents. Colette knew little about them. She had noticed them in the aircraft and later in the hotel; but had not spoken to them before the disaster. Now they were too remote, engulfed in their own pain and grief, and she couldn't help them.

The man began shouting; there was no sense or meaning to his words. His wife screamed with him as though his agony was hers, and then sobbed more desperately.

Someone yelled: 'For God's sake, do something for him.' The cavern walls tossed around the mingled cries.

Women nearby hid their faces in their blankets and held their hands over their ears. One of the two German nurses looked bleakly at her colleague, knowing there was no way in which the man's agony could be reduced. The Japanese dental surgeon who was changing the dressing on a woman's head injury glanced up quickly, tautened his mouth, then dropped his eyes again to the raw wound.

Eileen Spark moved closer to her veterinary surgeon husband, She spoke, quietly, almost pleading. 'Can't we do *anything* to help him?' There was a strange edge to her voice.

Robert Spark met his wife's eyes, then shook his head. 'Without drugs, nothing. He's dying.'

'I know . . .' She paused. 'That's what I meant. It would be kinder . . .' She left the sentence unfinished.

'He's not a horse, or a dog,' said Spark, shortly.

'We treat them better than people.' The level of her voice had risen and a man lying a couple of yards away, whom Spark had been bandaging, turned his head towards them.

Spark said, tersely: 'For God's sake don't make your thoughts public; you'll start a riot.' He saw her eyes moisten and knew her unspoken suggestion was only deep concern for the distraught man's suffering. 'It might be kinder, but we can't . . . I couldn't.' He reached to touch her, but she drew away, slightly. 'I examined him a little while ago. It can't last much longer.'

'It's so cruel,' there was a sob in her voice.

He nodded. 'Pain always is.' He took her shoulders and pulled her towards him.

11

Commissioner Bor had decided he would visit Postojna regularly, despite Minister Kalin. The Minister could insist that any newly available equipment was used in the villages until they had been cleared, but he hadn't said equipment or man-power already at Postojna should not be used to its best advantage. Bor intended to see it was.

He didn't particularly like Inspector Emile Zlobec. The man had the look of a ferret about him, and he moved with quick and jerky movements which Martin Bor found irritating. Within the framework of the old partisan movement Bor would never have given Zlobec a platoon or squad of his own. He doubted Zlobec's initiative and ability to act ruthlessly yet efficiently in an emergency. But the modern police force was not the wartime partisans, and Zlobec worked *exactly* to the official rule book. There had never been a complaint about his behaviour as a policeman, and he had taken and passed every examination. Even so, Bor had delayed Zlobec's promotion. Zlobec had applied for a place at university; he'd been accepted, and Bor forced to release him for three years. Zlobec returned with a degree, and the promotion to a senior rank could no longer be withheld. It did nothing to increase Bor's trust in the man.

'You have done well, Zlobec,' he said grudgingy when he'd studied Zlobec's minutely detailed report of the rescue work at Postojna. One thing about Zlobec, his reports might be lengthy but they were accurate. The Inspector had organised the man-power into rescue teams who worked the kind of shifts that would get the best from a man, and yet allow him just sufficient rest to continue the work for a lengthy period of time — weeks if so much was required. He had given a certain authority to men designated as foremen of the various groups, allowing them to decide for themselves on the spot the best way to go about their work. The trucks, the JCB and the two bulldozers were kept as a mobile unit, available for instant work on either the hotel or terminus sites, though most of the time they lifted rock away from the blocked tunnel entrance. With the help of the military, Zlobec had arranged field kitchens, a rest centre with bunk beds, and a small medical section where the injured could receive immediate help before being taken to the now overcrowded regional hospitals. There were a hundred and ninety seven men and women volunteers working on the site, plus the soldiers; in all, two hundred and forty eight. Zlobec had their names, nationalities and occupations listed.

Bor scanned the list, more from curiosity than for any other reason. 'Who is this?' He pointed to a name; Catlin, Joseph James; Nationality American. Occupation; Oil and Gas control engineer.

'A tourist, Commissioner,' said Zlobec, resentfully aware that Bor had examined his report in a critical manner. He knew the Commissioner was not particularly friendly towards him, though he had never been able to determine a reason. He assumed it was probably the age difference, and because Bor was one of the older generation, hard-line communists. 'I am making use of *all* volunteer labour who are capable of working. The American was here at the time of the earthquake, as a tourist; he has stayed and worked. He is not a very young man, but he works hard alongside the others, and he's no trouble.'

'He speaks Slovene?'

'No, Commissioner. He usually communicates with the work teams by means of signals.'

'I don't particularly like the idea of the tourists, especially foreigners, working on the site. It is preferable we use our own people.' By way of explanation, he said: 'The man could be injured and then there would be increased problems regarding our responsibilities. And, we know nothing of his background.

'I know quite a lot, Commissioner,' Zlobec said.

Martin Bor flicked his finger against Catlin's name as though the action would remove it from the list.

Zlobec continued. 'One of our volunteer workers has questioned him. Quite tactfully, I assure you.'

'At your direction, Zlobec?'

'Naturally. He may be very useful to us. He is an expert in the use of explosives; one of the leading men in the United States of

America. He is a specialist in dealing with gas and oil well fires. He knows about machinery . . .'

Martin Bor interrupted Zlobec. 'We have our own experts, Zlobec.' Bor could see difficulties arising from having *any* foreign expert on the site. If the Minister failed to send the necessary extra men and equipment, then the last people Bor wanted around the site were foreigners with the expertise who would aim authoritative criticism at the government. 'Show me where this man is, I want to speak to him.'

'Yes, Commissioner.' There was a glint of warning in Bor's eyes that Zlobec recognised with discomfort.

The office of the small press bureau which had been opened in Bor's headquarters in Ljubljana, was crowded. There were rows of seats, enough for twenty journalists, arrayed in front of a low rostrum. The seats were all occupied and many more newspaper men and women were standing in the narrow aisle and along both the walls. They blocked the doorway. There were two of Kalin's press officers standing behind their table on the rostrum; they were slightly dishevelled, having had to force their way through to the desk past the crowded journalists.

Rabuzin, the more senior of the two was attempting to answer the angry flow of questions. His knowledge of English was good, but he was flustered by the speed at which the many questions were hurled at him, and he didn't know all the answers. The journalists were aware of this weakness and were hoping that in an unguarded moment he would give them something new, something into which they could sink their teeth.

'We know about Idrija, and how you've brought in half the wheat crop from the east,' a man was calling from somewhere in the centre of the crowded room. 'You told us yesterday. And we've heard the Presidium statement. We want to know about our own citizens.'

'Of course,' nodded Rabuzin. He wished he was back in the peace of his department in Minister Kalin's offices. Normally he dealt with routine news stories from Slovenia, fed out through the national agencies; there was seldom any urgency in them, invariably no haste. 'As far as we know, all tourists have now left the area of the earthquake. You have full lists of any of those who were injured in the towns.'

'For God's sake, Rabuzin, that isn't the information we want . . . we want to know about Postojna . . . about the caves.' The man who was shouting at Rabuzin wore a cream linen suit and was wearing sun-glasses.

'Please state your newspaper or agency,' said Rabuzin, ignoring the man's questioning and using protocol as a defense.

'International Press,' called the man. 'My agency is still waiting for a full list of all the people who were killed in the caves. And we want a permit to allow our photographers to visit Postojna.'

There were murmurs of agreement from other journalists in the room. A woman, somewhere at the back, raised her voice, pitched higher than normal for clarity. 'We have a team of cameramen . . . television . . . we too wish to visit Postojna.'

Rabuzin raised his hands to silence them. 'Gentlemen . . . ladies . . . please. Some things are not possible; Postojna is a military area . . . photography is not permitted. Also, it was the epicentre of the earthquake and the entire environs of the caves are unstable.'

Someone shouted: 'Balls! Every damn tourist carries a camera at Postojna, and I've filmed on the lip of the Etna volcano; nothing is much more unstable than that.'

'What's the cover-up, Rabuzin?' Rabuzin recognised Max Castor, an American journalist who had been a regular visitor to the bureau since it had been opened. Castor had been on a political assignment in Belgrade, and had driven up to Ljubljana within hours of the earthquake.

'Mister Castor, there is no cover-up. You and the other journalists are allowed free movement . . . we ask only that you do not hamper rescue work in the towns and villages, and that you are self-sufficient and do not occupy the time and resources of the rescue workers and administration.'

'But we can't go to Postojna?'

'Regrettably, no. As I have already explained, the area around Postojna is classified as military. Owing to the earthquake it has been necessary for us to completely close that area . . . there is no mystery . . . none at all. We have given you the lists of the dead available to us. You know the difficulties we are having trying to establish if particular tourists are in the cave system, or have left the country. It will take time . . . many weeks . . . before we know for certain who has died in the caves.'

'How do you know if they're dead?'

Rabuzin's assistant saw the question as a cue. He unrolled a large sheet of graph paper and passed it to Rabuzin. Rabuzin nodded his thanks and held it up for the journalists to see. 'This is from the geologists . . . copies are available for all of you.' It was a careful piece of graphics, coloured and contoured like a map. Rabuzin pointed at it. 'This is a section through the mountain containing the Postojna caves. It shows the strata movement which has caused them to collapse. Here, you can see, the entire entrance tunnel is affected, and almost all of the main galleries and caverns. Here is the area where most of the tourists would have been at the time of the earthquake. You can see the strata slip, and collapse, is greatest in that section.'

'It doesn't prove anything,' a woman sitting in the front row of seats called up at him. 'We need to see for ourselves. It looks as though there might be plenty of places where a person could survive in those caves.'

'I don't deny that,' said Rabuzin. 'It is possible . . .' He regretted his words. The journalists picked them up immediately.

Castor was the first. 'What you're saying, Rabuzin, is that *you* believe there may be survivors.

Rabuzin threw the map onto the table and looked at his colleague in desperation. 'I . . . er . . .'

'Do you deny the possibility of *any* survivors,' someone shouted from the crowded doorway.

Rabuzin shrugged helplessly. 'I don't deny the possibility, gentlemen. But it is unlikely. You have all seen the geologists' statements, and the report from the Postojna Inspector of Police.'

'Mister Rabuzin . . .' The woman in the front row spoke. 'How many people do *you* think could have survived?'

'I have no idea . . .'

'Perhaps all of them?' It was Castor.

'Impossible . . .'

'Half?'

'I doubt if half could have survived!'

'You doubt, but you're not certain . . . and *you've* had *all* the information, Rabuzin. What are you holding back from us?'

'Nothing, gentlemen . . . I swear, nothing.'

'If you doubt that half the people underground at Postojna are alive, Mister Rabuzin, do you also doubt if half of them are dead?'

'I don't understand your question.'

'What are you doing to get the people out?'

'Everything in our power.' Inwardly Rabuzin cursed himself. He should have refused to answer any more questions for a few minutes until he had been able to collect his thoughts. He wondered how he would explain himself to Minister Kalin.

The journalists were looking pleased. Max Castor spoke again. 'Rabuzin, just what exactly is everything in your power?'

Rabuzin's junior, Otto Tihec, a former journalist himself, though only on one of the minor Yugoslavian journals, stepped protectively in front of his senior. A difficult situation had arisen and he realised Rabuzin had lost control of the conference. Unless Tihec acted quickly the press department would incur the anger of Minister Kalin; those responsible, including himself, would be certain to suffer. Minister Kalin could be vindictive, and had a long memory.

Tihec raised both his hands to silence the journalists. 'Ladies and gentlemen, I regret there is an official embargo on all news from Postojna.' There were angry voices, but he ignored them. 'It is only temporary and we will inform you when it is lifted. *Any* journalist who breaks the embargo will have his visa rescinded . . . and *all* visas of the journal, agency or company he represents.'

'When will this "embargo" be lifted?' shouted a journalist from the rear of the room.

'As soon as our ministry sees fit,' answered Rabuzin, seizing the advantage Tihec had established. 'A few days at most, but until we announce otherwise, the embargo is total. I repeat my colleague's warning, anyone who attempts to break this embargo will be expelled from Yugoslavia.' He softened his voice to a conciliatory level. 'We have our reasons, and I know I can rely on you all. There will be a further release of news of the Slovenian disaster tomorrow morning at the same time. Meanwhile, those of you who would like copies of this geological map should ask at the desk outside. Thank you all.' He turned and nodded gratefully at Tihec.

The cream linen-suited journalist in sunglasses, caught Max Castor's arm as he left the bureau. 'What the hell do you make of that, Max?'

'Bullshit, and tricky.'

'Tricky? I think those poor bastards at Postojna are alive, and they can't get to them. It's typical commie whitewash!'

Castor said: 'I agree.'

'Well, what the hell are we going to do?' He didn't wait for Castor to answer him. 'They'll monitor the wires and overseas calls. I think I'll try to drive out to Villach. Get the story through from there. You want to come with me?'

'No.'

'No?'

'Use your brains, Eddie. This lot don't play around. If your visa is cancelled here, you'll have trouble getting another for *any* Iron-Curtain country . . . and give your foreign editor a coronary.'

'But the story?'

'Balls to the story. It's good, and it's growing . . . we all know that. When it comes out, it's coming out with a bang. I want to be around when it happens.' He brought a small wire-recorder from his pocket and dangled it in front of the man's eyes. 'In here's the whole of the so-called conference we've just had . . . in a few days it's going to be worth gold.'

'A bottle of bourbon for a transcript? Two bottles?'

Castor smiled: 'Sorry baby.'

The member of the Slovenian Freedom Movement, an illegal organisation composed of right-wing students, stood in Commissioner Bor's Ljubljana office, awaiting the return of Bor's chief clerk. The Slovenian Freedom Movement was one of several organisations throughout Yugoslavia, all dedicated to the establishment of independence for their original states, and most for a moderate form of government freely elected by the people. An exception was the Croatian Liberation Army, which promoted anarchist ideals in competition with a fellow Croatian organisation with more socialistic aims of self-rule.

There was little interaction between the various groups, and each normally operated independently of the others. The anarchistic Croatian Liberation Army was the most violent, and had been responsible for many bombings and several ruthless assassinations. The Slovenian Freedom Movement was moderate and in many ways more successful. It continually angered the Presidium by the frequent publication and distribution of leaflets and newspapers criticising the actions of its Communist government.

Belonging to any of the illegal organisations was dangerous. Members faced long and harsh terms of imprisonment, if they were lucky enough to be brought to trial. The unluckier men and women died before the opportunity for any form of justice. It was known that several members of both Croation groups who had been forced to flee the country, had been tracked down by the Yugoslav Secret Police, and executed . . . in France, Germany,

Holland, and even as far away as the United States of America.

The young man waiting in Commissioner Bor's office, was not at that moment contemplating any specific subversive action. He planned to go to Postojna, and because he had some influence with Commissioner Bor's department, he was waiting for official permits which would allow himself and several of his student friends to pass through the road blocks which had been erected on highways in the devastated area. His influence came from his relationship with the Commissioner, for the young man was Alessandro Bor, his son. He had been waiting in his father's office for fifteen minutes while the permits were prepared. There had been no difficulty; the chief clerk, and most of the men in his father's administrative department had known him since he was a child.

He sat, now, on the edge of his father's desk and casually moved two or three of the requisition documents which sat awaiting the Commissioner's signature. A memo, addressed to the Minister of the Interior, Baraslev Kalin, caught his eye. He moved the requisitions aside with his slim fingers, and glanced at the memo. He frowned suddenly, and picked up the oblong of paper with its official police heading. He read the memo several times before replacing it on the desk. He stood and looked out of the small window, biting his lip for a full minute, his thumbs hooked into the leather belt of his jeans. He returned to the desk and re-read the memo. There was a small, dry-powder photocopier on a stand by one of the walls. He switched it on, wondering if the low hum of its motor would attract the attention of the clerks in the outer office. He decided it was unlikely they would hear it above the sound of one of their typewriters. He loaded the machine, looked quickly out of the window again, fed in the memo and made three copies. He returned the memo to its original position on the desk, covered it with the requisitions, and pushed the memo copies into his shirt front. A few minutes later, when he had received the permits, he left the office.

His friends, waiting outside, watched him arrive. He seemed worried.

'No permits, Alessandro?'

'I got them!'

'What's the trouble, then?'

'We'll talk about it when we get to Postojna and meet Lisetta. It ties in with what she told us on the 'phone.'

Catlin had the feeling he was being watched. He was working with two other men, and faced towards the mountain. Ahead of him the rubble had been flattened, many tons having been passed back to tipper trucks which dumped the rubble two hundred yards away on ground bordering the Pivka river. He ignored the feeling for a while until it became too strong, then he turned. Several yards away, beside the tailgate of one of the trucks, stood a man in uniform. His eyes, unblinking, were fixed on Catlin. He had a nicotine-stained moustache that drooped around the corners of his mouth, and he held his head a little to one side. He wore brown leather gloves, even though it was summer, and stood with his hands clasped in front of him. As their eyes met, the man uncoupled his hands and beckoned Catlin.

Catlin straightened himself and stretched. His muscles were regaining their tone and he had been getting a satisfactory rhythm into his work. He resented the interruption. He picked his way over the rubble conscious, at the sight of the man's impeccable uniform, that he must look a mess. His pants were torn and split and he was stripped to the waist. The sun had already begun to darken the unscarred parts of his skin. He wiped his hands against his thighs.

Bor watched Catlin approach him. The American was broad and heavily built, not the kind of American Bor had expected. Americans always seemed to be tall and have slim hips. This man was built more like many of Bor's own countrymen. He had a tough face, which looked as though it had been battered in several street fights, and the Commissioner was quick to notice the scars on Catlin's body. His arms were thick; those of a wrestler. Bor suspected the man was as tough as he looked. He nodded a welcome as Catlin stopped a few feet away.

'Mister Joseph Catlin?'

'Joe Catlin, yes.'

'I am told you have been working hard.' Bor began walking, a slow stroll away from the dust that lifted every time rubble was tossed clear of the site. Joe Catlin though about standing still and letting the man walk away from him, but decided until he knew what the man wanted he would tolerate what he considered a minor slight.

'No harder than the others.' He matched his steps to the man's.

'On the contrary, Mister Catlin, you have been . . . are an inspiration. I believe that is the word.' The man had reclasped his hands, but behind his back. He carried a leather covered baton like that of an army officer, but his uniform was similar in colour to the other police Catlin had seen around the site. The shoulder flashes matched those of the police officer he had seen at the administration tent.

'Who are you?' asked Catlin.

'Bor,' answered the man. He did not offer his hand. 'Commissioner of Police for this region.'

"Top brass," thought Catlin. He decided he'd met men like this before, in many countries. You gave them a uniform and they were quite prepared to make the fullest use of its authority. He'd handed out hundreds of dollars, path-smoothing his middle east operations, to such men. He wondered what was coming next.

'What are you doing here, Mister Catlin?' The man kept his pace even, but Catlin noticed he took a slightly longer stride with one leg than the other, though the limp was almost imperceptible.

'I take my vacations at disasters,' said Catlin.

The man laughed. 'I had forgotten you Americans have a strange sense of humour. It has been a long time since I held a conversation with your countrymen. I worked with them for a time, after the war. But, mostly with the British.' They were now seventy yards from the rubble and the Commissioner stopped. 'You haven't answered my question, Mister Catlin.' The voice was only fractionally less friendly, but there was an edge to the remark that was a warning.

'I had just arrived when the earthquake struck. I've simply been doing . . . my duty.'

'And excellently, too,' said Bor. This American wasn't nervous of meeting him. Many of his own people would have been hesitant when faced with a policeman of his position and reputation. This was no soft American, he decided. This was the kind who might have been a partisan had he been a Yugoslav, and been in the right place at the right time. 'You have done enough, Mister Catlin. Far more than enough. I shall pass on your name to our regional committee and I am certain you will receive their thanks.'

'I don't need thanks,' answered Catlin. I'm being run off the land, he thought, with surprise. Why, he wondered.

Bor laughed again, but the sound had no depth, like cheap theatre. He put a gloved hand on Catlin's naked shoulder. 'Mister Catlin, there is a limit to what is expected from any man. You are a guest in our country. We cannot allow you to labour like this. Where are you staying in Yugoslavia?' The hand remained and Catlin felt he wanted to push it away.

'I have a room at a hotel in Piran.'

The hand was taken away and Catlin was relieved. He didn't like being handled, and when the hand was disguised by leather it made it more distasteful. 'A pretty town,' observed Bor. 'Undamaged by the earthquake, though I fear they may have made use of your room, Mister Catlin, in your absence; I can arrange for it to be cleared at once. Do you have transport of your own?'

'A hired car . . . somewhere.'

'Good.'

So far the policeman had not actually asked Catlin to leave, and the longer he left the demand the more certain Catlin became he wanted to remain.

Bor looked at Catlin quizzically almost as though he expected Catlin to instantly say "goodbye", go leap into his hired car, and disappear in a puff of white dust down the rippled highway. Instead, Catlin said: 'I'm an engineer.'

Bor's eyebrows raised a millimeter. 'Yes, I am aware you are an engineer.'

'You need engineers on this site: A lot of them. And you aren't going to get those people out with a few hundred bare hands, a couple of antique bulldozers and half a dozen trucks. So far you're just making the place look tidier. In a month it'll be spick and span, and the people inside will be dead.'

'I am aware of the difficulties,' said Bor. So this was the first of many criticisms the American might make. It confirmed Bor's decision to get rid of the man, despite Catlin's knowledge of the people trapped alive below ground. Bor had considered the position carefully. There were delays everywhere, even if the man were to leave immediately it would take him almost a full day to get to Ljubljana, and then there would be at least a three day wait at Ljubljana airport. Thousands of tourists were still trying to leave the country — all at the same time — and the airport's capacity was limited. Now Bor knew that Catlin would first return to Piran, he could add an extra day to the time it would take Catlin to reach another country. He doubted if the American would be able to pass on any details of the plight of those below ground in much less than a week — even if it occurred to the man to do so. And in a week's time many things could have happened. Bor had already learned of the fiasco of the latest press conference; Kalin would be forced to release information soon. 'We have our own engineers, Mister Catlin.'

'Then where are they?' The American stared straight into Bor's deep-set eyes.

Bor held Catlin's stare, but ignored the question. 'Thank you again, for your help, Mister Catlin.'

Catlin was angry, now. 'Don't thank me, this isn't the right time for detente. Get me a drill rig and I'll supervise its erection. We can get down to those people from above . . . I'll willingly hand over to . . .'

Bor interrupted him. 'Mister Catlin, I am busy man. You are unaware of the size of our problem. You think the earthquake affected only these caves? It was a very big earthquake, Mister Catlin! Thousands of people have already died. Many more are still dying in the wreckage of their houses and factories, in towns like Postojna, Rakek, Cerknica. Pivka is almost totally destroyed. I have my orders and I intend to carry them out.'

'And how do your orders affect me?'

Bor swung on his heel and faced Catlin. 'My orders are to see all foreign tourists leave the disaster area, and go to safety.'

'Except those trapped in the caves . . .'

'Including those, if it is possible. Now please, I must ask you to leave.' Bor waved at a policeman standing some thirty yards away. The man stiffened and marched across. Bor spoke to him briefly in Slovene, then faced Catlin again. 'This police officer will take you to my office, and see you receive a pass which will permit you to cross the roadblocks when you leave.' He turned, flicked his baton up under his arm, and walked away.

Catlin watched him go, aware of the policeman standing awkwardly at his side. The man hovered uncertainly, knowing he must obey his Chief's orders but unwilling to hustle the friendly American who had worked so hard with them for the past few days. 'Okay,' Catlin said to him. 'Lead the way, buster.' By the tone of his voice, the policeman recognised his anger, and licked his lips uncomfortably.

The remains of Catlin's shirt were draped over his shoulders like a tatty poncho. He could smell the sweat in the material. He might have tossed it away, and left the site still stripped to the waist, but because the shirt was all he had apart from his pants and scuffed shoes, to abandon it would be like deserting the flag. He used a dangling sleeve to wipe sweat and dust from his face, scrubbing it vigorously across his forehead. He glanced at the piece of paper he had been given, with its official rubber stamp mark and scrawled signature, then began walking to the open space where he had left the Fiat. The ground was buckled and seamed, the tarmac surface hazed with deep cracks and ridges. The side of the car park was hidden behind a vast pile of debris that had been carried across from the destroyed hotel. He looked for Lisetta, but she found him. A rust-streaked bulldozer manoeuvred at the edge of the rubble, reversed its tracks and drove out ahead of him, its blade held high. He began altering his route to avoid it, but the engine died and a figure swung itself from the cab.

'Joe . . .' It was Lisetta, encased in dust-grimed and loose-fitting dungarees, a safety helmet tilted forward over her forehead. She ran to him and hugged him. 'You like new fashion for girl, eh?' She stood on her toes inviting him to kiss her. He tilted back the helmet, and did so. 'Good, Joe. Now we take rest together. I walk with you to get beer. I'm full of dirt and this machine shake much. I feel like bag of meat with no bones.' The dust had caked on her lips and as she smiled, he saw her teeth were darkened by a ridge of mud paste. He grinned at her strange use of English. She ran her tongue over her teeth. 'Ugh! It taste bad this earth.' She looked up at him again. 'Better, eh? You like?' She slipped her arm through his, then turned her head away, hawked and spat like a man. 'You excuse. You now come for beer?' She pulled at him.

Catlin resisted her. 'Sorry honey, I've been given the bum's rush.'

He saw her face furrow as she puzzled at his words. 'Bum's rush? What is bum's rush?' Her facial expressions were as colourful and lively as her personality.

Catlin spoke angrily. 'Your damn Chief of Police; he's thrown me off the site.'

'Commissioner Bor? He say you go? Why he say, go?' The edges of her mouth dropped, like a disappointed child. She tightened her grip on his arm.

'No foreigners . . . we're a liability.'

She took a moment to digest his words. 'Liability?'

'Another risk. He thinks he's got enough of us already in trouble, underground.' He was surprised to see tears building in her eyes, 'Heh, now . . .'

'But you are engineer! Good worker. We need engineer and worker . . . many such people.' She shook her head and one of the tears streaked a path in the dust on her face. 'He is mad, that Bor. What you say to him?'

Catlin put his hand to her face and smeared the damp dust on her cheek with his thumb. 'I told him his workers would cry if he sent me away.'

She pushed at his hand. 'No cry. Why I cry because ugly old man go away?' Her hand tightened on his and held it close to her cheek. Her dark eyes examined him. 'Not ugly old man.'

The action suddenly moved their relationship for Catlin. She was no longer just an attractive girl he'd had the good fortune to meet on vacation. Before, he had liked her, enjoyed her company. He found her fractured chatter amusing and an escape from his memories, and the horror of the present surroundings. She was educated and intelligent. Now, his feelings were much deeper; more positive. If he'd wanted the same kind of relationship he'd managed with other women over the years, he realised he should have backed away sooner. He knew it was too late now . . . too late to do it without hurt to both of them.

He said, gruffly: 'I guess Bor isn't going to begrudge me one more beer before I leave.' He turned towards the canteen and Lisetta fitted herself under his arm. He could feel the boyish muscles of her body moving as they walked.

He brought two beers to the small wooden table and sat opposite her.

She picked up a bottle, slowly. 'Many things no good, today, Joe. I think maybe no peoples ever come out from ground. My brother never come out. I lose him; I lose you.'

'The people in the cave *can* be rescued,' Catlin said, positively. He knew that in her present mood she needed reassurance. 'I started to tell Bor he should drill down to the people who are trapped. The suggestion didn't seem to interest him.'

Her mood changed instantly to one of keen interest. 'Drill down? How?'

'Straight in from above. A small bore drill to reach them quickly. Enough of a hole to get food and medical supplies down to the people.'

'That a good idea, but I no think we have oil drill.'

'You don't need one,' said Catlin, with certainty. 'There must be light equipment for sinking water bores, somewhere in the area. Maybe you even have equipment with a seismographic survey team.'

'And what Bor say to that?'

'I don't think he listened. He didn't give me time to explain what would be needed. He said you'll have your own engineers here in a little while.'

'Too late, I think.' Lisetta spoke the words as quickly as she'd spat out the dirt, then she softened her voice. 'You must not go. You must stay.' She started to reach towards him across the table to take his hand, but stopped the movement. 'You think I want you stay for me? Yes that so . . . but I want you stay for my brother . . . for the other people.' She frowned. 'When Bor say dance, men must dance . . . when Bor say go, men must go.'

'Like God.'

She smiled. 'Like God . . . yes, like a little God. Big Gods say to Bor when *he* must dance. Joe, where you going, now?'

He had to make a decision, and quickly. He could just say 'goodbye', knowing there would be sadness for both of them. It would be something he might regret as long as he lived . . . and there had never been regrets over women before. Or he could ask her to go with him; she might refuse, but he'd try. 'I'll go back to the Hotel Piran. Stay overnight, if they still have my room. Take a long hot shower, sleep, and then leave next day for Ljubljana. There's not a lot to keep me there, so I'll catch a plane heading west.' He watched her face, closely. 'If you came with me to Ljubljana, I'd want to stay longer. We could take it from there.'

It took her a few seconds to absorb his words and then the tears were back. 'I cannot do this, Joe.' She shook her head quickly and the tears fanned arcs on her dusty cheeks. 'I mean . . .' She put her hands to her face and spoke a few exasperated words in Slovene before she lifted her head again. 'I want to say beautiful things and I cannot. I can only say I want much to be with you; so much. But I cannot leave this place.' She hesitated and her dark eyes were wide, moist; frightened. 'You see out there, near cave entrance, one small old man who work with you? That my father. He has sixty seven years. He work all the time. Hands bleed all day. Near him is one woman; my mother. She work, too. Also work here my uncle and his sons . . . and my girl cousin. All family is here. I cannot leave now.'

'Then I'll wait for you in Piran.' Catlin surprised himself.

She met his eyes quickly, and wiped at the tears with the backs of her hands. 'You want wait for me?' He knew now she had been as uncertain of his emotions as he'd been of her own. 'Maybe long time wait, Joe.'

Catlin thought of Dallas and Leith. They'd survive, and at the moment the company's future didn't seem so important. 'I'm good at waiting.'

A thought startled her. 'Maybe they send you away. Maybe police say you no stay long in Hotel Piran.'

'I'm a very determined man. They'll have to put handcuffs and leg irons on me, and that won't be easy.' He managed to make her smile.

'I try hard to come soon.'

She walked with him until they were level with the bulldozer, then stopped. She avoided looking up at him and Catlin ruffled her hair with the palm of his hand. She seemed very small, child-like, in front of him. He stooped and kissed her. 'Take care of yourself, Lisetta.' She said nothing.

He was conscious of her watching as he walked away, feeling her eyes on him until he reached the Fiat. He started the engine, blowing a cloud of blue smoke from the exhaust as he revved it. She returned his wave, then turned away and slowly clambered back into the bulldozer's cab.

A few hundred yards from the distorted parking lot, Catlin stopped the Fiat at the roadside, and looked back. The destruction was hidden by the foliage of tilted trees. The mountain at this distance, seemed calm and peaceful. Catlin thought of the tourists trapped in the seeping darkness below the pine forests. He spoke aloud. 'Poor bastards.'

There was water dripping onto Berkley's shoulders and knees, it was cold but he hardly noticed it. He sat, his back pressed against a slab of rock that was smooth with a damp curtain of stalagmite, his knees drawn up to his chest, on a narrow ledge. Had he stretched his legs in front of him, from the knees downwards they would have dangled over the chasm that Serge Irano was trying to cross. There were sounds; empty sounds. The dripping of water and the occasional scraping of Irano's boots on the rock . . . the sound of breathing, deep with effort. There was a loneliness, even in the company of the other two men, and there was the strange, wet, dank, smoky scent of the caverns. Berkley wondered how men could find enjoyment in the exploration of places such as this. Caves and caverns had a strange beauty that was almost hypnotic, but how men and women could find pleasure in scrambling through ill-lit tunnels, forcing themselves through narrow crevices that drove the air from their lungs, and dangling above unknown depths on thin ropes, was almost incomprehensible. Berkley had always found it hard to understand those who chose to fight the elements. There were sufficient challenges in everyday life without making an artificial foe of a mountain, or a hole beneath the earth. He'd met men in Vietnam who seemed to enjoy placing themselves in positions of danger, almost as though they felt themselves immortal. They had usually died first, and done the least good. The successful battles he had seen, though he doubted if any battle could be described as successful from a humanitarian point of view, had been won by those who were carefully and intelligently brave, and who attacked their known enemy with caution, skill and determination.

He was watching the German, Struger, kneeling on a ledge a few yards to his right, paying out the climbing line to the guide, Irano, who was climbing upwards towards a narrowing section of the crevasse. Struger was a silent man who spoke little, although his English was quite good. Berkley envied him his climbing experience, for sections that made Berkley sweat with fear Struger treated with almost contemptuous ease, moving his body smoothly and surely across the wet rocks. Irano had been quick to notice Struger's skill, and the way in which the two men worked together made Berkley feel an outsider, and he knew it must have occurred to both of them they might cover a greater area of the system on their own. He was already half expecting they might continue the exploration without him, once they returned again to the main cavern.

He was surprised this thought angered him. There had been many times in the past few hours when he would gladly have been back in the cave with the others, but now he wanted desperately to remain part of this team . . . to be as good as the other two men. The thought of sitting uselessly in the main cavern, waiting, occupied only by his own thoughts and surrounded by so much pain and anguish, frightened him more than climbing.

Struger looked back towards him: 'More line.' Berkley let a few feet slide through his hands, and then Struger said: 'Enough.' The rope snaked along the ground for a few feet before rising in a gentle curve to where Irano was climbing.

They had been working together now for almost thirty hours. Keeping track of time was difficult and they rested only when they were either too chilled or too tired to continue. They had slept, for Berkley an exhausted and disturbed sleep, on a wet ledge somewhere in the cavern system a few hours before. Now, although Berkley was wearing an Omega, it was impossible for him to tell if it was daytime or night somewhere in the distant, real world over their heads.

They had explored a dozen passages leading away from the main cavern system. Some were through new openings that had been revealed when the mountain strata had moved. Others were through cracks or tunnels set high in the walls of the bigger caverns. In every case, so far, the passages had become narrower and narrower until even Irano's supple body could not be forced further along them. The present passage had gone deeper into the mountain than any of the others. Below, a long way below in the black depths of the crevasse, was the sound of running water. Irano had said he thought it must be a tributary of the Pivka for had it been the river itself there would have been a far greater volume of noise — and the air, even so high above the river's surface at the point where the men now stood, would have been disturbed by the churning water gulping its way through its siphons.

Irano was high above the two men, his feet clipped to a small ledge not wider than the thickness of a man's finger. His arms were stretched above him, his right fist wedged into a fissure in the rock. A foot above his head was the roof of the tunnel, while a yard and a half away from him was the far wall he was trying to reach. Two yards lower, across the chasm, was the entrance to a further section of tunnel, its floor rough and gashed with sharp recently fallen rock, which sloped upwards into darkness. Irano was wearing one of the safety helmets fitted with a small electric light that had been part of the caves' emergency stores. The light was powered by batteries carried hooked to the wearer's belt, or in a pocket. He turned his head and the shadows on the wall ahead of him moved; cracks appeared to deepen or were lost, handholds shrank or grew as the light played over them.

He reached sideways, across the chasm.

Berkley saw him take a deep breath, hesitate, and release his remaining handhold on the rock. His body was motionless for a fraction of a second and then fell outwards away from the rock wall. Berkley involuntarily gasped: 'Christ!'

Serge Irano's hands were pressed against the farthest wall, his body hanging above the chasm, and curving as his back and stomach muscles took his weight. He wedged himself, a bridge across the narrowed cleft.

Struger pulled in a few feet of line until it was almost taut. Irano's searching fingers found a minute hold. Berkley could hear him breathing heavily with effort, the tunnel magnifying the sound. Irano swung one foot clear of the ledge which had been supporting him, and with a long stride scraped the toe of his boot against the wall in an effort to find a new foot-hold. The ledge supporting the heel of his rear foot crumbled, and his body dropped downwards until he was supported only by the very tips of his fingers. Berkley heard him swear, softly, then his head turned quickly as he looked for new holds on the wall above him. There was a small crack in the limestone three feet to his left, which spurted a small stream of water. Irano groaned with the strain and began to swing his body sideways, like a pendulum, so his foot might reach the crack. Without warning his fingers slipped from the miniscule fissure. Irano fell.

Struger shouted, wildly, forcing himself back against the rock, and attempting to dig his heels into the polished limestone of the ledge. There was no sound from Irano. The line tightened. Struger yelped as the rope tore through his hands, biting deep into the flesh of his right palm before the coil of rope he had looped around his shoulders took the strain. He jerked forward and the short length of line between Berkley and himself tightened, Berkley staggered, then grabbed at the edge of a vertical crevice for support. There was a soft thud as Irano swung and hit the chasm wall in the darkness below them. The line skidded sideways along the lip of the ledge, raising a fine white line of steam. It caught in a sharp crack in the rock, and snapped. There was the horrifying sound of Irano's body bouncing from some hidden rocks deep beneath the two men, then, long seconds later, a distant heavy splash echoing and re-echoing from the chasm walls.

12

Catlin was asleep, but it was sleep wracked by dreams and memories bordering on nightmare. He relived the earthquake and the sights of corpses and dismembered bodies amid the wreckage; the back-breaking effort and exhaustion of the rescue attempts. His journey back to Piran had taken twice the time of his outward trip to the caves, before the disaster. Near Postojna, parts of the road had been destroyed, bridges had collapsed and been replaced by hasty military constructions thrown across the streams and rivers; villages were heaps of rubble through which rescue teams were still searching.

Piran itself was crowded with refugee families; there were no signs of the holidaymakers who had filled the streets and beaches only a week before. Catlin's own luggage had been packed, and placed in the hotel store — the clerks seemed surprised he had returned, and must have assumed he had simply fled the country, leaving his luggage behind, or that he might be one of the unlucky tourists still trapped in the cave. The Police Commissioner who had spoken to Catlin at Postojna had not contacted the hotel and it was only by bull-headed insistence Catlin found any accommodation in the hotel for the night, and that was on a camp-bed in what was normally one of the cleaning equipment store-rooms. The vacation atmosphere of the fishing village had disappeared with the tourists. All trucks and buses had been requisitioned by the military or the civil authorities, for the transport of medical supplies, food and rescue equipment to the devastated towns and villages. There was a shortage of food in Piran itself, even the bars had little to offer apart from the sharp Reisling produced in the local vineyards. Catlin had managed to buy a loaf of bread and a piece of garlic sausage and had washed it down, sitting on a rock overlooking the harbour, with a bottle of the wine.

There was no electricity in the town. Power lines from the generating stations many miles away had been destroyed, and the only lights in the town as the sun dropped, were from the occasional private generators or oil lamps and candles. People were off the streets early, and by nine-thirty, Piran appeared as deserted as the earthquake damaged villages Catlin had passed through on his return journey.

There was no hot water in the hotel, but Catlin had stripped in one of the public bathrooms, and had swilled himself down. Without electricity, he was unable to remove the four days growth of pepper and salt beard which bristled his chin, he could have bought a cheap razor but decided against it. He had clambered onto the camp-bed, pulled the blanket over himself, and been asleep within seconds.

The drumming was near his head. He heard it distantly, and with no recognition. It became part of his dreams, a hollow hammering as bodies were lifted into coffins, lids pressed down upon them and nailed into place. Sometimes the bodies moved and squirmed, resisting the efforts of those who sought to conceal them. The hammering was the fists of those trapped beneath the ominous coffin lids . . . knuckles rapping in desperation . . . skin bruising . . . nails being torn from bleeding fingers. The dream became a nightmare as Catlin felt himself lifted and realised he too had become one of the living corpses to be entombed alive. He struggled, gasping, fighting towards consciousness. There was a soft voice beside his face, insistent, pleading. He jerked himself back to reality.

'Joe . . . Joe.'

'God Almighty!' He shook his head vigorously, to clear the nightmare from his mind. There were strong fingers gripping his arm.

'Joe, it me, Lisetta.' Catlin fought away the jumbled dreams. 'It Lisetta . . . you remember; from Postojna. Lisetta Irano.' The girl's voice was urgent. A flashlight beam brought light to the small room.

Catlin shielded his eyes and levered himself onto an elbow. The camp-bed creaked a warning. 'Lisetta, what the hell?' He was still uncertain if this was dream or reality.

'Joe, I must have talk with you.' The light moved and she took her hand from his arm. He felt her body closer and her lips warm against his face.

He pressed the feeling of sleep from his eye-balls with his

middle finger and thumb. His mind began to function. He tried to see the watch on his wrist, remembered he had laid it on the floor beside the bed and reached and found it. He read the luminous dial in the reflection of the beam of light. The watch showed a little after one a.m.

He could sense Lisetta's nervousness as she spoke again. 'Joe, I must speak to you, but not here.' She swung the light beam around the room as though expecting to find someone hidden there.

'Okay, I'll dress.' He was fully awake now. 'Lisetta, what . . .'

She hushed him. 'I wait outside, near sea.' The flashlight beam swung towards the door and was gone.

Catlin struggled in the darkness to find his clothes. Something was wrong, something serious enough to bring her to him within hours of their parting; something that had nothing to do with their relationship. He wondered if she had come to warn him of his imminent arrest. Didn't the KGB like to do their house-breaking at dawn? Maybe the Yugoslavian secret police used the same tactics!

There were still a few oil lamps alight in the hotel corridors, in the foyer and behind the glass door of the night porter's room, and Catlin was able to find his way to the main door without difficulty. The night air was warm as he stepped outside. He paused for a few seconds until he could pick out the stars. A low moon, almost full, cast long shadows from the buildings. There was the hollow slap of the sea against the hulls of fishing boats in the harbour, and a hint of phosphorescence on the oily surface of the water. The girl was a silhouette, a small figure, hunched slightly as she leant against a concrete pillar near the steps to the sea wall. She turned at his footsteps.

'It is necessary I come to you quickly.' She said apologetically, and as he reached her she turned slightly and slipped her arm through his, drawing him further away from the dim light showing through the hotel windows. She kept walking, slowly along the narrow promenade towards the tip of the peninsula, past the closed and shuttered fish restaurants.

'How did you find me?'

'No easy. You say you stay at Hotel Piran, but the night worker not find your room number. Alessandro and me pay him much money to let us search. Many peoples sleep in cupboards and bathrooms. I lucky to find you.' The promenade had widened to a small square, the buildings now some fifty yards behind them. She stopped and faced the sea. It hissed on shingle beyond the concrete. There was the familiar port smell of stale fish and sewerage.

Catlin was wide awake now, the sea air which had at first seemed warm, had a chill to it that was finding its way through his clothing. Across the harbour and far out at sea, the lights of some cruise liner flickered as it headed southwards down the Adriatic. A group of fishing boats, acetylene flares on their sterns, drifted slowly half a mile away. Occasionally the shouts of their crews came on the light breeze.

'How did you get here?'

The girl pulled herself closer to Catlin's side, snuggling herself against him.

'With Alessandro. On motorcycle.'

'Uncomfortable?'

'Yes. I not like them in daytime. Night, they are worse.'

He had been waiting for her to explain her visit, but it was almost as though she was trying to avoid the matter; trying to soften him up first. 'Okay,' he said, abruptly. 'Why are you here? I don't usually have young ladies trying to find me after midnight.'

'We want you come back to Postojna.'

'Back? I've just been thrown out!'

'Official, yes, Joe. But I want you come back with us and help reach people underground.'

'Unofficially.'

'Yes, that is so.' The girl's voice was so quiet he had to lower his head to hear her words.

'Who's we? You and this Alessandro guy?'

'More. Many of us. Students . . . friends of mine.'

'And what does unofficially mean?'

'It means if you are catch near Postojna, Commissioner Bor will be very angry. You will be deported by police.' Lisetta had turned away from him, releasing her hold on his arm.

'And you and this Alessandro, and the rest of your friends . . . what about them?'

'I think we go prison for long time.' Her voice was even softer, almost a whisper.

'Prison?'

'Our Government is less strong against a foreigner.'

Catlin grunted, then half-laughed. 'Jesus! This is some idea you've got, Lisetta. You come in the middle of the night and wake me, to invite me back to a place where I might get myself arrested and tossed out of the country. It's the kind of thing that goes down well on a United States citizen's record. It's the kind of experience I can do without.'

'Joe, we need knowledge you have.' She caught his arm with both hands and held him, surprisingly strongly. 'If you no come back, then all people in cave die.' She spoke positively enough to jar Catlin.

'Hold on, Lisetta. Something I'm not taking responsibility for is the death of anyone . . . least of all several hundred tourists. This isn't even my country, it's yours. It's *your* government who are supposed to be doing the rescue work. If I ever *had* any responsibility, then your Police Chief took it away from me. And maybe I'm glad he did. If there are any problems now, they're his, and your Government's.' He had raised the level of his voice and she quickly held the tips of her fingers to his mouth. The movement surprised him.

'Joe, quiet. I explain.'

'Do that.'

'We have document . . . from Commissioner Bor's office. It say people trapped at Postojna are not so important. They no make the great effort to rescue them. They are, I think you say, expendable.'

'Expendable? No-one is expendable . . . expendable is a military word, like "waste", not a civilian expression.'

'Joe, this Military Government. Not exactly military, but our President is also head of our Armed Forces. This is communist dictatorship. The paper we have is letter, from Commissioner Bor to Minister of Presidium, Baraslev Kalin . . . he a man very close to the President. It confirm conversation Bor had with Kalin two days past. Bor told he must concentrate all effort, all manpower and resource, on assisting only the towns and villages to be normal as quick as possible. That is Commissioner Bor's prime work; the caves are nothing to these men.'

'Why?' asked Catlin, disbelievingly.

'We don't understand exact, we guess. I think we find out in a day or two from people we know. But, Italian radio say our Regional Committee in Slovenia refuse *all* offers of outside help . . . offers from most of European countries, America and Russia.'

'Refused all offers of help? God Almighty, that's crazy! You need all the help you can get . . . the International Red Cross, Green Cross, all the food and medical help there is. You need machinery and technicians.'

'We need, yes, but we have refused them. It sound crazy to you, but we think maybe our Government afraid. Our political situation is delicate. It become much more delicate now President Tito is gone. We are communist country, but we not think ourselves Soviet satellite . . . Yugoslavia is independent. But Russians want make more strong the east bloc, and they be happy to find excuse to invade Yugoslavia. The Government maybe say if Russians see us not capable of helping ourselves in this problem, it may be the excuse Russia need. There are some people here who *want* Russian communism in Yugoslavia. We hear also, one of People's Representatives, a woman, Anna Morolec, has been arrested. We don't know why, but she very liberal and she may have fight againt the Regional Committee decision.'

'You seem to know a lot.'

'We students. It is our business to know.'

'What about Skopje,' asked Catlin suddenly. 'You accepted aid when you had an earthquake there.'

'That before Vietnam.'

'What the hell had Vietnam to do with Yugoslavia?'

'Vietnam important to Yugoslavia, Joe. America withdrew in Far East. Now our Government, and the Soviet Government, believe America will never again put herself in external war; only fight if her own country or people are in danger. Also, at the time of Skopje, there are many internal problems in the Soviet Republic . . . battles for power between leaders.'

'And how in hell's name did you find out about the Government's plans. They sound to me like the sort of thing that's usually classified information.'

'Alessandro found this memo. On his father's desk. Alessandro Bor is son of Commissioner Bor.'

'And Alessandro is the one with the motorcycle.?'

'Yes.'

Catlin rubbed his hand across the bristle of his chin. Dallas seemed a million miles away, Ma MacDougal in the Leith office nothing more than a misty childhood memory. He knew the wisest thing he could do now, for his own personal safety and comfort, would be to refuse the girl and make his way home the following day. Fighting oil wells was one thing, but you could calculate the danger; fighting foreign governments was another far more dangerous game. He had even refused a cautious approach from the CIA some years before; dabbling in other countries affairs was too often fatal.

'Before you make up your mind, Joe, let me tell you more . . . figures. On the telephone link to the cave this afternoon, we are given list of all peoples alive, today. One hundred and seventy nine peoples are Americans, eleven British . . .'

'Thanks,' interrupted Catlin, coldly. 'That's real helpful.'

'If you can get this hole down through the mountain Joe, to them, you can give them life. As you say, once hole is made, they can be sent medical supplies, food, and even electricity for light and heat. They can live for many weeks. We can force Government to rescue them. They not refuse if we managed to do this thing.'

'The alternative is to let the international press see the document you have. Get them to exert outside pressure.'

'There is no time. First we must convince the press the document is genuine. Our Government deny it. Maybe we never find proof to satisfy newspapers. Our Government has a quick way to lose people who cause it embarrassment. Anna Morolec is example. Meanwhile, people trapped will die. Rescue, if it come at all, come too late for them. Have you thought what is like for them down there, beneath mountain . . . alone in a wet, dark place, no food . . . sitting in hole waiting to die?'

'Cut it out. I've done as much thinking as yourself. As for dying, I've been there, and I've seen it happen.' A quick picture of Mike O'Donovan flashed in his mind; two halves of a body divided by a smoking steel plate. The stink of burnt flesh. A little more than a week ago O'Donovan had been alive. His shroud had been the silver heat-reflecting suit that caught the desert sunlight as they loaded him into the coffin. Joe Catlin had avoided looking at the tortured face behind the mica mask. 'How would we work?' he asked, his voice level.

'From the mountains. We have place, there. The mountains are prohibited military zone, but no reason for army to send patrols — no reason for anyone to be there, now. Two of our men have already gone to Ljubljana, in car. They think they know of equipment you want, in Geological Department of the University. They return quickly. Others search for things you need, but we are only guessing until you tell us what you want.'

'Do they know the area well?'

'Simon, the one who goes back to Ljubljana, and two others, spend much time there. They are pot-holers, like my brother.' There was excitement in the girl's voice, and her dark eyes glistened almost as though they had stolen the phosphorescence from the sea. She squeezed Catlin's arm.

He grimaced at her. 'Give me half an hour to pack, and I'll meet you in the square.'

'I think you are already pack. I tell Alessandro to do this when I wake you. We know your car, it must all be inside now.'

'And what would you have done if I'd refused?'

The girl laughed, softly. 'I think I throw your baggage into sea.'

13

The cavern where the trapped people had survived was over two hundred yards in length and a hundred wide. From a point where the railway platform ended, in the waiting area, the cavern floor sloped steeply upwards towards the far end. This mound of jumbled ancient rock should have been a warning in itself of the possibility of catastrophe, for long ago the stalactite covered rubble had once been part of the roof of the cavern, which had collapsed through earthquakes several times throughout the history of the caves.

Three small fires burnt amongst the rocks on the steep slope of the cavern. The fires were small, but their warm glow gave some comfort to those who huddled around them. The wood had come from the wreckage of the canteen, and the huts that had held the cave's emergency equipment. Over one of the fires simmered a steel container of boiling water; the only warm drink. There was no coffee, the container had been crushed beneath falling rock that had exploded the gas cylinder and killed the canteen workers. There was no more sugar or food; the canteen normally stocked little underground, most people preferring to eat when they had returned to the surface where they could enjoy picnics in the hotel gardens, or on the banks of the Pivka river.

Not all the people trapped within the great cavern could sit around the three small fires at the same time, though most preferred to be somewhere near them. The warmth of the three fires was for the injured, and there was insufficient wood to permit more of them to be built. Occasionally, a man or woman accompanying or carrying a child, would ease their way carefully past the injured people, to stand for a few moments in front of the flames, rubbing their child's hands or knees or attempting to dry out their damp clothing. They were all conscious of the needs of others and seldom stayed for long.

Yacho Kristoff was dying. He knew it, and the thought made him angry rather than sorry for himself. Here was an opportunity when, as senior guide, he could have proved his value as a leader and now the chance was to be lost. It would have been nice, later, when they were rescued, to have been able to stand in a bar and have some of the older men point him out as the one who had led the people trapped in the caves. It was usually the other men who had been pointed out to Kristoff . . . 'That's Strakosec . . . he was one of the partisan leaders,' or 'Isn't that Petar Cec, great grandson of Luka Cec, the man who found the most beautiful part of the caverns?' No-one would be able to point to Yacho Kristoff.

The thought of dying did not frighten him. He would be glad when it happened; the pain inside him was continuous and almost unbearable. It was there when he lay back, unmoving, supported against a rock . . . it was a terrible searing agony if he moved.

He had seen the British veterinary surgeon but the man had been unable to help him.

'It hurt me here.' The man was examining the deep purple bruise across Kristoff's lower chest and stomach, probing it gently with thick, strong fingers; unlike those of any normal doctor Kristoff had ever encountered.

The man had nodded, silently, and his fingers had probed deeper.

Kristoff winced with pain. 'There . . . that place, it hurt much.'

'I don't usually get so much help,' acknowledged the Englishman. 'My patients don't talk.'

'I talk.' said Kristoff. 'Here where rock hit me. What rock do?'

'A lot of damage.'

'You fix?'

'I can't do anything.' The man looked helpless and Kristoff felt sorry for him. He had watched him working with the other injured, and without medical equipment it was impossible for the man to do much more than dress the wounds and attempt to set broken bones. There were no surgical instruments in the medical stores, only a few bandages, antiseptic ointments, slings and splints. All had soon been used.

'I die?'

'If we can't get proper medical help soon. I think you've ruptured your diaphragm, and also a lot of blood vessels. You're bleeding a lot, inside.'

'Blood go into stomach?'

'Into your intestinal cavity.'

'It very bad,' said Kristoff. He thought for a while. 'You cut and let out blood?'

'It wouldn't do any good.'

The man had left him shortly afterwards, and Kristoff had lain back against the rock thinking. It seemed stupid to die when outwardly there didn't seem to be much of a reason. At first, he had hoped the animal doctor was wrong, but after a while he knew the man's diagnosis was correct. It hadn't taken Kristoff more than a couple of hours to adjust to the idea that he hadn't much time left. There were things he still wanted to do . . . he would have liked to live to see his grandchild; his daughter was pregnant and the child was expected in another month. Kristoff hoped the child would be a boy. Perhaps, then, it would be named Yacho, after himself.

He wondered what it would be like to be dead. He'd seen people die. Some died quietly, just as though they were going to sleep; others died noisily. He knew his own death would be silent. He had called Tor Sarbo to him, but the man was now so terrified by the entire situation he was barely sane, and gibbered as stupidly as the monkeys Kristoff had watched in the Ljubljana zoo. Kristoff hadn't bothered to tell him what the doctor had said; he doubted if Sarbo would even have understood him, certainly he wouldn't have cared. Perhaps, Kristoff decided, he would explain it all to Serge Irano when the man returned. He might not always agree with Irano, but the man was strong-minded and a good leader. He could take over when he was dead.

Kristoff stared at the light of the fires. Although he was too far away from them to feel their warmth, he was happy knowing that the warmth was there. Winter was always better when it could be spent round the crackling flames of a good log fire. He could smell the perfume of burning pine cones.

Colette Marishall had been watching the passage along which Serge Irano, Carl Struger and David Berkley had clambered so many hours before. Time dragged in the gloom of the caves, and although she had busied herself helping with the nursing of the injured, there was little more she could do. She had tried sleeping, but closed eyes brought vivid pictures of torn and broken bodies, memories and regrets of her last hours with the two dead girls.

The photographic session in the caves had been *her* idea. She could easily have found some other location, and the two girls would still be alive; Angie with her cool beauty and Fudge with her bubbling enjoyment of life. David had sensed her feeling of guilt and had done his best to relieve her of its weight, but it remained inside her to be reborn in her moments of fear and loneliness. And the loneliness grew in his absence.

There was a faint glow in one of the narrow tunnels at the lower end of the cavern, like a winter moon attempting to break its way through a bank of mist. Colette stood watching it, surprised to find she felt as nervous as if she was expecting a midnight lover. A flashlight beam scored the cave roof, wavered and was then extinguished. She picked her way quickly down the steep slope. The light flashed again. Her stomach muscles tautened as the swinging beam revealed only two men.

She called: 'David?' There was unfamiliar panic in her voice.

'Yes!'

She was almost sick with relief as he replied. She reached him seconds later and found herself with her arms around him. He didn't push her away, but seemed glad at the warmth of her welcome. Struger stepped past them, then flicked on the beam of his own flashlight. Colette looked up at David Berkley. 'There were three of you. Where's the guide, Irano?'

Berkley shone his light at the ground. Its beam was already yellowing as the batteries exhausted themselves. 'He fell,' he said slowly. 'A couple of hours ago.' He began walking up towards the firelight and she stayed close at his side.

'Dead?'

'We climbed down to try to reach him. There wasn't a body.'

'Then he might be . . .'

'He hit some ledges first, and then fell into a siphon. It disappeared underground. There was a lot of blood on the rocks. He couldn't have survived.'

It was impossible to see his face clearly so far from the dim orange glow of the fires, but she could sense his fatigue. He stood for a while, staring back into the darkness. She knew he was thinking about the death of Irano. She stayed silent until he spoke again.

'Where's the chief guide?'

Colette pointed to the right of the highest of the fires. 'Over there.' She could see the German, Struger, standing above Kristoff, beyond the firelight, talking. As they reached the men, the German turned and spoke. Colette saw that the senior guide Kristoff, was crying.

'I told him about Irano. He says now we stop looking for a way out. It is too dangerous for us.'

Struger had removed his helmet and there were beads of moisture on the bald part of his head. A black line showed where the plastic headband of the helmet had sat. He was watching for Berkley's reaction and Berkley was conscious of the man's unblinking eyes. They gave no hint of Struger's own feelings; it was like staring into a pair of camera lenses.

'What do *you* think?' Berkley asked. He worked hard to keep any sign of emotion from his own face.

Struger noticed the effort and smiled, slightly. It was the first sign Berkley had seen that there was humour somewhere inside the man. The smile was gone quickly. 'For a man who begins, you climb okay. I think we rest, then we try more.'

Berkley nodded. 'That suits me, too.'

There was an odd feeling deep inside his mind that suggested if Struger had said no, then he would have gone on searching, alone. The fear of the caverns had not grown with Irano's death, surprisingly it was as though the enemy had revealed itself for the first time, and was not the indefatigable foe he had imagined.

Mihunokada was angry and there was a bitter edge to his voice as he spoke. 'They are back, and they have not found a way. One of the men, the Yugoslav guide, was killed in a fall. The American and the German did not continue on their own. They have returned.'

Nito, one of the party and a man of Mihunokada's age, rocked slightly on his heels. 'We have as much right as any others to try to find a way out. We cannot sit here and wait to die. I have my wife and young son with me. There is no more food, not even for the children. If we waste time now, we will be too weak to try later.'

Kaguri nodded. The two men were right. The more people who searched for a way out, the better the chances of success. He had approached the chief guide with that suggestion only a few hours ago, and had requested a couple of the guide's flashlights. The guide had refused, and had told Kaguri that although he agreed with him in principle, there were too few flashlights for any to be spared; and also, he thought it was safer for those with no climbing or caving experience to remain in the main cavern. Kaguri had not argued, but had decided to wait until the search party returned.

'The other party has been looking for a way out through the old system,' he said, deliberately. 'Perhaps there is no way left open in that direction. If we are to begin searching, I suggest we try to follow the river. We have no climbers, but it is likely we have strong swimmers.' He knew it had become important for the young and active members of his group to at least try to help liberate their compatriots. It would strengthen the morale of the older Japanese, too.

'I swim, Sensei.' Mihunokada answered quickly.

'And I.' The voice belonged to Yamada, a stocky dark-skinned man. He spoke with the clipped accent of the Tokyo suburbs.

'Then you two will go,' agreed Kaguri. 'Two is sufficient. The remainder of us will wait.'

'I can swim, too. Let me go with them.' It was Nito, the married student with the son; the friend of Mihunokada.

'Two only.' Kaguri spoke flatly, to remind the young man of his place. 'There are no flashlights available, but this does not matter if you are to swim. There are matches and candles. Matches can be made waterproof - their heads must be dipped in hot wax. You will swim with the current. At times the water runs beneath the rock, but it passes through caverns and caves, and it is there that you must find air.' He lifted his head and looked at Mihunokada. The young man's eyes reflected the distant fires, and the shadows set them deep beneath his forehead. Mihunokada smiled and his teeth showed. 'You are probably going to die,' warned Kaguri.

'You told me death could sometimes be the highest honour, and in any case, I would rather look for death than allow it to come searching for me,' Mihunokada answered.

'Avoid death, don't look for it. You are not doing this for yourself, you are doing it for all of us.' Kaguri paused and looked towards the firelight. 'And by all, Mihunokada, I mean *all* the people here in this cave. . . no matter what nationality. This is not war, and *you* are not seeking glory.'

Mihunokada felt himself blushing. Kaguri, like his own father, seemed to be able to read his thoughts.

'I have lasted longer than you,' said Yacho Kristoff to his feet. He tried to move them again, but they remained motionless, two leather parcels of useless bone and flesh below the torn legs of his trousers. They did not even look familiar anymore. The boots which Kristoff kept so carefully polished, were scarred and dirty.

So he was to die from the feet upwards, thought Kristoff. First his feet and legs, then his stomach . . . his chest. At what point, he wondered, would he be really dead? Would he be dead when there was no more pain in his abdomen? Or perhaps when it was possible for him to breath without feeling he was sucking fire into his lungs? When he closed his eyes, he could see the inside of his small apartment in Postojna. He could even smell his wife's cooking, and hear the constant chattering of the budgerigar that lived its life away in the small cage hung above the radio. But when he opened his eyes, he could see only the huddled groups of miserable tourists, their shoulders drooping beneath damp blankets, their hair lank, faces streaked and dirty. The voices were a hollow murmur in the cavern, and Kristoff's nose detected not the aroma of kebab and rice, but of sweat, excreta, filth and the decay of death.

Serge Irano is dead before me . . . like my feet, thought Kristoff. Irano had been the most alive of all of them only a few hours ago, and now he was dead. Serge Irano! Who would have believed it? Irano the rebel; Irano the pot-holer. Plenty of the girls who worked in the hotel Jama would be tearful when they heard the news. Serge Irano was popular . . . he was single . . . had been single. Plenty of the girls would have liked him for a husband. 'It doesn't matter about my feet,' Kristoff said to himself. 'It matters, though, about Irano.'

There was a shout from a bundled figure sleeping in a nest amongst the boulders. A dark shape moved and shook the sleeper to consciousness. Kristoff was surprised at the number of people who shouted, screamed or cried in their sleep; he wondered if he did the same. He glanced down at Mallek and Sarbo, sitting side by side, like children on a croft floor. Mallek ground his teeth when he was asleep, and Sarbo played with himself beneath the blanket. It was surprising what you learnt about people when you were forced to spend a lot of time with them. Like the tourists, for instance; normally a guide hardly spoke to them. They were clean and washed, tidy and shaven. They smelt of perfume, or after-shave. Very few stank. Tourists weren't normally even people; not real people. Tourists were things that came and bought tickets, wandered about the caves and made strange noises. Then they left. The tourists here *weren't* leaving, and they *were* identifiable . . . like the woman in the market who sells tomatoes, like the man who sells fish . . . the bar-owner . . . the neighbour you see but don't speak with. People, just people, thought Kristoff.

He wondered what was happening above ground. He had used the telephone a few hours ago when he was still able to move. Mallek had helped him. He'd had a short conversation with Zlobec.

'Are there any more dead, Kristoff?'

'Two more, Zlobec. Another Austrian, and one of the British.' Kristoff had deliberately left the title from Zlobec's name. It was something he wouldn't have done if they'd been face to face. Now the thin voice was too distant to make him nervous. He had never liked Zlobec . . . in fact he disliked all of the police who were stationed at the cave site. 'The Austrian was Franc Bressler. Address, eight five Brukkenstras Vienna. His wife is down here. I have no identity papers for the Englishman, but his name is Morrison . . . James Morrison.'

'Any more problems?'

'There aren't any *more* we *could* have,' Kristoff had said, angrily. What the hell had Inspector Zlobec expected, an outbreak of bubonic plague? 'We've been here three days. We don't have food left . . . not even sugar. We have a case of slivovitz, so we can all get pissed. And by the way, there aren't any medical supplies left except for about twenty aspirin tablets . . . half of the contents of the cabinets were missing when we opened them. They were either pilfered by some bastard, or incorrectly stocked.'

'I'll look into it,' Zlobec said, as though Kristoff was reporting the theft of the medical supplies on a normal working day.

'Damn you, Zlobec. Don't look into it . . . you think there'll be fingerprints on the damned cabinets? Just get us out of here! What's happening? How near are you to us? We can't hear you tunnelling!'

'Commissioner Bor was here earlier.'

'Did he move any fucking rocks?'

'He was most concerned.'

'I'll bet he was. Did you lick his arse, Emile Zlobec?'

'There's no need to be disrespectful, Kristoff.'

'Arrest me,' suggested Kristoff, helpfully. He had pictured Zlobec's face, red with anger.

Kristoff chuckled at the memory of the conversation, then tried to move his shoulders to a more comfortable position against the smooth rock. The action made him gasp, but suddenly the pain stopped. Kristoff knew that for the first time since the earthquake he would be able to sleep. He smiled at the thought, closed his eyes and let his head droop forward until his chin rested on his chest. Kristoff was dead.

The two pieces of corrugated asbestos sheet made a small and uncomfortable shelter on a ledge of rock seventy yards away from the fires, and in the darkness of the entrance to one of the collapsed tunnels. Berkley had dragged the material from the wreckage of the hut, and now one piece acted as a floor, and the other was wedged like a lean-to on the rock shelf. The ends were held in place by heavy splinters of limestone. The asbestos was damp but not wet, and the sloping piece that acted as a roof drained away the water dripping continuously from the walls.

'You can get cancer from asbestos,' Colette had remarked as he pulled the pieces from the rubble of the bar. She took one of the sheets and dragged it after him.

'You can get hurt jumping off moving trains,' he'd answered.

She followed him to the ledge of rock. 'Why so far from the others?'

He had begun clearing debris from a level section of the smooth rock. 'Basic insecurity. I need a place of my own . . . even in this damn cave. And I can do without crowds.' He wasn't exaggerating. A strange personal familiarity with the cavern was developing, the smell, the sound of the continually dripping walls and stalactites, the murmur of the people. With the familiarity came the need for a small private corner of his own; a place to come back to whenever he and Struger returned to the main cave . . . a place he could promise himself for a few subsequent hours of respite when the going, out there, got tougher than usual; his personal reward system.

He slid a piece of the asbestos sheet into place on the rock. 'This is Berkley's pad . . . right here.'

Berkley's pad! Not a sumptuous Manhattan apartment, but two pieces of corrugated asbestos! She'd wondered, a couple of times back in New York, what the famous David Berkley's home might look like . . . it wouldn't be anything like this, and yet he seemed as satisfied as if he'd just taken the lease of a penthouse. He seemed to be waiting for her to say something, she wasn't sure what. The damp air was suddenly thicker, heavier. She spoke quickly, feeling herself blushing; grateful for the half-light of the cave shading her face. 'Everyone seems to snore. It's difficult to rest properly up there.' She looked back towards the centre of the cavern. There was enough light to see the slope of rubble rising away from them, and amongst the rocks the dark heaps of figures, like bundles of old clothing on a city dump. She took a deep breath and said: 'You'll need a housekeeper.' He laughed and she was confused, feeling a need to explain herself better. 'This place is always damp. If two of us used your shelter, it would be warmer. We could share the blankets . . . double one of them underneath us. We'd keep each other warm.' Dear God, she thought, he knows now I want him. I should have kept silent, waited until he made the first move.

Berkley understood. 'I was trying to find enough courage to ask you. Thanks.' She saw the glint of his teeth as he smiled. 'I was going to finish the place, then strut around it crowing, with my feathers all on end, until I managed to entice you inside.'

'Idiot,' she said. She felt the knot in her stomach relaxing. She peeled the damp blanket from her shoulders and laid it on the asbestos. The cool air made her shiver. She climbed into the shelter. He swung himself up beside her, and spread his blanket over the two of them, then pushed his arm around her and pulled her close. She could feel the heat of his body against her and snuggled her head into the pit of his shoulder. The corrugations of the asbestos were hard against her right hip and she moved to find a little more comfort, putting her arm across his waist.

'Home is . . .' she began, then stopped. By the deep even sound of his breathing, she knew he was already asleep. She smiled to herself; there were a lot of girls back in New York who would envy her in his arms. Then she remembered she might die in the depths of the mountain as Angie and Fudge had died, and pressed herself closer to him, and was suddenly more afraid than she had been since the first moments of the earthquake.

'Ralph?' Sheila Hubertson spoke softly into her husband's ear. They were cuddled together between two boulders, their blankets shared and wrapped double around them.

'Honey!' Ralph Hubertson acknowledged her whisper. He had his head cradled on his right arm, and his neck was so cramped he thought it would dislocate if he moved quickly. He eased himself around, feeling the uncomfortable dampness of his trousers against his knees and ankles.

'Why don't you think that God is Love?'

'I'm not even certain God is God,' he muttered. His wife Sheila liked religion as a topic of conversation, and seemed to have the habit of waiting until he was involved in something before she raised it. Usually it was during a televised baseball or football game, or when he was at the most exciting part of a book. Just now he had been dozing and dreaming, a semi-conscious kind of dream where he was sitting in the sun just relaxing and watching bees and insects visiting summer flowers.

'Mary Baker Eddy wrote that God is Love,' said Sheila.

'I know, honey.' Sheila had shown no interest in religion until her mother had begun slowly dying. An old family friend had taken her along to a Christian Science Reading Room. After that she had begun attending their meetings regularly and increasingly avidly. That had been almost ten years ago, and since then it seemed to Ralph Hubertson there had never been a single day when she had not quoted Mary Baker Eddy or one of her disciples, to him.

'Maybe she was wrong.'

'Wrong?' Christ, thought Ralph, now was a fine time for his wife to begin doubting.

'Well, if God was love, there shouldn't be so much suffering in the world. Things like this wouldn't happen to innocent people.'

'There are reasons for everything,' he replied. He moved so he could get his arm around her. It was difficult, she wasn't a light woman and didn't help him by easing her back away from the rock. 'We don't know the overall plan of things. We're not capable of judging the actions of God, whether he's love or not.'

'I don't see that. If God is Love then his actions should be loving.'

Hubertson wondered where the conversation was leading. Sheila's arguments were usually on more basic subjects. He thought quickly. 'Well, suppose God is like us . . . one great big body, and all us humans are just cells in the body; minute cells, like tissue cells. If we move a hand, say to stroke someone we love, we destroy hundreds of cells and have to replace them. Maybe God is like that . . . he does something good or kind and a few thousand of his cells need to be rebuilt.'

'That's a good thought, Ralph.' She paused and then said: 'But it doesn't account for some things, like why I've got a lump.'

'A lump?' He was startled. If his wife mentioned any ailments at all, it was usually only the discomfort of the haemorrhoids she'd had since the birth of the children.

'Here.' She prodded herself. 'On my breast. The right breast.'

He turned his head towards her and although he couldn't see her face he could feel her breath, warm, against his cheek. 'You've got a lump? How long have you had a lump?' There was a sick feeling in his stomach. His question had been a confession to himself. It had been a long time since they had made love, slowly and carefully; a long time since he had explored her body with his hands. Age and familiarity had bred carelessness. Love-making was a quick lifting of her thick nightdress to her waist.

'A while,' she said, almost guiltily. 'Feel . . . no, just there. Gently, Ralph, it hurts a little.'

The lump was almost the size of an egg. Uneven in shape, he could feel it hard in the soft flesh of her breast, beneath her blouse. She had loosened her bra and the breast sagged. Hubertson resisted an exclamation. 'How long have you had it?'

'I noticed it three months ago.'

'Three months! Why didn't you see Doc Wilson? Why didn't you tell me?'

'I didn't think it was important. I mean, well, of course it was important, but I thought it would be all right. I saw a practitioner.'

'A practitioner isn't a doctor, Sheila. You should have seen Doc Wilson. He could have got it fixed.'

'The practitioner was helping me fix it. A lot can be done with prayer and thought. I think it would have been healed, if I'd really believed . . . really, really believed.'

'But you do really believe. Good God, everything has its limitations, even religion. Religion is good for some things, not so good for others.'

'I know, and that's the trouble. I tried believing, but it doesn't work. That's why the lump has got bigger.'

'Nonsense. The lump has got bigger simply because it needs medical treatment. Don't worry about it. Now that I know too, it's something we can share.' The thought made him sick with dismay, but he hid the emotion. 'Maybe a couple of injections . . . at worst, a small operation, and everything will be just fine.'

'It's cancer, Ralph, I know it's cancer; just like Mollie Happinger's. They'll cut it off, Ralph . . . cut it clean off.' Her voice rose, hysterically.

'Stop it, honey. Stop.' He pulled her close to him. 'It won't be like that. The minute we get out of here I'm taking you straight home. Thank God we've got good insurance. We can afford the best. You see, it'll be okay. A week or two in hospital at the most. Maybe only a couple of days. And don't start doubting that God is Love.'

'But why would he give me a lump?'

He could feel her fingers digging into his side, as she held him tightly. 'Maybe just to let me know how much I love you. How much I need you.'

The shoulder bags the two men carried had been made for camera equipment. Each now contained a plastic, screw-topped canister that had been used for displaying boiled sweets in the underground canteen; there were three unused candles in Morei's container and four in Yamada's. Both had a supply of waterproofed matches. The candles lasted three hours apiece, and if used singly there was enough light for twenty-one hours, as well as that provided by the candle which Morei now carried in the bottom half of a broken glass bottle. Morei's bag also held three pieces of chewing-gum.

The men had exchanged their blankets for anoraks they had borrowed from other members of the Japanese tour. Yamada's boasted "Datsun", in fluorescent lettering across the back, an indication of the employer of its former owner. Yamada also wore a red baseball hat, its peak reversed to deflect dripping water from his neck. Morei had his head wrapped in a white square of cloth, knotted at the back; its black caligraphy was the name of his sports club. His dark blue nylon anorak fitted him loosely, and he had rolled it up at the cuffs.

The departure of the two Japanese had revealed the death of the senior of the guides, Yacho Kristoff. Kaguri had visited the man to ask his advice on the route the men should attempt. He had found the body of Kristoff already stiffening. The man's death had not particularly disturbed Kaguri; there had been little enough leadership from any of the guides since the earthquake. What food there had been in the cave, they had handed out in the first day, although Kaguri had felt it should have been kept for the children. The guides, apart from the youngest who had been killed while searching for a way to escape, had shown hardly any capability for leadership. The two remaining guides were useless; when he had shown them the body of their colleague, one reacted by weeping hysterically while the other, a lumbering and sullen man, clumsily tossed Kristoff's corpse across his shoulder and lurched away into the darkness like some Frankenstein monster with its victim.

Kaguri helped himself to the candles, taking only a few. Yamada and Morei would either succeed in a matter of hours, or have no use for light. He had no illusions of their chances of success. He had found the German climber, Struger, resting in the shelter of a fallen stalactite, on the rubble slope; the man was so deeply asleep Kaguri had difficulty waking him. Told of Yamada's and Morei's intentions, Struger had shaken his head pessimistically and warned of the dangers — the body of the guide had been swept into a siphon and he was certain no-one could survive the raging torrents hurtling beneath the rocks — but then he had shown Kaguri the entrance to tunnels at the lower end of the cavern. The German had not yet searched them himself but thought they ran deeper into the mountain, and certainly in the direction of the underground river.

Senta Kaguri returned to Yamada and Morei, gave them the candles and the waterproof containers, and told them of the route Struger had suggested they might try. They had bowed their goodbye as formally as if they were leaving the company of a priest, but Kaguri frowned as he watched them. He had seen the same keen expressions in men's eyes before; there had once been long lines of enthusiastic youths, bowing stiffly to their senior officers before racing, cheering their Emperor, to the cockpits of aircraft on the flightdeck of a Pacific carrier. The young men had gone, knowing they could never return. It had been Kaguri's reason for seeking a transfer to submarines; the teenage pilots came and went like the spirits of moths flitting between the tombstones of a graveyard, without form or identity.

The route Struger had suggested was blocked, the tunnel ending in rubble, two hundred yards from the main cavern. Yamada and Morei retraced their steps then followed the gorge that had originally been crossed by the collapsed Russian Bridge. For the two men, it was a horrific few minutes as they had scrambled over the debris of twisted steel girders, concrete and broken bodies. Blood stained water still seeped from the rubble, colouring the rocks so they looked like brown Cararra marble, and there was a sickening odour of decaying flesh in the damp air.

Further into the tunnels, they had paused to listen. In the distance they thought they heard the sound of water, but it was so faint it might have existed only in their imaginations.

The two men, Morei and Yamada, although not friends, had

known each other for some time. Morei was the elder, by a year. Both lived in the same suburb of Tokyo, and had attended Waseda University. Now they spoke only when necessary, and Yamada seemed content to allow Morei to lead.

For half an hour they had been following a twisted metal handrail that showed itself occasionally above the debris of the collapsed tunnel roof. It was hard, tiring work, scrambling over loose rock and shale with only the poor light of a candle to help them. They had reached a section so low that both had been forced to wriggle through on their stomachs, Morei with the candle held before him, and Yamada in darkness, following. When they were at last able to stand, the light had shown a large cavern, with the floor sloping away to the left. They had slid down the mud and found another section of tunnel at a lower level leading almost back the way they had come. It was high enough to allow them to walk upright, except where collapsed sections of wall reached nearly to the roof, and over which they were forced to clamber. Now the sound of water was unmistakable. They could feel movement in the air, and the temperature was lower.

They reached the underground tributary just as the first candle guttered and the wick fell sideways in the melted pool of wax. Morei replaced it from his container. It had been three hours since they left Kaguri in the main cavern.

The mouth of the tunnel opened onto a ledge, ten feet above the water of a narrow river, at most three meters wide. It was impossible to estimate its depth. The current would have been undetectable, had it not been for small patches of foam drifting past them at little more than two miles an hour — walking pace. To their left, upstream, was the sound of water thrashing against rock.

Yamada said: 'Waterfall.' He tried to see farther into the darkness. Below him, the water was black, and the river might have been bottomless. The froth drifted past, faded beyond the candlelight, and disappeared.

'We'll swim.' Morei moved along the ledge to a point where the rock sloped closer to the water's surface. 'It will be faster than trying to follow the river on foot.'

Yamada made no comment. He was nervous, even a little frightened, but he had no intention of revealing his apprehension to Morei. He bit the inside of his cheek, using the pain as an anaesthetic for his fear. He had volunteered to search with Morei, and once he had done so there could be no honourable way to withdraw the offer. He had spent the last hour convincing himself he was already dead. It had not been too difficult; there was nothing familiar in the caves and the tunnels, nothing to persuade his mind it was wrong. He was already dead, and now there was nothing more of any greater consequence that could happen to him. He had used the technique once before only a few days ago when he was in the airport lounge at Tokyo. It was his first aircraft flight, and although he greatly wished to visit Europe the thought of trusting himself to a huge piece of metal which hung in the sky was not appealing. He had spent the waiting time hypnotising himself into the belief he had died, then, when the aircraft had taken off, he had said to himself; 'I am dead, so if this thing crashes, it doesn't matter. It will just be a quick way of getting my spirit down to earth again.' He had felt much happier, and had been pleasantly surprised when the aircraft made its first landing at Singapore and he found he was still alive. He was dead again, now. He was twenty-years old, and a walking corpse. The thought was amusing him. It was strange, he remembered, when the earthquake had happened he hadn't even thought of death. He'd thought of fear, but not death. He hadn't even thought of death afterwards, only of the fact they were trapped and would somehow be rescued. It had taken two full days underground before he had begun to think perhaps rescue would not come from outside . . . and even then he hadn't thought of death, only escape. He had decided to die, now, in the tunnels as they led him deeper into the earth. It was a strange place for a draughtsman to die. He laughed, and the sound echoed crisply from the opposite wall of the ravine.

Morei looked at him quickly, then said: 'Keep near to the walls. Swim slowly.' He slid into the water. His anorak billowed as air was trapped in the folds of material. His shoulder bag floated. He held the candle in its bottle, carefully, above the surface. 'It's pleasant. Warmer than the air,' he commented.

Yamada followed him. The walls of rock seemed to tower above the hidden roof. He trod water, then followed Morei. The current led them gently along the tunnel. The sound of the waterfall behind them, diminished. There were only the hollow sounds of the soft splashing of their own movements, and the soporific lapping of the stream against the rocks of the tunnel wall. They drifted for several minutes, perhaps for two or three hundred yards, when Morei spoke again.

'The roof. It's lower.'

Yamada looked upwards. In the candlelight he could see the rocks, shining two yards above them. Morei swam on, and the roof seemed to press down as though some mechanical device lowered it until it was only inches from them.

Morei stopped and grabbed a handhold on one of the rock walls. The current swung him round, tugging at his legs. His head was only inches from Yamada.

'Well,' Morei asked. 'Do we go on, or back?'

Yamada was surprised. It was a question he hadn't expected. He had assumed he was to follow Morei. He looked into the man's eyes, but they were deliberately expressionless and gave him no help. 'I am happy to go on.'

'The rocks will touch the water in another few yards,' warned Morei. 'You can hear it sucking air down with it. It may open up again in a few yards, or it might be a pipe all the way through the remainder of the mountain.'

Yamada thought of the alternative. They could work their way back upstream. It wouldn't be easy. The current was just about equal to the speed they might swim. They would find handholds to help them but it would be exhausting and at the end, when they hauled themselves out of the water and back on to the ledge, they would have failed, and somewhere they would have to begin again. As a dead man, it was better to follow the river. Besides, why should Morei attempt to force the decision to retreat on him? 'We can try it. I can hold my breath for a little over two minutes. Perhaps longer. There may be pockets of air trapped near the roof.'

Morei nodded. His mouth was just above the water, and his hair was long enough to be trailing in the stream. He let go of the bottle and candle. It drifted away for a few yards, tilted and sank, leaving the men in darkness.

This is really death, thought Yamada. Soon I will be greeted by the spirit of my grandfather.

'Float on your back. Protect your face with your hands. When there are only a few inches of the air left, take deep breaths then turn, dive, and swim strongly. Don't get your clothing caught.'

'I'm ready.'

They splashed away from the rocks. Yamada stretched his hand above him and felt his fingers trailing the slippery roof of water-polished stone. The air gap lessened until his hands touched the water's surface and his face at the same time.

He heard Morei gasp, blow noisily like a water-polo player and then call. 'Now!' There was a deep echoing splash and Yamada knew he was alone. He took three deep breaths, and on the third swung himself over. The back of his head hit the rock. He swam downwards, feeling the air trapped in his clothing lifting him. He had the sensation he was about to swim headlong into the unseen rocks, and tried to keep his arms a little way in front of him. The roof of the tunnel dragged against his shoulders. Something struck him violently on the side of his head, and he almost gasped with the pain then realised it was one of Morei's feet. His lungs began to tighten. He heard a shout, the sound carrying through the water.

'Air . . . air. Yamada, where are you?'

Water swirled around his head. He lifted it cautiously and his face felt cold. He took deep breaths, gratefully. 'I'm here.' The water was splashed, nearby. A hand grabbed at his jacket and pulled at him.

'Take hold of the rock.'

Yamada reached sideways. His fingers slid along the smooth surface until he found a grip. He spat water from his mouth, and coughed his lungs dry. 'I can't feel the roof above my head,' he said.

'Nor I.' There was so much echo in the tunnel, it was difficult to understand the distorted speech. 'It sounds high.' There was more splashing as Morei moved downstream away from him. 'I am trying to find a way up the rock.'

Yamada let go his hold and swam across the stream. It was still only a few yards wide, but his feet could not reach the bottom. The darkness was so total, that for the first time he realised what it must feel like to be blind. The rock through which the stream moved was polished and slippery. He began to swim gently, with the current again, his arms outstretched in front of him. It was comforting, womblike.

'Where are you?' Morei's anxious voice was several yards behind him.

'Drifting,' he replied, softly. He remembered a line of a poem and wondered how it would sound with the strange accoustics and in such complete darkness. 'The night is an ocean, and rivers leading to it are the sorrows of men.' He had seen the words written in beautiful caligraphy on the painting of a moonlit fig tree.

There was frantic splashing as Morei caught up with him. 'You fool, Yamada. If we lose each other, we lessen our chances of sucess. Perhaps we should tie ourselves together.'

Yamada decided he didn't want to be tied to anyone at that moment. The water was still warm, and the darkness surprisingly comfortable. He lifted his hand and felt the cool rock above him once more. It began sloping towards the water's surface. He said: 'We must dive again, soon.' He leant his head back to make the most of the lowering roof. He heard Morei swear, then breath deeply. He waited until the rock touched his forehead, then filled his lungs.

The siphon narrowed and the current increased, twisting him sideways, forcing him against one of the tunnel walls, crashing him into an underwater boulder. He wanted to breath; so badly he even considered taking a lungful of water. Stars sparked in his head and a deep pain raced through his chest as though his lungs were about to explode. He shouted, silently and airlessly, in the black water. He tried to swim upwards but the harsh rock drove him down. There was a deep thudding in his ears, a gigantic pulse which seemed to throb throughout his whole body. He swam forward with the current, desperately, fiercely, willing his arms and legs to give him just a few seconds more strength and power. He broke the surface of the water with a great shout that reverberated from the walls of a cavern. He pressed downwards with his feet, and found rock beneath him. The action was so explosive he threw himself upwards and out of the water, to land gasping on some unseen beach. He lay, his face pressed into the sharp pieces of rock and the clean air cut into his lungs as though it were acid.

There was light, a few yards away. A match flared, like a haloed comet, dimmed and then flickered. Yamada moved his head and saw Morei, kneeling, a candle tilted towards the match flame. The wick caught, spluttered, and the light brightened. He pushed himself up from the rock beach onto an elbow.

'I thought I was about to die,' said Morei, and Yamada saw he was grinning.

'I, too.' He stood, stiffly, and stumbled on the jagged slabs of rock that had been recently displaced somewhere above them in the cavern roof. He staggered across to Morei. 'That was a long swim, underwater. Perhaps three minutes. Another ten seconds and I would have been finished.'

Morei lowered the candle near to the rocks, then looked quickly at Yamada. 'Are you bleeding?'

'No . . . at least, I don't think so.' Yamada had felt no wound. He examined himself. 'No. Why do you ask?'

Morei wiped his hand on a piece of limestone and then stared at it. 'There's blood on this rock. Look.' He slid a finger across his palm. There was a congealed, dark mass. He smelt it. 'It *is* blood.' He squatted and rinsed his hands in the stream then stood, holding the candle aloft. He picked his way over the rocks. He stooped quickly and picked something from the rubble. 'A flashlight. Only the guides have flashlights. This one is smashed.'

'Perhaps it belonged to one of the guides who was killed during the earthquake,' suggested Yamada.

The rock wall stretched above them into darkness. Morei moved the candle close to a fissure in the rock. 'No, there are marks here. Someone has climbed this rock. It must be the place where the guide was killed . . . the guide with the American and German. They said he fell, and was swept away in a river.'

Yamada felt sick. 'Then we have reached no-where. If we climb here, we will be back with the others.' The hours of dangerous work, the swimming of the terrible siphons, had been for nothing.

14

Lisetta had slept most of the way in the Fiat. Joe Catlin had hardly noticed; there were many questions he wanted answering, but following the dim light of the motorcycle ahead, over the rough roads, took all of his concentration. She awakened once they had left the rippled tarmac surface, and bounced along a rough track that seemed to be through a long tunnel in dense pine-woods. The Fiat's headlights were weak, and the lenses coated with dust. Eventually the motorcycle slowed almost to walking pace and turned off the track into a small clearing. Alessandro levered it onto its stand and walked back through the Fiat's head-lights to Catlin's door. He pointed towards a thick patch of bushes.

'Drive it in there, then leave it. We'll hide it for you.' He strode away, kick-started his motorcycle and rode it, standing on the footrests, deeper into the woods.

Catlin shrugged, put the Fiat in gear and edged it into the crack-ling bushes until branches squeaked against the grey paintwork. He switched off the motor.

'And now?'

'Alessandro take his motorbike up more, but we walk,' said Lisetta, brightly, 'Leave key, they will want it.'

Catlin wondered about "they", and the need to hide the Fiat, but before he could question the girl she had climbed from the car and was lifting his suitcase from the back seat. Catlin joined her. As his eyes adjusted to the darkness he could see the heads of the trees set against the edge of a rocky gorge. There was the sound of tumbling water below, mingling with the night calls of crickets in the thick undergrowth. A low moon hung just above the trees, warm-looking, reminding him of autumn evenings of childhood. The air was heavy with the scent of pine. He swung the suitcase on to his shoulder as Lisetta switched on the narrow beam of a flash-light.

She led him across the small clearing, towards the gorge. The sound of the water grew until it drowned the chirruping of the night insects. The light flickered on a narrow path that at times was only a yard away from the edge of the river, and which twisted through the woods on its rocky bank. There was no point in talking. The river tumbled noisily through narrow rock gorges, filling the air with sound and a damp warm mist. The ground was soft underfoot. After a quarter of an hour the path turned away from the river and led up an increasingly difficult slope until Catlin was forced to scramble over rocks up a steepening track following a bramble-filled cleft in the side of the gorge. The sound of the water below softened, until he could hear the girl's laboured breathing a couple of yards ahead of him. The ground began to level out and the stony path beneath their feet became a carpet of pine needles under a canopy of trees once again. The girl paused and Catlin was grateful for a rest. His thighs ached with the effort of the climb, and his lungs seemed to have been stretched until they hurt. Now he was glad of the coolness of the night air.

'This way.' He followed her through thickening undergrowth until, for twenty or thirty yards, it became necessary for him to force a path through scrubby young pine and thorn bushes that were tangled together. The girl shone the flashlight on a steep out-crop of lichen-coated rock. A thin crevice bit into its surface. She swept the light ahead of them. 'Here,' she said. 'This is house of Erasmus.'

Catlin eyed the opening doubtfully, but followed her. The cave entrance was narrow, barely wide enough for his shoulders unless he stooped. The girl's light showed a sandy floor, and the rocks at his sides were polished with the passage of countless men and animals. After several yards the cave widened and there were worn steps cut into the surface of the rock, hollowed at their centres by centuries of use. The steps dropped steeply downwards and then the passage opened suddenly into a wide cave, some forty feet in diameter. The girl stopped and shone her light on a kerosene lantern, set on a square slab of rock. The lantern was unlit, but its wick was smoking.

'Alessandro?' The girl called softly. 'Alessandro?' There was an echo to her voice.

A pebble was dislodged in the darkness as someone moved. A

cigarette lighter clicked a small flame and illuminated a youthful face. A hand carried the flame to the lantern and as its wick caught Catlin found himself facing half a dozen young men in its soft yellow light. He recognised the motorcyclist, Alessandro.

The man who had lit the kerosene lamp stepped forward and spoke to Lisetta in Slovene. She turned to Catlin and smiled an explanation. 'These are my friends. They hear us coming and think we are the soldiers.' She swung the flashlight beam around the cave walls. 'This is Erasmus's house . . . his cattle rooms . . . his water well . . . his strong fortress.'

'Which of your friends is Erasmus?' Catlin asked.

The girl laughed. 'Erasmus, he is dead, Joe. He die more than four hundred years ago.'

Catlin stared at the bleak cave. The floor sloped away into darkness. 'I'm not surprised.'

'He was robber baron.' Lisetta indicated the watching men. 'These my friends . . . students, mostly.'

'Do they all speak English?'

'Alessandro yes, and they can manage a little.'

'I'm pleased to meet you all. This is some hideout you've got.' He could make out the men's possessions piled on rock slabs that seemed to have been quarried from the sides of the cave . . . blanket rolls, rucksacks, packages and parcels stacked by the walls. He was feeling tired after the steep climb up the cliff and sat himself on a smooth shelf of rock on the sloping floor of the cave. It was dry and warm as the cave was set high from the wet valley floor a few hundred feet below.

Lisetta spoke to one of the men and then turned to Catlin. 'He will make coffee for you, Joe.' She sat beside him. 'This place is historic, Joe. It is a cave some of our partisans use in war — the Germans never find them. And down there . . .' She pointed into the darkness. 'Is a real castle. A castle made in the rock mountain. We are above it.'

'It is broken,' explained one of the young men. He squatted opposite Catlin, leaning back on his heels, a stocky, swarthy man who looked very Italian. 'The earthquake . . . it breaks the castle. Now you can reach this place only from above. This way you come inside.' He held his hand towards Catlin. 'I am Stane.'

Catlin took the hand and found the grip powerful and firm.

Alessandro was speaking quietly to Lisetta and Catlin noticed while he did so the others watched in an uncomfortable silence. Stane, the man who just introduced himself, squatted beside

Catlin. He saw Lisetta's face stiffen and then her shoulders seemed to sag. She looked away from Alessandro, quickly, dropping her head a little.

Stane whispered. 'It is bad news for her . . . her brother. He was guide in cave.' Catlin nodded, remembering how he had felt embarrassed when she had told him there were people alive below ground, and he had corrected her for assuming they would all be rescued. 'Her brother is killed looking for place to come out of cave. He falls sixty metres.'

Lisetta was standing, staring into the darkness. There were no tears. Catlin wished there was something he could say that would help, but he knew sometimes consolation was best given with silence. He wanted to gather her into his arms but he resisted the intimacy in front of the other men.

'They tell police today . . . last night . . . on cave telephone. Also another guide he die. Things get very bad in caves.' Stane turned and spoke with the others. They seemed more relaxed now Lisetta knew of her brother's death. Catlin realised it was still something they found hard to accept; death was always alien to youth. Stane faced Catlin again. 'You know what Alessandro has found in his father's office?' Catlin nodded. 'Bad . . . very bad,' growled Stane. 'Our Presidium has too many old men. All old friends; communist nepotism is national sickness. How can Yugoslavia make progress when old friend's loyalty prevent criticism.'

Lisetta shook herself as though she were awakening from a deep sleep. She turned and questioned Alessandro. 'What about the others? The ones who go to Ljubljana!' Catlin realised she was using English so he would be included in her conversations.

'How can we know? Simon and Mileta have been gone since eight o'clock last night! We can't expect them before this evening . . . perhaps later. They must use the long route and then they need to find transport for the equipment at Ljubljana. I give them also a list of other things they must find . . . batteries and lights, clothing, food. It will take them time to collect all together.'

'How many of you are there?' Catlin asked.

'Nine, with Lisetta. Two engineering students, and a motor mechanic . . . the rest of us study things which are not so practical, but we know Postojna area, and the caves, and we do anything you say. We have maps; not very good detail, but they will help you.'

The roof of the cave had lightened and Catlin realised that outside dawn was breaking; a fissure some twenty feet above them let the rays of the dawn sun enter the cavern. There was the pleasant smell of coffee in the air. In a corner of the rocks a few yards away, a gas stove hissed under a tin pot and Catlin saw one of the men pour steaming liquid into plastic cups. The man brought one over and Catlin took it gratefully.

Alessandro spread a survey map on the ground by his feet, and lit another candle beside it, sticking it to the rock with a puddle of hot wax. 'This is the mountain above the caves. I have been working yesterday, trying to find the exact position of the main cave. It is not possible to be totally accurate. The only maps we have of the caves are graphic, and they are not made to scale.'

'That isn't good.' Catlin examined the map, closely. 'If I don't drill exactly above the cave then we'll just go on down into solid rock. We have to hit the cave roof. A few yards to one side won't do.'

'We know,' agreed Alessandro. He knelt and prodded a slim finger at the map. 'Here, the ground has sunk. Here is crater, quite a few meters across; new crater. There are many old ones, where there has been subsidence in the past, but this one is new. It must be above an important cavern collapse, and we think it can be above the Briljant cave, near the railway terminal.' He pointed at the map again. 'Here, on this place, more towards the entrance, a lot of the ground has moved. Many trees have fallen. There is less surface damage to the rear of the system, towards the Crna and Pivka caverns.'

'What depth are the caves?' Catlin asked.

'They vary. The deepest may be two hundred and fifty meters below the highest point of the mountain; towards Pivka, about one hundred meters or a little less.'

'A hundred meters!' A man could run a hundred meters in just about ten seconds, thought Catlin. A hundred meters of rock was something different. For the people below the ground, a hundred meters of rock was a formidable tomb.

'But limestone,' added Alessandro, as though he read Catlin's mind. 'Not so hard, and much of it fractured.'

Catlin pursed his lips. 'That doesn't necessarily help. A cutter will go through limestone fairly quickly, but if the strata bends away or worse still if it lies almost vertical to the drilling with soft layers between, then it can swing the drill out of a true line and you're liable to get pipe fractures.'

'We can go to examine the place.'

Catlin looked at his watch. It was not yet five a.m., and he hadn't slept. 'You said your friends would be back with the equipment this evening. That gives us plenty of time. I need rest. Wake me at eight o'clock.' He finished his coffee, then stretched himself back on the sloping floor, pillowing his head on his suitcase. The ground felt surprisingly soft.

Mihunokada had been silent for several minutes and Yamada could see his shoulders quivering as the cold air struck through the man's wet clothing. Yamada's own teeth were chattering and he made no pretence about his discomfort. He swung his arms violently to keep the blood circulating in his arms. His fingers were already numb. 'If we stop here, we'll freeze to death.' He knew that was an exaggeration, but movement, any kind of movement, was preferable to sitting on wet rocks in cold and soaked clothing. The water had been warmer. 'You think we should climb here, and try to get back?' In deference to Mihunokada's obvious taste for leadership he avoided making a definite suggestion.

Mihunokada stood and pulled his wet anorak tighter around himself. His shoulder bag seeped a thin stream of water that splashed onto the rocks at his feet. 'If I were alone, I would go on.'

Yamada smiled to himself. Here was Mihunokada, Kendoka champion of the University, an arrogant man whom the other students had disliked rather than respected, avoiding a positive decision. It made Yamada feel much happier. He was not the son of a great martial arts teacher himself. His father was a shoemaker. Yamada, like most of the students, had played Judo but he had never felt the same sense of tradition the sons of the more aristocratic families seemed to find in their sports. Yamada played Judo simply because it was a way of proving himself against them. He had never been interested in the more martial types of training, the Aikido, Kendo, or Kyudo. Mihunokada's reply gave him confidence. He spoke lightly. 'I, personally, do not intend to return to the others.'

Yamada stared at him for a moment. 'Of course we should not return. There is no point.'

'Absolutely no point.'

'We should go on down the river.' He looked at the dark water as though he could see below its surface. Further downstream was the sound of water thrashing itself against rock; a cataract, or another siphon. Morei had trained as an athlete since he was seven years old. He was fit and muscular, and knew the depth of his stamina. He had fought many times in contests, and latterly had won most of them. But fighting a man, armed with a bamboo shinai, did not require the kind of courage he sought now. He had been astonished to find himself terrified during the first underwater swim along the siphon pipe. The second had been no better, and he had now placed himself in a position where more were inevitable. He had expected Yamada to insist they should return to the main cavern, now it was not possible to do so. Yamada was a surprising man. He had watched him fight in inter-university Judo tournaments, but had noted there was a point in his efforts beyond which he seldom pressed. He won occasionally but lost quite as frequently, as though winning was not the purpose of the contest. 'Are you ready to go on, then?'

'Quite ready,' answered Yamada.

Morei unscrewed the plastic jar, squeezed the life from the wick of the candle and replaced it in the container. He fastened it back in his shoulder bag and stepped into the river. It shelved deeply and he lost his footing, sliding down the rocks and dropping into the deeper water in midstream.

'Mihunsan?'

It was the familiar form of address, but Morei was in no position to object. 'I'm all right.' He swam slowly against the current until Yamada climbed in beside him. 'Let's go.'

The water, although warmer than the air, now seemed colder to Yamada, and his wet clothing was dragging him deeper. He thought about trying to remove his anorak, but decided the action would be too dangerous. The sound of rushing water was closer now and the current gripped him. He heard Morei shout wildly, and then the water swept him sideways, crashing him against a rock ledge. He took a breath and cradled his head in his arms. His leg hit another boulder and then he was tumbling over and over, rolling between rocks, being bounced by the swirling torrent from one boulder to another. Suddenly he was falling, somersaulting. He managed a desperate breath, choked on half a lungful of water, and was then pounded into the depths of the underground whirlpool. He struggled wildly, kicking upwards with all his strength. He hit the roof of a tunnel and the rock grazed his face. There was no air, only the swirling water and the rocks smashing him deeper. The water roared in his ears, like the terrible sound of the earthquake. There was air again. He knew it was air because as he thrashed his arms there was no resistance, but he could not draw it into his lungs. The wet cloth of the anorak was wrapped around his head. He dragged it away from his face and his first breath rasped in his throat. He retched a stomachful of water. It took him a full minute to recover sufficiently to swim weakly towards the side. His hand touched a series of small, sharp-edged rocks. He found a hold and half-dragged himself from the water. He spat phlegm and bile from his mouth, his chest supported on a narrow ledge.

He called: 'Mihunsan?' There was a groan several yards away, barely audible above the sound of the water. 'Mihunsan?'

'Yes.' There was no strength in the voice.

Yamada moved himself along, traversing carefully and keeping a firm hold of one rock until he was certain of his grip on another. After a few yards he felt the bottom beneath his feet. The broken rocks sloped upwards, but the current seemed to run through them. He found Morei's leg beneath his hand, and the contact startled him.

'My shoulder bag is missing.' Morei's voice was strained.

Yamada dragged himself from the water and searched for his own bag. It was still around his shoulders. He unfastened it, and took a candle from the container. His hands were still so wet he was afraid to try to light the matches. He shook water from them, found a small crevice in the rock where he could wedge the candle, and then tried to strike one of the matches on a rock. The damp limestone provided no friction and the match failed to light. He took a second, opened his mouth and scraped the waxed phosphorous against the sharp edge of his front teeth. The match flared. He sheltered the flame then lit the candle. Morei lay next to him, his head back on the rocks. He held his chest with both arms.

'I broke some ribs.' The muscles of Morei's cheeks and jaw were rigid with agony, but he forced himself to sit upright. Yamada could hear the sharp squeak of the man's teeth as he gritted his jaw. 'The pain will go soon.'

Yamada pulled aside Morei's anorak. He did not resist. He saw the man's shirt had been ripped, and he eased it from the waistband. There was a long dark bruise across the chest, running from the centre of the breastbone to the armpit. He traced his fingertips carefully over the ribs. He could feel the fractures on two of the bones, but they were not much out of line and it was unlikely they would have damaged a lung. He said: 'I think you have two broken.'

Morei said: 'Shit.' He arched his back, and was unable to conceal a wince as the pain of the movement caught him. He rubbed his hand across his chest.

Yamada lifted the candle and held it above his head. The stream seemed to run beneath the rocks on which the men sat. They were like some huge sieve, and were obviously part of another roof fall. They might have briefly dammed the stream, but it had soon swept away the smaller debris and found itself a path through the obstruction. Time would wear the boulders smooth and gradually the stream would remove them all. The two men were in a wide cavern, with the pile of fallen rock stretching across its width like an uncertain bridge. Yamada could see Morei's shoulderbag a few yards away near the centre, wedged between the boulders.

'I see your bag, Mihunsan.' He stumbled across the rocks towards it. Something pale moved in the darkness and Yamada stopped. He held the candle high again, and took another cautious step. There was movement. He was uncertain what to expect. Something slithered over the top of a flat rock, inches from the water. Some kind of reptile which Yamada had never seen before; a pale, crawling thing. He moved towards it slowly. It rose, like the head of a cobra . . . pronged at its extremity. Yamada's mind recognised it with astonishment. 'A man,' he shouted. 'Mihunsan, there is a man, here. Alive.'

'It is the guide.' Morei knelt beside the man and touched his face. 'He seems dead. His skin is cold.' He shuddered, he had not yet become used to corpses, and this one felt like a dead fish.

'I saw his arm move.' Yamada put his fingers against Serge Irano's neck. 'And I can feel a pulse.'

Irano's body lay half in the water, which swirled around his waist. His head and shoulders were resting on the rocks. His left arm was twisted grotesquely behind his back, and his face seemed to have been squashed sideways. Blood stained his neck and chest.

'Hold the candle closer,' insisted Yamada. He pulled open his anorak and ripped a piece of cloth from his shirt. He wiped Irano's face carefully, then opened his swollen lips; the front teeth were jagged. 'He has a broken jaw . . . nose too, probably, and perhaps a cheekbone.'

Morei stared at the twisted arm. 'He has more wounds. With these sort of facial injuries, it's likely he has a fractured skull as well.'

Yamada eased a fragment of broken tooth from Irano's lower lip, and dabbed with the cloth. Irano's eyelids fluttered, but remained closed. Yamada slid his hand behind the man's neck and felt for broken bones. To his relief the spine felt intact at that point. He continued to examine him, stripping the torn clothing from Irano's battered body. The man's arm was broken in several places, with splinters of bone puncturing the flesh at the shoulder.

'He is certainly dying.' Morei rubbed his hand against his own broken ribs.

'We are *all* dying.' Yamada moved Irano's arm, cautiously. He folded it across the man's chest.

'You have a negative attitude to everything.' complained Morei.

'Negative?' For the first time Yamada reacted angrily. 'You think it is negative to acknowledge our death?'

'It's negative when we have been sent to find a way out for our friends.'

'Sent to find a way out? Morei, you're foolish! Don't you realise *why* we were sent away? Don't you know what Kagurisan was thinking?'

'He was thinking that the strongest should find a way for the weak; that is why he sent us.'

Yamada shook his head, his hair sending a spray of water through the candle flame. 'You and your Samurai bushido, your tradition of bravery and strength. It is a tradition of conceit! You are so superior you cannot even reason like normal men. Kagurisan sent us because the fact their own countrymen are seeking a way out for them is enough to raise the spirits of our people . . . and because you and I were making the others more aware of the horror and their own future death. By sending us, he was exiling us; dismissing us.'

'That's not reason, that's nonsense!'

'Kagurisan knows there is unlikely to be a way out. This man here . . .' he jerked his head towards Irano. 'He knows the caves better than anyone. He was looking in the most likely places.'

'Kaguri understood that, and that is why he suggested we try along the river.'

'For what purpose, Morei? Is your Sensei Kaguri also so foolish he believes the women and children will be able to swim underwater as we have done? Is he also stupid enough to think that even if we find a way we will be strong enough to swim back *against* the current to show the others the route they should follow?'

Morei thought for a while before he spoke again. 'So Kaguri gave just the two of us a chance to live, even though all the others may die.'

'Yes, perhaps. But he was well aware we, too, are more likely to die than live.' Yamada pulled off his shoulderbag, and then his anorak. He stripped the remains of his shirt from his chest.

'What are you doing?'

'Tying this one's arm to his body, and then I'll try to bandage his jaw.'

'You're wasting your time. It would be kinder to kill him with a rock.'

Yamada swung round quickly and faced Morei. 'What do you think you are Mihunsan? D'you think you're a God, to decide whether a man shall live or die? You think this is still your Samurai civilisation where you can claim the right to a peasant's life? You and your kind make me sick. You study your ancient martial arts, and talk of Budo and chivalry, and you conveniently forget your much respected Samurai was little more than a mercenary who would change sides in the middle of a battle if it suited him. Wake up, Morei, and join the twentieth century.'

Morei was startled at the outburst, his face set, and he stooped, picked up his bag and began to walk away into the darkness beyond the rocks. Yamada watched him, then leant forward and began to wind a strip of the torn shirt around Irano's arm. A rock moved and grated and he looked up quickly, half expecting to see Morei standing above him with a boulder poised in his hands. Instead, the man faced him a few feet away then squatted. He looked shame-faced and said: 'We will wait with him. It should not be long.'

Yamada knotted the cloth, tightly. 'No, we will take him with us.'

'With us? You're crazy!'

'Maybe. But I told you earlier, I have already decided I am dead. And as a dead man, I am not too concerned about the future. The Yugoslavian is not dead, but he is unable to choose for himself. I speak for him. He is going to take his chances with me.'

It had been the month of the festival for the water spirits, the time when the villagers, whose rice fields bordered the streams and rivers, made offerings of straw fish to the spirits who controlled their harvests and therefore their lives. Kaguri knew it was in the month of the water festival because the story was his family history, passed carefully and accurately down through generation to generation. It was the story of a brave and honourable ancestor, and throughout Kaguri's life, when there had been need for courage and determination, he had retold himself the tale. He did so now, in the darkness of the cave.

It had taken place in the time of Hideyoshi, four hundred years ago; in a time when all farmers had been disarmed and when there was no intermingling between the classes in Japanese society. It had been in the period of the two wars againt Korea. Kaguri's ancestor had been a great warrior, a student of war, but a man of great patience. The invading armies of Hideyoshi had been repulsed with terrible losses by the Korean defenders, and the survivors of the huge armies, each of more than a hundred thousand men, had been forced to retreat in their boats. A few Samurai had chosen to remain rather than suffer the dishonour. Kaguri's ancestor had been one of them.

In the sandy bay of Kuishu was a pinnacle of rock, eighteen metres in height, its base polished smooth by a million years of the action of the sea, but its small peak sharp and jagged; difficult to climb. Five of the Samurai fought their way back to the base of the rock, the sea around them pink with their own blood and that of the enemies who fought against them. On the polished rock ledges they stood together and faced the entire enemy army. They could have been killed by the archers, but that would have implied cowardice by the Korean commanders themselves. The fighting was knight against knight, sword against sword or naginata. One by one the Samurai died. At last there remained only Kaguri's ancestor. In the waves before him washed the bodies of twenty nine of his enemies. He was forced higher up the narrow pinnacle of rock, until he stood alone on its peak. At first, some of the Korean warriors attempted to reach him, but he cut them down. They still did not use their bowmen. They built their camp-fires on the sandy beach, and waited.

Kaguri's ancestor, although wounded, did not bleed to death. He knelt on the pinnacle of rock, his sword ready, his eyes continuously open, and his face towards his enemies.

He remained unmoving for many days. The Koreans continued

to wait. They held feasts on the sand near the water's edge, taunting the thirsty Samurai by draining their wine flasks into the sea or throwing food to their dogs. Kaguri's ancestor remained so still and impassive they wondered if perhaps he was already dead. They sent a young warrior to climb the rock. He fell from the summit with his head, right shoulder and arm, severed from his body by the power of a single blow from the Samurai's sword.

On the eighteenth day following the battle, it rained. The Koreans, now joined by peasants from the surrounding countryside who had learnt of the Samurai's fate, numbered many thousand. The Samurai's face and lips were swollen by thirst, his skin, burnt black by the sun, peeled from his cheeks below his helmet. He made no attempt to suck the rain water from his clothing, or drink from the small pools which formed in the crevices of the rock. After a few hours the rain stopped; the Samurai remained motionless.

Three more of the Koreans tried to reach him. He killed them all.

On the twenty first day, the Korean commander offered him an honourable position in his own service should he surrender. The Samurai did not reply.

When the twenty seventh day dawned, the beach was deserted. The Koreans had returned to their towns and fortresses. Below, tied to the base of the rock, they had left a small boat, its sails furled but ready for use; it was provisioned with water and food. In it, Kaguri's ancestor had returned to his homeland.

There were other such men, in the history of Kaguri's family. He knelt and let his mind consider their deeds, and for a while the cavern which held him ceased to exist.

15

The ground where Joe Catlin was standing was unnaturally spongy. It felt unsafe, as though a thin crust of earth hid a quagmire beneath. The plateau, a little below the highest point of the mountain, was scrubland, with open areas of coarse grass and bracken burnt crisp by the sun and interspersed by patches of low scrub and short-bodied, tilted, pine saplings. Outcrops of brown and grey limestone pushed upwards through the undergrowth, or stood like jumbled masonry amidst the dusty green of the stunted trees.

Ahead of him the ground was hollowed into a wide basin over an area of several acres. Fresh, jagged scars showed on the surface where the earth had moved, sunk or risen. Wide fissures and cracks zig-zagged in all directions. Trees teetered, fighting for a hold in the thin layer of soil above the tormented rock, like motionless survivors on a silent battlefield. It was possible to see the main path of the earth movement by the broad path of crumpled ground and the sagging pines. It was impossible to walk across the area in a straight line; some of the million cracks were only a foot wide and a few inches in depth, but others were wider than a man could jump, and reached deep into the rock beneath.

'And the caves are somewhere under here?' Catlin stared into a crevasse large enough to swallow a truck. The sun was noon high, its heat beating down from a cloudless sky. The air was still, and he was sweating. He wiped perspiration from his neck and chest with a handkerchief. It had been a five kilometer uphill scramble through the pinewoods to the mountain plateau, and walking had never been Catlin's favourite pastime. His canvas leisure shoes were beginning to look like those of a hobo; his feet were blistered. Lisetta, and the men, all wore strong boots.

Lisetta passed him a canteen of water. He opened it and felt the warm water swill the dust from his throat. The liquid tasted of aluminium. He rinsed his mouth and spat into the dust before handing back the container.

'Somewhere below us now.' Alessandro pulled the map from his pocket and opened it. 'The highest point of the plateau is there.' He pointed to Catlin's right. 'And ahead, in line with those fallen trees, is the entrance to the caverns. You see, they swing left at that point and then straighten for about one and a half kilometers. The main caverns must be somewhere under this area.'

'And this sunken ground is all new?'

Lisetta answered him. 'Yes, all new. Before the earthquake comes, it flat here. The highest ground was the ridge, the one above the cavern entrance.' She turned and looked behind them. 'That other ridge small, more small than it is now. Behind it, the ground goes down towards Planina town.'

'There are five sections of caves, below this mountain.' Alessandro said. 'Postojnska Jama, Otoska Jama, Megdelena Jama, Crno Jama, and the Pivka Jama. This area is right in the centre of the systems. The Pivka river runs through underground, away over there to the right. There are one or two streams below us, tributaries of the Pivka, but they are very small.'

'And the cave systems are joined?'

'They were,' answered Lisetta. 'But I think not now.'

'To be accurate, not all links had been confirmed, but they were believed to be joined.' Alessandro pointed at the map again. 'There was an underground river link between Megdelena Jama and the Crno and Pivka Jama's. It has never been explored.'

'This place . . .' Catlin swung his arm in front of him. 'Have you searched it for new entrances?'

'Yes. Mileta and Simon, the men who have gone to Ljubljana, and these two, Branko and Stane; they have been searching.' He spoke again in Slovene and one of the two men answered him, at considerable length. Alessandro turned back to Catlin. 'He says there are many new entrances. They have been searching them until yesterday. Most of them end after a few metres. Some of them are promising, but the openings inside them need to be widened. It will take a little time for them to get deeper.'

'It's going to be hit and miss trying to drill into the main cavern.'

Lisetta spoke. 'But for you this is possible, Joe.' It was a statement; Catlin recognised her total belief in his capabilities. It warmed him, but made the thoughts of defeat even less acceptable.

'Yes, it's possible. Anything is possible, with the right equipment.' It would be easy, Catlin thought, if this were the USA. By now there would be thirty drilling rigs set up in the area. One of them would hit the right spot. But here, with no experienced drilling operatives and God knows what kind of equipment, he wasn't feeling very optimistic.

'How much time it take?' She sounded like a small girl on a hated Sunday School outing, wondering how long before the parents would take them home.

Catlin stooped and picked up a piece of the limestone. He stared at it closely, then weighed it in his hand before tossing it away. 'It's a very porous rock. Much of it will be broken up below ground; there's a fair amount of rubble and chippings and a few feet down it will probably be very wet. With a good drill it could go thirty to forty feet a day. Possibly a little more, providing we don't get breakages.'

'Thirty to forty feet a day! Not much more than ten meters!' Alessandro sounded disappointed. 'It could take six or seven days. And if it is the wrong place, then another seven days . . . and seven days more. Maybe the idea is no good.'

Lisetta translated to the others and they looked grim-faced.

'Who would have the most accurate map of the cave system?' Catlin asked.

There was a brief discussion between Lisetta and Alessandro. 'The Cave Commission, or the Slovene Speleologist's Society. But the Speleologist's Society is in Ljubljana, and we can't contact Simon or Mileta until they return later today,' the girl said.

'Then what about this Cave Commission?'

'They had an office here, but . . .'

'But nothing,' said Catlin. 'If you want this idea to work we have to get good maps. Do you know anyone there who might cooperate?'

'The main local office of the Cave Commission was destroyed in the terminal building. I doubt if anything was salvaged.'

'A good map is vital,' Catlin explained. 'These friends of yours, the ones who have gone to Ljubljana. They're trying to get hold of the University rig, right? Well, it isn't going to be the kind of rig that drills deep holes, fast. It'll be a light rig, the kind your geological department uses for its teaching programmes. In some respects, that's good. It means it will be very portable, and light;

but it will probably have a low drilling rate. Alessandro is correct, it'll take time and we can't afford to make a mistake by drilling in the wrong place. A few hours spent now in getting the right information, may save us a week later on. We have to remember the poor devils have been down there four days already.'

'There is a possibility,' said Alessandro. He looked thoughtful. 'I think it is certain there will be a map of the cave system in the police offices, at the cave entrance. The wooden offices in the grounds; they were only a little damaged, and they still use them.'

'The officer in charge is Inspector Zlobec. He not co-operate.' There was disappointment in Lisetta's dark eyes.

Alessandro turned and spoke to the other men. One of them shrugged, looked doubtful, then spoke. One of the others said a few words. There were several minutes of discussion before Lisetta's face brightened and she turned quickly to face Catlin.

'They say they get map from police office. They steal it.' The idea seemed to amuse her.

'When?' Catlin asked.

'Tonight,' said Alessandro. 'There is only one officer on duty, during the night. You've seen them yourself, they spend most of the time in the tent where they provide food. Inspector Zlobec only returns to the site once each evening. He comes at about ten o'clock.'

'What you want to do, Joe? Is there more you want to see up here?' Lisetta had moved closer to him.

Catlin shook his head. 'There's nothing I can do without the equipment and the map. That river we crossed, below the cave, does it have somewhere I can swim?' Catlin's shirt was sticking to his back and the thought of cool water was inviting.

'I show you.' Lisetta spoke to the men, and then again to Catlin. 'They will stay here. They search the new openings, and meet us later.'

The sun was below the top of the limestone ridge, and the woods were shaded. Near the river, Catlin and Lisetta had walked through a campsite; it had been full to capacity with holiday-makers on the day of the earthquake. Now it was deserted, its concrete roads cracked and twisted. A wrecked caravan, burnt and blackened, lay on its side crushed by a fallen pine tree. A swimming pool, its tiled sides shattered and its floor buckled and fractured had spilled its contents into the earth. A wooden bar and restaurant had collapsed on their surround. Across the valley were the remains of a whitewashed church, its r antiles hanging from the twisted roof and its bell tower tilted a crazy angle. Beyond was a rising slope of olive trees . . . indest

Half a mile upstream from the campsite the river w ide. the current slackened at a deep pool. Stony beache where it flowed at the winter level. A jay, rust-chested and winged, screeched noisily ahead of them as they followed through the pine trees.

The water was clear, and Catlin could see trout, almost motionless in the shallows at the pool edges. A kingfisher, a flash of electric blue, scraped the water's surface.

Catlin stripped off his shirt and hung it over a branch. The girl perched herself on a rock, nearby. She wasn't watching him but he was aware of a slight layer of fat over his muscles, and a squareness above his hips that had not been there a few years before. Working in the sun, stripped to the waist for the past few days, had added colour to his skin.

He unzipped his pants and stepped out of them. He thought about swimming in his shorts, then changed his mind, slipped them off and waded naked into the water. It was cool after the heat of the sun up on the plateau, but not too cold to enjoy. He leant forward and let the water take his weight, swimming slowly against the current. He rolled on his back and drifted, then swam again. He ducked his head and scrubbed his hair with his hands, then swam back to the bank. The air was warm and pleasant and he stood letting the water drain from him. He sat on the short grass of the bank above the stones and boulders. The girl's voice disturbed the vagueness of his thoughts. She sat down next to him.

'What is this . . .' He felt her fingers touch him lightly on his right shoulder and was suddenly conscious of the deep scars on that side of his body. He had worn them for so long he seldom remembered them.

'Burns.'

The girl's fingers moved. 'Terrible burns. What made them?'

'Oil fire,' Catlin explained briefly. He didn't enjoy discussing his injuries. 'A mistake I made, once.' He let himself drop onto his elbow so his movement took the scarred side of his body away from her. She moved closer and her hand traced the curve of the muscles across his back.

'You are very hairy man,' Lisetta commented. Catlin smiled, enjoying the light touch of her hands exploring his body.

a long line of baboons.'

ghed, then found another scar with her fingertips. is this one?'

co, sixty six.'

laughed again. 'And this?'

Alaska seventy five.'

She had moved around so she faced him again, leaning across his body. He lay back so she was resting on his chest. Her dark eyes examined his face.

'You look like fighter.'

Catlin grunted: 'Huh!'

'You are like me, Joe. You want always to fight things; your oil well fires, rocks, mountains. I watch you at Postojna, there you fight concrete and steel. You think to be best, you must always fight.'

'I don't fight anything, I just do a job.' Catlin could feel the roundness of the girl's breasts against his chest, her body warmer than his own. It was impossible to ignore. He pushed her black hair away from the side of her face; her skin was smooth, flawless, tanned dark olive where her slim neck met the curve of her shoulders. 'You make me sound like a monster with an obsession.'

'Obsession? I don't know what is that word. But monster, I don't think so.' She moved her head in his hand as an animal might when welcoming a caress, then leant closer to him. He felt her lips touch his neck. She wriggled gently, and her breasts were naked against him. There was very little weight to her body as she lay over him.

'But I think that maybe you are fighting me now, Joe.'

He rolled sideways, turning her onto her back, and supporting her in the crook of his arm. Her T-shirt was pulled above her breasts, they were as tanned as her shoulders. 'I've just stopped fighting,' he said. He slid his hand gently across the soft curve of flesh, barely touching the surface, feeling the hardness of her nipples. He lowered his head and kissed the hollow between her neck and collar-bone. Her body was young, firm, her stomach flattening between her hips. She stretched, peeling the shirt over her head, watching him with her dark eyes. He flicked the button of her waistband loose and let the zip run down. She arched her back as Catlin pushed the material of her jeans lower. She kicked her legs free, spreading them wide, her knees slightly raised as though her body was instantly hungry for him. He let his fingers enjoy the soft skin behind her knees and thighs until they found the moistness of her body. He sucked gently at a breast, his lips matching the rhythm of his hand. She gasped, and then held his penis so tightly that a moment of pain led the caress. She twisted in his arms, bringing her body across him. Her lips were around him, her tongue seeking and finding sensitive nerves. There was an urgent violence between them, now. He lifted her, bringing her mouth to his own, pressing her gently against him. Her strong thighs held him and she guided him into her body.

Afterwards, they lay back on the warm grass, the girl's head cradled between his chest and arm. They had not spoken for a long time and Catlin listened to the sounds mingling, the water in the river as it slipped across pebbles, the hum and chatter of insects in the warmth of the late afternoon. The urgency and strong need for sex was something Catlin thought he had left behind; it still interested him, but was something he easily buried in his work. But today had been almost a rebirth. He wondered if it was the girl's youth, a fire which her lack of years and her fresh young body gave to him.

She moved her head, then spoke. Her voice was as warm as the air drifting across their bodies. 'Why?'

'Why what?'

'I just think why I want you so much; with the sadness and the death . . . and those peoples, trapped in the mountain.'

'Death has nothing to do with making love.' Catlin was uncertain what the girl would like him to say. 'I've heard a fox dying of starvation will take more notice of a vixen on heat, than the food he needs. It's a physiological thing.'

'You make woman sound like machine made only to produce.' He could feel her stiffen slightly in his arms, and realised he should have been less direct.

'Biologically, they are,' he said, then added as an apology. 'But that isn't an insult. It doesn't degrade a woman.'

'It's a man thinking.'

'No, it's fact. Chauvinism is either sex denying the other his or her equal rights within a society.'

'And what, are men?' Catlin didn't answer her. 'I suppose you say man is for hunt.'

'No . . . the hunting bit is only man's means to an end . . . the reproduction bit . . . his side of things. He needs to collect mates, and the best way is to be able to provide for as many as possible. A good hunter could feed a lot; he probably had the pick of the girls in the community. To be a successful hunter he would need to be strong, cunning and skilful. He'd gain a reputation, and respect . . . and as a result, he would fertilise a maximum number of prime females.'

'And if he not hunt to catch his "prime" women, then he fight oil wells.' Lisetta sounded peeved. 'That make him attractive for women.'

'I'm not attractive, I was attracted.'

Her voice was soft again. 'That much nicer, Joe, but you may be very wrong.' She pressed her lips against his neck.

Apart from the serious injuries to Serge Irano's face and to his shoulder, Yamada could find no others. There was a slight trace of blood from one of the man's ears, and although Yamada knew little about medicine he agreed with Mihunokada that it might indicate a skull fracture. Had he found a man with such wounds, in a Tokyo street, he would have simply called an ambulance and let the attendants decide how he should be moved. Now it was different. The guide was probably going to die, as were Mihunokada and himself, so taking him with them would make little difference. If it was very bad for the man to be moved, then he would simply die a little sooner. He would certainly die if he were left behind, and taking him with them only gave him perhaps a thousandth of one chance in a million.

'Well?' Mihunokada looked at Yamada, questioningly.

'We carry him across the rocks to the water, and then we float him on his back . . . with us.'

'You're mad. He's dying now. The river will kill him more quickly. And he will drown the first time we try to swim a tunnel.'

'Perhaps.' Yamada knew Mihunokada was probably right. He could think of no way to get the guide safely through one of the siphons. The cave in which they were now resting dripped water continuously, like heavy rain, from its roof where many thousands of minute stalactites, none thicker than Yamada's little finger hung downwards. The water drops were cold; far colder than the stream which was warmed outside the mountain by the sun, and lost little of its heat on its way through. He shivered almost uncontrollably. 'We'll die too, if we stop here. Get hold of his feet and help me.' He thought at first Mihunokada would refuse, but after a moment's hesitation, the man stooped and took hold of Irano's legs. They carried him over the sloping pile of debris, until they reached a smooth limestone slab beside the stream. Yamada returned for the candle. He checked the waterproof plastic jar in his shoulderbag, but kept the one candle alight. He passed it to Mihunokada. 'I will pull the man. You try to keep the candle lit for as long as possible. When we reach a siphon we'll decide what to do.'

They eased the unconscious guide into the water. It was shallower than the former sections of stream and they were able to walk along with the man's weight supported between them. The sounds of their stumbling progress was magnified by the polished rocks. They managed almost half a mile before the tunnel roof dropped to within inches of the level of the water. The candle was now an inch-long stub in Mihunokada's hand. The low walls of the tunnel were vertical, and although their fingers and toes were now numbed and wrinkled white, they could find no ledges or shelves on which to rest. Irano was still alive, breathing with strange slobbering gasps. The congealed blood had washed from his skin, and his distorted face seemed to be carved from ancient ivory, stained yellow and blue by some primitive artist.

Yamada held Irano's head carefully between his hands, and began swimming slowly on his back. The current speed increased and he wondered if he would suddenly be hurled against some unseen rock which would smash him, too, into unconsciousness. Mihunokada swam beside them. The space between the water's surface and the roof of the tunnel was now less than the width of a man's hand, and no matter how hard he tried, it was impossible for Yamada to prevent the guide's face scraping the rocks where they dipped even closer to the water's surface. Mihunokada was blowing noisily, like a porpoise, as he swam; ahead was the growing sound of water tumbling and crashing over rocks. Yamada was tempted to let go of the injured man to protect himself, but the thought made him tighten his grip on Irano's head and kick more strongly, forcing himself along with the current as though to let the river know it gave him no fear.

The side walls pressed suddenly close, curling the water back on itself in two deep rolling waves, like the wake from the hull of a steamer. Mihunokada shouted, but his words were lost. The current swept the men along, crazily, turning and twisting them, tossing them together. The sound grew to a roar. The candle was extinguished and the darkness was all noise and power. Yamada heard himself screaming. The body of the guide was torn from his hands. Then the noise diminished quickly and the current became gentle.

Yamada shouted, wildly and desperately. 'Mihunsan . . . Mihunsan,' A hand grabbed at his clothing and he found himself close to the other man, their faces touching briefly in the diminishing waves. 'The guide; I lost him.'

'He's here. I'm holding him,' gasped Mihunokada. 'By his hair.'

The current was carrying them slowly again, and Yamada kicked his feet, but felt no bottom. 'Is he alive?'

'How should I know. He's with us . . that's what you want isn't it? Does it matter now if he is alive or not?'

Yamada began swimming across the current. The stream had only been a few yards wide at its widest. Now it seemed a great distance until he reached the rocks at the side. He called again to Mihunokada. 'Swim sideways . . . we must try to find a landing.' He heard Mihunokada's legs thrash the water, and spluttering as the man breathed heavily with the effort. They drifted another hundred yards before Yamada found a break in the rock wall that gave him a firm handhold. Mihunokada joined him in the darkness. Ahead there was a deep throated and ominous rumble as though the mountain roared its anger at the insolence of two such puny assailants.

Yamada scrambled at the rock, his feet finding a grip. His arms seemed too weak to support him, but at last he managed to pull himself from the water. He reached down and grabbed Irano's clothing, but wondered if he would have the strength to hold him. He stretched his legs behind him for balance. Mihunokada grunted with effort, as he tried several times to push Irano up onto the rock beside Yamada. At last he wedged himself between two pieces of rock and lifted Irano bodily with a great shout of determination as though he were attacking an adversary in a contest. A moment later, he slithered up beside Yamada like a wet seal. For several minutes the men lay, silent. Yamada, his face against the cold surface of the rock, could hear his own heart pounding; his lungs seemed as congested as if he had bronchitis. He spat his mouth clean, then fumbled with his shoulder bag. His fingers were so numb he could not feel the clasp and was forced to tear it from the material. With difficulty, he unscrewed the cap of the plastic bottle, and managed to shake out a candle. He struck one of the few remaining matches on his teeth, and sighed with relief as it caught at the first attempt.

A wide grotto stretched into darkness behind them. Above, the roof was high enough to be beyond the pale light of the candle. A series of vast stalactites were columns between roof and cavern floor, their round sides fluted and delicate in the yellow glow; a forest of dwarf stalagmites grew upwards from the rock. Demons, dragons, strange beings, moved to life with the candle flame. Everywhere the water dripped, splashing, running. And beneath the men's bodies the ground vibrated to the deep roar of the torrent somewhere ahead of them.

'Your ribs?' Yamada questioned Mihunokada.

'I'm not enjoying them,' admitted the man, wrily. He took the candle from Yamada's hand and held it near the guide's marbled face. The flame moved with the man's shallow breathing and Mihunokada shook his head disbelievingly. 'This man is very determined to live.' He pressed his palm, flat, on Irano's chest. 'His heart beats slowly, but it still beats. I would not have thought it possible.'

Yamada looked at the strange shapes of the limestone formations around them. Perhaps they were hearing human voices for the first time in the countless centuries the grotto had been in existence. The thought gripped at the tired muscles of his stomach and seemed to speed his pulse, but was lost instantly with the realisation he was there by neither choice or design. 'Perhaps it will be possible for us to find a way out from here, without having to swim.' He shook water from the folds of his anorak, but it was immediately replaced by the water dripping from the roof. His hair was plastered down his face and drops of water ran from his nose. It was like standing in a thunderstorm, he thought, only the rain which fell in storms was much warmer than the rain of the caverns. He wondered what it would be like to lie in warm sunlight again, and to feel dry ground beneath his dry body. Heat was what he needed . . . heat and warm food; a bowl of fish soup, and then thin slices of beef, grilled above the embers of a glowing Hibachi.

He lit a second candle, and then the stub of the third. No more remained in the plastic container, but the additional yellow light seemed to offer a little warmth even if it was only imaginary.

'I shall go and look,' he told Mihunokada. The man nodded, glad of the opportunity to rest his punished ribs, and to examine his injury more closely when he was alone. The pain in his chest was sharp with every breath, and there had been times when he was swimming when he could feel the ends of the rib bones grating against each other.

The continuous rain within the grotto threatened to extinguish the candle Yamada was carrying. He protected it with the plastic container and held it in front of him like a lantern. The floor of the grotto was smooth, running with water, and ice-cold. Yamada realised with surprise he had lost his shoes and was barefooted. He rubbed his toes over the surface of a stalagmite that was nothing more than a slight dome on the ground. It was a jellyfish on a wet beach, slippery beneath his unprotected feet. He shuddered and was angry with himself for allowing his mind to play when it should be keen and positive. Perhaps it was the eternal cold, the cold that could destroy a man by numbing his brain while making him think he was enjoying the last few pleasant moments of thought before deep and satisfying sleep. He shook his head violently, put the candle on a short stump of limestone and exercised briskly for several minutes, forcing his body to find the energy to jump and leap. He sang, loudly and untunefully, and felt better.

He walked away from the sound of the river, but the misty glow of the candles he had left beside Mihunokada were always visible between the stalagmite columns. He found the wall of the grotto, some seventy yards away from the stream. It rose, an unclimbable slab of veiled and splintered stalactite, above him. He followed it in an arc, until it reached the water's edge again some ninety yards above the point where he and Mihunokada had climbed ashore. But the stream he expected to find had widened to a broad river emerging from a tunnel on his right; across its width and only faintly visible in the light of the candle, water foamed and raged as it was forced towards him through a narrow gap between rocks. Whirlpools swirled on the black surface. As he walked beside the river the vibration of the ground became greater, and the roar of the river deeper and more threatening than it had sounded before. Spray filled the air, giving the candle flame a distinct aura, even within the plastic container.

Yamada stood on the edge of a gorge where the river was squeezed between rock banks that were like massive stone wedges. It swept past him at a terrifying speed as though it were sucked from below. Small out-juttings of the gorge's sides scored its racing surface with waves that darted like fish towards its centre. But the great roar of the water came from the rock tunnel into which it pounded, and from there also came the vibration

Yamada could feel not only in the air, but through the soles of his feet. He edged himself into the tunnel entrance. The light of the candle was just sufficient to show him the water dropping, hurtling as though it was being channelled to drive a giant turbine at the foot of a dam, into the curving throat of a massive siphon. He stared at it for a long time before returning to Mihunokada.

'Well? Did you have any luck?'

'This is not our stream.'

'Then what?'

'We have joined a river . . . it comes in to this cavern through a big tunnel. Much bigger than the tunnel we swam. We came down a tributary, like a drainpipe, and now we are in a bigger river.'

'The Pivka?'

'Perhaps. But I found no way out of this cavern in that direction. The current of the river would be impossible to swim against. It is more powerful even than the stream. We have our usual choice. We can stay here and die, or we can swim with the river, and also die.' He explained the terrifying siphon, and Mihunokada's face, as he listened, was impossible to read.

'The bodies of my family dead have always been returned home,' Mihunokada said in a matter-of-fact way when Yamada was finished. 'Perhaps the family have always been lucky. Even my grandfather's father who died in the rebellion, has his ashes in the family tomb. My mother was always sad about those who never returned. She wept for the soldiers who died and whose bodies never returned to Japan. She says their spirits wander the earth in loneliness.'

'My family are conveniently buried anywhere suitable,' replied Yamada. 'I've no idea where my grandfather might be buried . . . let alone my great grandfather. Maybe on a hillside above a village!'

Mihunokada stared at the dark stream. 'I only meant that perhaps if we go with the river, our bodies might be swept out somewhere, and found. That way, mine would be returned to my family.'

'As I am already dead my corpse is of no interest to me.'

'So you keep telling me. For the past day almost, I have been travelling with a dead man . . . no, two dead men. I'm not particularly impressed by your philosophy Yamada. I live until I die. I do not die when I am in a position to avoid it. I do not enjoy your make-believe. Dying mentally is a shield for your cowardice. A warrior who considered himself dead, could not fight efficiently;

he would give up, because there would not even be his pride to save.'

'I have enjoyed today far more as a dead man, than I would have done had I been living.'

Mihunokada stood. 'You make me angry, Yamada. Take off your anorak.'

'You want to fight me? Here?'

Mihunokada swore. 'No, you idiot. Give me your anorak. I'm going to wrap it over the man's head.'

'You'll suffocate him.' Yamada pulled the anorak from his shoulders, and felt the cold eternal rain on his back.

'It may just help him. It traps air, remember. Well, if he has a bag of air around his head, it could save him.' He took the nylon jacket and tied the sleeves together beneath the guide's arms, then pulled the material over the man's head and attached the waist draw-strings to the sleeves so that Irano's head was enclosed in a large bag. 'Keep it away from his face until we are in the water. When we get near the siphon try to trap air in the folds. It may work, but it probably won't.' He dragged off his own jacket, stood on one of the sleeves and ripped the tough material into strips. It was strong and by the time he had finished he was breathing heavily with the effort. He knotted the strips of nylon together until they made a rope some twelve feet in length. Yamada watched him, startled, as he stripped the remainder of his clothing from his body. His muscles glistened, sharply defined in the candlelight, and rippling as he moved. 'Strip off those rags of yours, Yamada. We will face the God of this mountain as naked as he must be himself.' Mihunokada's voice was strong and determined, and his new mood instantly infectious.

Yamada felt a strange happiness inside him, as though he had met an old friend whose company he enjoyed. He said: 'Yes, of course.' He unbelted his pants and stepped out of them, then pulled off his shirt and tossed it away. He flexed his stiff arms and legs.

Mihunokada threw him one end of the long strip of nylon 'Tie yourself on. Whatever happens next, will happen to all of us.'

Yamada knotted the nylon back on itself so there was a loop. He pushed his head and one arm through, and jerked the slipknot tight in his armpit. It was uncomfortable, but he was happy there would now be some positive link between himself and Mihunokada. He watched Mihunokada fasten the line around the guide's body and then around his own waist. He smiled and felt good when Mihunokada winked and grinned back at him.

'How many glasses of beer can you drink at one sitting, Yamada?'

'I once drank eleven.'

'Tonight, I will buy you twenty.' Mihunokada held his hand towards Yamada. He took it and felt Mihunokada's grip tighten powerfully.

They slid Serge Irano from the ledge and back into the river. The candles remained alight on the rock beside the discarded clothing and bags. They trod water briefly, supporting the unconscious man between them.

The current carried them towards the growing noise of the giant siphon, the water's speed increasing as the gorge narrowed. The candle-light dimmed behind them in the grotto and was gone. Currents beneath the water's surface sucked at their bodies, pulling them downwards into the depths. They kicked to keep themselves afloat. Yamada pulled the nylon anorak closer around the guide's head.

With a roar, they were into the great siphon. The water dropped away below . . . thousands of tons a minute deluging through a narrowing and descending tunnel.

Mihunokada felt he was falling for a lifetime. Something tore at his ankles, a rock smashed into his thigh and he felt bone snap and grind. Pain, blue white explosions of fire danced in his brain. He fought to hold his breath and prevent himself screaming with agony. The descent ended but the roar and the current made it impossible to guess at a new direction. There was another terrible pain in his testicles. The nylon strip holding him to the guide tautened between his legs. For several seconds the nylon held him against the raging current cutting deep into his groin, then he was released. The guide's body crashed against him and he grabbed at it with both arms. A smooth boulder rolled him sideways and then suddenly there was nothing; no sound, no pain, only darkness.

Mihunokada opened his eyes slowly. His body was one seething, throbbing agony. There was a continuous pain across his chest, while his lower abdomen and thighs felt as though they had been scalded. It took him several seconds to focus on something moving a few feet above his head; a robin, red-breasted, curious and staring sideways at him with jet-bead eyes, sprang from branch to branch of a twisted pine that was little more than a large bonzai. Across Mihunokada's vision flew a dragonfly, hovering, darting. The robin left its branch, swerved quickly near Mihunokada's head, and caught the dragonfly, carrying it high into an overhanging tree.

'If I am in heaven, then there is death here, too,' thought Mihunokada. He moved his head sideways. He lay in the shallows of a wide pool. A few feet away, a tree lay parallel to the water, it's trunk cracked through with the violence of its fall, and its green fernlike branches sweeping the surface of the river.

'I am alive.' Mihunokada spoke the words, and the sound of his own voice was further proof. He repeated the words more loudly. 'I am alive.' He pushed himself upwards and the pain was so sudden and sharp he could not prevent a cry of agony. He tried again, slowly and cautiously. The pain was still bad, but was just bearable. He ran his hand down his leg and felt sharp bone just beneath the skin of his thigh. He tried to feel his ribs, but the swelling across his chest was too thick.

He lifted his head and could see the far bank, rocky, boulder strewn, overhung with pine trees. He pushed himself backwards until he was sitting, supported against a rock, and closed his eyes.

The guide! Mihunokada felt at his waist for the strip of nylon which had bound them together. It was still there, a tight band that had worn skin from his hips. He slid his hand along the strip, and found it shredded and loose. He remembered the pain between his legs and the way he was held back in the current; that must have been when the nylon snapped. He looked quickly around. To his relief the man lay only a few feet away, water lapping around his waist; the upper part of his body resting on a fine gravel beach. Beyond the man, and hidden partly by a large boulder, was Yamada.

Mihunokada eased himself carefully sideways, gasping as pain ripped through his body. He reached the guide. Irano's face was still covered by the anorak. Mihunokada pulled it away. A slight pulse, visible in the sunlight, throbbed on the guide's neck.

'He's alive . . . we are alive.' Mihunokada shouted the words. 'Yamada . . . Yamsan . . . we are *alive*.' There was no movement or reply from Yamada. Mihunokada slowly worked his way towards Yamada's feet. He pulled himself up on a boulder. 'Yama . . . eeh!' The shout became a cry of horror. Yamada lay on his stomach, his arms widespread, with the nylon strip still tying him to the guide. But Yamada would never answer to his name. His body was headless. The stump of his neck seeped what little blood that remained in his body, into the gently moving river.

A corporal and two privates, of the Zagon depot, patrolling the woods at the base of the mountain close to Planina and the Pivka cave system, heard Mihunokada's scream. The corporal, standing on a ridge of high ground below the forest, swung his binoculars along the course of the river. He could just distinguish three people apparently lying in the water half a mile away, and little more than a hundred and fifty meters from the river's exit from the mountain. The area had been closed to visitors since the day following the earthquake.

'Bastard campers,' he grumbled. 'Go down and warn them off,' he told the privates. 'If they argue, then arrest them. And get a move on.' It would be nightfall soon and he was tired and thirsty after several hot hours on patrol.

16

The air was cooling, and the sun had dropped below the distant hills by the time Catlin and Lisetta returned to the rock fortress in the side of the mountain. For the first time Catlin was able to view it from below before climbing the steep gorge. He found the fortress impressive, a stern, white-stone building set into the mouth of an enormous cavern in a four hundred foot high gorge. Part of the entrance had been destroyed by the recent earthquake and a section of the crag above the gorge had dropped to crush some of the building in the gigantic cavern; but much of it still survived, poised above the river which flowed below it straight into the depths of the mountain. He could see why the place had been chosen to be the hideout of a robber chieftain; the upper section of the gorge, where the others waited in the cave, was easily defended from attack from the low ground, while the upper entrance was well hidden and narrow enough to be held by even a couple of swordsmen.

Catlin was glad of the distraction the fortress provided for him. He'd been climbing the rocky track, behind Lisetta, watching the sleek movement of her lithe body only a few feet ahead. She was just a kid, not some mature sophisticated woman from a big city. That line of argument hadn't helped him a few days ago; he wouldn't have been so interested if she'd been sophisticated. It was the freshness, the way she found enjoyment in everything, the way she always bubbled, that had reached him. She even liked his scars! A lot of women would have had the shudders, or at least pretended they weren't there. Life would be a lot of fun with Lisetta, even if it might sometimes, often, be unpredictable. He hadn't made love in the open air, tumbling in the long grass like that for how long? He couldn't remember when . . . maybe since he was a kid himself. It would often be like that with Lisetta . . .

they'd be walking on a mountain, be out in the car, and she'd want him; strange places, strange times. And he'd want her, and it would happen. No, she couldn't fit in with oil fires . . . with the constant danger of his work. And that's a lie, too, he realised. She'd damn well fit in, he knew it. She'd want to be with him, would expect to stand on the sideline, waiting for him . . . hell, he'd have to fight her to keep her from helping.

'It could work,' he said, aloud.

She stopped, a pace ahead of him and faced him, her eyes bright and alive. 'It work, Joe. I know it work.'

For a second he thought she'd read his mind, but knew it wasn't possible; at least, not yet. He said: 'What?'

'The drill . . . you and the drill.' She reached out and took both his hands in her own. He pulled her closer, enjoying the feel and scent of her body, locking her arms around him with his big hands. The dark eyes were only a few inches away. 'Joe, you will do it; I know so.'

Her confidence was almost material enough to touch; the kind that protected the naked feet of firewalkers from white-hot coals. He just said: 'Maybe.'

'No, no maybe. You do it . . . we do it.' She broke her hands free, reached up and clasped them behind his neck. 'Kiss me, Joe.'

They'd climbed the rest of the steep track, hand in hand, like young lovers, and Catlin felt good inside. He hadn't yet realised, but the compressed pellets of emotion formed by his last job, and O'Donovan's death, were already dissipated and gone.

Inside the cave, a pressurised lantern had been lit and the smell of kerosene was heavy in the air. Alessandro made no comment on their return, and simply introduced Catlin to the men who had only minutes before returned from Ljubljana. Stacked inside the cave entrance were several boxes, lengths of light steelwork and an engine on its carrying stretcher.

'Simon and Mileta have just returned,' he explained. 'We carried the equipment up from the valley. They managed to borrow an old delivery truck. We've hidden it in the woods. They have also brought petrol for the engine, and some lubricating oil.'

Catlin examined the rig. It was, as he'd expected, light equipment, meant for the drilling of shot firing holes for seismographic survey. It was British by manufacture and built by Boyles Brothers, a company which Catlin knew had recently been acquired by Dresser of Europe. It had a depth capability of a little more than two hundred and fifty feet.

'Is it good?' Lisetta questioned him, anxiously.

'Maybe! But only if we hit the right spot first time. We're likely to have to use this to its maximum capacity; it'll be working hard for light equipment.' Catlin opened the boxes; they contained sections of drill rod, each about five feet in length. He counted them quickly, then turned to Alessandro. 'They've brought only twelve pieces of drill rod. It'll take us down sixty feet! Nowhere near enough. It won't get us halfway to the cavern. And there's only one cutting head.' He knelt and examined the diamond-tipped teeth. 'You'll be lucky if this lasts. It's seen a lot of wear.'

Lisetta looked horrified. She glanced quickly at Alessandro. 'It will not do?'

'Sorry,' said Catlin. 'I can't stretch the rod, and I can't put new diamonds into the cutter. It's a disappointment. I'd hoped it would be in better condition, but the most important thing is the drill rod. Without that we can't go anywhere.'

Alessandro spoke furiously to Simon in Slovene and the man replied quickly, his own face angry. An argument began which Catlin was unable to follow. Lisetta joined in, her voice trembling with emotion. After several minutes she turned and spoke to Catlin. Anger thickened her accent, 'These two . . .' she waved a clenched fist at Simon and Mileta. 'They have been most stupid, but they have got more of those drill things coming.'

'Well, that's very good,' replied Catlin, hoping his exaggerated relief at this news might calm her.

'It is not good. Yes, well, perhaps it is a little good, but we are all angry because of *who* they ask to bring it.' Her forehead was furrowed, and her dark eyes glistened with emotion. 'They have asked Croats.'

'Who's Croats?'

'Croats. The Croats are . . . they are Croatian men from Belgrade, some from the Belgrade University.' Catlin half expected her to stamp her feet in fury. 'They are bad, Joe, very bad people these men of the C.L.O.'

Alessandro spoke, his voice calmer. 'Not all Croats are bad, Joe, but these men are members of an extremist student group. They want independence for Croatia . . . they have a reputation for violence. They are very nationalistic and dangerous men.'

'They won't get much mileage out of a few lengths of drill rod,' said Catlin.

'They will, they will.' Lisetta maintained her anger. 'These men will do *anything* to draw attention to their cause. They bomb, they shoot . . . they cause much trouble.'

'Students? I don't believe your government would tolerate . . .'

Alessandro interrupted him. 'Lisetta is right, Joe. Some of these men are students like us. They are a society for the independence of Croatia . . . a student society, basically, but they have members outside the university. They aim at a society based on anarchy. We have had some contact with them on only one or two occasions, but we avoid them if possible. Our goals are not the same. Simon and Mileta thought they were doing the right thing. They could think of no other way to get drill rods. It is bad, it has involved these men. They are bringing the equipment from Belgrade, and also some of their people they say will wish to help. That is not a good sign; they will try to capitalise on the project in some way.'

'There will be much trouble, I know this,' insisted Lisetta. 'They are always making trouble.'

'But, Lisetta Irano, they *can* bring forty more sections of the drill rod . . . and that is the most important thing,' said the man Simon, his English as good as Alessandro's. 'It's typical too, that their university in Belgrade should be better equipped than our own. If Slovene students require more rod, then they must borrow it from the local authorities and fill in many official forms.'

'When will this other rod arrive?'

Lisetta answered Catlin. 'Tonight, tomorrow . . . when these Croats think they must come.' She pouted. 'I'm sorry, Joe, it sound if I hate Croats; I don't hate. Many are fine people. It is just this group. They are . . . extremists. We, also, want changes, but there are better ways to get them.'

'Okay, okay,' said Catlin. 'I'm not interested in politics, only in drilling at this moment, and we're wasting time and energy. Let's get this stuff up to the drill site ready to start work. The less time we lose the better.' He turned to the group of men, picking out Alessandro with his eyes. 'You promised to get the other map I need, well we need it now.'

Alessandro translated and Stane looked at his watch, and then nodded. 'They will try.'

'Trying is no good,' warned Catlin. 'I get the map, or I can't drill.'

Oichi and Nohime were Kaguri's two daughters; Uesugi his thirteen year old son, born late in his marriage. The children's names were as old as his family. In the past few days he had thought of them often, and was glad they were safely at home in Hosokai. Oichi was the oldest, nineteen, and soon it would be time for her to marry. They had not spoken of it yet. A generation ago, Kaguri's own marriage had been arranged, to link together two suitable families. Any other bonding would have been unthinkable, and still was in the country districts. But Hosokai was a town, and Oichi a town girl with a modern education. Kaguri was aware that, traditional as he might want his family to remain, he would be able to do little more than advise his daughter when it came to the choice of her husband. But he knew she would act sensibly, and that was a comfort. The same would apply to Nohime, a pretty seventeen-year old. She would follow the example of her sister.

Uesugi was the one who would carry on the family name; carry it forward with the male Kaguri blood. There were other ways of maintaining the name if a family didn't have a son; a daughter's husband could adopt the name, and by doing so, also inherit much of the family wealth. By law, children now shared equally, but few families made their bequests with the recent legal exactitude. If you were a farmer, you couldn't split your hand into uneconomic parcels, nor as a businessman divide the responsibilities too thinly.

Uesugi? Kaguri wondered what the boy would be like as a man. He was still very much a child, pampered, even spoilt, by his mother.

'It is not necessary for you to take him to the dojo.'

'He enjoys it.'

'He is too young, only three years old.'

'He sits quietly, and watches. He learns that way.'

That had been ten years ago. He had begun teaching him kendo when he was seven; the child had showed promise, then. Lately, Kaguri wasn't too sure Uesugi would continue once he could make his own decisions. There was too much western influence in children's lives in Japan, today; television and films. Uesugi had already shown an aptitude and interest in electronics.

If I die, down here, thought Kaguri, then it is almost certain he will continue as a kendoka. In deference to my memory, my wife will encourage him, even though she doesn't appreciate the skill herself. She will consider it a duty to do so.

Children were a responsibility you accepted totally; a commitment that was always welcome. Too many daughters, though, could be expensive; in fact Kaguri knew of families who had begun saving towards their daughter's wedding gifts on the day the girl had been born. To have too many daughters, even in modern Japan, could keep a man poor.

Children! Kaguri stared across the gloom. Fifteen yards away a child was cradled in its mother's arms as she rocked it, comforting both herself and the infant. Children were the future of all families, the future of every race. Their terror, their fear and misery was so much greater than that of the adults. Adults could reason; hope. Children could only wait and suffer, without understanding. A man, a strong, trained and healthy warrior might survive, but children had no reserves of strength. Sadly, Kaguri had watched them grow weaker each day. There was no longer any energy to spare for play, even when their parents attempted to distract them. And Kaguri had seen children die before; killed by the terrible machines of war that wasted them just as their present starvation shrank their intestines and gnawed its way through their delicate tissue. Kaguri's submarine had been only twenty miles out at sea, off Nagasaki, when the first of the atomic bombs had fallen. He had seen the results; lived with them for many years. The slow deaths of the many children were as firmly imprinted on his memory as the shadows of some of the bomb's victims had been burnt into concrete walls.

The children down here in the caves, *must* be given every chance to live, Kaguri determined. Their help *must* be the priority. He would speak with some of the other men from the different groups.

Inspector Emile Zlobec was harrassed rather than tired. In the first few days following the earthquake he had been exhausted; not only by the sudden increase in his mental output, caused by the need to organise the Postojna rescue work but by the sheer physical difficulties of moving anywhere, and by anxiety for the well-being of his own family. It had been several hours before he had heard his wife and children had survived; the children being out of doors at their school, and his wife weeding the vegetable patch at the time of the disaster. The school, a prefabricated building, had been wrecked but miraculously no-one had died or been seriously injured in its collapse. Zlobec's bungalow had shed its roof tiles and cracked a few walls, but remained standing; by luck its foundation stood in an ancient and deep bed of gravel which had absorbed much of the movement of the surrounding earth.

Zlobec's routine at the Postojna site now allowed him a few hours sleep in his own bed. He was able to return to his home, for supper, at around eight o'clock in the evening; he could take his time over the meal, have a glass of brandy, and drive back to the site for a final quick check at about ten p.m. There seemed nothing likely to disturb the pattern of his days; the site was being cleared in what he thought to be a sensible and tidy manner. Most of the rubble of the hotel had been built into neat piles, and the terminal building was presenting no problems. It was possible a few bodies remained under the last few tons of rubble; some of the employees were still unaccounted for, but only three or four more. The rock slip of the strata at the cave entrance was fully exposed, but until more suitable equipment arrived to deal with it not much more progress could be made. He was unhappy about the people trapped below ground, and there were times at night when his sleep was disturbed by his thoughts. He knew the caves well and it was easy to picture the terrible scenes beneath the mountain. Daily he received the telephone reports from the cave; the growing list of dead, the continuous pleas for help. He wished the government would speed up its action and get the rescue moving more quickly. Surely it could not be long before they would act. He had expressed his thoughts to Commissioner Bor. It had been unwise.

'Zlobec, we're police, it is our job to maintain law and order, and to support authority. We are doing all of those things now. Order *IS* returning to the region. Don't question authority, Zlobec, and do not expect miracles. Just carry on with your work, as directed by me,' Commissioner Bor had said, with a more than slight tinge of exasperation in his voice. 'Now the military are involved, your constables can be used to patrol the damaged towns; send them to Planina, and Postojna town, and warn them of the possibility of looters. If any are found, they can be arrested, or shot if they try to escape. Minister Kalin has warned that looters must be dealt with severely.'

There would be no looters at the Postojna Cave site, Zlobec decided. He reduced the number of constables, normally on duty there, to one in the daytime and another at night. They found little to occupy themselves. Zlobec spent much of his time in the Postojna town depot. The town itself was depressing. Large sections had been evacuated where the buildings were still unsafe or had been demolished. Less than a quarter of the town's inhabitants were still able to live in their homes.

Zlobec sucked in his cheeks, and the action made his angular face unpleasantly like a death mask. He was sitting at his desk, resting his head against a telephone receiver. It was nine p.m., and he should have been home an hour before. He had been trying to contact Commissioner Bor for the past two hours. It was difficult to locate the man; he moved rapidly from village to village, supervising the work of the police and the military, and then making his daily report back to Minister Kalin.

An operator spoke to Zlobec. 'Inspector? We have found the Commissioner at Cernica.' The town was ten kilometers west of Postojna. 'One of the men is bringing him to the telephone shortly.'

'Good.' Zlobec yawned, then shouted: 'Salvitz!' A young policeman, little more than conscription age, poked his head nervously around the door of Zlobec's office. 'Get me a coffee, Salvitz.' The man's head nodded and the door jerked close.

'Yes?' It was Commissioner Bor's voice in Zlobec's ear.

'Zlobec here, Commissioner.'

'Yes . . . what do you want?'

"Pig", thought Zlobec. "You can't give me the common courtesy of my official title." He said: 'Something has happened here I thought you should know, Commissioner.' Salvitz, the young policeman came into the room, a cup of coffee balanced precariously in his hands. He had returned so quickly Zlobec knew it had to be instant coffee. He waved Salvitz towards his desk, impatiently. 'Two men, Commissioner. They have come out of the mountain, alive.'

'Out of the mountain alive?' Bor's voice was disbelieving as he echoed Zlobec's words. It made Zlobec more confident.

'Yes, out of the caves. One Japanese tourist, and the guide, Irano.'

'Wasn't he the guide who was reported killed?'

Zlobec was surprised. He sent the daily list of dead to Bor's office each morning, but didn't expect the Commissioner to read them personally. He had thought they would simply be buried in the files. he said, meekly: 'Yes, Commissioner, that is correct.'

'Then how did they get out?'

'There were three men; a military patrol from the Zagon

Barracks found them in the river at Planina, they had been tied together with strips of nylon cloth. One Japanese was dead, and the other, and guide Irano, alive.'

'You haven't answered my question,' snapped Bor, irritably.

'We think they swam.'

'Through the Pivka system? Impossible!'

'Well, we don't exactly know what happened,' admitted Zlobec. Bor always managed to make him feel incompetent although he knew he wasn't. 'Guide Irano is unconscious; likely to be for some time, according to the military doctor who examined him. He has a compressed fracture of the skull, and severe injuries to his face. He also has compound fractures of the right arm, collar bone, and shoulder.' Zlobec glanced at a scribbled note in front of him. 'He has other broken bones, in both feet, and is suffering from exposure. The Japanese is also injured. He has a broken thigh bone, and fractures of the pelvis and a number of ribs. He is suffering from shock and is sedated. The other Japanese was decapitated, probably by the nylon which bound them all together. The patrol found his head further downstream.'

'Why was the guide previously reported dead, if he was still alive?'

'It's confusing. I will ask for more information when we next have telephone contact with the cave system. According to the military telephonist, the people in the cave originally claimed Irano fell a long way onto rocks, and was then swept into a siphon. They said there was no way he could have survived. I don't have any more details. We'll have to wait until the Japanese is able to talk.'

'When will that be?'

'The doctor thinks he will be better when he has slept off the sedation. He will need surgery, tomorrow. It's good news, eh, Commissioner?'

'Where are the two men now?'

'In the military hospital at Zagon Barracks.'

'Good. I want a full security screen around them until I decide otherwise, Zlobec. To anyone outside the hospital, those two men don't exist. You understand me?'

'Yes,' said Zlobec, but he meant 'no'. He could see no reason to hide the escape of two people from the depths of the mountain. Their discovery had excited him. It gave just a little hope for those who were still trapped.

'No word of them to anyone, Zlobec. I'll speak to the Military Commander at Zagon, personally.' There was a pause before Bor spoke again. 'One other thing, Zlobec. Have you seen my son?'

'Alessandro?'

'Yes, Alessandro.'

'He was on the site, er . . . yesterday.' The sudden change of subject had momentarily confused Zlobec. He was uncertain as to whether he had seen Bor's son since.

'Is he still around the Postojna Jama?'

'I'm not sure.'

'No matter. If you see him, tell him to telephone his mother. She worries about him.' Bor replaced the handset on its rest. He was displeased with the news which Zlobec had given him about the escape of the two men; not that he resented them escaping and saving their own lives, but because they could stir to life the embers of a dying fire. If the newspapermen learnt of their existence, then even greater speculation would be aroused in the plight of those believed dead beneath the earth; re-kindle hope for those already mourned just when more recent international news was pushing the catastrophe of the earthquake on to the lesser pages. Countries who did not have citizens trapped in the caverns had now lost interest. Things were going exactly as Minister Baraslev Kalin had predicted.

Martin Bor picked up his telephone again. 'Get me the barracks at Zagon; Colonel Taufer.' He waited impatiently. The Colonel was dining in the Officer's Mess and it took some minutes to find him. At last Bor heard his voice. 'Colonel Taufer? This is Commissioner Bor.'

Colonel Taufer winced inwardly. He had met Bor many times, but found him an uncouth man. Like Bor, Taufer was not of an aristocratic family, few high ranking officers were in the modern Yugoslavian army; but he did try to instil a certain elegance to his manners and bearing. 'Yes, Commissioner Bor; delightful to hear from you again.' Hearing from Bor was never delightful for Taufer; the Police Commissioner, sharing partisan camaraderie with many of the members of the Regional Committee, had more power than even the military Colonel enjoyed. It was rumoured Bor was on first name terms with the highest members of the Presidium.

'You have two men in your hospital; a Japanese, and one of the cave guides . . . they were found in the Pivka.'

'Yes, Commissioner. Excellent news is it not? Although they

are both badly injured, I am assured they can be nursed back to health. I believe some plastic surgery is required for . . .'

'I'm not interested in their present condition, Colonel,' said Bor, coldly. 'I want a full security veil drawn around the two men. They have *not* escaped from the mountain, they were *not* found by your men, and they are *not* in your hospital. In effect, Colonel, for the moment they do not exist. No mention of them is to be made to anyone outside your barracks. Furthermore, I do not even want them discussed *inside* your barracks by any of your men.'

Colonel Taufer was about to ask on whose orders Bor was acting, but changed his mind. It might be an unwise subject to pursue. Instead, he asked: 'Are we to continue to treat them?'

'Yes, of course you will treat them.'

'We don't have all the necessary equipment for major surgery,' said Taufer. 'Also, although we have military doctors the patients will need skilled orthopaedic surgeons.'

'Use only the men on your staff, Colonel.'

'Very well.'

'And keep me informed. Goodnight.'

'Goodnight, Commissioner.' Colonel Taufer sat back in his hard leather-covered armchair. He selected one of his pipes from a rack on his desk, and opened his tobacco jar. He stirred the mixture, then rolled it carefully in his palms before methodically filling the pipe. He bit on the stem, lit the tobacco, pressed it down with his forefinger, and drew the smoke slowly into his mouth. What was Bor up to, he wondered. There was some game being played out, and he was simply a bystander. Worse, he wasn't even sure *what* game was being played.

It was almost midnight. The arc-lights in the area of the blocked cave entrance were set low and directed towards the mountain, as though the debris of the hotel and the terminal building were part of some strange Son-et-Lumière show. One of the bull dozers was parked awkwardly against a long mound of rubble. Another was still working, at a steady pace beside the terminal. Half a dozen workers tossed loose bricks and small pieces of concrete wearily into a truck. Another group of men stood resting around the JCB where two of the men were attempting to lever on one of its huge tyres. A number of soldiers, rifles slung across their shoulders, lounged beside the refreshment tent. There were no ambulances or medical staff to be seen, and the tents which had been erected for the injured and the dead, stood deserted.

Inspector Zlobec's prefabricated hut leant towards the mountain as though it was resisting the force of a gale. Electric lights, pulsing to the rhythm of a mobile generator, glowed yellow through the cracked glass of the windows. A police constable, his jacket draped over one shoulder and with his cap on the back of his head, leant against the doorpost.

Stane, Miki and Branko knelt in the undergrowth forty yards away, waiting. They had been there almost a full hour and were cramped and uncomfortable. The constable, for some reason, had not yet left the office. They watched him, mentally willing him to be thirsty, hungry, or have any desire which might get him away from the vicinity of the police depot. They heard his office telephone ring. The man turned and disappeared inside. They were close enough to hear his voice.

'Maria? Sweetheart! . . .'

'The bastard,' breathed Branko. 'It's his girlfriend. He's been waiting for her to call him.' He stretched his legs carefully, keeping himself below the height of a low bush. 'Why the hell didn't the bitch call earlier?'

'Out with her other boyfriend,' suggested Miki.

'Of course I want you, my chicken . . .' droned the constable's voice. 'Yes, later. When I finish here. A little after one . . . yes, yes, my love, it's late . . . but it's convenient.'

'He's married,' said Miki. 'He's . . .'

Stane silenced him. The telephone's bell jangled briefly as the constable replaced the receiver. They saw the man at the door again. He swung his jacket across both his shoulders, pulled the door closed, then began walking towards the refreshment tent.

'Go on you shit. Hurry up . . .' Stane watched until the man reached the tent. 'If he starts to come back, then whistle,' he told Branko. 'Right, Miki . . . keep low.'

They ran, stooping, across the open ground. Stane reached the door, and hoped it would be unlocked; the man had simply pushed it closed. He reached it and pressed the catch. It opened. Miki followed him inside.

'Where?'

'Try the filing cabinet, I'll search the desk drawers.'

They hunted furiously for several minutes. There was no time to be tidy; they tore documents from the files and scattered the contents of the desk and cabinets.

Miki spoke anxiously. 'Do they have a map, at all? Where did you see one?'

'I didn't,' Stane admitted. 'I just assumed they'd have one. For God's sake, this is the caves police station; they *must* have a chart of the cave system . . . they'd need one.'

'There isn't one in the files, and none in the . . .' Miki's voice hesitated then he spoke more loudly. 'Shit, we're blind! Look!'

Stane followed his pointing arm. High on the wall, above one of the desks and in an incongruous gilt and plaster picture frame, was a chart of the caves; so obvious and yet unseen in their hurried search.

'Get it.'

Miki ripped it from the wall. As he did so, there was a sharp whistle from outside.

'The policeman . . . get out.'

Miki paused at the door and peered out. He spoke in an urgent whisper. 'He's less than twenty meters away!'

'Go,' ordered Stane.

Miki burst from the door, Stane only a yard behind him. They had run several paces before the guard spotted them, a few more before he reacted. 'Halt . . . stop.' They heard his boots thudding on the hard ground, as they reached the edge of the forest area. 'Stop . . .' The guard shouted again. They were dodging the fallen trunks of the lower trees when he fired. The shot hissed above them and smacked against the rocks. There was another shot, and a bullet ricocheted from a tree branch, to hum its way angrily into the distance. Two more followed, and then there was silence and they had reached the higher ground above the collapsed cave entrance.

Miki was panting, scrambling up the rocks like a baboon pursued by a leopard. Stane heard Branko call from a tall clump of fern. 'This way . . . this way.' In seconds they were beside him. 'You two unhurt?' They had no breath left to answer. 'The guard is still down there. He didn't follow you. I can see him from here . . . he's running back to the huts. He probably thinks it's unwise to follow two of you into the woods. Rest for a few moments then we'll go back to the cave.' They leant gratefully against the rocks. Below they could see the site. The soldiers had unslung their rifles and were now hurrying towards the police office. 'Not too long, it may get hotter around here,' warned Branko. 'Did you find a chart?'

Miki turned the large and ornately gilded frame towards him.

'What the hell do you think I'm carrying? A Rubens?'

They were singing in the cavern, and the echoes were distorting the sound, passing it to and fro along the length of the vast hall, bouncing it from crevasses and grottoes in the fissured rock, spinning it from the smooth surfaces of the curtain stalactites until it sounded like the voice of the crowd at a football stadium.

Only two of the fires now burnt. There was only sufficient wood to keep them alight for another couple of days. The injured and the dying took all the warmth.

The song was international. The words were being sung in English, German, Yugoslavian, Swedish and even Japanese. Perhaps they had slightly different meanings, but no-one cared. The song was communication; it was people doing something together, it was a temporary anaesthetic for the situation.

At the lowest end of the great cavern, as far away from the singers as it was possible to get, a man stood on the stump of a fallen stalactite and shouted a wild sermon. He had been preaching continuously for the past three hours. At times he had a small audience of the curious; at other moments he was alone, shouting his prayers and his sermons to the shadows of the great cavern, and the darkness of the tunnels. He was a lay preacher, from Mexicali. His forefathers had been lay preachers since the days of the wagon trains; there was much family skill in the way he delivered his admonitions. The cavern reminded him of hell, and he was a man who found hell easily. The singing of the trapped, in such a time of anguish, could only be the work of the devil. For a while his wife had tried to silence him, but he had eventually wrenched himself away from her, leapt on to the stump of rock and, wild-eyed, launched his tirade at the punished humanity who invited the wrath of his vengeful God. His wife sobbed herself to exhaustion at his feet, until she was led away by his deserting congregation. Now he raged, alone and incoherently, spittle glistening on his cleft chin.

Colette and some of the women had washed in one of the many pools of water around the perimeter of the cavern. The pools were shallow and swirled murky brown when disturbed, but the mere action of cleaning themselves gave a mental boost to the women. All of them wished it were possible to wash their clothing, but they had learnt that once it was wet, it never really dried in the clammy air.

It was the beginning of the fifth day of their imprisonment and they had all been without food long enough for it to show. Colette had noticed that men who had been portly were losing the tyres of fat padding their waists. The plumper of the women were finding clothes hanging looser on their bodies; the already slim women, had a gaunt look to their faces and their eyes seemed to draw deeper into their sockets. Hunger was aging for the thin. For the adults, the worst days had been those at the beginning of their ordeal when stomachs were still used to regular filling. Now the habit of food was gone, and hunger was weakness and lethargy, a dull ache and the subject of dreams and nightmares. It was seldom discussed.

For the remaining twenty three children in the cavern, it was much worse. The youngest were barely able to understand the reasons for their hunger, and despite promises from near-distracted parents, continuously begged or demanded some respite for the unfamiliar pangs they were forced to experience. In desperation, one young German woman had tried to feed her long-weaned four year old from her empty breasts, and then, nearly demented by its suffering, had attempted to strangle the child to end its torture. Her husband had quickly intervened, and now kept the child cradled in his own arms.

The youngest children had begun the process of dying.

Kaguri and Meyer, an elderly German who spoke some English, Struger, Hubertson and Berkley, sat together on an outcrop of sloping rock near the towering wall of the cavern. The singing of the others was drowning the five men's conversation, and they were forced to speak louder than Kaguri would have preferred.

Struger and Berkley had spent most of the day exploring the smaller of the passages. The batteries of the flashlights were becoming weaker. When they were gone, and that would be in only another couple of hours use, then the two men would have to continue their work by candlelight; and climbing would then become more dangerous . . . perhaps even impossible.

Kaguri had requested a meeting of representatives of all the main groups of nationalities. Hubertson had been surprised to find himself nominated; he had never pushed himself to the front, and had been satisfied to sit in Sheila's company and isolate himself as much as was possible. He had felt he had little in common with the other members of his tour. He had not even wanted to visit Yugoslavia . . . would have been happier spending more time in Britain, or remaining at home working in his own garden.

He had asked Berkley to accompany him to the meeting with the Japanese. Hubertson spoke to Berkley every time he returned to the main cavern . . . usually he said the same things. 'Any luck this time?' Berkley would shake his head or shrug his shoulders. 'There's got to be a way . . . somewhere.' Hubertson persisted. Berkley would nod, and say: 'We'll find it. Sure there's got to be a way out, somewhere.' Or: 'It's a matter of time, just time. Don't give up.'

Berkley was important to Hubertson, important to all the people in the caves. With the passing of the days, the world outside became more distant, more unreal. It was real only down here . . . the pain and discomfort, the hunger and the misery, they were the real things. And the hope, that was genuine, too. But hope was Berkley and Struger, the two men you could watch trying to find a way out . . . the people you sat waiting for; any time they might return and shout: 'We've found it . . .' Hubertson needed the hope; he needed it for Sheila. So he was glad when Berkley agreed to join him, and Struger was there, too. It was good to have their strength.

Kaguri's English was almost faultless. He spoke his words clearly though slowly, kneeling on the rock. Hubertson had noticed him a few days before, and the man's calmness had impressed him, though he had wondered at the time if it was not simply a demonstration of oriental acceptance of fate.

'I think we *must* agree,' said Kaguri, his face unreadable so far as the Europeans were concerned. 'The guides who might possibly have helped us, are now all unable to do so. One is more frightened than our children; the other is mentally too slow to be decisive.'

'Decisive,' thought Hubertson. What decisions could we possibly make that might help anyone? We can hardly decide everyone is going to break out of this prison, or decide everyone should suddenly eat, when there's nothing left to share. Decisions are unnecessary.'

Struger cut into Hubertson's thoughts. 'We should lead, perhaps! But *how* can we lead?'

'Do any of you know what was said on the telephone last night?' Kaguri asked.

Berkley answered him. 'The big Yugoslavian just had a long talk with the operator at the other end. One of the tourists who speaks Slovene listened to him, apparently he spoke about stupid things. He asked about the weather, and if there had been rain on the maize crops. No-one had died, in the past few hours, so he gave no names. When he was asked afterwards what was happening about our rescue, he just said: "They keep trying, and say we must keep up our spirits." '

'Something has been bothering me,' said Hubertson. The matter had been in his mind for some time, now it jelled. 'I couldn't work out what was wrong for quite a while, then earlier tonight I realised. Back home on the television news programmes I've seen reports of things like mining disasters, train crashes; I've been in the army myself. When something like this happens, when there's death around, then someone usually offers the services of a Priest.'

Kaguri bowed his head in agreement with a rocking movement of the upper part of his body. '*Exactly* so. That is one of the reasons why I have asked you all to speak with me here. I am aware of religious practices amongst Christians . . . we have quite a large Christian community in Japan. In times of death or sorrow there is *always* a Christian Priest. One expects such a thing in our own religion. For some time now, I have been surprised that no Priest has tried to speak to his people . . . or if he could not speak in person at least send them words of comfort. But there is also another thing; I know quite well that as soon as my own family would have heard the news of my imprisonment in this mountain, they would have tried to get a message down to me . . . even though it might be only a single word on the cave telephone. And, no-one, not one of us, has received a message. It is as though we are already dead.'

The German, Meyer, spoke; he sat with his back towards the distant firelight and his face was only a shadow, but Berkley knew he was the husband of a woman who had been badly injured during the earthquake. She lay now, near the fire, paralysed by injuries to the lower vertebrae of her spine. Even if they were rescued, he doubted if she would ever walk again. The man's voice was bitter. 'What does this mean?'

'There are really only three possibilities,' suggested Kaguri. 'Our rescue is imminent . . . a matter of hours, and therefore a Priest and messages from our friends and families can wait, because nothing must delay the rescue. Alternatively, our rescue is going to be a *very* lengthy business, and messages from friends and the words of a Priest may be introduced later to boost our morale at some critical juncture.'

'You said "three" alternatives,' Hubertson prompted firmly,

but he had already anticipated Kaguri's words.

'The third? That we are not going to be rescued, because it is impossible!'

'But surely that would be no reason to prevent a Priest from contacting us.' Hubertson hoped Kaguri would have no ready answer, but he was disappointed.

'Our Shinto and Buddhist Priests do not lie,' said Kaguri. 'I assume that yours also, do not lie. Perhaps the people outside do not think it would be a kindness for a Priest to remove any traces of hope. There is, however, a final possibility which is the most unpleasant of all.' Kaguri paused, but it was because he wanted to delay his words rather than seek theatrical effect. 'We are already officially dead!'

'That's a very unpleasant thought,' admitted Berkley. The idea hadn't occurred to him before, but now it had been raised, it was frightening.

'It is possible.' The elderly German moved himself to a more comfortable position on the wet rock. 'With Yugoslavs, anything is possible. Many years ago, I was in the army here. They are strange people. Some of them have fire inside them; most are sheep. It would be characteristic for some of them to walk away from a difficult job. We could be, as you say, officially dead. It would make life easier for a lot of people.'

'But our government would not permit it.' Struger spoke quickly. He sensed a need to quash Kaguri's suggestion, urgently. If it reached the ears of the others, it would destroy all hope. And without hope the process of degeneration would accelerate. 'There would be pressure from the United Nations . . . besides, we are on friendly terms with Yugoslavia. They would ask for Germany's help, in a disaster.'

'I would have thought so,' agreed Kaguri. 'It is the spark of comfort that denies my idea. It is more likely, I believe, our rescue will take a long time.'

'But how long?' asked Hubertson.

'An impossible question. We are beneath a mountain of rock. I did not have much time to study it, but it was tall enough for me to notice the forest on its slopes. We are also a kilometer and a half inside; that was the distance the train travelled. As far as we know, the tunnel is blocked this end. It could be blocked for its full length.'

'More likely, only blocked in sections,' said Berkley hopefully. He knew he was trying to convince himself.

'Perhaps. But the rescue may still take many weeks.' Kaguri stared at the dark silhouettes of the men facing him, sensing rather than seeing their eyes examining him.

'They may give up.'

Kaguri shook his head. 'I think not . . . at least, not yet. If they are trying to rescue us, then they will continue their efforts as long as they hear voices at this end of the telephone link. When the voices stop, then perhaps they will cease their work.'

Hubertson had assumed, from the first moment the full extent of the disaster had become known, rescue would be fairly quick. Each successive day had dragged, seeming longer than its predecessor, but he had comforted both himself and his wife with the thoughts that perhaps each day was the last they might spend beneath the ground. To contemplate living for perhaps weeks, in this terrible environment was almost incomprehensible. His voice expressed his horror. 'But we have no food, we're starving now. In a little while people will begin to die of starvation.'

'That is why our meeting is important. This is our fifth day underground. We have reached a critical period for the survival of a certain section of our people,' said Kaguri. His eyes were on Hubertson, but he seemed to look through him.

'Our people', thought Berkley. It was an unusual expression, but it indicated Kaguri had accepted total responsibility for his own group and expected as much from the men who faced him now. The two words could only be used by leaders, spokesmen.

Kaguri continued: 'What we will discuss might be easier if we were of one ethnic party, but the division created by speech, background, even colour, is surmountable. We need to be single-minded if we are to survive, and our single-mindedness *must* be concentrated on our survival.' He paused for several seconds. 'There is something we may have to do; something upon which we must *all* agree.'

'What do you suggest?' Berkley asked. There was something fascinating about Kaguri, charisma perhaps, a calm inner power that was almost hypnotic. Berkley had the feeling he had known the man all his life.

Kaguri didn't answer at once. He thought for a few moments, choosing his words carefully, as though he were afraid of their effect on the listening men. 'We are anxious for our children.'

'The children are growing weak, quickly,' commented Struger. 'They cannnot last without food.'

'Regrettably, they will die first, unless they are fed,' said Kaguri.

'They can't feed on air.' Hubertson was beginning to think the conversation was pointless. He was well aware of the misery of the situation and could see no reason why he or the others should be forced to dwell on something which could not be alleviated. 'There is nothing edible left in the cave.'

'The children can be fed,' said Kaguri, positively.

Berkley understood him immediately. 'Yes, they could be.' Like Kaguri, he did not wish to develop the idea alone; it was unpleasant, no matter how he viewed it . . . but for survival . . . it had happened before.

'How?' Hubertson asked, naively.

Kaguri's face was a mask. 'There is meat!'

There was a moment of silence before Hubertson's realisation. His face muscles tautened with horror, then he spoke, his voice trembling, 'Eat human meat; feed it to the children? How could we do that? How could we live with ourselves afterwards? We don't have the right to inflict such a decision on children . . . how would they view us for the rest of their lives?'

'It happened in the Andes air crash,' Berkley reminded him. 'I read the reports. It wasn't pleasant, but people who would have died, survived.'

'It's unthinkable,' insisted Hubertson. 'We are supposed to be civilised men.' He added: 'All of us.'

Kaguri relaxed his face a little. 'Now you understand why we must *all* be agreed. It *is* barbaric and primitive, but I do not think we have a choice, for the sake of our children.'

'How long will they live, without food,' asked Struger. Children were important to him, not only because he worked with them. He respected them, and their naive basic honesty. One day he would have children of his own, and he hoped they too would respect him.

Kaguri said: 'I have spoken to the medical workers. The condition of the children is extremely serious; some may last only two or three more days at the most. Several of them, the smallest and lightest, are already very weak. The shock of the situation has not helped, and the weaker they become, the more likely they are to develop other sicknesses.'

'Pneumonia,' said Berkley. He was surprised he had not been disgusted by Kaguri's suggestion. He had heard of it happening in some Vietnamese villages after the defoliation programme, and at the time the idea had seemed repulsive.

'I don't think it is necessary yet, for adults.' Meyer's face was pale in the candle-light. 'Maybe later, but I think it is possible for older people like myself to last a week or two more. If we are not rescued by then . . .' He left the sentence unfinished.

'But the parents . . .' began Hubertson, still distressed by the idea. So many years had passed since his own children were young he was uncertain of how he and Sheila might have reacted, but he was almost certain that Sheila, with her usually strong religious beliefs, would have refused no matter what the cost.

'I have thought very deeply about the problem. The decision *cannot* be left to the parents. If only one of a pair were to refuse, the burden on the other would be intolerable. How could a husband agree and his wife disagree, and then the child starve to death in their arms . . . could they ever face each other again? The problem would be no less for them if they disagreed, but the child ate and lived.'

'Is it possible to do this without a parent's knowledge,' asked Berkley. Kaguri had obviously spent a lot of time considering the matter. It was still new to Berkley and the others.

Kaguri nodded his head only slightly. 'It is possible. You . . .' He raised a slim hand, pointed at Berkley, and then moved the finger to include Struger. 'You and he have been exploring the cave system. You know where there is a place where you can reach a river . . . where the guide fell and was killed. It is not impossible you might find the carcass of a deer, trapped in the rocks. Naturally, you could not carry it all back — it would be too difficult to climb with so much meat — you will bring back only a few strips of its flesh in a bag . . . enough for the children.'

Hubertson turned away and retched violently, his empty stomach wracking him with pain as all it could expel was thin bile. He shuddered, wiped his mouth and then apologised. 'You must forgive me . . . I'm not very much use in this discussion.' He moved as though he were about to leave, but Kaguri stopped him.

'Wait. You feel no different from any of us. It is not an easy thing to do, or even talk of doing . . . you have acted only as all of us wish to act.'

Hubertson was grateful to the man. His action had made him feel inadequate.

Struger spoke directly to Berkley. The two men had developed a close bond in the short time they had been exploring the system together. 'Well, David?'

Berkley recognised encouragement in Struger's voice, the same tone he used when helping him up a particularly dangerous or difficult pitch of rock. Struger had already made up his mind: an affirmative. Berkley nodded.

'The rest of you?' asked Kaguri, softly.

There were murmurs of agreement.

'Then, if it is necessary, in two days time,' he said. 'Until then . . . and afterwards . . . I think we should be prepared to remain silent.'

'No matter how long I live, I do not think I will ever wish to discuss this conversation with anyone,' said Meyer, uncomfortably. He was pleased the meeting was ending and knew he shared the same thoughts as Hubertson.

'We will put out another fire,' Kaguri said. 'The wood must be saved, and we must all search the cavern to find the smallest splinters that may be useful later.' He paused. 'Thank you gentlemen, for your understanding.' His words, and his tone of voice, were exactly those he might have used at the end of a manager's meeting in the factory at Hosokai.

17

Catlin heard the shots. They were distant, but a warm breeze swept them up the mountainside. He recognised them instantly. Had the sounds come in daylight he might have been only curious, but by night they tightened the muscles of his throat and brought an unpleasant dampness to his palms. Gunshots and darkness were harbingers of bad memories; another night, a north Korean bomb for defusing, an ambush and a fusilade of shots to tear life from his friends.

Lisetta, sitting beside him, gasped. Her hand tightened on his arm.

He spoke to her gently. 'Relax. Maybe it's just someone shooting rabbits.' Catlin knew they were pistol shots. 'They were a long way off.'

It was the second journey they had made to the high ground of the plateau. All the drill-rig equipment was now stacked, hidden beneath the greenery of one of the fallen pines. A lantern, turned so low it barely glowed, lit only the small clearing where they sat waiting. Transporting the engine, the drill-rig and heavy pipe had been exhausting work. Moving in the darkness through the woods, scrub, and over the broken ground had been difficult. The fresh crevasses, their sides steep and still crumbling, were ready pitfalls. Now all they could do was wait.

They had expected the three men to return sooner . . . Alessandro had thought the police guard took his break around ten o'clock. It was now well after midnight. The sounds of the shots were ominous. It was easy to picture three bodies lying bleeding amongst the rocks or on the scented pine carpet of the woods.

The night was warm, but Lisetta shuddered and pulled herself closer to Catlin, snuggling her head against his shoulder. She had not mentioned their lovemaking of the previous afternoon, but she was always close to him, moving to his side whenever they rested, reaching out to touch his arm in the darkness as though to reassure herself of his presence. Catlin knew their relationship had developed past the point of no return. He wasn't yet certain of the future but he wasn't regretting either the past or present as far as Lisetta was concerned.

An hour passed in silence as they sought the faintest sound from the surrounding woods that might bring them the knowledge of their friends' safety. They heard it together, a low whistle two hundred yards away across the scrub. Catlin felt Lisetta's body stiffen; the whistle was repeated twice.

'Stane,' Alessandro said, quietly. He whistled once, in reply. Moments later dry twigs snapped and there were the sounds of clothing brushing aside the undergrowth and low pine branches. The men were on their feet, alert and wary. A dark figure moved against the sky and a voice called: 'Alessandro . . .'

Alessandro answered, and the three men appeared from the scrub. They were dirty and sweat streaked, their clothing torn.

'Do you have it,' Lisetta asked, even before the three men had joined the group. Miki had removed the map from its gilt frame. He held the roll of paper towards Catlin, with a satisfied smile.

It was dawn, still early, and although the sky was lightening towards the east, the sun had not yet risen above the distant mountains. There was already form to the trees and rocks, and the increasing light was giving them substance and colour. Catlin was working on the two maps; they were spread across a flat-topped boulder. Beside them rested a waterproof compass that was part of one of the men's pot-holing equipment. It would have been easier and more accurate for Catlin had the compass been prismatic and he'd been able to sight through a lens to a distant landmark; but by checking each of his calculations several times, he hoped to make up for the instrument's deficiency.

Working by the light of the lantern, he had spent two hours transferring the major features of the landscape from the survey map which Alessandro had given him, to the chart of the cave system which Stane had removed from the police office. The job could have been done in minutes on a graphic artist's enlarger. Catlin had worked slowly and carefully. An error of an eighth of an inch on the map could result in his sighting the cave perhaps as much as fifty yards away from its true position. He thought of the equipment store in his Leith warehouse; survey instruments that would have made the job a hundred times easier.

'Will it be good enough?' Alessandro knelt beside him, staring at Catlin's pencil lines criss-crossing the map.

'Maybe.' Catlin scratched his nose, then rubbed it with the back of his hand. 'If I can find that sharp peak, and the high point of ground to the west, then I'm getting somewhere.'

For another hour he continued work on the chart, moving with it across the plateau until he could align the many reference points, returning to check and recheck their positions. It was survey by dead-reckoning, he admitted to himself, but there was no alternative. The hills rising to the north of the plateau were suddenly gold as the rim of the sun bit into the morning sky. Catlin, who had been staring at the horizon for some time, kicked a rock aside with his foot. 'We drill here.'

The patch of ground where he stood was almost level, but a few yards ahead of him it sloped deeply into a newly formed crater.

Alessandro looked at him questioningly. 'You sure, Joe?'

'Of course I'm damn well not sure. The initials J.C., stand for Joe Catlin, not Jesus Christ!'

There was a sudden movement in a large clump of bushes, and a shout of warning, in Slovene. Catlin didn't understand the words, but the meaning was clear. Alessandro stiffened, then raised his hands. There was another order, and the remainder of the men and Lisetta followed suit. A sudden burst of laughter followed their action. The pines were brushed aside and a party of a dozen young men pushed their way to the open ground of clearing. Alessandro dropped his arms, his face pale with anger and embarrassment. One of the newcomers stepped in front of him, slapped him on the shoulder and attempted to shake his hand. Alessandro refused and the man grimaced and turned to Lisetta. He made some quick remark and she answered him furiously, her eyes glistening dangerously.

'Who the hell are they?' Catlin asked. Their humour wasn't the kind that appealed to him. The man who had shouted, and Catlin thought might be their leader, was little more than five feet in height, dark skinned and heavily built. He had a Mongolian type of moustache. He carried a coil of climbing rope, slung from his shoulders, and wore black jeans and a dark sweater that made him look like a stocky Apaché dancer from a left bank Parisian bar.

Alessandro answered Catlin with a look of displeasure. 'The

Croats . . . the C.L.O., and more of them than we feared.'

The short man strolled lazily over to Catlin and stood a couple of paces in front of him. He eyed him up and down in a way that did nothing to improve Catlin's humour. Eventually the man held out his hand and then spoke. His English was understandable, but grammatically jumbled. 'You him American?' He jabbed a stubby finger at his own chest. 'This man, Sasa.' He tried to crush Catlin's hand in a bullying handshake. Catlin squeezed back and the man was pleased to let go, quickly. 'These my men, my old friends.' Catlin noticed he looked several years older than his colleagues. 'Them students,' said Sasa, following his gaze. 'Me no student; me shepherd.'

Alessandro looked scornful. His face showed his distaste. 'Shepherd! He's Sasa Miculik. He *was* a factory worker. He went to university for a year and studied political science. He's a member of the Croatian Liberation Organisation, and he's wanted by the police.'

'Ahhh!' Sasa Miculik turned quickly to stare at Alessandro. 'You know much.' He walked towards him, and shrugged the rope further onto his shoulder. 'And I you know. You are son of Bor, the Police Commissioner.' He turned his head and spat onto the rocks. 'I like shit on police.'

'Cut it out,' ordered Catlin. 'Do you have the drill-rod?'

'Yes, American, we have rod. Much rod, eh!'

'Okay, you've delivered it. We're grateful but we can manage on our own from here. Just pile it with the other material. There's no need for you to stay, and nothing you can do.'

'Nothing?' Sasa Miculik laughed, and several of his companions grinned. 'Nothing, American?' His voice became serious, 'You want rod, we stay. You no want rod, we go. You want guns, you want explosives? We get. We expert. We not student.'

Lisetta looked pleadingly at Catlin, but he shrugged his shoulders. There were too many of Miculik's men to contemplate taking the drill-rod by force, though by the look of the faces of his own party they would be happy to try if he made the suggestion. 'Right. If you're determined to stay then I'm not going to stop you. But I don't want any arguments or interference; I expect you to work. And you can forget the guns.'

Miculik smoothed his moustache with the back of his hand. His mouth smiled but his eyes remained hard. 'Of course, American. You boss. We work hard, American. You say, we do. You bet.'

Inspector Emile Zlobec was glad he had arrived at his office early. He had been called by his constable a little after midnight and had spent the rest of the night clearing the mess the intruders had left and checking through the scattered files and papers. It was now two minutes past eleven a.m., and a call from Commissioner Bor's secretary had summoned him to the telephone. A telephone call from Bor was unusual in itself, it was usually Zlobec who made the contact; a call so early in the day was exceptional. Had Bor found him absent, then Zlobec knew it might have provided even more future ammunition for his chief's dislike of himself. He sat waiting, his fingers drumming the edge of the desk nervously.

Bor's secretary said: 'Inspector . . . one moment, please.'

'Zlobec?' Bor's voice was hoarse, as though he had been awake all night.

'Yes, Commissioner.'

'I have a report that some of the C.L.O. have left Belgrade, and are believed to be travelling to Postojna.'

'The C.L.O.?' Zlobec was puzzled. He could think of no reason why any members of the C.L.O. would wish to visit his area.

'We've enough trouble without those bastards in the region,' snapped Bor, as though Zlobec was personally responsible for the problem. 'State Security contacted me half an hour ago. With their usual inefficiency, they've managed to let Sasa Miculik slip through their fingers. They planned an arrest during the night, but he'd already gone. They managed to extract some information from the student who was letting Miculik use his apartment. All the man knew was that Miculik was coming in to Slovenia, and he thought he had heard the Postojna caves mentioned.'

'Why Postojna?' Zlobec regretted the question, but he needed some form of answer.

'Why do the C.L.O. do anything? To make trouble, Zlobec! It's an opportunity for them to get publicity.'

'Do they know about the people who have escaped from the cave?'

Bor sounded angry. 'Possibly, but I hope not. Security has been excellent at my end, apart from some stupidity in the press bureau. I trust it has been as efficient at your own.'

'Of course, of course, Commissioner.' Zlobec hesitated. There was some news he had to give to Bor, but the present conversation hadn't made it easy. 'There was an incident here, last night.'

'What kind of incident?' The tone of Bor's voice was ominous, and Zlobec could visualise the man sitting at his desk, leaning forward with the familiar deep scowl on his face.

'A minor incident, Commissioner,' explained Zlobec. He could feel himself perspiring; the sweat beginning to bead on his forehead. 'There was a break-in at the office.'

'Which office?'

'Er . . . the police office.'

'Holy Mother,' breathed Bor. Although he was an atheist he had found no substitutes for traditional oaths.

Zlobec spoke hurriedly. 'The files were searched, and there was a lot of mess, but nothing much taken. All weapons and equipment are safe.'

'What was taken?' There was a dangerous edge to Bor's voice.

'A map.' A drop of sweat ran down the thin bridge of Zlobec's nose and he wiped it with his cuff. 'Just a map of the cave system; the official map. I had it framed, on the office wall. My officers and myself have checked everything else; nothing more seems to have been taken.' He drew in another deep breath. 'The constable on duty fired at the men. He saw two, but believes there might have been more. A military patrol searched the woods for half an hour, but found no-one.'

There was a full minute of silence at the other end of the line, before Bor spoke again. 'Well, Zlobec, what is *your* opinion of the break-in?'

It was the question Zlobec had been dreading. He had spent a lot of the night pondering, but had come up with no reasonble conclusion. He was not even certain the map had been stolen by the intruders; it could have been missing for a couple of days. It was kept in the general office which he seldom entered, and the policemen themselves had not been aware it had gone. Only the clean patch of wall had been a clue which Zlobec himself noticed; even then, there was a chance that it could have been shaken out of place by the earthquake, or perhaps removed by one of the off-duty constables or a rescue worker. It was only when all of the men had been called in, and the office thoroughly tidied and searched, Zlobec had finally decided it had been stolen. 'It would only be of use to someone interested in the cave interior,' he said. 'The Cave Commission and the military would have their own maps. There are also maps at the Pivka caves. In the circumstances, it's not likely to be of any use to anyone.'

'Except trouble-makers, Zlobec. I want the area patrolled

regularly by your men and the military. I'll call Taufer and tell him we expect fullest collaboration. I need to speak to him of the C.L.O., anyway. By the way, Zlobec; State Security informed me they found a few useful documents at Miculik's apartment. What is of more concern are the things they didn't find! Their . . . informant told them he had seen weapons, but they had been removed. This means the C.L.O. are armed, Zlobec. Bear that in mind.'

'What about Miculik?'

'What about him? Security want him, the State Police want him, but if he's in our area, Zlobec, then I want him.'

Unlike Inspector Zlobec, Colonel Taufer was pleased when Bor telephoned him a few minutes later. He had been trying to contact the Commissioner for the past thirty minutes.

'Taufer?'

'Yes, Bor.' The Colonel decided if the Commissioner could address him without a title, then he could do likewise. He was becoming increasingly angered by Bor's attitude.

'Last night's incident at the Postojna police office,' began Bor. 'It's possible the C.L.O. are involved.'

'That's hardly the responsibility of the military.'

'I know. But I have had some information from the State Security Department. Sasa Miculik is believed to be in this region . . . possibly at Postojna.'

Colonel Taufer's reaction was not what Bor expected. 'As a matter of fact, Bor, I don't give a damn for Sasa Miculik or the C.L.O., at this moment. To put it bluntly, Bor, the whole way your rescue operation at Postojna has been handled is horse shit.' Taufer regretted the vulgarity, but hoped it would indicate the depth of his displeasure. The Commissioner was sufficiently startled to remain silent and enable Taufer to continue. The Colonel recognised his advantage. 'It's been a disgrace from the start. I can understand the Committee's concern for the region, but there is no excuse for the way in which Postojna has been neglected. A load of nonsense about security, about priorities . . . and now the C.L.O. There are people who have been there for five days in that mountain, Bor, people who are alive, and who are guests in our country . . . apart from our responsibilities as their hosts, there is the simple matter of humanity. If we *were* doing everything possible to get them out, and it was still impossible, then it might be different. But we aren't, Bor. We haven't even got into first gear.'

'I see,' said Bor, non-commitally. He was surprised he didn't feel angry at Taufer's outburst.

'I've been two hours in the hospital unit, Bor. Two hours at the bedside of the Japanese tourist. He's conscious. You want to know something about horror, Bor . . . then come and listen to this man.'

'He speaks Slovene?'

'Of course he doesn't speak Slovene! This is a training camp, Bor, I have three hundred conscripts . . . and a lot of them are intelligent, well-educated men, right out of university.' Bor was quick to see Taufer's implication. 'There are children, women, inside that mountain, Bor, and they will soon be dying of starvation. There are injured people . . . and no medical supplies or doctors. Hundreds of them, Bor, not just a few. The telephone reports we've had from the cave system give no real indication of conditions down there. I am ashamed for all of us, Bor; ashamed for Slovenia and ashamed for Yugoslavia.'

'There are political implications . . .' Bor began. He didn't even feel like trying to make an excuse. Had he been less tired, he might have hung up on Taufer and then made an official complaint of the man's behaviour to the regional commander of military forces.

'Damn political implications and inferences! What have they got to do with these people's lives? And security! What in hell's name have two brave men got to do with national security? What possible reason do you have for insisting they are kept here in silence? They have families, Bor, families who have a right to know they are alive and safe!'

'I am acting on instructions. We all have to take orders, Colonel, and I am only following mine.'

'Then you are obeying an imbecile; for humanity's sake show some initiative,' snapped Taufer. 'Good morning to you, Commissioner.'

Bor stared at the dead instrument for some time before he slowly replaced it on the rest. He was feeling very old. He looked at the back of the hand that had been holding the telephone; the skin was brown, slightly mottled. He rubbed a finger along the sinews and noticed how the skin had lost its elasticity. Nicotine had stained the nails. The old wound in Bor's neck had stiffened with fatigue, making it uncomfortable for him to move his head. He massaged it with his hands for a few moments, then stood and slipped on his uniform jacket. He wiped dust from the peak of his hat and then walked to the outer office.

'Sir?'

'I'm returning to my home,' Bor said. He glanced at his watch. 'It's eleven twenty five; I'll be back later this afternoon. If I'm needed, you'll know where to contact me.'

'Of course, Sir.' He thought the Commissioner's voice sounded unusually considerate.

Bor didn't put his hat on his head, he carried it out to his car. He never bothered to use an official vehicle to transport him from his office to his home, preferring his own imported Peugeot, a small estate four years old. Using his own car made him feel as though he was away from his work a little sooner . . . a police vehicle somehow carried the job right to his door.

He parked the Peugeot ten minutes later outside the street door to his apartment. It was in a restricted parking zone, but all the traffic police knew the Peugeot's number. He climbed the steps wearily, and unlocked the door. There was the familiar smell of home and he heard his wife call, from the kitchen.

'It's me, Martin.'

She appeared at the kitchen door, wiping her hands on a brightly patterned apron, then came to him and kissed him welcome. 'You look tired. I was worried about you.'

'I thought I'd come back and bath, have some food and a cup of decent coffee,' he explained. 'I don't have too long. Have to be back in the bureau shortly.'

'Martin, you're killing yourself,' she complained. 'You can't keep on like this. Days and days without proper sleep.'

He unbelted his jacket and peeled it off, then dropped heavily into an armchair. 'I'm not a young man.'

She spoke from the kitchen doorway. 'I didn't say that, Martin.' He had always been sensitive about his age.

'No, I said it myself.'

She came back to him and stood by the arm of his chair. She put her hand on the side of his head. 'What's the matter?'

'As you said, I'm just tired.'

'I've seen you tired before; there's something else.' She walked through to the kitchen and returned quickly with a small cup of coffee. 'There's brandy in it.'

He took the cup and sipped the black liquid. 'I had an argument with Taufer this morning.' He automatically wiped coffee from his moustache.

'Taufer? Colonel Taufer?' He nodded a reply. 'But what can you argue about with Colonel Taufer? He's a very gentle person . . . and anyway, in regional matters your position is superior.'

'We didn't exactly argue,' admitted Martin Bor. 'He dressed me down.' She looked at him quizzically. 'Oh, Taufer was *quite* aroused. The trouble is, I agree with a lot of the things he said.'

'But everything is progressing well, I've been listening to the radio, and even today in the newspapers . . .'

'You should read some of the foreign press.' There had been a scathing report in the previous day's New York Times, with implications the Yugoslavian government was withholding information on American citizens. 'I had translations in this morning.'

'And *they* are worrying you? Martin, we all know about exaggerations in foreign newspapers.'

'This time, they are partially justified.'

She sat opposite him, close enough for her to reach forward and take the coffee cup from him. She held both his hands. 'You've been upset for days. It's not the organisation, I know you can handle that . . . you've done quite as much before, with security plans for state visits, the President's tours . . . what is it?'

Bor grimaced, uncomfortably. 'Kalin.'

'But Baraslev Kalin is a friend of ours. You've known him for more than thirty years.'

'He's become ambitious.'

'Baraslev has *always* been ambitious. He was as a young man, he's no different now.'

'I think, perhaps, he sees himself as a candidate for Presidency.'

She laughed. 'Baraslev Kalin! He's a good regional man, but I have never visualised him as President.'

'Nor I,' admitted Bor. He sighed and then said: 'He's underestimated the problems of this disaster. We aren't getting enough help for the region.'

'But that's not a difficult thing to remedy. Tell him you *need* more assistance.'

'It's not that easy; he knows what we need . . . it is deliberate.'

'Deliberate?' She looked at him, disbelievingly. 'Why?'

Bor shook his head. 'I don't have access to his thoughts, only his directives. And he's been good to us in many ways. He helped me a lot when I first joined the police force.' He looked uncomfortable. 'I owe him my loyalty.' He looked quickly around the apartment. 'We owe him this.'

'Nonsense. You would have been a success whether Kalin helped you or not . . . you have always been a determined man, Martin. A good party man when you were younger. You have a fine war record.'

'The war has been over a long time.' He shrugged, wearily. 'We old men are no longer needed . . . perhaps the country wants us to go. Perhaps it is time we were *all* retired so the young can take over.'

'That's silly talk. You have a lot to give, still.' She looked at his tired eyes. 'There's something else . . . something you haven't told me.'

He looked down at his hands, avoiding her gaze. 'I've never questioned an order. Not ever . . . not since the war. Sometimes I thought the orders were strange . . . or difficult to carry through, but I've never questioned. I know my limitations, I'm not a stupid man, and I've thought that if I didn't understand the reasons, then it was because someone better informed than myself *did* know. Now, I have orders which I think are wrong; orders which will kill innocent people as surely as if I shot them with my own pistol.'

'Baraslev Kalin's orders?' She kept the tone of her voice even, refusing to give any indication of pre-judgement.

'Yes.' He told her about Postojna and the people trapped in the cave system; about the two who had escaped by swimming the underground river, and the horrors he knew existed within the mountain. It took him a long time, and there were many pauses as he tried to find the words he needed. Annina said nothing until he had finished, then she slid herself forward off her chair until she was sitting at his feet, her arms resting on his thin legs, her hands holding his, tightly.

'Baraslev Kalin is a murderer,' she said softly when he finished speaking. 'A megalomaniac.'

'Anna Morolec has been arrested by the State Police.'

'Anna Morolec? At Kalin's request?'

'I assume so,' said Bor. 'I learnt unofficially. Bresek at the bureau informed me . . . said she was brought in three days ago. She argued strongly against Kalin at a special meeting of the Regional Committee.'

'Martin, that's terrible.' The grip on his hands tightened, and her voice warmed. 'You came back to tell me all this . . . I didn't need to question you, did I.'

He shook his head. 'You didn't need to ask, I would have got around to it. I suppose I . . .'

'Wanted to warn me before you put your own position at risk?' He nodded. 'You think it would worry me if you were to lose your job because you are an honest man? Because you have compassion and feeling? Do you know why I love you, Martin Bor? Because you are brave . . . because you were a hero . . . because you are the most honest man I have ever met in my life. And because you are a kind man, Martin. Those are the reasons. I did not marry you because there was a likelihood of you becoming the Regional Commissioner of Police.'

'If I am wrong, then it could be bad for us.'

'You are not morally wrong, Martin. It will be far worse if you take no action; you will be condoning Kalin's foolishness.'

Martin Bor smiled. The warmth inside him was proof of the satisfaction of their years of marriage. He leant forward and kissed the side of her head. He could smell perfume in her hair. 'I'll file a report, this afternoon.' He felt more at ease than he had for several days.

He leant back in the chair and closed his eyes. There was a lot to be done; a lot he *could* do. Annina was right, Kalin had become a megalomaniac . . . perhaps he was a little deranged. No, not deranged, it was just that Kalin had set his ambitions too high, and then become obsessed by the route he had chosen. Bor had seen it happen with other men, but never before at such a level of authority. Perhaps it indicated a small weakness in the system of Regional Government, but that shouldn't be possible.

Postojna! The caves must now be his priority. Taufer *had* been right; tourists *were* guests . . . not only guests, but people who were important to Yugoslavia. They were ambassadors, every one of them in their own small way. It wouldn't matter if they weren't, mused Bor. They were human beings in desperate misery . . . the same kind of human beings who had rotted and died in the extermination camps so many years ago. He had taken risks for freedom then, and by God, he would fight again now.

He pushed himself quickly to his feet. He felt rested, as if he had slept for a full day. He called to Annina: 'I'm going back to my office . . .' He was outside the apartment and striding down the steps towards the Peugeot before she had time to reply.

The Boyles X-ray rig was in position and erected by a little after two p.m. It was not a complicated structure, and had been relatively simple to construct. The petrol-fuelled engine started on the second swing on the handle. Catlin let in the clutch and the first section of rod above the diamond-tipped cutter fed quickly through the thin layer of top soil, into the ground. A foot deeper it hesitated and slowed its descent as the cutter hit the rock. Even so, in the soft surface material it cut quickly and fifteen minutes later a second length of rod was screwed into place. The cutting speed was slowing with every inch, as the rock became more firmly compacted, and eventually levelled out to a rate of half an inch a minute. Catlin checked a mark on the length of revolving rod, against his watch, and felt satisfied. The cutting rate was higher than he had expected, though he was aware it might be reduced at greater depth. Without any additional problems to slow its progress, there was a good chance the drill would reach the upper part of the cavern in four days. He was not prepared to be more optimistic, but there was always the chance the route of the cutter would pass through existing cavities in the porous rock, which would greatly decrease the time.

Half an hour before he had ordered the engine started, he had made one more final check on the position of the drill site. Rechecking his map references he had again found the position of the erected drill rig in the anticipated area of the cavern. Short of using a skilled surveyor and good, professional equipment, there was no improvement he could make. Using branches of the fallen pines to mark the area of the underground cavern, the drill site was situated as near as he could estimate to its centre. This gave him a tolerance of inaccuracy of almost thirty yards to either side of the drill rig situation, and fifty yards ahead and behind. With good surveying, this would have been more than adequate; with only his eye and the small compass to help him, he knew he could still be drilling into solid rock at the perimeter of the cavern. It was an unpleasant possibility.

The drill rig itself had been well hidden by Sasa Miculik's men. Catlin had noticed the Croat had worked with an almost military efficiency, and all his men followed his orders without hesitation; Miculik may have been unpopular with the Slovenes, but there was no doubt about the admiration of his own followers. They responded to his orders as quickly as if he were an officer in an army; something which Catlin found ominous. Within a few minutes they had dragged fallen pine trees and bushes from the area around the rig. The trees had been built into a screen which, from only a few yards away, completely shielded the rig and deadened the throb of its small engine. Any smoke from the exhaust drifted through the branches and was dispersed by the rising heat of the ground. Even if the military should decide to search the area Catlin was confident that, with the rig's engine stopped, a man might walk within yards of the equipment without discovery of its existence.

Miculik had also posted guards. It seemed sensible and Catlin had not objected. From the high rocky ground a few hundred yards to the north of the rig they could survey the entire plateau, and Miculik himself seemed happy to keep away from the actual physical work of the drilling operation.

The operation of the drill rig was simple. All it required was that fresh rod should be fitted when the cutter had bored itself deeper into the ground, the engine topped-up with fuel at regular intervals, and the working parts of the rig lubricated. Handling the light lengths of rod did not present the kind of problems experienced on full scale rigs where overhead lifting equipment was required to manoeuvre the heavy gauge tube. Here the rod could be moved by hand, one length weighing no more than a few pounds.

By evening the drill had sunk thirty three feet; the engine had not missed a beat and Joe Catlin was keeping his fingers crossed.

It began raining just as dusk fell across the mountain plateau. Since late afternoon cloud had been building across the horizon, pressing heavily on the distant mountains and gradually filling the sky. The sound of thunder had grown until it could be heard above the thudding of the engine, and as the light faded sharp spears of lightning crackled from the dark base of the low cumulus.

There was no build-up from light rain to downpour. One moment it was humid and uncomfortable, the next a torrential rainfall slashed down into the pines, shaking the light branches and splattering from the rocks. Within a minute the soil was waterlogged and small streamlets flowed across its surface, cutting away the sharp edges of the new crevices and fissures in miniature waterfalls and torrents.

Catlin, his ginger hair plastered against his head, and water dripping from his nose, ears and chin, his clothing already soaked, worked to get a waterproof cover over the engine. He managed with Lisetta's help, and the two of them crouched under a shelter built of tree branches. There was so much sound conversation was impossible. The storm was overhead, so close the lightning and thunder were coupled. Catlin was praying that some bolt of lightning wouldn't choose the rig as a convenient conductor to the wet earth. It hadn't occurred to him there was a risk to his own safety, he was concerned by the knowledge of the destruction such a lightning strike would cause to the irreplaceable equipment. He could feel Lisetta flinching at each blast of thunder, as though she were a child experiencing her first winter storm. He held her close to him.

The rain storm lasted for half an hour, and then slackened to drizzle. The thunder died away, and the lightning played on the distant clouds that had brought early night. Catlin was cold and uncomfortable. He could feel Lisetta shivering next to him. A few yards away the engine throbbed, and he could just see the drill-rod revolving beneath the tree-shrouded rig.

There was movement in the bushes. Alessandro emerged, a storm cape thrown across his shoulders and pulled like a hood over his head. 'Bad. . . very bad weather. Will it affect the drilling?'

'It will probably slow things down a little.' Catlin stood and shook water from himself like a half-drowned dog. 'Where are the others? We need them. We have to take up the rod and check the cutter.'

'Up? All of it?' Alessandro was aware of the depth of rod in the ground.

'If we don't, we may find we're wasting valuable time by trying to cut rock with a blunt head. Get your friends. We'll need some help.'

'Three are underground,' said Alessandro. 'Branko says they've found an interesting fissure. It's new, but it's running down in the direction of the cavern. Your map is helping them, but this weather is bad. Much water will be draining down through the caves. Dangerous for exploring. The tunnels flood quickly.'

Catlin nodded. He pushed the rig gearbox to reverse and watched as the drill rod began to work itself out of the ground. His job was to look after the rig, and get the cutter down through the rock as quickly as possible to the cavern below. If any of the group were stupid enough to cause problems by getting into difficulties in a pothole, they would have to look out for themselves. Catlin had problems of his own.

Berkley spoke quietly. Normally there was a continuous murmur of sound in the vast cavern amplified by the smooth rock and the countless limestone formations. There was always someone talking, crying, or snoring. But there had been a strange silence for the past hour as though death had already stilled his fellow prisoners. He said: 'It's raining! It's night-time, almost midnight, and it's raining, up there.'

"Up there," thought Colette. "Outside is up there." She could barely see him in the gloom. Only one fire glowed, sixty yards away across the cavern. 'Rain? What a wonderful thought! How do you know?'

'Listen . . . water.'

She held her breath. He was right, she could hear distant splashing, the hollcw sound of running water, an increase in the tempo of the constant dripping from the cavern and tunnel roofs. 'I used to hate rain back home. Rain, and people in the subway in wet clothes; how they smelt. You know, when we get out of here I don't think I'll ever ride a subway again. I don't think I'll go anywhere I can't see the sky. I don't think I'll ever shut a window, or close a door. Maybe I'll just live in the open like a hobo.'

'You've been mind reading.'

'You want to be a hobo?' She giggled. She couldn't picture him in tattered clothing. David Berkley in New York was one of the most fashionably dressed visitors to Lady Ahead's offices. She was amused for the first time since the earthquake.

'Well, almost. Things can never be the same for any of us. When I came back from ''Nam it was with a different set of values to those I'd had before. I wonder how often a person can keep changing them?'

'All your life, I guess.'

She saw his body move against the distant glow of the fire. 'I'm finished with photography.'

'Finished?' You're the best in the business.'

He didn't respond to the flattery. 'I was talking with Carl. He feels the same. Maybe we've all changed a lot. He's thirty eight. Works as a history teacher. He's finished with that, too. Ski-ing's his hobby. He's quitting teaching. Say's he'll work in a mountain ski school in the winter, work with his hands in the summer, or as a climbing guide. He thinks he'll be unable to work indoors.'

'You'll change your minds when we get out.'

'No. Not me, and not Carl. I know him pretty well, now. He'll do it.'

'And you? You're going to be a hobo?'

'No, not a hobo. Maybe a bum.'

'How?' She closed her eyes and rested her head back against the damp rock. She found his voice soothing.

'I've saved a bit. I'll sell my apartment . . . the Ferrari. I used to go on fishing trips with my Dad . . . a place called Blue Lake. I'm going back.'

'To fish?'

'To live. New York isn't living, there's too much stone . . . too much concrete.' He thought for a moment. 'Too many caves.'

'And what'll you do in Blue Lake?'

He didn't answer immediately, but after a while said: 'Just grow things.'

'Things?'

'Kids. Chickens; maybe hogs. I could farm trout.'

'David Berkley, trout farmer.'

'Say it again.'

She laughed. 'David Berkley, trout farmer.'

'It sounds good.'

It was after midnight before Joe Catlin left the drilling rig in the care of Mileta and Branko. The rain had now completely stopped, and the sky cleared, bringing a little night warmth to the plateau and life to its countless insect population. There was a fresh clean smell to the night air, and a light mist was filling the hollows of the plateau with silver pools in the moonlight.

Catlin stripped off his shirt and walked back through the pine woods. His skin dried, tingling, as though he had just towelled himself after an ice cold shower. He paused on the high ground above the plateau, to look back. The storm was just a thick band of black above the horizon. The stars seemed to be close enough to touch, and a bright, full moon gave crispness to shadows across the rock and open ground. He knew the position of the drilling rig, but was unable to see it in its camouflage of trees and shrubbery; the throb of its engine was beyond earshot. Lisetta waited, a few paces ahead of him, knowing he was enjoying the sharpness of the night, drinking it in like chilled and sparkling wine.

'Good?'

'Yeah . . . good.' He took several deep breaths. The night landscape was unreal. The moonlight making the fissures in the collapsed ground even more distinctive, and the mist pools adding bizarre touches of surrealism with gaunt pines leaning at crazy angles above the drifting surfaces. It had been a long time, thought Catlin, since he stood and looked at hills at night. He was a specialist in bars, not landscapes.

There was excitement in the cave when Lisetta and Catlin arrived a few minutes later. He didn't understand the conversation between Simon and Lisetta, but when Catlin had changed into dry clothing Simon came over and sat next to him.

'It's good news, Joe. The men who were searching underground, they have found a deep entrance to the system. They don't know how deep, but it looks promising. And they think they can hear the cutting of your drill in the rock. This passage, is narrow though, and very difficult.'

Stane had joined them, bringing bowls of hot soup for Catlin and Lisetta. 'We nearly drown after rain,' he said, grinning. 'Much water come off mountain. Flood small passage quickly. But we hear drill . . . grrr . . . grrr . . . grrr. Above, someplace. Maybe we race you down, huh?'

'What about Miculik?' Catlin asked. The fiery Croat's presence was still disturbing him. He could sense trouble ahead.

'Out, with his men,' answered Alessandro. 'Some of them are on the mountain, others are above us, guarding this cave entrance. He says they're watching for military patrols.'

'If that was all, then I'd be pleased,' said Catlin. 'But there's something else. You said he'll try to promote their cause; well, watching patrols isn't going to do that. He'll have something else in mind, if you're right.'

Simon made a wry face. 'I think perhaps Sasa Miculik is reforming himself; to be more like us.'

'Snakes not change,' warned Lisetta. 'Miculik kills with bombs. I not happy he stays here. Miculik is dangerous, like a cobra snake.'

'Bombs?' queried Catlin. 'Miculik in person?'

Alessandro nodded. 'Two years ago a bomb was placed in the Central Station in Belgrade. Two people were killed, and several were injured. Miculik was responsible. There were other bombings. That's why the police want him. But we can do nothing about him. In this country there are many people who feel degrees of dissatisfaction with our government; many small organisations such as our own, who hope their efforts will change things. Sometimes the organisations must work together . . . we have contacts with many . . . some right wing, left wing. . . the one thing we have in common, is we wish to make changes.'

'Overthrow your government?' asked Catlin.

Lisetta looked horrified. 'No, not us!'

Alessandro explained. 'Some underground organisations do . . . but not us. You cannot hate people who genuinely think they are acting in your best interests, and you cannot preach revolution without hate. In many ways ours is an honest government, but it is ignorant. It has many faults but the one we fight against is delusion. Our leaders talk communism, but want socialism. They want increased productivity and wealth, but limit incentive, they worship freedom and yet the majority of the prisoners in our gaols are political.'

'That is why here is important, Joe,' said Lisetta enthusiastically. 'Because bombs is no good. Because we show our government that sometimes what is too big for them, is not too big for . . . for little people.'

'Freedom of the individual to take responsible action, without state bureaucracy,' Alessandro added.

'One more thing I'd like to know,' said Catlin. 'If it weren't for your politics, would you guys be here right now?' He immediately regretted asking the question; it was unnecessary.

Alessandro's eyes caught his: 'Would you be drilling if only communist Slovenes were trapped in the caves?'

Catlin felt his face redden. 'I asked for that. The answer's the same for us all, I guess. Yes.'

Catlin was restless. The cave was silent, but for the past two hours he had been lying awake beside Lisetta, his back against the rock. His mind still guarded the spinning drill rod, and his ears remained tuned to the steady throb of the engine. Eventually, he left the cave and walked back, alone, to the rig; Mileta and Branko were adding more rod. Catlin stood and watched them for a few minutes, then kicked himself a nest in the scrub ten yards away. He stretched himself on the damp, springy branches. The sound of the drill rig was reassuring; within seconds he was asleep.

18

Days and nights for many of the people trapped in the cave had ceased to exist with the collapse of the entrance. Some, the determined or methodical, marked the passing of unseen days by their watches, some scratched lines on rocks, or chipped marks in pieces of wood. Time passed quickly while they slept; awake, it had no progression. No sun or moon traced a crossing on a sky, no habits remained to provide orientation within a twenty-four hour day. Without light, or darkness, sleep or rest came only when exhaustion dulled senses; without food there were no mealtimes, no movements of the bowels.

A few knew it was the sixth day; for all it was worse than its predecessors. It began with disaster, it began with a minor fault on the telephone system.

Mallek had been chatting to a military operator; his conversation pointless and inane. The line crackled.

Mallek, slow thinking even when well-fed, and more stupid now he was starving, stood and swore. In an attempt to correct the interference on the wire, he kicked part of the control box. The result was a complete loss of communication. Struger had found an electrician amongst the German group, and for the past three hours the man had been checking the instrument's internal connections; without success. There were no electrical maintenance tools in the cavern's emergency stores. The man had admitted to Struger he was unlikely to be able to repair the equipment. Communication with those outside the cavern had been lost; the feeling of isolation became total. It had been impossible to conceal the disaster, Mallek had made too much fuss.

Struger had broken the news to the Germans, Berkley to the Americans and English.

'But, Jesus . . . what now?'

Stay calm, Berkley thought. Panic is infectious. 'It doesn't mean anything. The telephone isn't important. They're still working just as hard to get to us.'

'But we won't know anything . . .'

'We don't need to know anything. The telephone was only a bonus. The telephone isn't digging us out, or providing us with food and medicine. Losing it won't make any difference.' It did though, even to him; but he wasn't going to admit it. 'Just rest easy. All we have to do is keep calm and wait.' He lied: 'The last we heard was it wouldn't be too long.'

It was a relief when, half an hour later, he and Struger left the main cavern to attempt a route along a higher section of tunnel above the collapsed Russian Bridge. It was at Struger's suggestion, and Berkley was pleased to agree, although previously Struger had dismissed the tunnel as unlikely. Berkley felt that Struger was experiencing the same disturbing emotions as himself, and needed only an excuse to get away from the others. It was better when the sounds of the cave were behind them.

A little after mid-day, Paul Ukley of Oregon City, whose bronchitis had worsened and developed into pneumonia two days previously, died.

It was almost an hour before those sitting or lying close to him realised his laboured breathing had ceased.

Twenty minutes later there was another death. A three year old Italian child stiffened in the arms of the British veterinary surgeon, convulsed violently and, despite the man's frantic efforts to restart its heart beat, was gone. He stood with it awkwardly in his thick arms, as he might have held a dead lamb, before passing the small body to its sobbing mother. There were tears on the surgeon's face.

Few people were capable of diminishing Minister Baraslev Kalin's confidence or ego; Jano Vulas, Secretary of the Presidium of the League of Communists, member of the eight-men Presidency, was one. The two men had been political rivals for many years, and Kalin knew Vulas was a certain contender for the unique presidential leadership which Kalin hoped, one day, to possess. He viewed Vulas's situation with envy; it set the man several rungs higher on the political ladder than himself. He did not feel the important status had been earned. The dislike between the two men was mutual.

Kalin faced Vulas now. It had been a five hour drive to the

Party's Zagreb offices where he had been instructed to attend in a curt early morning conversation with Vulas's personal assistant; that in itself had been a calculated insult.

'Leave immediately, Kalin, Secretary Vulas expects you here this afternoon.'

There had been no indication of the subject of the meeting, and almost in panic Kalin had ordered his own office staff to pack the official automobile with any material which could possibly be of interest to the Presidium Secretary. He had spent much of the journey consoling himself with the thoughts that perhaps Vulas merely wanted a report of the salvage operations in the devastated northern region. It was not a personally convincing calculation, and by the time the official automobile, with its red licence plates, reached the Party's gothic offices, Kalin's suit was creased and damp with perspiration.

He had been kept waiting twenty minutes in the ante-room, before being summoned into the Secretary's office. It was a large room, the walls panelled in oak and the ceiling high and ornately plastered. A marble bust of Tito stood on a column in one corner, to the side of Vulas's large leather-covered desk. Behind the desk, and draped with crossed flags of the Republic, was a painting of the late President in his wartime uniform.

Vulas did not smile a greeting. His handshake was formal and cool. He indicated a stiff-backed chair facing him. There was a microphone on the desk, and Kalin knew it was connected to a concealed tape recorder. It did nothing to add to his confidence.

Vulas said: 'I have had a report, Kalin.'

Kalin nodded. The feelings of uncertainty and anger were mixed. At the moment he felt like an errant schoolboy facing his school principal; it was distasteful. But one day, he swore, the positions would be reversed.

'Regarding the disaster in Slovenia.'

Kalin had a sudden feeling of relief. It had been six days since the earthquake and everything seemed to be progressing as he had planned. His mollification was misguided and short-lived.

'The report has been made known to the Presidency. They are extremely angry, Kalin. The mishandling of the entire business is a national disgrace.'

Kalin committed himself to defensive attack. 'I have been acting in the best interests of Slovenia and Yugoslavia, Secretary. I know of no inefficiency; the entire operation has been smoothly conducted. All telephonic communication has been restored in the region, many bridges have been replaced, certainly on the major roads, and food and medical supplies are going through to all the places where they are required. Naturally, medical resources are strained, but in the circumstances . . .'

'I am talking of the dishonour you have brought on our country, by the way you have seen fit to deal with the calamity at Postojna.'

'Postojna!' The word was like a blow to Kalin's solar plexus.

Vulas turned papers on the desk. 'I have here a State Police report on the detention of Anna Morolec. It forces me to question your sanity, Kalin. I interviewed her two hours ago, and ordered her immediate release.'

'Secretary, I have been acting only in the best political interests of the State.'

Vulas almost shouted. 'Political interests? You have no right to consider political interests. Only the Presidency Committee, or the entire Presidium of the League of Communists has the right to make political decisions. Are you not aware, Kalin, of the importance of the United States of America, to Yugoslavia?'

'They are not communist, Secretary,' Kalin retorted. He knew Vulas was making the most of the opportunity to discredit him. It was one way of reducing the field of opposition.

'Nor are the West German Republic, Kalin; nor most of our neighbours. It has taken us many years to establish rapport with the western powers. You dare to make a decision which jeopardises the future of our country. Every possible effort should have been made to rescue their citizens trapped at Postojna. It should have been the priority; every available man and machine should have been used in their rescue, even at the expense of our own citizens.'

Kalin tried bluff. 'There *has* been a continuous rescue operation, at Postojna, since the day of the earthquake, Secretary. Commissioner Bor is personally responsible and I believe him to be a competent man. I do not think he is guilty, as you suggest.'

'No, Commissioner Bor is *not* guilty, Kalin.' Vulas slid open a drawer of the desk, pressed a switch and sat back in his armchair. He looked at Kalin, contemptuously.

There was a low hiss of sound from a speaker at the side of the desk.

'But the news is good, Minister. The people were believed dead . . .' It was Commissioner Bor's voice.

Kalin remembered the conversation and silently cursed the

inventor of tape recording equipment. His stomach felt empty and he had to make a determined effort to retain the contents of his bladder. He should have realised Bor would protect himself by recording every radio or telephone call from a superior. He heard his own voice: 'Stay in Ljubljana, Bor. It would be sensible if . . .'

A minute later Vulas silenced the recording. 'Nero fiddled while Rome burnt; Minister Kalin takes his Regional Police Commissioner out to a restaurant! I'm glad, however, Martin Bor has habits similar to my own. A record should be kept of everything, don't you agree, Kalin? This tape recording, and his own report, was delivered to my office last night by one of his messengers. I heard from the State Police immediately afterwards . . . a wise move by Commissioner Bor, Kalin.' Vulas stood, and pressed one of the battery of buttons on a console on his desk. Almost immediately his assistant appeared at the door accompanied by two men whom Kalin knew, instinctively, were plain-clothes State Policeman. 'Your resignation is accepted, Kalin. I am now faced with the task of attempting to salvage the honour of our country. You, however, will attend a meeting of the Presidency who will decide your future. In the meantime, you are to be escorted back to Ljubljana and placed under house arrest.'

On the plateau above the cavern, in the late afternoon, the drill-rod of the rig began to operate strangely. It was fortunate Catlin was standing within a foot of the operating lever and was able to act immediately to prevent its self-destruction. The drill-rod, which had been revolving steadily following the cutter inch by inch into the rock, jerked several times, the engine speed increased suddenly and the rod abruptly dropped six inches. Catlin snatched the gear lever to neutral, and swore loudly.

'What's wrong?' Alessandro who had been sitting a few yards away, was instantly on his feet.

'We've lost cut. I think we've hit a fissure or maybe an underground cave. If not, then we've lost our cutting head.' Catlin let in the clutch, slowly. The machine began revolving, then the rod dropped again, its clamp jamming and squealing against the rig platform. 'We're cutting air. That's good, we gain easy depth.' He stopped the cutter and added another five foot section of drill rod. He let in the clutch. 'Steady . . . if we let go too fast, then the unsupported length of drill-rod above the cutter will bend and we'll lose the lot.' Alessandro nodded. 'Another thing; if the cutting head is following the edge of a fissure, then it will force the drill-rod out of true. If that happens, then the tube will snap. Never let the drill take control; you're the boss, not the machinery.' He put his head close to the revolving rod. 'When this sort of thing happens, listen carefully to the noise of the drill. If the cutting head is being forced out of line by one side of a fissure, then you can hear it cutting unevenly, like it's taking little bites out of the rock. If it's cutting air, then there's no sound. Drilling in regular rock produces a regular sound. Right now the drill head isn't cutting, so we have to lower it steadily. We don't know what it will meet next.' He stopped the machinery and added another length of rod. In two minutes the cutting head had dropped six feet. There was another twenty feet of air before the drill head picked up rock; first with the uneven sound, and then with the steady grinding of the normal cut.

Lisetta had been watching, closely. 'Twenty eight pieces of drill-rod, Joe. That means we're down over forty meters.'

'One hundred and forty feet in thirty hours. That's good but the earthquake has made it easier. It ground a lot of the strata into rubble and the drill head doesn't have to cut as much as it would through solid material. But don't get too optimistic. Optimism has made a lot of oil men bankrupt.'

A hundred feet below ground, and twenty yards further west than the spot where Catlin was standing next to the rig, three of the Ljubljana students were slowly edging their way along a narrow crack in the distorted rock. They moved only an inch at a time, twisting and wriggling, to force their way forward through a crevice only eight or nine inches in width. They had discarded most of their clothing thirty yards back, and were near naked. Sharp edges of freshly broken rock scored red lines along their skin, and bit deep into the straining muscles. Beams from the headlights on their helmets illuminated the coloured strata.

Stane was leading. His helmeted head was wedged against the rock and he was trying to find purchase with the edge of his boots. Ahead of him the tunnel seemed to open slightly; another two or three feet and he should be able to move more easily. Behind him was Milovan, grunting with effort as he tried to lift himself over a raised hump of sharp limestone.

Stane called: 'Quiet . . .'

Simon, the third of the men shouted from behind Milovan, his voice anxious, 'What's wrong?'

'Quiet, both of you.' Stane pressed his helmet harder against the side of the passage. 'The drill has stopped.' The steady grinding, like the distant sound of pebbles chattering in surf, was no longer ahead of them.

'Maybe we're just further away from it.' Milovan's voice was muffled by Stane's body.

'No, we should be about right.' Stane found grip for his right boot, gave a groan and heaved himself through the narrow gap. There was an instant feeling of relief as the pressure was released from his chest and he was able to breath deeply once again. He pulled himself into the wider passage on his elbows. 'There's a steep pitch here.' His headlight showed an older, undamaged section of tunnel. He found enough height to crawl forward on his hands and knees. The floor dropped away in front of him and ended at a deep crevasse cutting across the fissure at right angles. He lowered his head so the beam could shine downwards.

'What's there?' Milovan was still caught in the squeeze.

'A drop. About twelve meters. But it still looks good.' He shone the light upwards. 'It's an old waterway.' The roof was still coated with a limestone deposit and thin pencil stalactites dripped continously. A ledge of limestone protruded by the side of the crevasse and the split rock offered good hand and footholds. In normal circumstances he would have used a rope, but the only one they had carried lay with their clothing behind them. He swung himself over the side. Milovan's light flashed a few feet away.

'It doesn't look too bad.'

'The fissure breaks out at the bottom.' Stane forced his hand into a deep crack and then clenched his fist to give him a strong hold. He swung his legs sideways towards a section of broken rock.

'The drill's cutting again,' said Milovan. 'I think very . . .'

He didn't finish. There was a sudden explosion of sound. Rock chippings and limestone rubble burst from the roof above them. Milovan protected his face with his arm, and stared upwards. His light beam caught glistening movement.

'Jesus Christ . . . the cutter!' Milovan saw sharp-edged polished steel teeth tearing at the air only inches above his friend's shoulder. They dropped slowly towards him like the claws of some medieval instrument of torture. Milovan yelled: 'Move . . . move fast.'

Stane glanced sideways, saw the gears and struggled desperately to find a new grip on the rock. The teeth were now only an inch from his body. He snatched at a narrow ledge, almost beyond reach, and twisted himself sideways. The movement gave him only a few seconds respite. His feet scrabbled at the slippery rock face. There was so much sound from the mechanism close to his head he could not hear Milovan's instructions; he saw the man's hand held out towards him, the fingers hooked in readiness. He let go his hold on the ledge, and grabbed at the wrist, feeling Milovan's hand lock round his forearm. He kicked himself away from the rock as the teeth of the cutting head smashed into the plastic of his helmet. The beam of Milovan's light blinded him but he felt the man dragging him upwards. A moment later he was sitting beside him, breathless, on the lip of the tunnel. The two men watched the revolving shaft as the cutter head lowered itself towards the base of the pit; abruptly it stopped its movement and there was silence.

'What the hell's going on along there?' Simon's anxious voice seemed to roll along the tunnel as he forced himself through the tight squeeze to join them.

Milovan answered as Stane began seeking a safer route down the shaft. 'It was Joe Catlin's American sense of humour. He tried to drill through Stane's head.'

'Milovan pulled me out of the way,' called Stane.

'Only because I thought you'd damage the one cutting head Joe's got!'

Sasa Miculik was lying on his stomach between two grey outcrops of limestone, high above the site of the demolished cave terminal. Beside him was Lojze Bosilj, an eighteen year-old student from Belgrade. Bosilj was a thin, weedy youth; his father was an attendant in one of the Belgrade hospitals, and Lojze Bosilj was one of nine children. He had begun his studies in economics less than a year previously, but saw Miculik as a more ready solution to his own problems.

Miculik was watching the suddenly increased activity on the site below him.

Half an hour previously, a column of fifteen heavy transporters had arrived, all marked with the insignia of the state owned haulage companies. Eight of the transporters had carried men; Miculik estimated there were at least a hundred and fifty of them, construction labourers by the look of them. Some wore safety helmets and the bright fluorescent orange jackets of road workers. The other seven transporters carried equipment, amongst it three giant bulldozers. A number of smaller vehicles had arrived shortly afterwards, including two identifiable as those of the regional police. There were three state vehicles with the official red plates.

There was no time wasting. The occupants of the official cars had spent a brief time in one of the wooden buildings a hundred yards from the demolished terminal, and had then moved in purposeful groups to various places on the site. The workers were already separated into teams, the bulldozers unloaded and the equipment stacked. One of the bulldozers, a vehicle, judging by its great size, normally used for land clearance on motorways, was already tearing aside the remaining rubble at the foot of the cliff. Its blade lifted great slabs of reinforced concrete as ferociously as a starving tiger shark attacking a victim.

From his viewpoint five hundred feet above the terminal, Miculik could hear the shouts of the men, and the growing rumble of the heavy machinery.

As they watched, a military vehicle — built like a World War Two Jeep — swung itself from the distant road and bounced across the buckled tarmac of the parking area. There was more movement beyond the trees; a number of grey, canvas-topped military trucks lumbered towards the site.

Lojze Bosilj eased himself back from the edge of the grey rock, as though the military activity were being directed at him personally. 'What's happening?'

Miculik didn't reply. He didn't know the answer, but he was determined to find out.

Commissioner Bor was feeling happier. His conscience had been a burden over the past few days, and he had never agreed with Kalin's decision. He knew now he should have gone above Kalin's head at once, and cursed himself for his weakness. He had become too complacent, too satisfied with the system, too unquestioning and comfortable; he had put the danger to his own position ahead of the lives of those trapped beneath the mountain. He hoped now the delay had not been too great. He stood by the door of Zlobec's office, and watched the growing scale of activity as more and more men and equipment arrived to dig their way into the mountain. There were government engineers directing the gangs of men, checking stores, working on plans and schemes to bore their way through the rock. Full information regarding the plight of those trapped alive in the caverns had been released to the international press, and in just one more day, he had been told, heavy tunnelling equipment and skilled operators would arrive from Italy. Truckloads of machinery were already hammering down the German autobahns, and would cross the Austrian Alps near Villach in another twenty-four hours. It was like watching a vast army assemble in the days before an invasion. It made Bor warm inside.

'Commissioner!' He turned. A grey-painted military staff car had drawn up behind him, the sound of its arrival drowned by the machinery on the site. Colonel Taufer leant from its rear window. 'Good evening.' Colonel Taufer was shouting, then changed his mind and clambered out of the car. He brushed his clothes straight. 'Thank God, Comissioner Bor. This is what we wanted, eh?' It was necessary for him to talk loudly over the thunder of the engines. Bor nodded his agreement, he saw no reason to hold a grudge against Taufer. The man had been right; the catalyst Bor had needed. 'What's happening about security? I've had no recent official directives!'

Bor leant closer to the Colonel without moving his feet. 'My instructions are that we must wait for the orders of the Presidency, so I think it will be wise to be particularly tactful. Officially, contact with the survivors underground has only been made in the past few hours. Keep the press away from the two men you've got, for a little while, anyway. But I see no reason why their escape should be kept secret much longer. If your doctors wish, they can call in help from the Ljubljana medical clinic. From noon tomorrow, I have been told, all foreign press will be allowed to visit here. Naturally, we don't want them at any of the military establishments.'

'Of course not. This is much better, Bor, much better. I was hoping you'd get things going.' He raised an eyebrow. It was a small dig.

'It was bound to take time,' answered Bor. There was no need to give the Colonel more of an explanation. He would learn about Kalin's disgrace soon enough.

'What about the C.L.O.?'

'Sasa Miculik?'

'Yes.'

'No more reports, Colonel. Could be the information was inaccurate. There's been no sign of him, or any of his members, in the towns. All my men have been warned to keep their eyes open.

What about your patrols?'

'Nothing . . . apart from the incident the other evening. I doubt if that was anything to do with the C.L.O. Their men tend to shoot back. We've got regular daylight patrols out on the area, but they've reported nothing out of the ordinary.'

'Let's hope it stays that way,' said Bor. Sasa Miculik and the C.L.O. were an additional problem he could do without.

Kaguri remembered the advice he had received in his youth from one of his teachers. There had been several times in his life when the master's words had pushed their way to the forefront of his memory. Always he could picture the time when they had been spoken. He had been kneeling in a line of fellow pupils in the Tokyo dojo. It was a place of strict reigi, discipline, and he was sitting carefully, his body vertical, unmoving. In front of him was his 'men', the heavy mask; to his side, his bamboo shinai. The pupils were still wearing their body armour and their heads were wrapped in their hachimaki, the cloths that acted as helmet paddings and sweat bands. The teacher, a man already in his sixties, had been discussing zanshin, awareness, the ability to be always on guard. He had turned the subject to courage.

'If you must look for it, if you need to ask yourself if you possess this quality, then you have already sown the grains of doubt in your mind. Once courage is doubted, it has been lost. Go into battle, go into your lives, with the knowledge that you will win.'

Standing in the chill dank of the caverns, Kaguri, for the first time in his life, questioned his own courage. 'I am not about to die', he told himself. 'I am not facing a sword or a gun. I am not wounded. But I am afraid.'

It was not physical fear, but something deeper, more inexplicable. He was not fighting for his own life, but the lives of others. The unnerving thought was that he was fighting himself.

He waited for the return of Berkley and Struger.

The two men returned to the main cavern, and a horrifying task. Their exploration of the tunnel had only proved Struger's earlier suspicion; it led upwards, but gradually ended in a series of small, impassable fissures. The two men found Kaguri waiting for them near the cavern entrance.

'One of the children has died.' Kaguri lowered his head slightly, as if in deference to its memory.

Struger swore softly in German.

'Of starvation?' asked Berkley. He had the same dull feeling inside him he'd experienced before battles in Vietnam; a kind of sick numbness.

'Perhaps. The Englishman says more will die soon.' Kaguri stared at the two men but they both avoided his gaze. 'Our decision has already been made,' he prompted.

Struger said: 'Ja,' and bit his lip, nervously.

'Then come . . .' Kaguri turned away.

There were fifty six complete bodies in the short length of tunnel that led away from the lowest end of the great cavern, they were all that the survivors had been able to recover. Many more were buried beneath rock. There was also an unpleasant pile of dismembered trunks and limbs. The bodies, and the torn pieces, were wrapped in bloodstained blankets, but despite the chill of the damp catacomb there was a nauseating stench of decomposing flesh, and the corpses were swollen; pressing against their thick wet shrouds like ripe chrysalis.

The three men wore cloths wrapped around their faces, covering their mouths and nostrils, but they did little to reduce the sickening odour. Between them they carried the corpse of Paul Ukley. The body was not heavy; Ukley had been a lightly-built man, and weeks of illness had slimmed him even more. Transporting him across the broken ground was difficult; rigor mortis had set him in a crouched position, as though in death he hunched his body to protect his ravaged lungs.

They carried Ukley to the farthest end of the passage, where the roof sloped to the floor in a jumbled mass of fallen rock. Berkley was experiencing a new kind of fear, not now the fear of battle or personal danger, but a more terrifying kind of fear, deep inside himself; a fear which questioned, a fear which was revulsion at what he knew must be done.

They knelt beside the body and pulled back the blanket. Ukley's head was tilted at a slight angle as though he queried their actions. His arms were pulled tight across his stomach, and his knees were raised. He looked like a man with stomach cramps, his eyes half-open and his lips drawn back from even, white dentures.

'God, forgive us,' breathed Struger. He turned the beam of the flashlight so Ukley's head was in darkness.

'It may eventually prove harder for us to forgive ourselves.' Kaguri reached forward and began unfastening Ukley's belt.

Berkley watched as Kaguri undressed the lower part of Ukley's body. It seemed to glow yellow in the light of the lamp. Berkley's stomach heaved, and he swallowed quickly. He wondered how the other two men were feeling. He had no doubt Carl Struger was as horrified as himself, but Kaguri showed nó emotions.

Struger had the knife; he had purchased it in Munich only three weeks before. It was made of Solingen steel, ground to razor sharpness; he had bought it because it incorporated a pipe tamping tool. The short blade was intended for use in reaming out tobacco tar. A longer blade would now be more useful.

His hands were shaking and the beam of light fluttered across Ukley's legs. Struger cursed himself, then placed the flashlight on a rock. He had difficulty opening the blade with his broken thumbnails softened by the continuous damp air. Kaguri took the knife from him.

Berkley forced himself to watch, feeling if he turned his head away it would be inexcusable cowardice. He felt Struger's broad hand tighten on his wrist as though the man expected to feel the agony of the steel in his own flesh.

Kaguri drew the blade firmly across Ukley's thigh. To Berkley's relief, no blood flowed; Kaguri might have been carving a joint of raw beef. He cut more deeply, first across the muscle and then downwards until a clean slab of muscle could be lifted from the bone. He laid it on the rock beside the flashlight. It looked like a five pound piece of rump steak, one surface pale and coated with fine dark hair. He grunted and moved closer, on his knees, to use the rock as a butcher's palate. He skinned the joint, then cut it into a dozen narrow strips like raw pemmican. He packed the meat into a plastic bag Berkley had found in the demolished canteen, then passed it to Struger. The German took it without comment, pushing it quickly from sight beneath his torn jacket.

They re-wrapped Ukley's corpse, carefully knotting the blanket around his body with strips of cloth. Kaguri stood, stiffly, then found a small pool nearby and washed his hands for a long time in the shallow water.

When he spoke again, his voice was pitched lower than normal. 'Go. Do not come back for seven or eight hours. Wash the meat before you return. And remember, you found the carcass of a deer.' Kaguri knew he had conquered himself.

David, you can't go so soon. You haven't rested.' Colette was almost begging.

'It's become urgent . . . and Carl has an idea about one of the passages.' He was dreading the next few hours.

She felt his depression. 'Is there something wrong?' The warm concern in her voice brought him closer to tears than he'd been since childhood.

'Nothing.' He tried to sound convincing but it wasn't easy to lie to her; lies were out of place in the relationship that had developed. He wanted to crouch beside her in the small shelter he had built, feel her warm and close, and tell her of the terrible thing that had to be done.

'You shouldn't go now, David,' she insisted. 'There must be others. Let someone else go with Carl, for a change. Perhaps you're ill.'

'I'm okay. Just feeling tired.' He straightened himself. 'I'll get over it when we start moving.'

'You can't go on like this, you're exhausted. It's stupid, you'll kill yourselves. You and Carl should *both* rest. No-one else is doing anything. Look at them, they just sit around all the time.' She saw his determination, and realised there was a reason he wasn't prepared to share. It hurt a little.

She held his hand, and walked with him across the cavern until they met Carl. When the two men left, Berkley didn't look back; he knew she was watching them. They had gone no more than four hundred yards along one of the now familiar tunnels. They found a ledge sheltered by an overhang and rested there.

For a long time the two men sat in the darkness together in silence. Berkley thought Struger was sleeping, the man's breathing was even and shallow. He was surprised when he spoke.

'I saw my father last night.'

Struger had never mentioned his family before. Berkley answered: 'In a dream?'

'Maybe a dream . . . but I saw him.' There was a strained quality to Struger's voice, as though he were forcing himself to tell Berkley.

'Your father is at home in Germany?'

'No, he is here.'

'Here?' There was something in the way Struger had answered that made Berkley hesitate. 'He is one of the tourists?'

'No. He died here . . . a long time ago . . . in the war. They blew up this place.'

'The petrol dump!'

'Yes. He was inside when it happened. They never found his body.'

Christ, thought Berkley, I imagined it was bad for me! Struger has been living for the past six days in his father's tomb! He said: 'Strange things are happening to all of us. The continual poor light doesn't help. I find my eyes see things in the darkness that don't exist. Perhaps it's a form of hallucination.'

'No, this wasn't hallucination,' said Struger. 'I went, last night, down one of the lower tunnels. I was walking, and someone was walking a little behind me. I thought it was you. I turned, and he was standing there. I didn't recognise him at first, perhaps if he'd been in his uniform . . . he was wearing a suit and his clothes were neat and pressed. I knew it wasn't one of us . . . he was too clean. Then he held out his hand and I saw a special gold ring on his finger. I knew who he was, then. I think I said something, but he was gone.' He paused. 'You think I am mad, maybe?'

'No, I don't think that.'

'I think I must be a little mad, but I have had unpleasant thoughts since last night. My father, he died here over thirty five years ago, and I saw him, still here in these caves. David, has he been here, in this damned hole for all that time? Will he still be here a hundred years from now? And will I be here with him?'

It was late evening, but all of Alessandro's men were gathered around the drilling rig. Stane was talking rapidly, waving his arms and grinning. Alessandro laughed, then spoke to Catlin.

'We nearly killed him. The cutter broke through the roof of a cave, just above his head. He thought there was another earthquake!'

'Does he know what time that was?'

Allessandro questioned Stane before replying. 'About four this afternoon. That would be the last time the drill was, as you say, cutting air.'

'And we've added another fifteen feet since then.' Catlin thought for a moment, then rubbed his hands across the stubble of his head. 'Yeah, that's good; great.'

Lisetta smiled. 'Tomorrow maybe we get through to the cavern. I know my Joe do this.'

Catlin frowned theatrically. 'Never count chickens or oil wells, Lisetta.' He was always nervous of predictions. There were still many things that could go wrong; a sheared drill-rod was only one of them, the engine might fail, or the head become too blunt to cut the rock . . . he stopped considering possible calamities. 'We'll need work shifts for the night . . . I'll stay on until midnight, then Alessandro and one of the others until four a.m. Simon can take over then. But I'm not leaving the rig, I'll be right here. If the slightest thing goes wrong, wake me; I want to know about it . . . and fast. We're down over two hundred feet, and it's been all luck since we started. Luck isn't easy to get . . . I want to make sure we keep what we've got.'

It was night. The moon had not yet risen and the air was still and humid. Five men crouched beneath the whitewashed walls surrounding the military base at Zagon. They had been waiting silently for two hours, since the bugler had sounded 'lights out' for the trainee inmates. No night patrols had left the base. Orders had been shouted, and the guard at the main gate had been changed. There was no sound from the buildings, or from its parade ground with the rows of parked transports and light tanks. Apart from the guardroom, and a few of the buildings inside, the place was in darkness.

Zagon Barracks were familiar to Vodnik, the man kneeling beside Sasa Miculik; he had spent four months of his compulsory military service there as a transport clerk. Four hundred and fifty men normally occupied the billets; three hundred trainees, and one hundred and fifty of the regular training staff. The regulars were specialists in training, driving, vehicle maintenance, weapon training, foot-drill, or clerical duties. Guard duty was the tedious task of the recruits.

There was one guard outside the main gates. Miculik had been watching him for fifteen minutes. The man carried his automatic rifle slung on his shoulder, and was standing with his hands in his pockets. A single lamp bulb, naked in a socket above the main gate, illuminated the soldier. He had been motionless for some time. Now, he took his hands from his pockets, looked furtively around and then began walking towards the hidden men. They pushed themselves tighter against the walls.

The man stopped ten feet away, still silhouetted against the electric light. He ducked his head and a match flared. A cigarette glowed. The guard turned and looked back towards the main gate. Miculik stood, silently, then ran forward.

The guard heard him but it was too late. Miculik hit him across the neck with the butt of his pistol and the man collapsed, tried to struggle to his knees, then fell face downwards on the sandy path.

There was no talk between Miculik and his men. They followed him to the main gate. He stopped, pointed briefly at the light, then ran on into the barracks. One of the men swung the barrel of the guard's rifle upwards and the yellow electric bulb exploded with a soft plop.

Miculik paused beyond the guardhouse. Vodnik pointed to a building at the far side of the square, past the rows of transport. There were two guards standing together in front of one of the trucks. Miculik signalled his other men, pointing into the darkness beneath the body of the first truck. He worked his way towards the guards, on his stomach. Vodnik was beside him. They could hear the low conversation of the two men; they were discussing football.

They rose behind the two guards simultaneously. Miculik sliding his arm across one guard's face, muffling his terrified shout. He hit him high on the head with his pistol. It took three blows before the man's legs gave way and he sank to the ground. Vodnik was in difficulties; the guard he had chosen was strong and Vodnik was having trouble keeping his hand across the man's mouth. Miculik jerked the guard's bayonet from its scabbard and drove it upwards into the man's chest. Vodnik felt the man sag, and released his grip on the guard's head. The man began screaming. Miculik swore, drove the guard's head down into the gravel, stabbing wildly. The man's brief scream died to a gasp. The two men pulled the bodies under the truck and lay there, their pistols ready. No-one came to investigate the sharp cry of the dead guard and, after several minutes, Miculik ducked from beneath the transport and ran across to the building. It had sliding doors, fastened by large steel bars and a padlock. Miculik's men joined him. One pulled a hacksaw from the front of his tunic and, after wrapping a piece of cloth around the lock, began sawing at the hasp. It took twenty minutes to cut through the tough steel.

Vodnik slid back one of the doors, and the men moved inside. Miculik shone a flashlight around the room. There were several stacks of wooden cases and rows of weapons in racks. Miculik indicated the boxes he wanted, then lifted several automatic rifles from a rack and tossed one to each of the men, cradling a machine-pistol for himself beneath his arm. He swung another across his back; took two plastic grenades from an open box and stuffed them in his pockets.

The boxes were heavy and it took the men all their strength to carry them. They hefted them onto their shoulders and followed Miculik back into the night.

They had reached the second row of transports, thirty yards from the main gate, when there was a shout. A flashlight beam swung across the open square and stopped on the face of one of Miculik's men.

The operator of the flashlight was as startled as the man he had illuminated. 'What the hell? Who . . .'

Miculik fired his pistol three times. The beam of light spun upwards and a man shrieked in agony. More lights flicked on at the barrack windows. A door was flung open, and several men ran towards the vehicles. A spotlight hurled a sudden white arc towards the vehicle park.

Miculik began running. He stopped at the gate and let his men pass him, then he bowled one of the grenades, underhand, towards the trucks. It exploded beneath the body of the nearest, tossing it upwards in a sheet of white flame as the fuel-tank split and ignited. He lobbed the second through the window of the guard-house. There was a shout from the room and then the hollow crash of the grenade as it exploded.

The young guard Miculik had stunned outside the barracks was on his knees, his hands to his injured head. Miculik grabbed him by the hair and shouted at Vodnik. 'Here . . . I want this one.' Vodnik ran back, pulled the guard up by his arm, and between them Miculik and Vodnik dragged him into the darkness.

When they were in the woods on the mountain slope, half an hour later, the flames of the burning vehicles in the barracks were still visible as a red glow against the sky.

A full six hours had passed, from the time Berkley and Struger had left the main cavern. Now the two men worked their way deeper into the cave system to where they knew a waterfall gushed from a fissure in the limestone and tumbled down a steep-walled chasm.

Struger pulled the packet of meat from his pocket. He tipped it out on the rock as though it held some unknown form of disease. He knelt, staring at the red strips in the dimming light of the lamp, and Berkley knew he was willing himself to touch them. He didn't interfere; it was important to Struger he should succeed. After a couple of minutes, Struger picked them up, quickly, and held them beneath the gushing water. They were limp, like the thin bodies of dead reptiles, slippery between his fingers. He shook the water from them, then let them drain before wrapping them in a clean piece of cloth. Berkley watched, knowing that even though his own stomach craved nourishment, he would be unable to eat this kind of food.

There was excitement when they returned to the cavern. They gave the explanation Kaguri had suggested, and it was accepted. They had found the body of a small deer trapped in some rocks in an underground stream; there was only sufficient meat for the children, but it might be possible to bring more the next day.

Both Berkley and Struger were relieved when they finally managed to escape from the gratitude of the children's parents.

Colette had met them, on their return, joining them as their light flickered at the end of the tunnel. Berkley knew she had waited there, alone in the darkness for the whole time they were away. She was pleased, for the children's sake, when he and Struger explained their find; proud that somehow providence seemed to have rewarded Berkley's courage and persistence.

Now she walked back with him to their shelter. Berkley sat on the rock ledge. He slumped forward, his face in his hands, and sobbed.

'David? Why? You should be happy, you've given life to the children . . . that deer was a Godsend.' She paused; her mind caught a little of his guilt and horror, it brought realisation. She put her hand quickly to her mouth. 'Oh, no!' She knelt in front of him and pulled him tightly to her breast. 'David, there wasn't a dead animal.' She felt him shake his head. 'Oh my God . . . my darling . . .' She held him, rocking him as though he were a terrified child.

19

'An armed raid on Zagon Barracks!' Martin Bor ground out his cigarette butt in an over-flowing ashtray on his desk. A police orderly, a man in his middle twenties with close cropped hair and a sallow complexion, stood waiting beside him, a steaming cup of coffee in his hands. He was nervous, standing rigidly at attention, his eyes fixed on the angry Commissioner like a frog hypnotised by a viper. Bor was ignoring him, holding the telephone so tightly his knuckles were white. 'Of course I heard the explosions, Colonel. They could be heard in Postojna town. Some of my men are already on their way to investigate. What the hell happened?' He took the cup from the orderly, drained it in one swig then thrust the cup back and waved the man away. 'Four dead and seven wounded . . . the bastards! The armoury? No, damn the trucks, Colonel Taufer, what's missing from your armoury? Weapons . . . yes, but *what* weapons? Automatics! Grenades and explosives! Yes, I'm quite aware you're also an ordnance depot, just tell me what explosives were taken. Plastic and detonators . . . time pencils! Jesus Christ, Colonel, we have enough trouble with the C.L.O., without handing them more explosives and weapons! Of course it's the C.L.O., I warned you they were operating in this area. Damn you, Colonel, weapons and explosives in the hands of terrorists *are* my business. I'd like a full report, with a complete list of all the stolen equipment . . . yes, now . . . in an hour at most. And get as many patrols as possible, immediately. I want every inch of mountain and forest searched by tomorrow evening.' He paused as Colonel Taufer disputed his authority over the military, then cut in on the man, wearily, 'Colonel it is essential we co-operate, and the question of which one of us has the greater authority is of no importance. We both want Sasa Miculik . . . we want him and the rest of the C.L.O.

For the first time, we've got them out in the open.' He was pleased to hear Taufer agree with him. 'Good, Colonel. And we should keep our radio operators tuned to both the police and military wavelengths. I suggest we share a joint headquarters. He replaced the receiver and shouted towards the door. 'Sergeant!.'

The door opened so quickly it was obvious the man had been standing just outside.

'Sir?'

'Find Inspector Zlobec and bring him to me.' The man turned to leave but Bor stopped him. 'Sergeant, I want all of our men back on duty . . . I don't care if they're sick or dying, I want them here immediately. And arrange for reinforcements to be brought in from all the surrounding towns as soon as possible . . . all of them fully armed. And I want a military helicopter available for search work as soon as it's daylight.'

The man hesitated.

'Get the hell out of here,' shouted Bor.

The dull thuds of the explosions had been barely audible above the throbbing of the rig engine, and Catlin and the Slovenes had hardly noticed them. Milovan, Stane and Simon were underground again; they had removed some of the rubble from the section close to the drill, and were now trying to follow the crevasse even deeper. Behind them, the cutter was already out of sight, noisily chewing its way deeper into the soft rock over the cavern.

It was still dark, but toward the east the sky was beginning to lighten. It was a little before three a.m., and Catlin was feeling exhausted. He was aware that now was the time of maximum risk for the entire operation. The drill was working close to its limit. The light-walled tube of the drill-rod was under enormous stress, and should the cutter jump a fault in the rock, or suddenly embed itself into a hard strata, then the drill-rod would fracture and recovery might be impossible. The small engine and gearbox were under full load,; had they been new and well-maintained this might not have been a problem, but the engine showed signs of neglect, and there were no spare parts amongst the equipment.

There had been no sign of the C.L.O. leader, Sasa Miculik, for several hours, though one of his men had strolled down from the rocks just after midnight to watch the operation. The Slovenes had ignored him and eventually the man had left them and gone back to his post.

Lisetta Irano had been in the cave where Catlin had sent her to rest earlier that night. She had returned to the drilling site just after two a.m., bringing food and a flask of coffee for the men. She had mentioned the explosions, and that she thought she'd heard gunfire and seen the glow of fires in the sky while walking through the woods, but all had been quiet for the past hour.

Sasa Miculik's arrival was startling. There was a sudden crashing in the bushes behind the drill rig, and Miculik burst into the clearing thrusting a stumbling and terrified young soldier in front of him. Behind were a group of his men, their faces blackened with charcoal, their chests heaving for breath after their run across the mountain. Alessandro shouted a protest in Slovene as Miculik hit the soldier with the butt of a machine-pistol and forced him to the ground at Catlin's feet.

Miculik looked as though he was insane. His dark eyes were wide and there was saliva froth around his mouth, sweat furrowed the black powder on his skin. He waved the machine-pistol dangerously, and then pressed the barrel against the head of the soldier. For a long moment, Catlin thought he was about to shoot the man, then Miculik seemed to relax. He let the barrel drop and stared slowly around the group of men.

'What the hell have you been doing?' Catlin asked, angrily.

Miculik laughed wildly and brandished the weapon above his head. 'Fighting, American. Fighting for Croatia, and freedom.'

'Oh my God,' said Lisetta, quietly.

Miculik shouted again at the soldier and the man babbled a long and near hysterical reply.

Lisetta looked quickly at Alessandro.

'You see,' said Miculik. 'This government do much, but always too late, eh?'

Alessandro explained the soldier's words to Catlin. 'A lot of heavy equipment has been brought into the site . . . on Presidency orders. Our national government has only just learnt there are people still alive below ground. Equipment is coming from Italy and Germany . . . tunnelling equipment, and all the labour they can get.'

'It took time,' said Catlin, wrily. 'But at least it's happening.' He looked at the terrified prisoner. 'Now what about . . .'

'And more,' interrupted Miculik. He kicked at the crouching soldier and the man flinched. 'Two people come alive from cave. Now in barracks. Both much sick. One Japan, one Slovene . . . a guide.'

‘A guide?’ Lisetta spoke quickly. ‘Which guide?’

‘How I know which guide? A guide . . . almost dead . . . men swim out in cave river.’

Lisetta tried to question the soldier, but the man only shook his head and wept silently.

‘He knows nothing. He is fool conscript.’ Miculik cleared dust from his throat and spat into the bushes. ‘They fools.’ He waved the machine pistol. ‘We have plenty weapons, my friends. Plenty good guns and bullets. Miculik will protect you, American. Miculik fight for freedom.’

‘Guns are not necessary. We don’t need guns,’ Alessandro spoke angrily. ‘If you want to fight a war, then go fight it on your own. We want nothing to do with violence.’

Alessandro’s anger was infectious and Lisetta shouted furiously at Miculik in Slovene. The man’s face stiffened and his hands tightened on the gun. For a moment Catlin thought Lisetta was about to attack Miculik with her bare hands. Miculik thought so, too, and stepped quickly backwards. Catlin took Lisetta’s arm and pulled her away from the man. ‘I don’t know what she said, but it probably goes for me too. I’m allergic to guns . . . I don’t like them. I don’t like you either, Miculik. Take your men and get the hell out of here.’

Miculik grinned, but there was a warning in his eyes. He brought up the gun suddenly, aiming it at Catlin’s stomach. Catlin felt his muscles tauten, involuntarily; he could almost read the man’s mind, and expected at any second to see the bright flash of flame from the muzzle and then feel the searing agony of a bullet tearing through his flesh. ‘Maybe *you* should, how you say American . . . push off?’

Catlin shrugged. ‘It’ll be a pleasure, Miculik. Now your government is taking some action the best thing I can do is to hand the drilling over to them. I guess your government is going to overlook our trespassing on their military property if we’ve given them a few extra days time to get the people out.’ He turned away from Miculik and then stopped and leant towards the kneeling soldier. ‘You won’t be needing him. He can come with us.’ He took the man by his shoulder and began lifting him to his feet.

The barrel of the machine-pistol rammed into his side, and Catlin felt a sharp pain as the foresight tore the skin across his ribs. He swung round quickly, his fists bunched. The muzzle of the weapon was less than an inch from his chin and Miculik’s eyes dared him to attempt an attack. There was a movement from

Alessandro and Miculik shouted an order. One of the Croats jumped forward and smashed his automatic rifle against Alessandro's head. The young man fell to his knees with a groan and clasped his head in his hands. Blood trickled from between his fingers.

'You bastard,' swore Catlin. 'What the hell do you want from us? We're no good to you. We don't want you around us. Go and start your war and leave us alone.'

Miculik lowered the gun slightly. He grinned. 'I want you, American.' He jerked his head toward the rig. 'I want you, and I want this thing. You make this work right . . . for me, eh?'

Lisetta spoke. 'You see what he want, Joe?' She spoke to Miculik in their own language. Miculik didn't reply. 'He not care about the people dying underground . . . he only think about his Croat liberation . . . his anarchy. He want this hole made for propaganda, so he can say the rescue was led by C.L.O, and when he reach the people below, he say they live only because his brave C.L.O. fight against government to rescue them. He is murderer who would like to be known as saint.'

Before Catlin could move, Miculik struck Lisetta across the mouth with the back of his hand, then swung the gun again at Catlin. 'This your Slovene whore, American? Then you tell her be silent, or I kill her . . . kill all!'

Only the danger to Lisetta prevented Catlin from attacking Miculik. He had never felt hatred so strongly before nor fought so hard to control anger. He swore silently Miculik would pay for the blow and insult; pay heavily. He kept his eyes on the man and moved carefully to Lisetta's side. He put his arm around her shoulder, protectively, and spoke softly. 'Take it easy, baby.' She was shaking with fury, her face white but for the scarlet smear where Miculik had struck her. He held her tighter. 'Easy now . . .' A time would come when he would even the score, but it would be later. Right now Miculik was using his bullying tactics to impress his own men as well as threaten the Slovenes. He was inviting an opportunity to kill.

'You listen him,' warned Miculik. He glared at Catlin. 'You, American, you make this drill go for me, eh?'

'I'll stick it up your ass first.'

Miculik spoke over his shoulder and three of his men stepped behind Catlin and Lisetta. Catlin began to move, but Miculik raised his gun again aiming it between Catlin's eyes. Catlin felt his arms seized and held behind his back.

Miculik handed his machine-pistol to one of the men. 'You think I make jokes, American?' He spoke to his men in Croatian and two of them pulled the young soldier to his feet, supporting him between them by his arms. One of them passed Miculik a long-bladed knife. Miculik stood in front of the soldier, the man was slumped forward, his chin resting on his chest.

'You don't have to prove anything to us,' Catlin said quickly. 'Leave the kid alone.' He sensed Miculik's intention, but hoped the man was bluffing.

'He is C.L.O. enemy.' Miculik grabbed the youth by his hair and pulled his head back. With an almost casual movement, he drew the edge of the blade across the soldier's throat. Blood spurted from the man's neck and Miculik stepped quickly aside to avoid the spray of dark liquid. The soldier struggled wildly but the two men held him. He tried to scream but choked as he sucked his own blood into his lungs.

Catlin heard Lisetta groan. The soldier's struggles weakened and his legs collapsed beneath him. Miculik spoke sharply to the man holding him and they let him drop onto the blood splattered ground. The soldier kicked several times, his body flopping like a stranded fish and then he was still.

Catlin was sickened. Miculik stepped in front of him and Catlin felt his captor's hands tighten behind him, on his arms. Miculik raised the bloodstained knife and held it a few inches from Catlin's throat. For a few seconds Catlin thought he was about to suffer a similiar fate to the dead man, but Miculik grinned then wiped the blood from the knife on Catlin's vest. The tight hands on Catlin's biceps relaxed. He took a deep slow breath. One of the men passed Miculik his machine-pistol. He spoke to Alessandro in Slovene and Alessandro replied. Miculik nodded and gave an order to his men. Three of them disappeared through the scrub.

'So, maybe I don't need you, American. Instead, that one I keep.' He pointed at Branko who had been standing silently beside the drill rig. 'He drill for me, eh?'

'Until you hit trouble.'

Miculik smiled coldly and tapped his hand against the butt of the weapon. 'I think I don't get trouble, eh?'

There was a new scent in the damp air of the cavern; the smell of food. It brought back forgotten pangs of hunger, wetted mouths uselessly with saliva, entered even the dreams and nightmares of those who slept. The aroma was a temptress, calling and promising, but giving nothing; the siren of old, returned to seduce the living, to death. For those few who knew its origin, it was the aroma of horror.

Soon there would be only darkness, thought Colette. There were few candles left in the guide's stores. Only two or three were kept alight, and they burnt continuously. And with darkness, she new people would die; give up. The darkness was a future of terror; almost beyond the limits of imagination. Before . . . before the earthquake, darkness had always held the promise of light. The darkness ahead, was final.

She shuddered.

Thirty yards away were a group of fellow Americans. She could barely see them in the gloom. She watched the hunched silhouettes, remembering how, only a week ago, they had been spruce and affluent holidaymakers. Now, the women were as wretchedly filthy as herself, their eyes dull and sunken. The faces of the men strained and dark-stubbled; the bodies of all painful with boils and ulcers from the constantly damp clothing and the friction of the rock beneath them. People degenerated quickly, under stress and away from their familiar environment. She understood now how refugees could look like hobos only days after having been forced from their homes.

'I read a book,' David had said. 'A book about a woman who was in solitary confinement in a Russian gaol for nine years. No-one spoke to her, not even the guards. They didn't let her wash for months at a time . . . there was no toilet in her cell, nothing. She lived, and she survived mentally, because she simply refused to accept the situation as real. She lived the whole of the nine years in a world she built for herself in her mind. She came out of the imaginary world, the day she came out of the prison camp. They couldn't do anything to hurt her, or shame her, while she was hidden inside herself.'

'I don't think I can do that.'

'Nor I,' admitted Berkley. He turned, easing her body closer to him. 'It's something people from mid-Europe might be able to do, perhaps orientals as well, but it doesn't suit the westerners. We're mentally built to look forward.'

'So there's nothing for us, now?'

'We plan! We think of the good things we're going to do, later.'

'Like your Blue Lake?'

'And the fish and chickens. . .'

She was going to add 'and kids', but she stopped herself. She took his hand and brought it to her lips, running her tongue gently between his fingers, then guiding them to her breast. He responded gently, and the cave began to lose form and reality.

The two Croatian guards were sitting either side of the Slovene group in a small clearing below the rocks three hundred yards from the drill rig. The rig itself was well hidden by the trees and shrubs which had been piled around it as camouflage a few days before, and it was barely possible to hear the sound of the engine in the still dawn air. The guards, two of the youngest men in Miculik's party, sat with automatic rifles across their knees; Catlin watched them closely. They held their weapons as though they were strange new toys, and he suspected they were unfamiliar with them. One of the guards, little more than a schoolboy, was flicking his rifle's safety catch on and off with his thumb and obviously found the weapon heavy in his hands.

Catlin had no doubt the rifles were loaded, he had watched one of the men slide a full magazine into his weapon, and lever a round into the breech. He also knew the men would obey Miculik's orders to shoot if they had cause. But neither of the men were experienced soldiers; the situation was as unfamiliar to them as it was to their captives. At the moment they were both nervous, twitchy, and any sudden movement was likely to provoke them. But they would eventually relax, and when they did so Catlin intended to act. For the moment, he would wait. He had decided Miculik was mentally unbalanced, but as Lisetta had said, the man's main concern was the publicity he would gain from cutting through to the people in the mountain. There was a possibility that in success he would be magnanimous and allow his prisoners to leave as some grand but condescending gesture. Catlin did not intend to give the man that satisfaction.

He smiled grimly. For years he had insisted he, and his men, should remain isolated from any political problems arising in countries where they worked. His policy of neutrality had saved his team's lives. And here was the policy-maker himself, Joe Catlin in person, part of a dangerous conspiracy, because he had failed to obey his own rules. He glanced at his watch and made a calculation. It was evening in Texas, time when his office would be closed and some comfortable bars open. But the thought was not as inviting as Lisetta. She was sitting a few yards away beside Alessandro, but Catlin could feel her eyes on him, and sense her emotion. He knew now she loved him; why or how it had begun no longer mattered.

There was a change to the rhythm of the engine and the clank of drill-rods banging against each other. Catlin frowned.

'What's that?' Alessandro looked up at him.

The nearest guard glared threateningly at the men, but Catlin ignored him. 'I'd guess they're pulling up the drill.'

'Pulling it up? Why?'

Catlin shook his head. Branko who was operating the rig had insufficient experience to diagnose a problem unless it was serious enough to be obvious. 'Maybe they fractured the tube. If so, then that's Miculik's drilling finished.'

'Somebody comes,' warned Lisetta. Three men were walking towards them through the scrub. She corrected herself. 'It is Stane and the others. Miculik has brought them up from underground.' Milovan's and Simon's headlamps were still alight in their helmets and the three men looked dirty and tired. They had been underground for several hours. Behind them walked one of Miculik's men. He waved them into the group with his rifle.

Stane smiled at Alessandro and spoke in Slovene.

Lisetta translated for Catlin. 'Miculik's men go down into the system and bring them out.'

'Ask them if they know why Miculik is bringing up the drill,' said Catlin.

Lisetta did so, and seemed startled by Stane's reply. Catlin saw Alessandro look quickly at the man. 'Miculik will use explosives to break through to the cavern below.'

'He's what? The man's crazy!'

Lisetta questioned Stane again. 'Miculik thinks drill will take too long. He has much explosive to blast in the cavern roof, he says.'

'How much explosive?'

Alessandro answered. 'Stane says he saw three boxes. Maybe fifteen kilos a box.'

'That's over ninety pounds! Jesus wept,' swore Catlin. Ninety pounds of explosive, used in the two hundred foot depth of the drill hole and in rock already fractured and loosened by the earthquake, might blow in a huge section of the cavern roof with terrible effects on those trapped below. 'The man's a lunatic. If we've set the rig position correctly, and are above the cavern, then he's going to kill a lot of the people he's supposed to be saving,' Catlin said, grimly. 'Tell one of the guards I want to talk with

Miculik . . . and fast.'

Alessandro spoke to one of the men who shook his head in reply.

Catlin got to his feet and the guards swung their weapons at him, threateningly. 'You tell them that I talk to Miculik, or they're going to have to kill me now.'

Alessandro spoke to the men again. One of them finally nodded and then indicated to Catlin with his gun barrel that he should walk ahead of him to the rig. Catlin did so, and the guard followed.

The rig engine was idling in neutral when they arrived. Branko and two of Miculik's men were stripping off drill-rod while Sasa Miculik stood watching. He turned as Catlin approached, and glared furiously at the guard behind him. The man explained, nervously.

'So you want speak to me, American.'

'You're damn right. I hear you're planning to use explosives in the drill hole.'

'It more quick.'

'It's more crazy. Another few hours and you'll have a clean drill hole through to the cavern. If you use explosives, then you'll wreck the drilling operation . . . you could block the hole and waste all the work.'

'I save much time. Time I have not. Plastic explosives, I have much.'

'It's too risky, Miculik. This mountain is nothing more than a heap of rubble. The cutter's been going through it as though it were loose shale. God knows how the cavern roof survived the earthquake. You use explosives now, and it may all drop in . . . you'll kill the people below.'

Miculik shook his head, then made a sour face. 'I, what you say, take chance, American. All life is chance. They die, I die, maybe you die. Maybe you and me hero . . . all people live. It is chance, like poker.'

'Let me carry on with the drilling,' begged Catlin. 'I'll drill for you. Give me a few hours and I'll get the cutter through to the cavern. A neat hole and no-one hurt.'

Miculik spoke to the man who had brought Catlin to the rig. The man signalled Catlin away with a jerk of his head. 'You go,' said Miculik. 'Go and wait. You see, Sasa Miculik is always right . . . like God.'

'Not this time,' warned Catlin. He turned and walked away.

When he reached the clearing in the rocks, the others were waiting; the guards watched his arrival curiously. He moved his hands vaguely in reply to unspoken questions. 'Like Stane said, Miculik's going to blow the hole. I couldn't make him change his mind.'

'And the people will die,' asked Lisetta. He saw she was fighting to hold back tears of disappointment.

'Maybe.' Catlin paused and then said: 'I'd say probably.' He avoided looking at the guards and continued to speak to Lisetta without altering the tone of his voice. 'Do these three understand us?'

Simon, standing to Alessandro's side, answered. 'I think they do not . . . perhaps one word or two.'

Catlin turned and pointed back towards the rig as though it were the subject of his conversation. He kept his voice level. 'We have to get down to the cave entrance. Get a warning through to the people in the cavern on that underground telephone. Move real slow until I shout, then act . . . fast.' He turned back to face them, and stepped sideways so the nearest guard was only a pace away to his right. The second and third guards were behind Stane and Alessandro, sitting on one of the outcrops of rock. One held his rifle across his knees, and the other had his weapon propped vertically, its butt on the ground between his feet. Not all the other Slovenes would have understood Catlin's conversation, so only three or four could be relied on to help him. Catlin knew it was risky. He tried to make himself appear relaxed and then walked a couple of paces across the clearing on a line which would take him close to the nearest guard. The man moved away from him. As he did so, Catlin shouted: 'Now.'

He dived sideways at the man, barging him with his shoulder. He felt the hardness of the guard's rifle against his upper arm and grabbed him wildly. There was another shout from behind him. He could not see the other men, his arms were wrapped around the guard, his head under the man's chin. The man fell backwards and the end of his gun barrel scraped down Catlin's cheek. The guard kicked at him and began to scream. Catlin clamped a hand over his face, forced the man's head sideways with his left arm, and swung a punch with his right fist. He was kneeling on the man's chest. The punch glanced from the side of the guard's head, but failed to stop his struggles. Fingernails scored down Catlin's neck. There was movement at his side. For a brief moment he thought one of the other guards was standing above him, but a hand clenching a rock swung past his face and thudded against the guard's skull. The man's struggles stopped and he sagged backwards. Lisetta knelt beside Catlin. He pushed himself up off the unconscious guard. The girl stood, staring down at the man, horrified by her own violence. One of the other guards lay back against a rock, his head twisted sideways at a strange angle. The third man, the youngest, lay on his stomach, his face buried in the earth. Simon was kneeling on his back, with one of the man's arms twisted almost to his shoulder blade. The guard was alive, but when he moved Simon increased the pressure. Alessandro kicked one of the weapons aside, picked up the other and aimed it at the young guard. He spoke quickly in Slovene. The guard's head jerked in agreement and Simon slowly released his arm and stood up. The guard remained spreadeagled on his face, but moved his arm to a more comfortable position.

'Did I kill this one,' asked Lisetta, softly. There was anguish in her voice.

Catlin put his arm around her. 'He'll live.'

'Mine didn't.' Alessandro's face was pale and he spoke breathlessly. He wiped the back of his hand across his mouth. Once the three of them had made the first move, the other Slovenes had joined them. The guards had been quickly overpowered.

Catlin picked up the rifle a guard had been carrying. It was Russian. He slid open the breech and saw a cartridge already in place. He checked the magazine clip; it was full. A lever on the side allowed a selection of single shot or fully automatic fire. 'Do you know how to use these?' he asked Alessandro.

'We must all serve in the military. I was a cadet . . . Simon has already done his conscription. But not the others . . .'

Catlin looked across toward the hidden rig. There was no sign of movement in the bushes which surrounded it; the sound of the engine must have drowned the shouts of the guards as they were attacked. 'Will you come with me?'

Lisetta's eyes met Catlin's, and he could see her fear for him. 'You go to fight them? No Joe, you mustn't.'

'I don't have any choice. I put the hole there, that makes it my responsibility. I have to stop him from using it to kill the people we wanted to rescue.' There had been a dozen men with Sasa Miculik, and three of them were now out of action. When Catlin had been taken to the C.L.O. leader he had seen only two other men with him, apart from Branko. With luck, all the others were stationed as lookouts up on the ridges. It might be possible to capture Miculik without a fight — if he could be surprised while his attention was occupied by the movement of the explosives. Catlin hefted the automatic rifle in his hands, trying to regain the familiarity he'd once had with weapons; the rifle still felt clumsy.

The morning air was clean and cool. Catlin took a breath and smelt the scent of the pine woods. He remembered the last time he had stood on a hill with a rifle in his hands; it had been a long time ago, a far off place, and it had been raining. Here there was no stink of previous battles. He said abruptly: 'Let's go,' and began a slow zig-zagging run towards a low outcrop of rock pushing upwards through bracken and scrubby trees. To reach it he had to cross a wide clearing, and hoped if there were guards above on the ridges they would mistake him for one of their own men.

The rocks were closer now. Catlin began to feel confident; once he got to them, it would be possible to wriggle forward on his stomach, through the brush, until he reached the rig. He heard and saw the bullet strike, before the sound of the shot and Miculik's lookout's cry of warning. There was a hiss, then an explosion against a rock a few feet ahead of him and to his right; chippings of limestone spun into the air, while the bullet ricocheted away to the distance with a low whine. The sound of the shot followed, echoing from the wooded slopes. The hidden guard's cry of warning was high-pitched and eerie. Catlin dropped to the ground. A second bullet smacked against the root of a sapling a foot from his shoulder. He rolled sideways to find better cover; there was a burst of automatic fire from the trees ahead. A body crashed against Catlin, knocking the breath from his lungs with the impact. The body moved, kicking itself off him; it was Alessandro.

Catlin turned his head as another long burst of fire followed. Simon was running towards them bullets kicking up dust around him; he dived at the rocks like a football player. He was on his knees at once, to fire a single shot up towards the guard on the ridge.

Alessandro said: 'Mileta is trying to get that one.'

'What the hell with?'

'He has a knife from one of the men.'

'How many rounds do these things hold?' asked Catlin, lifting the automatic rifle and resting it on a crevice between two of the rocks.

'Twenty. Don't put it on automatic or you'll use them too quickly.'

Catlin lifted his head and as he did so a bullet chipped away the rock a few inches from his face, one of the splinters tearing at his ear-lobe. It stung like a wasp. He swore and tried to see the man who was shooting; he was hidden somewhere in the broken trees close to the rig. Catlin moved his position slightly and instantly a machine-pistol opened fire from the scrub, the bullets spraying the rock in front of him. He pressed himself against the ground, wishing he was smaller. He heard Miculik's voice, shouting from the direction of the rig.

'He wants us to surrender,' said Alessandro.

'Tell him, no way.' There was movement in the bushes, a quivering of a spray of pine twigs. Catlin fired three quick shots to cover a narrow arc where a man was hidden. There was a scream of pain and the branches parted. A man staggered forward several paces, then collapsed on his face. Catlin was disappointed it wasn't Miculik.

There was a wild cry from the distant ridge. Mileta stood on a narrow rock ledge, jubilantly waving his arms above his head, his legs straddled. '. . . He must have killed the lookout.' Alessandro spoke enthusiastically.

'For God's sake, warn him to get . . .' began Catlin. The youth was in the open and must have been in clear sight of Miculik and the men hidden near the rig. Before Alessandro could react there was a single shot. Mileta's arms stiffened above his head, then like a diver on a ten meter board his body folded forward and somersaulted downwards to crash through the tops of the spindly trees. They heard the thud as it hit rocks below. Alessandro groaned.

At the far end of the outcrop Simon jumped from behind some rocks, his automatic rifle at his hip. He ran forward towards the rig, spraying the trees surrounding it with a hail of bullets. Catlin knew there was unlikely to be another opportunity to get to the cover of the woods to his right. He scrambled through the bracken bordering the rocks. Behind, Alessandro fired two shots in quick succession, then followed. They reached the cover of the trees and the rising ground leading to the edge of the plateau.

Catlin scrambled up the incline, and stopped by the thick shattered trunk of a fallen tree. He could now see the clearing behind the drill-rig. Three men crouched beside a pile of boxes. He recognised one as Miculik, and took a steady aim at the man's chest. Just as he squeezed the trigger, Miculik moved, suddenly. The bullet passed between his body and arm, and struck the man behind him, spinning him backwards into the undergrowth.

Dry branches cracked to Catlin's left. Alessandro charged past him down the slope towards the clearing. He was sixty yards from Miculik who saw him coming and dropped to one knee. The other man turned and leapt into the dense scrub beyond the rig.

Alessandro began firing as he ran. Catlin watched the bullets puffing sand some yards from the kneeling C.L.O. leader; the youth's shooting was wild. Catlin took aim again, quickly, but before he could align his sights on Miculik the man's machine-pistol spurted orange flame. Alessandro's legs seemed to be swept from under him. He fell sideways through the branches of a clump of pine saplings, to disappear in the undergrowth.

Miculik fired a long blast through the low trees, stood, then walked cautiously forward. Catlin's foresight followed him, picking a spot on his head where the dark hair swung down across the cheekbones. His finger tightened on the trigger. Miculik had still not seen him and must have thought the first bullet had been fired by Alessandro.

'Miculik. . . ' The voice was Alessandro's. The youth leapt to his feet several yards to the side of the spot where he had fallen. Miculik turned quickly to face him, a burst from his machine-pistol tearing through the undergrowth around the young Slovene.

Alessandro stood, facing the raking fire of Miculik's weapon. His own automatic rifle fired steadily. Miculik staggered backwards as one of the bullets hit him in the centre of his chest. His heel caught a fallen sapling; bullets from his machine-pistol sprayed upwards. Momentarily he tried to regain his balance. Alessandro fired again; this time a single shot as his magazine emptied. The bullet smashed up through Miculik's jaw into his brain, exploding outwards in a mist of blood and bone. The body dropped, kicked once and was still.

Catlin raced down the slope. Alessandro stood swaying. He let his rifle drop, then sank to his knees. Beyond him the bushes were thrust apart and Simon appeared, his own automatic held at his shoulder and aimed at Alessandro's back. Catlin realised he must have mistaken his friend for one of the C.L.O., and was about to fire. Catlin shouted: 'No . . .' He was only twenty yards away and still running. Simon swung to face him, the rifle still ready. He seemed to hesitate as though he might yet fire, but as Catlin approached he lowered the muzzle of the weapon, slowly.

'Jesus,' swore Catlin. 'I thought you were going to shoot us.' He knelt beside Alessandro. 'Are there any more of the C.L.O.?'

'One escaped . . . I missed him as he ran past me. He went up towards the ridge. There must be others, maybe two more . . . they could be at the pothole. They shot Branko when we attacked. He is dead, beside the rig. I think Mileta is dead, also. Where is Alessandro wounded?'

Alessandro was gasping with pain. 'In my leg; here in the thigh.'

There was the sound of feet behind them in the scrub. Lisetta and Miki appeared, breathless. 'We saw from the hill,' explained Lisetta. She dropped beside Alessandro, and gasped at the sight of the blood pumping from the wound in his leg. 'I think I see Miculik run away with his men.'

'He didn't run.' Catlin jerked his head towards the fallen trees. 'He's over there. His career as a terrorist is finished.' He stripped off Alessandro's belt, ripped apart the bloodstained jeans and strapped the leather around his thigh. The blood flow slowed. 'Get thick pads of cloth and tie them hard over the wounds. Don't leave that tourniquet on long or you'll cut off the blood supply to his leg. Get the others and carry him away from the rig.' He looked at Simon. 'Where are their explosives?'

'I looked . . . the boxes are empty,' answered Simon. 'They must have already placed them in the pothole.'

'Fuses?'

Simon looked bewildered, not understanding Catlin. Lisetta explained in Slovene.

'Ah!' Simon disappeared into the shrubbery surrounding the silent drill-rig. He was back a few seconds later and passed a slim tube towards Catlin. 'They have these . . . there is a box of them . . . it was open, and some are missing.'

Catlin examined the cylinder of metal. It was half an inch in diameter and several inches in length. There was a knurled screw at one end, marked around its circumference with figures. Catlin stood, quickly. 'Let's get away from here . . . come on . . . all of you.' He slung the rifle across his shoulders by its sling and stooped, picking Alessandro up, as though he were a child. Alessandro yelped with pain. Catlin ran across the clearing. He kept going until they were a hundred and fifty yards from the rig, then he stopped and lowered Alessandro to the ground; he was unconscious.

Catlin held the cylinder towards the others. 'This is a time-pencil. You twist the cap and set it against one of the numbers. At the chosen time it detonates. Miculik has probably set the fuse, and we don't know how long its going to be before the explosive goes up . . . when it does, that rig is going to come out of the ground like a champagne cork.'

'The people in the cavern must be warned, now,' said Lisetta.

'You go,' Simon stared at Catlin. 'You go with Lisetta. We stay and look after Alessandro. If C.L.O. men come, we can be ready. You can explain about explosives, better than us.'

'Okay.' Catlin had no way of knowing how Miculik might have set the detonator; it could be anything from half a minute to ten hours. He gave Miki his rifle. 'I won't need this; you might.' He looked down at Alessandro. 'Take good care of him . . . and Simon, make sure all of you keep well away from the rig or the pothole.'

They ran, stumbling across the rocks and forcing their way through the light undergrowth of the sparse woods. They reached the highest point of the ridge in thirty minutes and Catlin was glad when the ground levelled and finally began to drop away in front of them. Less than a mile ahead, and below the now thickening pine forest was the cave entrance, but here the large trees on the slope had been more affected by the earthquake. Great sections of the surface earth had broken away and avalanched from the rock beneath; the trees were jumbled at crazy angles, entangled and interwoven in places, inpenetrable. Lisetta and Catlin scrambled and climbed over the fallen trunks, forced their way through the jagged and broken branches, and slid down the loose shale surface of the exposed rock. And at any moment, Catlin knew they might hear the sound of an explosion from behind them on the plateau.

There was no word of complaint from Lisetta, although he heard her gasp with pain as sharp needles of pine or jagged rocks tore at her skin. His own hands were bleeding, and salt sweat bit into the grazes across his chest and neck.

They met the patrol two hundred yards above the cave entrance; a line of grey uniformed men clambering upwards over the loose rocks. Catlin found himself facing a startled young soldier aiming a rifle at his chest. There was a hoarse command from a few yards away. Catlin understood the tone rather than the words. He carefully raised his hands above his head.

Lisetta shouted in Slovene, but her words brought a further command from a tough looking sergeant who had now joined them. The sergeant carried a pistol and indicated he would enjoy the opportunity of using it. Lisetta spoke again, pleading with the man. Catlin heard her mention Commissioner Bor and then name his own nationality. The sergeant called his patrol and had them searched. He found nothing; Catlin had no papers or possessions in his pockets. The sergeant refused to be hurried.

Lisetta had been speaking while she was searched, and the sergeant was a little more relaxed now he knew they were both unarmed. He called a radio operator and gave him instructions. The man slid out the aerial and began a conversation with his base. The Sergeant took the instrument and by his attitude it was obvious he was speaking to an officer. A few seconds later he ordered his patrol and prisoners down the hill towards the cave site.

The sound of heavy machinery made the air vibrate. Catlin barely recognised the Postojna entrance site. Half a dozen giant bulldozers were clearing the remains of the debris of the terminus building. Teams of men loaded trucks with the rubble and there was a constant flow of vehicles between the bulldozers and a hill of wreckage at the edge of the parking area. A mobile crane swung aside the heavier slabs of concrete, and it was already possible to see where the main entrance to the caverns had been. A chain of men were passing pit props along their line to a deep crevice above the entrance, and tubes from a pair of compressors fed power to miners working out of sight under the lip of the mountain.

Catlin was astonished at the number of military and police guards patrolling the area of the site. They stood in pairs, their weapons cradled ready on their arms, every thirty yards around the entire perimeter; it was as though they were expecting an attack at any minute.

The sergeant who was escorting Lisetta and Catlin pushed them ahead of him and his patrol. The other guards watched curiously as they were marched across the open ground below the terminus. There was no point in conversation, they would not have been able to hear each other above the noise. The guards were bunched around them closer now, as though to identify themselves as the captors of the two prisoners. Escape would have been impossible; they were watched from every direction by armed guards and police.

The noise softened as they crossed the car park towards Inspector Zlobec's offices. As the patrol approached, the door opened and Commissioner Bor stepped outside, flanked by the Inspector and an armed constable. Bor gave no sign of recognising Catlin when they were halted in front of him, and then stood in silence for a full half minute before he spoke.

'So you are connected with the C.L.O. terrorists. You will regret the company you keep, Mister Catlin. You will also regret not taking my advice to leave our country.' He faced Lisetta. 'What is your name, woman?'

'Just a minute, Commissioner.' Catlin interrupted him. 'We came down here for your help. There isn't any spare time . . . you have to act at once. The people in the cavern need warning.'

Lisetta spoke: 'There will be explosion. They will be injured . . . killed. The Croatians, they put explosive into the mountain.'

'Silence . . . I believe *you* are both members of the Croatian Liberation Organisation. I also believe *you* were responsible . . .'

'For God's sake, Commissioner. Your son has been fighting the C.L.O. for you. There isn't time to waste . . . you have to act at once. It may already be too late.' Catlin felt like picking the man up by his collar and shaking him.

'My son . . . what do you mean, my son?'

Lisetta answered. 'Alessandro is wounded, some of his friends are dead. They try to stop Sasa Miculik from blowing up bore hole we drill in the mountain. Mister Catlin is working with us . . . we are students from Ljubljana. The C.L.O. try to take control . . . we believe Miculik attack Zagon Barracks last night and steal explosives. He put them in our bore hole and fit a time fuse.' Lisetta was speaking desperately.

Bor stared at Catlin, their eyes meeting. 'This so, Mister Catlin? How much time have we got?'

'I don't know; it's fused with one of your military time pencils. Miculik put ninety five pounds of explosive, I guess something like forty kilos, into the bore. We were down to over two hundred feet . . . eighty meters maybe. Not far above the roof of the cavern. The fuse could have been set a couple of hours ago. The people below ground have to be cleared from the cavern at once; I don't know what will happen if the charge blows.'

Commissioner Bor spoke quickly to one of the men at his side. He made the man repeat the order and then sent him away, at the double, towards the terminus. 'They will be warned at once, Mister Catlin.' Bor frowned and looked at his watch. It was ten thirty a.m. In five hours time he was expecting a visit from the President, who had announced he was to tour the devastated area that day. Bor sighed inwardly. The President would have already been informed of the attack on the barracks, and now there was another problem. Bor took out a pack of cigarettes, lit one then offered the packet. Catlin shook his head. Bor said: 'Where is Miculik, now?'

'Lying on top of the mountain,' answered Catlin. 'Dead.'

The answer surprised Bor. He put his head on one side like a quizzical terrier and his eyes narrowed. 'Sasa Miculik dead?' The news, if it was accurate, was the best he had received for many days.

'Your son, Alessandro, killed him.'

Bor seemed to have forgotten the mention of his son's injuries, but Catlin's statement obviously startled him. 'Alessandro?' He looked at Lisetta. 'Is this true?'

'Yes. Miculik have pistols when he comes. He get more from barracks last night. Your son and our friends attack their guards, take weapons and fight Miculik. They fight him, very bravely,' added Lisetta. She added: 'Mister Catlin lead them.'

'And all the C.L.O. are dead?'

'Perhaps three have got away. They're still on the mountain. The others are dead or wounded.'

'So . . .' Bor thought for some time before he spoke again. He dropped the cigarette butt and ground it into the dust with his polished heel, then he straightened the bottom of his tunic. His manner had softened and he seemed embarrassed. 'How is my son hurt?' He asked, quietly.

'Not too badly. He was shot in the thigh. The bone is damaged and he needs attention, quickly.' Catlin hesitated then said: 'He stood and faced Miculik who was using a machine-pistol. Alessandro killed him *after* Miculik had shot him.' Catlin noticed Commissioner Bor's eyes had lost their usual hardness, as though the man was daydreaming.

Bor's mind was, in fact, on a scene imprinted on his memory thirty five years before. He was standing on a mountainside, amongst the rocks. He could smell the scent of the crushed heather beneath his feet, the sweetness of the plants mingled with the rank smell of cordite smoke from the weapon in his hands. A few yards lower down the slopes lay the mangled bodies of the rightist guerrillas he had just killed with a grenade. The long war was finally over and a new country would be built on the wreckage of the old. Bor felt jubilant. He cheered loudly and waved to his companions further down the slope. There was the sound of movement on a patch of shale to his left and he turned quickly. There was a man facing him . . . a thin-faced man with a short beard, wearing the remnants of a uniform of the King's Alpine Corps. The man screamed one word: 'Communist', and then aimed his Luger at Bor. Bor was too shocked to experience fear. He saw the flash of the pistol and felt the hammer blow of the bullet.

In his mind he suddenly viewed the scene as a spectator. The man in the uniform was Sasa Miculik; the victim, his own son, Alessandro. The fear which had been absent thirty five years previously, welled over him now. He struggled to control emotions he had forgotten.

The breathless return of the policeman he had sent to the site of the terminus building snapped Bor back to the present. The man shouldered his way through the group of soldiers standing around Lisetta and Catlin, and spoke quickly. Bor angrily slapped his leather baton against his boot.

'The telephone,' Lisetta explained to Catlin. 'Is not working.'

'It hasn't been working since almost midnight.' Bor's face was darkening with anger as he spoke, but it was not directed at Catlin. 'The fool of a military operator didn't make a report. He hoped the fault would clear itself.'

'If we can't warn the people, then we have to try to stop the explosion,' said Catlin. 'Can you get a bomb disposal man from the military barracks?'

'Bomb disposal? I doubt if they have such a specialist,' answered Bor. 'But I can try.'

Catlin felt his stomach muscles tense. 'Wait,' he said, quickly. He pointed across to the helicopter. 'That thing yours?'

'Yes . . . I have the use of it.'

'Get me back up the mountain. Maybe I can defuse the explosive.'

'No . . .' Catlin felt Lisetta take his arm, protectively. 'No, Joe . . .'

Bor frowned. 'I think it would be unwise, Mister Catlin.'

'Explosives are my work,' insisted Catlin 'I learnt about the stuff in Korea.' Inside his head it sounded like someone else talking. 'You've no choice, Commissioner. I don't have either. Just get me up there.'

Bor frowned, thought for a moment and then said: 'I agree, Mister Catlin.'

The grip on Catlin's arm tightened. 'Joe! Please, Joe.'

'It's okay, honey. You wait down here. Have a few beers ready for me.' He unwound himself from her fingers, then kissed her cheek.

Fifteen minutes later, the military helicopter was swinging north along a ridge which forced it upwards to the mountain plateau. Below, large sections of demolished forest lay scattered above freshly exposed rock.

The armed police patrol hunched uncomfortably in their seats, their backs pressed against the vibrating fuselage as if it offered them safety. Catlin crouched beside the open door, wind sweeping past his body, clawing at him. The voice in his head spoke again. 'All you need now, buddy, are hot lines of tracer bullets coming up at you.'

20

He heard them in a dream; two vast armies facing each other across a deep valley, shouting their obscene threats, a continuous roar of angry sound. He awakened to the shrill pitch of a woman's shriek . . . despair, not fear. Figures swirled beyond the thin glow of the remaining fire, and the wavering orbs of haloed candle flames. There was movement everywhere on the rising slope of the cavern. Berkley pushed himself into a sitting position on the narrow shelf and felt Colette's arms tighten around him in her sleep, resenting the chill that replaced the comforting warmth of his body. The indistinct figures on the tumbled rubble were strange underworld monsters, hooded against the moist atmosphere, their blanket clothing like dark bat's wings. They seemed to be dancing some demonic ritual. Berkley had been in a deep sleep, exhausted by the strenuous exploration of the countless passages and by lack of food. Now he had difficulty separating reality from nightmare; he thought perhaps like Struger he was experiencing a hallucination. The noise intensified, stalactites and countless rock surfaces turning the voices to insane satanic chants.

From the tumbling mass of fallen columns something crawled and scuttled its way towards him, he saw it only as a moving shadow silhouetted against the dim light. He snatched up a broken sliver of limestone, its edge sharp as a razor, and waited, knowing that the total darkness of the ledge protected Colette and himself.

There was a groan from the shadow then it spoke, its voice a harsh whisper. 'David? It's Carl . . . for God's sake, David . . . where are you?'

'Here.' He reached out and touched the damp clothing on the man's back. Struger jerked, startled at his touch. 'What's going on, Carl?'

Struger's hand gripped his arm, his strong fingers digging painfully into his muscles. 'Quiet . . .' Struger pulled Berkley closer to him and he felt the German's breath against his cheek. 'They've gone mad . . . all of them, insane. They want to kill us.'

'Us? Who?'

'Me, you . . . Kaguri . . . they've killed Hubertson, already.'

'Hubertson?' Why should anyone want to kill Hubertson, wondered Berkley. Hubertson was too mild to offend anyone.

'He couldn't remain silent about Ukley . . . about the meat.' Struger kept his voice low. 'Maybe his conscience . . . he told his wife, and she became hysterical, shouting about God and Christianity. Others heard her. People were shouting, getting more angry . . . out of control. The father of the small, blonde boy, he attacked Hubertson.'

'But his son was the weakest . . . he was dying.' Berkley remembered the child, its pale skin almost translucent, and its thin body nothing more than bones wrapped in clothing. The British veterinary had pointed the boy out to Berkley . . . the child was naturally thin and had no reserve of fat. 'This boy can't last another night without food,' the Veterinary Surgeon had said.

'It made no difference.' There was a tremor of horror in Struger's voice. 'The man tried to strangle Hubertson, but he didn't have the strength . . . no-one attempted to stop him, they just watched; then two others suddenly grabbed Hubertson's arms and pushed him down to the ground. They held him, and the child's father picked up a rock and smashed it down on his head . . . not once, but many times, until . . . my God . . . it was bad.'

Berkley said nothing. He could feel Struger trembling.

'They are shouting that they are going to kill the Japanese, Kaguri, and then they will come looking for Meyer and us. It is pointless, stupid. We only did what was necessary to save children, soon everyone may have to eat flesh, or die.' He sighed deeply. 'Perhaps it makes no difference if they do murder us . . . we have to die anyway. Maybe it is better to let them kill us quickly. At least a dead man has no more hunger and pain.'

There was howling from the people on the far side of the cavern, shouts of anger distorted by the weird accoustics. Berkley could see figures moving but the light was too poor for him to distinguish their individual actions. He knew the Japanese kept themselves together beneath an overhang of rock beyond the fire, and it was there the mass of people seemed to be heading.

'We should try to help Kaguri.'

Struger stiffened. 'There's nothing we can do. There are too many of them . . . thirty or forty . . .'

'I'll wake Colette; do you have your light?'

'No, I had no time to find one.'

'There's a bundle of candles on the ledge; and matches. Take them all . . . I have my helmet light. Go along the passage to the section where Irano fell. Get Colette across the gorge and then take the right fork beyond the crevasse. I'll follow as soon as I can.'

Berkley found his helmet and removed the small battery-powered light from its crown. He hesitated before discarding the helmet, it would have been useful protection for him but was too easily identified. He slipped the light and battery case into his pocket.

'What's happening?' Colette's voice was confused.

'Go with Carl; he'll explain . . .' Berkley reached into the darkness and touched her. Her small warm hand found his own. 'Don't worry, I'll be back with you soon.'

He followed the lower walls of the cavern, working his way carefully in the gloom around the end farthest from the crowd on the hill of rubble. The animal sounds of their voices rising and falling, billowing through the still, damp air, amplified until Berkley felt these must be the sounds of hell. He wrapped his blanket closer, draping the top of it over his head like the hood of a monk's robe. He was closer to the crowd now, and there was some light from the candles on the rocks.

He could see the terrified party of Japanese, huddled together against the wall of the cavern; the women crouching, the men attempting to protect them from the rocks thrown by their attackers. He recognised Kaguri, the man had thrown off his blanket and stood facing the crowd, a three foot length of metal rod in his hands as though it were a sword. His torn clothing and swordsman's stance made him a wild figure amongst the strange scenery. On either side of him stood several other men, some holding splintered rock or pieces of debris as weapons.

A man at the head of the attacking crowd was shouting, and now Berkley was closer he could distinguish the words. The man, was screaming: 'Yellow bastards . . . stinking yellow cannibals . . .' He stooped and picked up a large fragment of stalactite, hurling it at the huddled figures beyond the defensive line of men. There was a scream of agony from one of the kneeling women; it was as though it were a trigger that set Kaguri in motion. He swung the metal rod vertical and leapt forward, sure-footed even on the broken ground. The crowd in front of him scattered, but the stone-thrower was too late. Kaguri swung the heavy rod downwards. The first four inches of metal hit the man on the junction of collar-bone and shoulder; Berkley heard bone snap with the sharp sound of a breaking twig. The man screamed and fell backwards, rolling down the slope. Kaguri forced the crowd further away. A man stumbled over a boulder, then yelped as Kaguri's weapon smashed his kneecap and the taut muscles pulled the shattered bone apart. The crowd retreated. Kaguri stopped and watched them go. A yard away, the man with the broken knee moaned as he dragged himself through the rocks.

Berkley crept forward in the shadow. Nito, a Japanese who had been fighting alongside Kaguri heard the sound of his approach and leapt towards him. Berkley threw off his hood and raised his hands. The Japanese stopped his attack but failed to recognise him. Berkley called, quickly. 'Kaguri . . .'

Kaguri turned. Berkley saw the man was bare-footed, but seemed unconcerned by the limestone fragments that cut and tore at his feet. His toes seemed to dig into the surface of the rocks as he moved over them. There was arrogance and pride to his bearing that had not been so obvious before.

'Berkley . . .' Kaguri spoke his name with a soft nasal pronunciation to the "k" in its centre. 'I think you are unwise to visit us. You must go, at once.'

'You can't stay here, they'll kill you.' A stone hissed from the darkness and shattered behind them. 'Can your people follow me?'

'They will follow me,' answered Kaguri. 'And I can follow you.'

'We can go to one of the passages. It's narrow. You'll be safe . . . safer, down there.'

'Good.' Kaguri nodded, then spoke to the men. They hurried to the main group. There was a shuffling movement that brought another volley of rocks from the crowd higher up the slope of the cavern. One of the men grunted as a baseball-sized lump of stone thudded into his side. The shouting was loud and angry again.

'Go,' ordered Kaguri. 'We follow.' He called to the others in Japanese and they moved from the shelter of the wall. The hail of stones grew, bouncing from the rocks, shattering against stalagmite columns. Berkley moved as fast as possible in the gloom of the lower part of the cavern. Behind he could hear the Japanese following him, the rattle of loose rubble beneath their feet, the occasional gasp or cry as a stone found its target, the moans of an injured man or woman. It took fifteen minutes to reach the narrow entrance to the tunnel; Berkley could have walked it in two had he been able to use his light. Once inside, he connected the battery, shone the light ahead, then waved the Japanese past him into the darkness. The tunnel was eight feet in width, but narrowed along its length until only one man at a time could force his way through.

Outside in the cavern, the noise had died away. The silence was ominous. Berkley knew the demented attackers who were following would see the faint glow of light, and know which passage he had chosen. Until the Japanese had passed through the narrow section and crossed the gorge beyond, they were still in danger. Pebbles rattled, a few yards away, outside the tunnel entrance. Berkley shone his light towards the sound. It illuminated the anger-distorted face of a man, half-crouching, his arm drawn back to hurl a rock into the tunnel. As the light blinded him, the man dropped his missile and dived sideways to the shadows.

Kaguri spoke. 'You go on. Lead them. I will stay here until you are inside.'

Berkley said: 'Tell them to keep to the right hand wall for a hundred meters. Not to move to the left, there's a deep chasm.' Kaguri shouted the instructions in Japanese.

Berkley pushed his way past the frightened men and women and swung the beam of his light along the narrowing tunnel. There was an unpleasant familiarity about the route, he had travelled it many times in the past days; it even smelt different from the main cavern. Here the air had a mustiness to it, as though fungi grew on the damp walls and the dripping ceiling. The Japanese moved silently, but behind there were wild cries echoing along the tunnel like the tidal bore of a river.

He saw the glow of Struger's candle ahead of him on the far side of the gorge, and a few seconds later heard Colette call his name, anxiously. He waved the beam of light as an answer.

'You brought them all?' Struger thought of the narrowing tunnel behind him; in hours it would become fouled, impossible to inhabit. There were no caves, no caverns; the nearest water was the river at the bottom of the deep crevasse. Berkley helped the first of the Japanese onto the rope bridge he and Struger had constructed across the gorge, the day after the Guide Irano's fall. Struger raised his hands, almost imploringly, then shook his head and reached towards the woman clutching the rope.

Minutes after they had all crossed, Kaguri appeared, padding out of the darkness of the tunnel like the sallow wraith of a Samurai. His lank black hair, which he normally kept tidy with oil, hung down over his ears. Only the remnants of his vest draped the lean muscles of his shoulders. His skin glistened with perspiration and the moisture of the caves. A dark bruise scarred the upper part of his chest and blood oozed from a wound high on his right cheek.

'Are they still following?' Berkley held Kaguri's wrist and swung him across the black chasm.

Kaguri scrambled onto the ledge beside him before he answered. He wiped sweat and blood from his face with the back of his forearm. 'I have managed to discourage them. They aren't carrying lights. Perhaps they will calm down when they have more time to think, then . . .' He stared down into the chasm. 'If they persist, it will not be too difficult to stop them crossing here.' He put a hand on Berkley's arm. 'I . . . we are all grateful for your help.'

'I'm ashamed it was necessary.'

'Ashamed? There is no need to be ashamed. You are ashamed because some of your countrymen attacked us? No . . . you should not have such feelings! They are sick people . . . weak and desperate, and they are frustrated and afraid. It is the reason why a wild cat will tear its bowels out when caught in a trap. And there were not many of them throwing the rocks . . . only a few crazed people. I am the one who should feel ashamed, for fighting them.' He lowered his head. 'A man is always learning about himself . . . I thought after so many years I could contain my anger, and I am disappointed to find I cannot. I have been trying not to kill those who were hurting us, but my rage was growing. If you had not arrived Berkley, then I am certain I too would have become a murderer.' As Kaguri looked up, Berkley was surprised to see there were tears mingling with the sweat and blood on the man's face.

Above, high on the mountain plateau, the waving figures of the four young Slovenes guided the military helicopter to a landing area two hundred meters from the drill-rig. The machine dropped slowly, its rotors swirling a cloud of brown dust and dead pine needles beneath it, the down-draught twisting and bending the tops of the thin saplings and forcing the watching men to shield their faces and wrap their clothing tighter around their bodies. Wisely, they had piled the weapons they had taken from the C.L.O. terrorists in a heap on the ground some yards away, for even before the machine finally settled the armed police pushed past Catlin in the doorway and leapt to the ground; their own weapons were ready for use as they surrounded the Slovene students.

Catlin clambered from the machine as its skids settled into the soft earth. Bor was not so agile, waiting until one of the crew gave him a hand to climb down. His old wounds were stiff with fatigue.

The police were now searching the Slovenes, running their hands over their bodies, turning out their pockets with professional expertise. Catlin found Simon, his hands clasped behind his neck as he was searched by one man while another kept him covered with a machine-pistol. 'Where's Alessandro?'

'Over there, with Miki,' answered the youth. He grimaced at the touch of the policeman's hands.

'Is he okay?'

'Yes, Joe. We stopped the wound bleeding, but he must be taken to hospital, quickly.'

'Sure,' said Catlin. 'As soon as we can. How difficult is it to get down to where Miculik's men laid the explosive?'

'Get down to . . .' Simon looked startled. He half-lowered his arms, but the policeman prodded him with his machine-pistol and spoke angrily. Catlin signalled him away and reluctantly the policeman allowed Simon to relax. 'Why?'

'Because we couldn't warn the people down below. I have to reach the explosive, and try to get the time fuse out.' Catlin kept his voice even. 'I need to get to it fast.'

Bor had joined them and was standing a few feet away. 'So this one speaks English.'

'He knows the tunnel where Miculik placed the explosive. I need some information from him.'

'You won't be able to stop the fuse, Joe.' Simon warned, urgently. 'Too difficult, too dangerous. It's better you don't try.'

'I'll decide that when I see it. I just want to know how to get there.'

'This one will lead you.' Bor spoke to Simon in Slovene and the young man nodded a reply. 'He volunteers!'

'I know the cave, Joe, and if I lead you it'll save time. It is good I come with you.'

Catlin was surprised at Simon's sudden enthusiasm and wondered what Bor had threatened. He said to Bor: 'He's *your* responsibility, Commissioner,' and then to Simon: 'Okay, thanks for the offer.'

'You will want tools, Mister Catlin?' asked Bor.

'No. If I can reach the detonator, I can remove it by hand. If it explodes once it's out, it won't do much harm.' No harm to those in the cavern, perhaps, but it was still powerful enough, if it detonated, to kill the man who held it. Catlin knew he would be gambling, something you never did with explosives if you wanted to reach old age. He was gambling, too, on the way Miculik's men would have laid the charge. He hoped the explosive was packed into the hole first, and the detonator fitted into the last few inches; it was the way most amateurs would do the job. If there was an expert amongst them, then the detonator would be deep inside the charge and there would be nothing Catlin could do.

Catlin had seen films of cave exploration on television programmes back home. He had always thought it a crazy sport, in the same category as mountaineering and hang gliding. Catlin took risks himself, but they were risks tempered by experience and calculation . . . and he got well paid for taking them. Now, working his way along a narrowing tunnel behind Simon, his views were confirmed. The first thirty foot of the descent had been along a series of step-like ledges leading deep into a newly formed fissure on the mountain plateau. From the bottom he had glanced upwards; he had seen Commissioner Bor's silhouette against the bright sky. Bor's views were similar to his own, for he saw the man shake his head slowly before he stepped backwards out of sight. The first of the tunnels was pitch darkness after the sunlight, and even the helmet light seemed feeble until Catlin's eyes became more used to the gloom.

Catlin's bulk was a disadvantage. In sections where Simon's slim frame could pass through without difficulty, Catlin was forced to struggle, compressing his chest and shoulders and using all his strength to ram his body through the small spaces between the rock walls. The mountain seemed to press in on him, and he could almost feel the weight of rock above his head. The deeper into the mountain, the wetter the rock that surrounded them became, until, where the tunnel widened, a steady stream of water ran down the walls to disappear along polished rock channels cut by its own action on the rocks of the cave floor. Catlin could see little beauty in the place. They crossed a wider section of cave, piled high with rubble over which Catlin was forced to crawl on his hands and knees, then reached yet another narrow section of tunnel, the walls so close together Catlin doubted if he would get through. The roof dropped sharply until there was only a gap little more than a foot square.

Catlin said: 'Jesus wept!'

'It's all right,' Simon called over his shoulder reassuringly, his voice hollow in the confines of the tunnel. 'It was worse. We cleared it.'

'Thanks.' Catlin answered sarcastically.

'Don't fight the rock, Joe. Make yourself relax and don't tighten as you go through. Work with your feet, not your shoulders.' The light ahead of Catlin diminished as Simon slid forward into the tunnel on his stomach.

Catlin followed, feeling the cold damp rock against his body. 'Think small,' he said to himself.

In the last five yards and ten minutes, Catlin felt he had aged twenty years, but then the cave roof lifted and the section widened until he was able to stand. Simon waited a yard ahead of him.

'There . . . see where the drill broke through.' The man's light shone upwards revealing a jagged black hole. 'The cutter came out there.'

'This is where they put the explosive?'

Simon looked downwards and his light illuminated a wide shaft a few yards deep. 'At the bottom. There is a rope fixed here. We can go down.'

'Not we,' said Catlin, firmly. 'Me. I go down alone. You go back up to the surface. I can find my own way out.'

'I stay.'

'Suit yourself; I haven't time to argue.' Catlin eased himself over the lip of the drop and caught the rope; it was thin and wet. His hands slipped and he dropped a yard before he was stopped by a narrow ledge; he kicked himself away from the rock and jumped the remaining six feet. He found the bore-hole in the centre of a small section cleared of rubble, then knelt and stared down, shining the head-light into the darkness of the narrow hole.

'You see it?' Simon had joined Catlin at the bottom of the shaft.

'You're not one for taking hints, are you son,' said Catlin, wearily. 'Yeah, I see it . . . about two feet down.' He lay on his side and pushed his arm down the bore, stretching to reach the fuse. 'You're going to regret being here if the fuse has been sensitized for movement.' He could remember types he'd encountered in Korea that could be set to detonate several hours ahead, but which would go off the instant they were touched. The Koreans liked to use them in lumps of pebble-filled plastic explosive hidden under the bodies of American or British dead. He could feel the knurled cap of the detonator with the tip of a finger; he slid his hand around it. The plastic explosive felt like cold putty. He pulled the detonator carefully, feeling the suction of the plastic explosive gripping the slim tube of metal for a few seconds before allowing it to move.

Catlin knew that now was the time when fear could kill, for a trembling hand might jar the time-fuse into action. He willed strength to his fingers; the fuse moved again, smoothly. He slid it upwards. It was clear of the plastic explosive. He rolled over on his back, drawing his arm quickly from the bore-hole. The fuse, like a metal-bodied ballpoint pen, glistened in his head-light. 'Got you, you bastard.' He sat upright, shone his head-light along a thin crevasse branching out from the shaft, and tossed the fuse deep inside. He watched for a few seconds, then took a deep breath. Explosives didn't frighten him, but defusing someone else's work when the setting of the fuse was unknown was like playing Russian roulette with an automatic pistol. He could feel his heart thumping deep inside his chest.

He stood, glanced down at his hands and noticed they were shaking.

He grunted. 'I'm losing my touch.' Then said: 'Okay, let's go. There's nothing more we can do down here.' There was no hurry now, one of the military demolition teams could remove the explosive from the bore-hole; it was safe without the detonator.

The thin rope cut into the burns on his hands as he pulled himself up out of the shaft. He eased his chest over the rim and wriggled clear of the edge of wet rock. He had an uncomfortable feeling all was not well, that he had overlooked something vital. He wondered if Miculik could have set two separate charges, or used two fuses, one pushed deep into the plastic explosive. His searching fingers within the bore-hole had found only one. He dismissed the thoughts; it had been many years since he had defused explosives and he decided age was giving him too much imagination.

Simon had not yet joined him. He looked back over the edge, his light searching the shaft below. Simon, kneeling beside the bore-hole, stood quickly.

'What's keeping you?'

'I was curious,' answered Simon, his face in the beam of Catlin's light. He turned away then reached for the rope, swinging himself upwards with little difficulty. He was alongside Catlin a moment later. He didn't wait for him, but moved into the narrow tunnel, dropping to his knees and crawling through the narrowing passage. Catlin had to move quickly to keep up with him.

The tunnel became 'V' shaped, wider at the top than the bottom. It tightened against Catlin's body as he turned himself on his side, his feet scrabbling in the narrowing section as he forced himself through the gap. Beyond there was a little more room, though the tunnel remained the same awkward shape. Catlin could see the soles of Simon's boots a few feet ahead of him.

An unpleasant thought was developing in Catlin's mind. He called: 'Wait,' but Simon ignored him. There was more height to the tunnel. Catlin dived forward and caught Simon's ankle. The young man kicked at him with his free foot, the boot ripping skin from the back of Catlin's hand.

Catlin swore and grabbed the leg with both hands, pulling himself further along Simon's squirming body. The man twisted himself and punched at Catlin's head, but in the narrow confines of the tunnel his punches lacked force and Catlin buried his face in the man's legs and took the blows on the back of his head. He reached up and managed to get his left hand around Simon's throat, then with the right, he grabbed the man's testicles and twisted, hard. Simon screamed with pain. Catlin forced Simon's head back, and managed to move further along his body until he lay over him, his weight forcing the slimmer man into the narrower section of the crevasse below. Catlin's back was tight against the roof of the tunnel, Simon's wedged above the narrowing lower part of the 'V'.

The beam of Catlin's head-light shone down onto Simon's face, distorted by the pressure of Catlin's grip around his neck, forcing his head further backwards until his neck threatened to break.

'Suppose you tell Papa,' growled Catlin. 'What should I know?'

Simon tried to shake his head and Catlin relaxed his hold slightly on the man's neck. 'Nothing . . . you're crazy . . . let me go.' His voice rose to a yelp as Catlin's right hand squeezed his testicles again, twisting them between his thighs.

'Think fast,' warned Catlin. 'They feel like they're coming off.'

Simon was sweating, beads of moisture forming on his forehead. Catlin wrenched at the man's crutch, brutally. 'A fuse . . .' Simon's voice was shrill with agony. 'I put in another fuse.'

'You little bastard . . .' Catlin's memory filled in the missing pieces. Simon had been the one to bring Miculik to the drill site. The extra drilling equipment had been nothing more than an excuse. And when Alessandro had killed Miculik, Simon had appeared with his rifle aimed at Alessandro . . . it had only been Catlin's shout of warning, and his own rifle, that prevented Simon from killing the boy. Simon was one of the C.L.O. 'How much time on the fuse?' There was no reply, the man twisted his body beneath him trying to move Catlin's weight. Catlin tightened his grip in the man's groin. 'How much time?'

'Four minutes . . . I set it at four minutes . . .' Tears of pain were running down Simon's cheeks.

Catlin swore: 'You lousy shit!'

There was movement at the extreme range of Berkley's light. He could see a man, creeping forward in the gloom, and behind him others. They came towards the gorge slowly, moving along the narrow ledge, feeling their way close to the dripping wall of the tunnel.

Berkley shouted: 'Get back. Go back to the cavern, leave us alone . . . these people have done nothing.'

The leading figure stopped, staring at the light.

'You're dead Berkley . . . you, the Kraut and the Jap. We'll get you first, and then we'll get the others.' The voice was hollow, the man's face almost emotionless, pale as a white slug in the beam of the light.

'For God's sake, it had to be done. There was nothing else . . . no other way of keeping the children alive.'

'Children? Our children, Berkley, not your children! You and those other filthy perverts . . . making them eat corpses. Now you're going to die . . .'

From the darkness a sombre voice called: 'It is the way of the Lord . . . those who shall choose to follow the path of Satan will feel the wrath of Jehovah upon them . . .'

A two-pound fragment of limestone spun out of the darkness of the tunnel to shatter on the ledge at Berkley's feet. He felt Kaguri's hand on his arm pulling him back away from the gorge.

The figures on the ledge moved closer.

The shock wave hit them simultaneously, knocking the breath from their bodies, driving into their sinus and ear passages as though they were in an aircraft which had suddenly dropped a thousand feet. The man who had been shouting at Berkley was knocked off-balance, he stumbled, clasped his hands to his head, lost his footing and fell sideways into the gorge. His scream mingled with the sound of the explosion, magnified as it swept along the length of the tunnel. Berkley staggered back against the wall of the cave. Behind him, people cried in sudden terror.

The reverberation of the explosion died away. The candles had been extinguished and only Berkley's light took darkness from the tunnel.

He heard Colette's voice beside him, surprisingly calm. 'Is it another earth tremor?'

Kaguri answered her. 'No . . . I think not.'

A match flared and Carl Struger held it to the wick of one of the candles. His hand shook as he did so. The wax-soaked string caught and the flame grew. Struger watched it and then spoke excitedly. 'Look . . . look here at the flame.'

The flame of the candle was not vertical; it leant sideways, the tip of the orange cone bending in the direction of the main cavern.

David Berkley's mind took several seconds to understand the significance of the flame's movement. Then he spoke softly. 'There must be a draught . . . my God, there's a draught along the tunnel.' He turned his head, trying to feel a breath of air against his cheeks, but after the many days in the damp atmosphere of the cave they were too insensitive.

Kaguri shouted in Japanese and there was a murmured reaction from the people behind him in the darkness.

'Please God, let it be over.' Colette's voice begged softly.

Berkley put his arm around her and pulled her close against him. 'I think maybe they've reached us.' He held her tightly, knowing she was crying.

Catlin had known there was no time left; no time even for thought. He'd felt only the first blast of the explosion as it drove along the narrowing tunnel, striking from deep in the crevasse below him. The force of it beneath the length of Simon's body rammed him upwards against the unyielding roof of the passage. There was no more awareness.

Not all of those who had been trapped in the cavern survived the explosion. Nineteen more tourists died, as well as the man who had fallen into the gorge. Catlin had drilled accurately. The explosive was placed directly above the most crowded section of the cavern.

The survivors did not leave the cave immediately; it would have been impossible for most. The explosion blew in a section of roof, and the escape route was eighty feet above the cave floor level. The first to reach the cavern, by means of rope ladders, were the military; young doctors, medics. Following them were a police rescue team with electric floodlights, food and dry clothing.

The passages through which Catlin had squirmed, were widened by tunnellers with tungsten-tipped hammer drills.

Twenty four hours after the explosion, the first of the tourists were brought to the surface; the others followed, as quickly as the rescue workers could carry or lead them through the passages. They sat, or lay in the open air blinded by the sunlight, confused by the activity and noise. Red Cross men and women took them to helicopters and lifted them away from the mountain to the hospitals of the towns. Most of those who had been trapped would never meet each other again.

Sheila Hubertson would live; her tumour was not malignant. But she was a widow, and lived with the awful knowledge it was her own hysteria that had brought about the death of her husband, Ralph, only a little while before the rescue. Many months of psychiatric treatment would eventually lessen her grief.

Senta Kaguri discharged himself from the hospital two days after climbing unassisted from the caves. He had cabled his family, and knew he was as capable of rebuilding himself physically as any of the hospital's doctors. He had no wish to continue his vacation away from Japan. He wanted to return to Hosokai, see and touch his children, watch his wife busy with the housework. He would then go, for just a few days, to Kyoto, to the Ryoanji temple. There was a garden of contemplation, studded with eight carefully placed rocks, its sand surface combed to fine patterns. He wanted to compose his mind, prepare it for the year of work that lay ahead in his factory. With the expanding market for Yoshuabi products, it was certain to be busy. In two months time there were the National Kendo Championships; his pupils must be prepared for the arduous contests.

Carl Struger, David Berkley and Colette Marishall, had stayed together. Colette had been separated from the men in her first days in the hospital, but now, on the morning of the day they were to leave, the three of them sat in the hot sun in the hospital gardens.

Struger, pallid and still gaunt, would be home in Germany that evening. His fiancée was already at his house waiting for him. They planned to marry immediately. His teaching career was over. He had no intention of ever returning to his school. 'Hedy has made arrangements with her father,' he told them. 'We will stay a week or two at my home, and then go to the mountains. There is work for me. The ski school has agreed to accept me as an instructor this winter. It will be good to work outside.' He looked enquiringly at Berkley. 'And you?'

'I have to go back to New York and sort out my business.'

'No Blue Lake?' Struger sounded surprised and disappointed.

'Yes, it's still Blue Lake. I have to do a few things first. Sell my business, equipment, settle a few affairs. Get married.'

'Married?' It was Colette who questioned him now. He had been affectionate to her, but they had not talked of the future; the past was still too close. And he had never mentioned a fiancée.

Carl was watching them, interested. She realised the two men had become closer than brothers during their times together in the dark tunnels, and David had obviously already discussed her with Struger. She felt her cheeks colour. She couldn't meet Berkley's eyes.

'There can't be a Blue Lake without you,' Berkley said.

'I think that is true,' added Struger. 'He loves you very much.'

'I was going to tell her, myself.'

Carl Struger laughed. 'David, if you want to be first to the top of a mountain, then you must climb the last fifty meters very surely, very quickly.'

'One hell of a partner,' grunted Berkley. 'You promised to teach me to ski, not to propose.'

'Now I get to kiss the happy woman,' asked Struger, brightly.

'Oh no you don't,' Berkley turned to Colette. 'Well?' She nodded, happily. He took her in his arms.

Inspector Zlobec stood in the parking lot at the Postojna site, and stared at the sloping face of the mountain, at the twisted and already sun-scorched undergrowth of trees that had once clad its steep sides.

He had just supervised the clearing of his wooden office, seen the documents and equipment neatly packed for transfer to his new office on the outskirts of the township.

The bulldozers had left the cave site, as had the military. There was more important salvage and restoration work for them elsewhere. No-one alive remained inside the mountain; even the corpses, those that could be found and reached, had been removed and were now buried in a plot in the Postojna cemetary. The bodies still inside the cavern would remain for a long time.

It would be good, he thought, to be away from this place. Too many people, over such a vast period of time, had died in the darkness of the caves. He remembered the history. The archaeologists had found bones . . . of cave bears and palaeolithic man, in the mud of the caverns. Men had died there thousands of years ago. They had died there in the last world war, in the attack of the partisans . . . and because of that, more men died in the villages. Now, there were the recent deaths, and the unrecoverable bodies of those buried beneath thousands of tons of rock.

The caves were closed. It would be many years before they were reopened, and by then they would no longer be his responsibility.

Many things were changed, he decided. Even Commissioner Bor. He had seen the man return from the mountain, seen the strict and emotionless disciplinarian, walking beside the stretcher, his hand holding that of his wounded son while tears streamed down his face. Bor had shown he was human. It was said that he had even insisted on staying in the operating theatre while the surgeons treated the youth, and had remained at his bedside until he was certain of his recovery.

Zlobec walked slowly towards his car. He paused, took the twisted silver case from his pocket, and lit a cigarette. Perhaps the mountain, the caves, had finished with killing. The C.L.O. no longer existed; those of the terrorists who had been captured alive, now awaited justice of the courts. The young Slovenes who had drilled into the mountain, with the red-haired American, had already been pardoned. Their bravery in fighting the terrorists had prompted leniency. Zlobec turned the case slowly, so the sunlight reflected from the bent polished surface. It was more than he needed as a memory of the disaster. He slid it back into his uniform, straightened himself, then quickened his pace. He did not look back.

21

It was sixteen days before Joe Catlin regained consciousness. Sixteen days within which a team of surgeons brought together by the directive of the Yugoslav Presidency, removed shattered portions of his skull and replaced them with titanium plate; they set eleven fractures of ribs and limbs, and re-shaped and wired his jawbone.

His first spell of consciousness was brief; just long enough for him to realise somehow he was still alive. He lay, unmoving, watching a blurred shape a few feet away, seeing it move closer and feeling the soft touch of fingers above an eyebrow. He made no attempt to assess his injuries; he knew they had to be considerable. He felt exhausted, as though he had been working strenuously for a long time. He knew it would be good, just to sleep.

He awoke again, twenty four hours later. There was a dull ache in his head, and soreness in his throat and nasal passages. He swallowed and felt hard plastic at the back of his tongue. He tried to move his jaw; it didn't function, and the action was accompanied by a stab of pain below his left ear.

His eyes focused, slowly. He thought it wise not to try to move his head, but could see a green plastic shade over an electric light in the ceiling above him. To one side he managed an inverted view of some kind of drip, its thin tube running towards him. He felt the bed move, and looked downwards. He could see a figure, but refocusing his eyes to a shorter distance took him a few moments. He recognised Lisetta, and winked. She winked back, then smiled.

He tried to speak, but it was only a dry croak.

Lisetta moved closer. 'Don't Joe. Wait a little.'

He made another attempt to speak, but it seemed his larynx didn't want to function.

She smiled down at him. 'If you *must* say something, then whisper.'

He didn't nod, he knew it would be painful. He let a breath slip from his lungs. 'Hi, Lisetta.'

'Hi, Joe.'

His mind focused almost as slowly as his eyes, but he knew how to handle it; there'd been other accidents, other hospitals. He took his time.

'How much of me is left?'

He was pleased to see the smile remain on her lips, it confirmed her words. 'You're all here, Joe; a little broken, but complete. Doctors very happy with you . . . it take time, but you not try hurry. I wait; no matter how long time. I want be Mrs. Joe Catlin.'

The muscles that should have made him grin jerked at the wires and caused him to wince. 'That's some idea!'

'You no want?' As always, the instant emotion. This time, hurt.

'I want. You bet I want.' Her smile returned and her eyes glistened. Catlin took a deep breath. It was painful. 'How long was I unconscious,' he asked.

He saw the smile drop a fraction. Her hand gripped his fingers below a plaster cast. 'A long time, Joe. More than two weeks.'

Two weeks, thought Catlin. My God, two weeks unconscious! His mind dwelt on it. What the hell could happen in two weeks? He was stuffed full of tubes; no wonder his throat and nasal passages were painful! He had a strange mental picture of an operating theatre, men and women in green robes working on a body beneath harsh lights. Had he seen it happen to himself? Had he stood away and watched his own operations . . . the pictures seemed real. Had the body, bulky with wrappings, bloodstained and silent, been his own? He blinked the scenes away and saw Lisetta staring down at him with concern.

'Joe?'

'I'm okay! What about the people in the caves?'

She smiled again. 'They're out, Joe. The explosive broke in the cavern roof. Bor's men were able to bring them out through the opening.' She didn't think it necessary to tell him yet of those who had been killed in the roof fall that followed the explosion. 'Many already go back to their own countries. A few are here, in the hospital . . . they had a very bad time.' A terrible time, more terrible than perhaps anyone would ever know she told herself.

There had been a rumour they had been forced to eat human flesh . . . a body had been found with strange wounds, but not one of them would talk of it when questioned by the rescuers. They never would admit it now, it was a secret they would always keep to themselves; a horror they could not share with those outside their own experience. 'Joe . . .' His eyes swung up to her face again. 'If it not very hard for you . . . if it possible . . . Commissioner Bor need something for completing his report. Simon was killed, but both of you are found a big way from the explosion and laying as though you are returning from the place. What happen down there?'

Catlin was watching her as she spoke. He decided she was beautiful; she was life . . . the life he wanted. The hell with oil wells! He tried concentrating on her question, but couldn't remember the moment of the explosion; the micro-second of his life when the blast of ninety pounds of plastic explosive struck upwards from the depths of the wedge-shaped passage in which he and Simon had fought. Nor could he know how Simon's body had taken the main force of the blast below him, cushioning him just sufficiently to survive, even with his terrible injuries.

He tried thinking about the final few minutes that still remained in his memory. He wanted to make his mouth smile, but bandages and wire held it stiff. 'Tell the Commissioner I forgot about Murphy's Law.'

The end

THE DEVIL'S ALTERNATIVE
by FREDERICK FORSYTH

'Whichever option I choose, men are going to die'. This is the Devil's Alternative, the appalling choice facing the President of the USA and other statesmen throughout the world.

As the gripping story gathers momentum, the reader is transported from Moscow to London, from Rotterdam to Washington, from a country house in Ireland to the world's biggest oil tanker which threatens to pollute the whole of the North Sea. The climax is the most exciting that even this master story-teller has contrived, and the last-minute surprises in the concluding chapters take the breath away.

0 552 11495 2 £1.95

GENESIS
by W.A. HARBINSON

There is a global conspiracy of such enormity that those who encounter even its outermost fringes are inevitably contaminated. A conspiracy based on incredibly advanced technology of Earthly origin. A conspiracy dedicated to the eventual enslavement and subversion of humanity as we know it. A conspiracy with one man — old beyond nature, powerful beyond measure — at its core. A consipracy stretching through time — across icy polar wastes and jungle hideouts . . . into the cold vacuum of space itself. A conspiracy poised to turn life on Earth into a chilling nightmare of living death. Unless . . .

GENESIS

is the once-in-a-lifetime novel of searing terror and explosive excitement. Based on little-known but indisputable fact, it is more — much more — than a gripping, frighteningly plausible story. It is the reading experience that will alter the way you look at your world — and your universe . . .

0 552 11533 9 £1.75

SEVEN MINUTES PAST MIDNIGHT
by WALTER WINDWARD

The compelling novel of a perilous plan to snatch one of the highest-ranking Nazis from Hilter's infamous Bunker. The Horsetraders — a small team of British and American crack-commandos. The Operation — a simple trade-in: life and liberty for double-agent 'Valkyrie' in exchange for vital information about Stalin's post-war ambitions and the location of Germany's hidden gold reserves.

But only when they were actually in Berlin would one of their team — a woman — be able to recognize 'Valkyrie'. And as Berlin crumbled and blazed all around them as the Russians moved in, the Horsetraders discovered that one of their own team was a fanatical Stalinist agent . . .

> 'SPLENDIDLY DETAILED WAR-TIME THRILLER . . . CREATES A MOST INGENIOUS CLIMAX'. British Book News.

SBN: 0 522 11474 X Price: £1.25

TYPHOON
by JOHN GORDON DAVIS

Elemental, Passionate, Surprising and Strangely Moving: An extraordinarily powerful novel by the author of HOLD MY HAND I'M DYING.

Hong Kong. Nine years have passed since the dramatic events of *The Year of the Hungry Tiger*. Jake McAdam has left the Hong Kong police. But the appearance of Vanessa Storm Williams, an American journalist, draws him back into the violent and sinister underworld and involves him in a tragic love-affair that will change his life, and the lives of those around him, irrevocably . . .

And through the long, hot summer of passion and terror, Typhoon Rose moves relentlessly across the South China Sea towards Hong Kong and its awesome shattering climax . . .

0 552 11185 6 £1.25